I0621707

Maker of Sunshine

ONLY FOR LOVE REMIX

SUBIRA MILES

HUN BUN LOVE

MAKER OF SUNSHINE

All rights reserved and proprietary. This book or parts thereof may not be reproduced in any form, stored in any retrieval system, or transmitted in any form by any means—electronic, mechanical, photocopy, recording, or otherwise—without prior written permission of the author and publisher, except as provided by United States of America copyright law.

Submit requests for written consent to the Author and/or Publisher.

Send all requests to GNICHELLEBOOKS@GMAIL.COM

Note from the Publisher: This is a work of fiction. Any resemblance to actual historical events, persons living or dead or references to locations, persons, events, or locations is purely coincidental and used fictitiously. Other names, characters, circumstances, places and events are imaginative and not intended to reflect real events.

Copyright © 2019 by G Nichelle

Remastered Copyright © 2025 by Subira Miles

All rights reserved.

No portion of this book may be reproduced in any form without written permission from the publisher or author, except as permitted by U.S. copyright law.

CHAPTER ONE

Nailah

"Are you there?" she asked. Regina on speakerphone, but her excitement for me attending an art show was loud enough to be heard across the parking lot.

Eyeing the pristine modern building with bright white paint, vines of ivy crawling up the sides, petite manicured bushes, and huge, crafted doors, I took a deep breath. It was a new reality for me. Some days, it still shocked me that I had made it. I was still standing, and my new professional life with exclusive gallery visits and fancy dinners was real.

I heaved the door to my well-loved Lexus shut and walked through the parking lot to the sold-out event.

"I'm in the parking lot right now," I answered for the third time. Last week, when Regina invited me to attend in her place, she added an appointment on my work calendar and an alarm on my cell phone. This morning, before I sat down at my desk to work, she reminded me of all the beautiful art pieces on exhibit. She brought lunch to my office for the sole purpose of reminding me to shave. When I asked her why hairless legs were required for a trip to an art gallery, she gave me a sly grin and said, 'You never know when someone will want to view your pieces.' She wasn't talking about art either. Regina was in a meeting when I left the office, but she texted me a note about wearing something flirty.

"Jermaine Timmons and Naeem Matthews will be there tonight. Take advantage of the opportunity."

"Did you say Naeem Matthews will be at this event? I'll be in the same building with two future basketball hall-of-fame players?" I stopped mid-stride to ask.

I looked over my outfit.

"You better be glad that I love you like a step-sister. Otherwise, I'd be backing my ass up and down those halls trying to bring home a rich baby daddy."

The uneasiness I had about attending this gathering of the well-to-do returned. Regina had made it seem like I was doing her a favor by attending.

"Didn't your date with the baseball player conflict with tonight?"

"Why I gave you the ticket doesn't matter," Regina dismissed, "I refuse to let you remain a hermit."

If my eyes could roll any farther, I would be able to see behind me. Maybe I haven't attended any events since moving to the city. Perhaps I haven't been out since cell phone cameras were a modern wonder. That doesn't qualify me as a hermit. I go to work. I go to the grocery store. I go to the movies. Alone, but I go.

"Going out is overrated."

More than once, I thought about slipping into my baby blue yoga pants and furry black slippers for a comfy night on my couch. I could live vicariously through her exploits and reality show television if I needed excitement.

"I only agreed to this so your ticket money wouldn't go to waste, and I wanted to see Ernie Barnes' paintings from Good Times on display."

"If you think I paid for anything, you were fooling yourself."

"What? Regina, how the hell-" Before I could finish, she cut me off.

"Quick. Put me on video chat to see what you're wearing."

Regina's glammed-up face popped onto the screen, and for a second, envy circles me. She makes it seem so easy to look so beautiful. Perfectly manicured brows, glowing flawless makeup, and a flawless smile leads me to re-evaluate her invitation to visit the spa with her. Sometimes, in a good way, she reminds me of the women that surrounded me when I was a kid. The women got made up, dressed up, and ready to party every day like it was a uniform. Regina could write a book on how to party and look good.

"You look nice," I tell her as though A, she doesn't already know, and B, there is ever a time that she doesn't look nice.

Regina's lips twist up in a knowing smile. "Don't even try to get me off topic. This call is about you. Your compliments won't work."

I allow my shoulders to shift down and practice rolling my eyes as far as possible.

"Alright," I mutter. Regina gives me a hard time, but I know it comes from a good place, so I comply.

I look around the swelling parking lot.

People are in various stages of positioning their vehicles, stepping out of chauffeur-opened doors, and entering the building as I play with the phone camera.

"Let me see," Regina insists.

I extend my arm to angle the phone to see my skinny jeans, tunic top, and flat strappy sandals best.

"I thought we talked about this." Regina's disappointed eyes close for a brief second before reopening.

"What's wrong with my skinny jeans and top? I'm cute." At least, I thought I was.

"You need to pop the top off of all that bottled-up sexy and serve a nice man tonight," she suggests. "I can't even tell if you have breasts under that muumuu covering up everything."

"I'm going to look at art, not auction off my body parts," I reminded her yet again.

Regina twists her lips to one side and shakes her head again.

"You're impossible."

Childish as it may be, I stick my tongue out at her as I reach the curb.

"I have to hang up now. The sign says no cell phone use and no flash photography," I explain, but I want to avoid repeating her *let loose* lecture.

"Go ahead. Ignore my sage wisdom-" Regina starts.

"I'm hanging up now," I cut in.

I end the call and neatly tuck the phone into my pocket. Although the phone causes a slight bulge, my long, flowy shirt hides it. It hides all of my curviness, so I liked it until that conversation.

I pat my shirt down and straighten it before taking a few steps toward the looming metal door to the upscale gallery.

"Let me get that," a large masculine voice interrupts.

I hear his hurried steps behind me and wonder who would go through the trouble of a sprint for me.

I look over to see one of the most dream-worthy men who can use two feet. I bet that even his toes are fine. Although I have to tilt my head up slightly to really view his face, it is worth the effort. Smooth, tawny skin lay perfectly over his soulful eyes, crafted jawline, and firm, full lips. A neatly trimmed goatee distinctly framed his mouth like a work of art. I would have paid the price of admission just to see him and even pawn valuables for a touch.

"Um...." I stutter, temporarily taken aback by his good looks. "I got it. Thanks."

Before I can place a hand on the extended iron handle of the door, he brushes it away. Flutters of happiness skitter through me, and I am not in the least bit irritated by this stranger's touch.

"What kind of man would I be if I did that?" his smooth forehead furrows as he dismisses my notion of independence.

A sexy man. I kept that tidbit of information to myself. Pretty men are the worst, and on the sexy meter, this man was reading at a hundred.

I give him a half smile and allow him to do what he is determined to do.

"After you," he charms.

Before stepping through the door, I give the man another once over. Sometimes, in my life, I must admit I am wrong. Regina will never hear it from me, but she may have been right. I should have worn something more appealing.

"You look nice, by the way," he says as we enter the foyer. "I disagree with your friend."

"What?" I cough, nearly choking on the saliva that I've successfully functioned with for twenty-eight years.

Of course, he had heard a piece of my conversation with Regina. In my world, anything embarrassing about me is displayed for the world to see.

"Thank you," I manage to say, even though his closeness is distracting. "I wish my friend could hear you say that."

We pause between the two sets of doors, and the good-looking stranger places a hand on my shoulder. It is calm and nonthreatening. Although I generally don't allow people to touch me, his light graze doesn't cause the skin-crawling reaction that others do.

He pulled back the second set of doors, and the nice stranger smiled and ushered me through.

"I like a woman with a little mystery." He winks while holding the door.

Ahead of the gallant man, I enter the gallery with a prize-winning, cheek-hurting smile. I haven't pulled out a smile this wide since second-grade picture day.

"Well, Mr. Sherlock," I gush with an embarrassed chuckle. "I appreciate your interest in mystery and your chivalry."

"No problem." Laughing, he gives a mock bow. "You have a nice night."

The sweet man with the kind words walks off into the crowd, most likely to find a beautiful woman to solve.

CHAPTER TWO

Nailah

When my world is about to shift, I get a strange feeling that's hard to explain - it's churning in the pit of my stomach, an acute awareness of my surroundings, an etching of every detail into my memory, and a strange itching in my left palm. My grandmother used to say that my special feeling meant that money was coming. On those days, we would walk the four blocks to the nearest corner store to play the lottery. She never won a jackpot, but one time, she did hit the numbers for three hundred dollars. As I got older, I realized that my 'something special,' my 'weird feeling' was about more than money. The same upset stomach and itchy-palmed disorientation had marked every major turning point in my life.

As I walked further into the expansive art gallery, I knew something about the *Lives in Color* showcase would be significant to my life. The exposed brick walls, strategic lighting, and artsy people moving about awe me. The people were just as interesting as the art. In the small, dusty Texas town where I grew up, people didn't usually look like a live version of a magazine ad or a music video.

I don't know where to begin. Everything is new, fresh, and unique—even the people. Back in Brook Bonnet, there were about five different types of people. Everyone could be categorized, dropped in a life slot, and their whole existence is totally known. In Dallas, and especially in this art gallery tonight, people are matchless blends of color, style, and centrism. Unique is an understatement for the people and the art. Every piece of pottery, every painting, every picture that I can see adds to the fabric of a beautiful history mostly tucked into the back of America's closet.

I take a glass of wine from a waiter with a floating tray and peruse the place. I wonder where my Mr.Sherlock went. He is the perfect eye candy. Since I came here to look at nice things that I can never have, I might as well sneak in a few more peeks of the sexy man who holds doors for strangers.

In my search, I notice a slender man in a trench coat. He is the only one who looks out of place as he stands near a hipster-inspired group. The walnut-colored man, oddly dressed for the warm July weather, snatches my eye because, really, who needs a trench coat in Texas year-round?

The guy blinks in my direction a few times, gazes as though he may recognize me, but then quickly flits his eyes away.

That was weird, but artistic people are often different.

Continuing my scan of the room, I notice a couple clinking their glasses together in a toast. They chuckle as though life has no cares and smile at each other like they are the only two in the room.

I take in a deep breath. I don't fit in here, but I saunter into the gallery a little farther anyway.

I used to believe that someday, I would be one of those happy, love-struck people. I used to believe that someone would come and save me from the sadness that clouded my life. So far, I have had to be the maker of my own sunshine.

I walk toward the left to view an exhibit of local artists.

A soft jazz number adds to the ambiance, and I am proud to be in the presence of so many beautiful people. It's like watching life through a filter. Laughter hops around the room amongst the excited hum of murmurs, and I lose myself in the beauty of the moment.

After another good glass of sweet wine, I make my way through an alcove of traditional African art from Ghana. When I stroll over to a series of replica sculptures from Augusta Savage, I notice that the same weird-eyed, trenchcoat-wearing man is right behind me. Automatically, I slide my nails over the inside of my hand at rapid speed.

Maybe if I ignore him, he will go away. Maybe he is not really watching me. Maybe he just happens to be near me again.

Turning away from his gaze, I move to look over a smaller representation of a sculpture called *The Harp*. The lined-up busts of people are the strings of a harp, and the hand holding them is a base. The original piece, by Augusta Savage, is a work of marvel, but even the replica is amazing to review. The intricate lines defining the eyes and the width of the nose capture a somber hope. The same hope for survival that I recognize in myself.

It felt like eyes were crawling over my skin. Not able to shake the creepy feeling, I turn to scan the room.

Trench coat man has pinpointed me again. With his laser-like precision, he could burn a hole in the side of my skull.

Shifting my weight from one leg to the other, I try to remain natural and examine the art piece longer. If this were my sofa, and I were watching me on TV, this would be the part where I screamed at the stupid female lead to 'Take your tail to the house! Only crazy people who like to eat other people's fingernails stare like that!'

However, I wasn't at home.

The next time I move to a new city that is twelve times the size of my hometown, I will make sure to pack a buddy. So far, a few weeks into life in a new city, I have made one friend: Regina. She's my coworker, but within the first five minutes of meeting her, I felt like she was the sister that I never had. I was my mother's only child, but Regina makes me wonder if we may have had a common father. Knowing what I do about my dad, it's not such a far-fetched idea.

I look over my shoulder casually. The strange man is still there. Standing between two paintings with his eyes glued to my neck, the man sent an unnerving chill through my spine. To be on the safe side, I move to the largest room and key in on where the security guards are. Growing up, I had to deal with creepy guys on a regular basis, and I learned two things: know what your resources are and always have an exit plan.

Scanning the room, I look for possible ways to escape the gallery without being noticed, and I examine which objects could possibly double as weapons.

I position my keys in my front pocket for easy access. If the man stepped out of line, a few strategic jabs with my car key would lay him out. Instead of just finding an evacuation route, I find an added bonus. Standing in a group near an exit was the sexy Sherlock, who opened the door for me. Runway-ready women and court-day-clothed men crowded near them. Looking down at my frock, I understand why Regina was concerned.

One woman was suspiciously close to my sexy Sherlock. Are the two together? Is she his type? I may not be as perfectly trimmed as the stacked woman, but I definitely have a great shape.

Briana Matthews is married to the NBA player Naeem Matthews. With three budding children, her life seemed so much like a fairytale that, for two seasons, she had her own reality show. That was five years ago. The show ended amid rumors of Naeem's drug use and his trade from the superstar Los Angeles team to the Dallas Colts. I had watched season one of their reality show but stopped when season two began. No matter how much the couple boasted about their great life, Briana's eyes never smiled. Women can be great pretenders, but the truth will eventually leak through.

Standing next to Naeem in the gallery, Briana held onto her husband's arm, but her eyes were held by the alluring man who opened the door for me.

I practice my eye roll and sip more wine before looking at the beautiful people again.

When I was a kid, for the few years that my father was around, we would sit and watch basketball. Even after he was gone, I continued to have an affinity for the sport and the home team, the Dallas Colts. I don't catch every basketball game, but I catch the commentary every day. Naeem Matthews and Jermaine Timmons are a powerhouse duo. They played college ball for the same team and went to play professional ball on separate teams but wound up in Dallas together. One of my favorite commentators said that the two were an unstoppable force. They had taken Dallas to the championship four times in the last five years and won three of those titles.

Sexy Sherlock was comfortable among them. Laughing slightly and hugging many of the people in the growing crowd, he eased his hands in and out of his pockets to clap backs and squeeze shoulders like they were family.

His smile is amazing, and I find myself grinning because he is.

When mega realtor Reginald Strong joins the group of stars, I want to sneak out my phone to snap a picture. I don't, but who would ever believe that I was in the same room with basketball players and an arena owner? Everyone in Brook Bonnet would just assume I was exaggerating the truth.

A tap on my shoulder interrupts my reverie.

I spin on my heels to confront the perpetrator with a glare.

In general, I am an easygoing person, but there are three things that instantly swap my chill mode for attack status. Number one, don't touch me unless I invite you. Number two, no matter how down I may be, I can get up on my own. Since nothing is for free, I don't accept charity. Number three, I need to know what is happening at all times, with no surprises.

Standing there, a crooked smile plastered to his face, is the man in the trench coat.

Watching the parade of stars had taken me off my guard. Damn, I should have run while I had the chance.

"I'm Warren," he proudly pronounced as though he were waiting for me to applaud. Trench coat, Warren extends his arm for a shake.

I look down at his small, thin hand and then back to his face.

I don't bother to be nice. I learned a long time ago that entertaining fools only makes you a member of the group.

"First of all, Warren, you don't know me, so don't touch me," I speak calmly, as his hand dangles as useless as wet flaps on a cardboard box.

"Also, I don't speak with strangers or strange men. Since you ring the bell in both categories, I'm going to turn around and continue my peaceful night without you stalking me. Mmm-kay?"

His eyes narrow as though he is determining how serious I am.

"Stalking you?" he repeats like the words taste dirty.

"Have a great night, Warren."

Spinning on my heels, I about-face and walk away.

"Wait!" Warren shouts above the room-level murmurs.

If it were only a yell, if it were only words, then I could move on. I could keep walking and act like the incident didn't happen, but it wasn't just a shout.

I hear Warren's footsteps behind me, and I quickly learn that he has long nails for a man. Twinges of pain shoot through the muscle of my shoulder with the pinch of his fingers digging into the tissue. Fear flashes through me as childhood memories flood my mind.

"I'm talking to you," his words are almost as tight as his grip. "You don't get to walk away from me."

It has been a long time since any man attempted to harm me. Warren had just crossed all of my lines and onto a landmine.

If sweet and sanity each had a light switch in my brain, his actions just shut them all off.

CHAPTER THREE

Tyriq

When I see the sweet woman that I opened the door for getting fiery with a strange man, I excuse myself from Naeem's admirers and head over. It was really none of my business, but she intrigued me.

Earlier, I saw the odd man watching her, but I didn't pay much attention to his fascination with her. I had been admiring her myself. She favored the famous model Jubilee, that I couldn't wait to see each week on a modeling contest show that my cousin made me watch. Something about the killer body she was trying so desperately to cover, and the curve of those full lips kept my eyes wandering back to her. I've been wondering what she tastes like since she called me Sherlock.

"Is there something that I can help you with?" I asked the man dressed in a trench coat.

I move forward, effectively coming between the man and my mystery beauty.

He squares his shoulders, taking a stance before looking in my direction.

"This doesn't concern you," he used his big man voice to say.

I look back at the determined, steel-eyed woman and then back to her follower.

"That's where you're wrong," I explain before planting my feet. "Anything having to do with my friend here concerns me."

He seemed to weigh his options and then relented with the right decision.

"Fine. You can have the bitch." He looks in her direction. "Regina was right, you do need to get you some dick."

"Call me a bitch again," she dared as she lunged out toward that idiot.

I slide a strong arm around her waist, pulling her back.

"Whoa there," I chuckle. "Let's chill."

People in the gallery begin to take notice. Most steal a glance at the small commotion, while the nosiest stop and sip their champagne like a boxing match is about to ensue.

I lift a hand toward slow, slew-footed Chuck, the security guard making his way over and nod. I come to the gallery often, and I helped him with some free medical advice once. He owes me a couple of favors.

Chuck nods back and moseys on in another direction.

When I'm sure she won't attack, I let her go.

"Are you alright?" I question.

"I'm fine," she huffs. "I just need to murder someone."

"Who? Ol' boy? I don't think he'll be a problem again."

"Not him, my *former* friend," she exhales loudly. "She obviously tried to set me up with that fool and didn't even tell me."

She rolls those beautiful eyes of hers.

"I'm running around thinking he's a stalker, not just an asshole," she continues before sucking her teeth.

"Wow," I manage to whisper, but not because of her words. The woman is magnetic. The slant of her eyes, pronounced cheekbones, and tapered nose seem perfectly symmetric. If I painted her face on canvas, I could sell it for millions.

"Thank you for your help," she says, adjusting her clothing. "I could have handled it, but thank you for stepping in."

"I see how you would have handled it, and you're too pretty to go to jail."

She shrugs. It amazes me how soft and tough she is at the same time.

"Do you want to make a police report?" I check. A surge of protectiveness courses through me, and instantly, I want to make sure that nothing happens to the sweet and mighty woman.

"I'm good," she says. " Thanks again."

Then she walks away as though our conversation is over, as though we're done. This is new. In most cases, girls are like smeared glue; the only way to remove them is to peel them away.

"Just a second," I say and wait for her to respond. I didn't want to be an unwanted company.

"Yes?" She looks back, and her sweet smile is there, but she doesn't stop walking.

With that blessing, I skip a step up to her.

"So, when I'm telling my heroic story to my friends later, what do I call you?" I ask.

"So, you're a hero now?" She slows her steps to dart those sexy eyes to the side and fold her arms under her covered yet conspicuous chest.

"Chivalry is what I do." I noticed that she still has not given me a name. "Who are you, princess?"

"I'm no princess," she quietly remarks.

There is a story behind her downward gaze, something that seems to be weighing her down. I want to know what it is. I want to see her smile again.

"Friends call me Lew," I tell her. "Is it alright if I hang out with you?"

"I don't know," she draws out the vowels in the last word as though I asked her a question about quantum physics.

"Come on," I push. "You can't say no to your charming Sherlock. That's not how the story goes."

She stops walking and allows me to admire her one more time. I can tell that she is sizing me up, looking at all my details to determine the bigger picture of who I am.

I allow it.

"I guess," she shrugged. "With that big ego, you can't get too close to me anyway."

I laugh, but the wound is real.

"Is that what you think of me?" I ask as we stroll on.

"You don't look in the mirror often?" she questioned. "I know you've seen yourself before. You look good, and you know it."

I place a hand over my heart and catch her eyes with mine.

"Hunks have hearts, too," I tease.

"I just mean that it doesn't seem like there is much that can puncture your pride." She blinks her thick lashes over her chocolate brown eyes, reminding me of a baby doll.

"You're doing a good job," I laugh. "I thought I was charming you."

"Well, don't believe the hype," she quipped and showed two perfectly symmetrical dimples.

"Why so brutal?" The woman had insulted me a handful of times in so many minutes, but I wanted to know more.

"Me, brutal?" She shakes her head, her shoulder-length hair flowing with it. "I'm just being honest."

"Honestly, brutal."

An innocent grin brings her dimples out of hiding again.

We stroll together at a comfortable pace. She examines the art, but for me, she is more interesting than everything in the gallery—even Briana.

I wasn't expecting Briana to attend or be here with her husband, either. I would have brought a real date. Even though we broke up in college, no other woman ever had my attention like she had- not until tonight.

"Are your friends going to miss you, Charming?" she asks as we pass by a group of people.

I shake my head no but scan the room anyway.

"But if a woman does pop up to hug me, it's just my little cousin. She might be a no-show."

"You were supposed to meet a girl cousin here, huh?"Those beautiful lips poke out to the side.

I can tell that she doesn't believe me.

"What's wrong with that?"

She shrugs.

"This place gives me date vibes with the dim lights and wine."

"My cousin and I come here for different events. She's always looking for decor for her interior design business. Besides my brother, she's actually my best friend."

"It just sounds like an old-school mack line." She stops and takes a stance imitating a man. "Yo' honey, that's just my cousin. Don't trip."

She returns to our slow stroll.

"Who have you been hanging out with?" I laugh. "Who says 'mack' and 'yo honey'?"

Her laughter lifts through the air and makes me smile.

"Did you not hear me say 'old school'?" She placed a hand on that hidden hip. "Men with a whole bunch of girl cousins and play sisters always have some tired lines."

"What? At some point, we need to discuss these people you know." I laugh. "Mali is the only girl out of six boys."

"That's a lot of kids." Her eyes widen. "How many siblings do you have?"

"Three brothers. My Aunt has two boys and one daughter, but we were all raised together."

I am blessed with a grin in my direction.

"I'm an only child," she says. Her smile fades as her eyes fall toward the ground.

Again, I want to know what happened to her.

We move to the Ernie Barnes section of the exhibit, and I can see the excitement in her eyes as she recognizes one of my favorite paintings—the reason I follow art at all.

"Sugar Shack!" she exclaims, pointing at a picture of people with exaggerated arms and legs dancing in a shack.

We pick up the pace to get as close to the painting as the ropes allow.

"Man, I used to watch Good Times reruns religiously," she reminisces. "I really thought JJ could paint too."

"Nope. It was Ernie Barnes who completed many of them," I add. "This has to be one of the most recognizable artworks ever."

"I love it," she says. "I want to break out and sing the theme song right now."

"Do you really know the words?"

"I know," she spouts, and I get the full picture of her figure when she plops both hands on her hips.

"Alright. If you're that confident in your skills, let's wager."

Her eyes narrow suspiciously.

"A friendly wager," I add. "If I know more words than you, then you tell me your name. If you win, then I'll take you out to dinner."

Her chuckle is just as satisfying as a song.

"No fair," her words fall over chuckles. "You win either way."

She licks those lips. The lips that I want to taste.

"Would you like to wager something else?" My voice falls out deep and husky without my intention. I probably sound like the old hustlers that she knew.

She met the intensity of my gaze, and I sensed that she was feeling what I was feeling.

Suddenly, I wish that we were somewhere more private. She could tell me her thoughts, and I could show her body what was on my mind.

"There you are, Lew," the familiar female voice interrupted.

I inwardly cringe.

Briana had on her best fake smile and brought her annoying ass husband along for the ride.

Something about Briana's catty grin makes me want to grab my mystery princess and run.

"You disappeared on us," Naeem adds, clapping a hand on my back, but he doesn't look at me. His eyes are on her, the beautiful woman standing next to me.

Naeem and I haven't been friends in a long time if we ever really were. Working with the team as medical staff kept us in the same circles.

Yeah." I step closer to my new friend. "I didn't want to be away from my girl too long."

I place a possessive arm around my mystery princess' waist. She doesn't bristle or move away; she just melds into the side of my body as if she belongs there.

I catch her eyes and send a silent message with a slight eye twitch, pleading with her to play along.

"That's nice," Briana dismissed with no trace of kindness. She doesn't acknowledge the woman at my side, and she only looks at me.

There is another moment of awkward silence before Naeem moves the party along.

"Glad to see that you didn't disappear," Naeem shrugs.

"I'm still around," I sniped.

"Nice to meet you-" Naeem pauses and extends his hand, waiting for my mystery princess to respond and shake.

She grins.

"Likewise," she says as she places the hand that she should have used to shake his onto my chest.

She dismissed the hell out of his smug ass, and that shit turned me on in a major way.

Naeem and Briana moved away.

Briana's backward glance is quick enough for her husband not to notice but long enough for me to know that she is not happy. If Briana could shoot fire from her eyes, both Mystery Princess and I would have been burned to a crisp.

"So, your ex-girlfriend is Briana Matthews?" my mystery princess questions as she steps out of my embrace. "You used to date the wife of basketball superstar Naeem Mathews?"

A coolness sweeps into the space where she stood, and I sincerely want to have her warmth pressed against me again.

"Yeah," I grunt.

"Wow," she says as we move forward. "That's impressive. I used to watch their reality show about their marriage and kids."

I just nod. I hated that damn show. Everything about it, and about the two of them, was as fake then as it is now.

"You must have dated her a long time ago. She's always going on and on about how she and Naeem fell in love during college."

I ignore her last comment. I don't want to talk about Briana. I don't want to even think about Briana.

"Thanks for playing along," I thank her and decide to use her interest as an advantage. "I'll tell you the full story if you tell me your name."

"Hmmm." She acts as though she is considering it. "That's alright. It was fun enough seeing the pissed-off look on her face when you hugged me."

"So, it's like that?" I conclude and question.

"Oh," she gasps. Those pouty lips move into a perfect circle and take away my concentration. "Look at that painting!" she switched the topic and stepped away from me.

I followed her because there was no other option.

CHAPTER FOUR

Nailah

The painting My Miss America by Barnes makes my feet stop. I stand straight and still. It's my first time ever to see it, and the painting is powerful. The brown-skinned, red-dressed woman in the picture is standing tall, her muscles magnified, as she moves forward with a bag in each hand.

I slip closer to the painting, examining as much of it as I can without touching it.

I feel like I know this woman. The determination in her face, the power in her thighs, and the strong lines in her hands resonate with me. I had seen women like her too many times on my block not to connect to her resigned expression. The lone woman carrying the load. Life conditions her to be strong. She carries it all because there is no one else around. I know what it is like to carry a lot and be alone. It is tiring, but it has made me strong.

Lew pulls me closer to his side by hooking his arm around my waist again, and I swear that I want to faint on the floor. Tingles shoot up from my private parts like fireworks on the Fourth of July, and my mind is cluttered with images of kissing this man until he can't speak.

"What are you thinking about?" he asks.

"Me? Thinking?" I choke out. Again, until meeting Lew, my saliva and I worked well together.

His naughty smile tells me that he must be a bit of a mind reader.

"I thought you were honest, princess," he says in that deep, husky voice again.

He's too near for me to breathe normally. I want to move so that I can speak, but I like his touch way too much. Maybe he's only touching me to make his ex-girlfriend jealous. Why else would he so interested in me?

I scratch at my palm.

"I was thinking about how much I connect to this painting," I tell him. It is true that I was at one point thinking about the painting.

He takes another thoughtful glance at the art.

"How?" he asks.

"I'm alone a lot." The words slip out with more sadness than I intend, but I can't help it. "Sometimes, I feel like I'm destined to be alone."

He nods and looks down at me as though he can change that.

The immediate lurch in my gut caused me to place a hand over it to make sure that it did not disconnect itself.

"You know," I begin, "this is not a science fiction movie. Just looking at me like that doesn't drain knowledge from my brain, or pain for that matter."

My joke loosens the intensity slightly, and the gorgeous guy, Lew, grins.

"Tease all that you want," he states. Eyes still glued to mine, he traced the side of my arm with a gentle finger. "One day, I will find out."

My intuition tells me that there is something about this man and this moment that may have a lasting effect. My mind knew better. He wouldn't look like that if he knew who I really was. The longing in his eyes would wither away and die if he knew my past.

Tamping down words about undeveloped feelings, we move forward quietly. There is no awkwardness, just pervasive peace.

The next painting is of a young boy sitting on the cracked steps of a multi-layer brick apartment building in a blighted neighborhood. His face, resting on his hands and bent knees, is sad. His wide eyes are brimmed with tears, and he looks all alone. He reminds me of a child that I worked with once. Social workers often catch a bad rap because of the laws that we have to follow, but I genuinely care about the children I support. After what happened to me as a child, I make sure that I do more than required to ensure the best outcome for kids.

I sigh at the picture and the hopelessness that I know the child would be feeling. I can see myself, past and present. Is that what I am destined to be, alone? It makes my heart hurt to think of that. I may not believe in the fairytale love, and I would never admit it to Regina, but I would like a partner, someone to confide in, laugh with, and enjoy life with.

"I don't like these kinds of paintings," Lew offers.

"Why? These are my favorite."

"It is another painting of despair," he says, throwing a hand to the side.

I can tell by the confidence in his eyes that his opinion is definite.

I look at the painting again and then back to Lew.

"How can you not see the value in this painting?" I ask. "The reality of the situation is so sad."

"So, you're one of those?" he scoffs.

"What? A human who has emotions and understands empathy?" I return with an upturn of my lips. "Artists paint their reality, and to me, the reality of this painting is saddening."

"But is that the only reality?" He shifted his leg in the way those pretentious men do when they plant into a point. "Why just reality? Why not paint above that? I have eyes. I can see reality. Why not paint a better future?"

"So, we should only paint hope?" I question him. "What about those who can't see hope? What about paintings that people can relate to?"

He folds his arms, and his biceps bulge.

I pause in reverence and give praise for the masterful work of a man in front of me. I want to reach out and touch him.

My tongue involuntarily slips across my lips. The man may be an arrogant ass, but he sure is an aesthetically pleasing one.

I regain a bit of my resolve and clear my throat before continuing.

"The only way to change something is to thoroughly understand it," I clarify my earlier point, "To understand it, you have to see it from all angles, analyze it. Art allows us the privilege to look at ourselves from different perspectives."

He unfolds his arms and pushes his hands into the pockets of his pants. My eyes travel across the stretch of fabric outlining the bulge of his muscular thighs. I wonder what other big muscles he may be hiding.

"Yes," he agrees.

I snatch my attention back to his eyes. Bad girl. Focus. I have to focus on his face.

"The problem is that the only perspective being pushed since the seventies is this downtrodden, welfare, single strong woman, and lost child agenda," he says and then steps forward.

I can feel the heat pulsate from his well-dressed and sculpted body. Why are all of the cute ones assholes?

He continues, but because his nearness limits my ability to speak coherently, I step back.

"If every image paints us as dejected souls struggling to survive, this is what the world will view us as, and eventually the view we will have ourselves," Lew eloquently expounded. "Hope. We need positive ways for change, not another litany of problems."

Just as I am about to give the man my litany of problems with him and his theory, I stop.

I step away from him like he has the plague. Another thought forces its way through.

"What's wrong?" Lew asks.

I narrow my eyes at the handsome man who had a lot of words to just randomly walk into an art museum at the same time as I did.

"Doctor or lawyer?" Anger and humiliation fight for the top spot, and I plop a hand on my hip.

He has to be a set up. This smart, perfect man couldn't have found me on his own and wanted to spend all of his time with me.

"What?" His eyebrows row together.

"Alright, Lew. Are you a doctor or a lawyer, and how do you know Regina?" I say the words slower this time.

He allows his perfectly shaped head to fall back as he laughs.

"Who is Regina? I don't know-"

"Don't even try it," I cut him off. "She's good. She sent the crazy stalker guy first so that you could rescue me and shine," I shake my head. "Her plan is not going to work."

This time, he doesn't laugh, smile, or look in any small amount amused.

"What plan?" Lew whispers. "Who are you talking about?" He swivels his head around as though someone could be watching us.

"It's alright. The gig is up. I've figured you out," I insist, taking a step forward.

I look his face over and try again. The bewildered concern and confusion in his eyes made me think that I was wrong.

My saliva and I have yet another malfunction. This time, there is not too much. This time, it has dried up and left the building. Even my spit doesn't want to associate with my mouth and this foolishness at the moment.

"My friend, Regina. Didn't she send you here on a mission to be my baby daddy?" I rechecked and waited for him to tell me about Regina's plan.

"No," he said as though I was both hard of hearing and understanding.

Heat burns through my throat and flames across my face. I pivot as quickly as possible and make a line straight through to the exit.

"Wait! What's your name?" I hear him yell out.

I am going to kill Regina.

I had come to the museum on my own, just the way that I had come to the city, just the way that I had come into the world, and tonight was confirmation that I would leave it just the same.

CHAPTER FIVE

Tyriq

C ell phones have made the art of hanging up on a person nearly nonexistent. They just sucked all the joy right out of it. I wish that I had one of those super large old-school house phones with a handset so that I could smash them together and make real noise. Pushing a button is different from the click and clank sounds of crunching a handset onto a base.

If Briana ignores one more of my calls, I am driving to her house. I've tried nearly ten times to get ahold of her with no success. Every five rings of her line, I hear the haunting sound of her professional alter ego saying, 'Hello, this is Briana Matthews' on her voicemail.

"Calm down, brother." Trystan closed his book and looked up from a hospital waiting room chair.

I plop down in the chair next to him.

"You alright?"

I let my head fall into my hands and take in a deep breath.

My frustration with Briana is only the tip of the iceberg when it comes to what I am feeling. My mother being in the hospital prompted my parade of phone calls to my ever-busy ex-mistress to begin with.

Trystan claps my back.

"I guess it's a good thing that Terrence went back with Pops to talk to the doctors," he adds. "At first, I wondered why the doctor in the family wouldn't want to try and take over."

I shake my head.

"I'm a primary care physician," I explain. "I haven't done trauma or surgery in years." In addition, it is my mother. The fussing, cussing churchwoman who loves her community and her family even more. I don't want to face her and see the hundreds of things that can go wrong. I don't want to hear the doctors sing the same tune of 'We'll see what happens' as I used to. No, it is better that Terrence is back there. He is unflappable. No matter the situation, he gives the same standard expression: flat.

"I get it," Trystan adds, pushing his glasses up on his nose. "It would be like me jumping in a prosecutor role when I specialize in human resource and corporate law defense."

I agree without really paying attention to his legal words. Trystan has always been this geeky, super smart person, top of his class at every level, and damn near perfect. When Crystal, one of his mentors at the law firm he went to work for, popped up pregnant, I would have testified under oath that she was lying. It turned out that Trystan was the father and the two married.

Both Crystal and Trystan left the firm and now have two kids.

"It's okay," my three-year-old nephew says while taking his short steps over to me. He is the spitting image of his father.

"Thank you, little man." I high-five Trystan Junior and then slide my palm across his to end our special handshake.

"You know," I look over at Trystan, "it used to weird me out how much this little person is a miniature version of you. Now, I think it's kind of cool."

Trystan's left eyebrow lifts near his hairline.

"Not the original Dr. Fly guy, basketball superstar, got every girl wanting you player," he pinpoints. "You, who used to say that children are anchors meant to pull your youth and happiness into an abyss of sadness."

I cover a yawn and lean back in a chair.

"I'm not signing up for birthing class, but I have evolved some. Having a little person may not be as totally life-draining as I thought before."

"You need some rest, brother, or a chocolate bar. You are definitely not yourself today."

I've been in the hospital for nearly five hours now, and my body reminds me that sleep is required.

TJ maneuvered the walk back to his mother without taking his eyes off the game, scrolling across his kid-colored tablet.

I have three brothers. Terrence is the oldest at thirty-three. I am second in line. Trystan is a year younger at thirty. Twenty-eight-year-old Tyson is the youngest of us and the most unsettled.

Other than my family, the private hospital waiting area that I asked for is quiet. We are all waiting for news about our matriarch, our rock, the woman that keeps us all together.

My mother, who is forever an independent woman, decided to drive to the grocery store alone at midnight because she didn't want to wake my father. She was out of cinnamon for the neighborhood's famous peach cobbler she promised for the bake sale. My mother's car was T-Boned three blocks from the house as she passed a major intersection. Her husband and all four sons gathered at St. Parks Memorial Hospital hours ago to learn about her condition.

My head jerked forward when I woke up startled.

"You sleep, Uncle 'Riq?" TJ asks in his small voice from across the room.

He's taking a break from his tablet and watching me. His mother, Crystal, smiles over in our direction.

"I was explaining to him that he should be sleeping." Crystal looks over to me and then at her son. "Even Uncle needs a nap."

"I'm just resting my eyes," I repeat the words that older people told me when I was younger.

TJ giggles before getting back to his game.

Crystal rubs the little one's back and gives him a worn but adoring smile.

A twinge of longing aches in my chest. There is not one person for me to call who will answer to comfort me.

I shouldn't be upset with Briana. It's my fault for even thinking that she would be there for me. She has never been what I needed, only what I wanted.

The words from the mystery princess at the art gallery a few nights ago loop through my mind: 'Maybe I'm destined to be alone.'

"Where's my sister?" I hear Aunt Pat's voice ring through the tiled hall. It's always been that people heard Aunt Pat before seeing her.

"Aunty Tat!" TJ says, bounding up from his mother's side

Crystal sighs and allows TJ to run toward his great-aunt's voice.

"What's going on with my sister?" she questions after only stepping one foot into the waiting room. "Tyriq, why ain't you in there running things? You're a doctor. You need to make sure that my sister is getting proper care."

Behind Aunt Pat is her only daughter and my favorite cousin, Mali. She shakes her head.

"Slow down, Aunty." I stand up and give her a hug.

Aunt Pat gives my shoulder a squeeze.

"She's just out of surgery," I explain. "There was a tear in her spleen. She has some bruised ribs, but she'll be alright."

"Ya'll should have called me earlier," Aunt Pat fusses. "I need to know about my family."

A family vote via a group chat happened among the adult kids, and we decided to tell Aunt Pat about the accident after my mother's condition was stable on purpose.

"We're here now, Mom," Mali soothes.

"The doctors know that she's my mom, and they are taking extra care of her," I explain.

"Nobody will take care of her like her son," Aunt Pat huffs.

She positions herself in a chair, her large black purse taking up the width of her lap. She pulls out the hand-sized wooden cross that she carries and begins whispering prayers to herself.

"Hey cousin," Mali says, walking over to give me a hug. "How are you holding up?"

"I'm fine," is the answer that I give to her. Years of experience give Mali the advantage of understanding my moods. We are the same age, born seven days and seven hours apart. Aunt Pat uses that to explain why we've always been in sync with each other.

"Why the frown?" she questions.

"I'm not frowning."

"This line in your face says otherwise," she says, poking at my forehead.

I swat her hand away.

"Is there something about Aunt Shirley that you're not telling me?" Mali whispers before checking to see if her mother is paying attention to our conversation.

Aunt Pat is lost in her prayers.

"No," I answer with a shake of my head.

The door to the waiting room opens, and my older brother Terrence walks in. His long locks are twisted back into a knot at his neck, usually softening his menacing look. Not today.

"Mom is doing well," Terrence announces to everyone. "She's a little groggy from the anesthesia, but she is good."

"Thy will be done!" my aunt shouts, lifting her hands into the air.

Aunt Pat gives Terrence a hug.

"Everything is going to work out," Terrence coaxes.

"I know it will," Aunt Pat adds assuredly with a wobble of her head.

Terrence nods towards the hallway.

"Come grab some coffee with me, brother."

I don't like the look on his face. Instinctively, my chest tightens. When I worked in the emergency room, I gave out bad news to families every hour repeatedly without a blink of an eye. Now that my mother is on the table, dread pinches at my nerves and confidence.

I caught Mali's eyes. She knows the drill. She has to keep her mom occupied while we figure out a plan for the situation.

"Hey, Mom, let me show you this idea for my new tattoo while we wait," Mali calls out to Aunt Pat.

"Oh no, you won't. You will not get any cuts or marks on your flesh," Aunt Pat explains in her outdoor voice to Mali.

Terrence and I walk into the hallway before I can hear the rest of Aunt Pat's lecture. I owe Mali big time for that one.

As soon as we are away from the waiting room, I brace for the news.

"What's happening?" I ask, but I'm not sure if I really want to know.

Terrence walks with me a little farther to a coffee stand before saying anything. He is quiet as he orders a small black cup of wake-up brew.

"What name for the order?" the barista asks.

My brother gave his name and paid, and we walked to the other side of the counter where the "Pick Up" sign hung.

Fortunately, there are only a few people moving about.

"Mom is waking up, but they can't keep her blood pressure high enough for her to stay conscious."

I swallow back some of the worry that I feel and attempt rational thought. I file through a list of a few simple, non life ending reasons in my mind to calm myself.

"Do they know what the problem is?"

"The hope is that the medication used to put her under for surgery is the culprit. The next few hours are critical, and the move to intensive care for monitoring is happening as we speak."

"Alright," I say to my brother. You can head back in there with Pops. If things haven't improved, I'll update the family in another hour or so."

"Lew?"

I'm almost afraid to turn around. I have a few skeletons buried in this hospital, and a few of them need help staying buried.

Terrence looks around me and gives me that knowing smirk.

"I'll text you if there are any changes, little brother," he says. "I see you have some things to take care of."

Hope builds briefly inside of me like a tower. Maybe Briana saw my missed calls, heard my messages, and hurried over to comfort me. Maybe I could finally have someone.

I turn around, ready for whatever the situation may be.

When the mystery princess from the art gallery smiles at me, an instant need to be near her overwhelms every other feeling coursing through me.

"Princess," I sweep her up in a hug like we've known each other for years. "What are you doing here?"

She falls into my hug as though she were made to be in my arms.

Her warmth pressed against me, and her arms stretched around my neck, stirring up other emotions.

"Work," she says, lifting a badge clipped to her shirt.

I let her feet touch the floor again and look her over.

She is wearing an ill-fitting pair of slacks and a white top that could also pass for a short dress. Even in the oversized clothing, I can tell that there are some knock-out breasts hiding in the folds of the material.

"What do you do?"

"I'm a social worker," she explains. "I'm on call this week, and the hospital had a case that needed immediate attention."

"Are you done for the night? Any more cases? Can you hang out for a little bit?"

She lifts a cheek in hesitation.

"I was just about to grab a coffee before heading home."

"Let's grab a cup." I nod toward the coffee counter.

Again, I am face-to-face with the barista.

The barista clicks across the computer register to ready for her order.

"Your name?" he asks.

I look over at my mystery princess and smile.

She looks from the barista to me and back to the barista.

"Are you a CIA operative or something?" I ask. "What's up with the name?"

She sighs, but there is a tinge of laughter in her resignation.

"What name would you like me to add to the order?" the barista asks again, his voice just as flat as the look in his eyes.

"Nailah," she says plainly.

Before Nailah can take money from the dowdy slacks that she has on, I pull out a bill to pay for it.

"I got that." I slide a crisp bill into the palm of the clerk.

"You really don't have to do that," she says, fumbling through a satchel and then her pockets.

"It's just a few bucks." I place a calming hand on her arm. "It's not much, Nailah. No big deal."

"I don't need any handouts."

I tilt my head to review her face.

"Are you always this nice to people who buy you coffee?"

"I appreciate it," Nailah says in a kinder tone.

We step away from the counter, and when I face her, an emotion that I cannot read flickers across her eyes before she speaks again.

"It's actually nice to see you," she says.

She winks a smile at me, and I notice her left dimple peeking out.

"When I saw you standing there today, I knew that it was fate."

"Really?" I question. "The Olympic sprint that you took from the gallery says otherwise."

She looks away.

"Was that a blush?" I wonder aloud.

Nailah doesn't answer but at least looks up at me again.

"I apologize for running out on you," she rattles off quickly. "I shouldn't have accused you of being a hookup from my friend. You started to seem too good to be true and-"

The barista calls her name, interrupting the few nice words I have gathered from the woman since our meeting.

I watch as she walks away, and I swear I see a swish of her hips beneath the cloak of her slacks, but I am not sure.

Quickly, she picks up the coffee, turns, and takes long strides in the opposite direction.

"Wait," I say, catching up with her. "Is that it? You're just going to leave now? I learned your name, and you're trying to disappear?"

I fall in step with the retreating Nailah. The thought of never finding out what the woman is hiding under all of that clothing is bothersome.

"You want to know more about me?"

"Yes." I wish I had a game buzzer to ring. Finally, she is starting to understand.

She narrows her apprehensive eyes, and I want to run a hand across her wrinkled brows.

"Even after how we met?" she questioned.

"Especially after how we met." I step closer. "If you knew my family, you'd understand why I'm a fan of different. I want to get to know you more, that's all."

Nailah shrugs, and she slows her pace so that we can walk side by side.

"My shift is over. I wanted to grab some coffee before driving home," she stated, holding up her coffee. "Why are you here?"

Worry for my mother squashes over the excitement I feel about seeing the mystery princess again.

I guess she notices the change in my mood and walks toward a bench.

"Let's sit," she suggests.

We take a seat on the bench together.

"What's going on?" She sips on her coffee.

I sigh as earlier feelings of angst and concern bubble up through my chest.

"Well, my mother-" The words won't come out.

I learned a long time ago that showing a woman your weakness leads to her leaving you.

Nailah has telling eyes. As beautiful as they are, if the spitfire woman is not saying what she's thinking, her eyes speak instead. I read the caring concern there and made the decision.

"You don't have to tell me anything that you don't want to. You look like you need a friend."

Nailah slides her manicured hand over the back of my knuckles.

I swallow back the lump of emotion threatening to make itself known and try to resolve the anxiety swelling inside of me.

She places her coffee down on the bench and scoots closer to me.

"You know my name now, so you owe me. Talk to me," she coaxes.

Nailah wraps both hands around mine.

"My mother is strong," I begin, but I have to stop and breathe.

Nailah drags a slow hand down the side of my arm.

"To have a son like you, she has to be."

I like that she is encouraging.

The late hour, the long day, and the fact that my mother is not made of steel hit me all at once, and I feel like a weak ass kid.

I swallow again and lean into the woman sitting next to me. Something about her warmth is calming.

"So, this is why you're a social worker, huh?" I ask and catch her eyes with mine. "You make everyone feel safe with you?"

She shrugs.

"Maybe."

Nailah slides into the space between my shoulder and arm, and I pull her into me. I nuzzle into the vanilla scent of her neck as she slides her palms up and down my side, pushing down my building emotion.

I am not sure how long we stay like that and at what point I fall asleep, but when I wake up, Terrence is tapping my shoulder, and Nailah is gone.

CHAPTER SIX

Nailah

Just getting out of the car and walking into work has become a master yoga class. As a social worker, I am constantly on the move with the bounds of casefiles stuffed with paper. This morning is no exception, especially since I took over one of the busiest areas of the city from a woman who just retired but had practically stopped working a year ago.

I bump my hip against my car door to close it. A soft click of metal lets me know that contact is made, but the mission is not accomplished.

I lean a hip up and use my ab muscles to bump up the twenty folders that begin sliding out of their cradled position in my arm. I balance the carrier of coffee in my left hand, my laptop between my chest and forearm, and a folder-full satchel on my right shoulder, which is starting to slip toward the sliding folders.

Using my left foot, I mule-kick back to close the door completely.

"Sorry, Lucy," I apologize to my beloved car.

I have had Lucy the Lexus since I was sixteen, and she was nearing middle age then. She was a gift, free and clear, and I know I wouldn't have made it without her. She has been a shelter and a friend. Now that I am twenty-eight, Lucy needs all the love she can get and a good portion of my paycheck for upkeep.

Today, I just need to make it to my office, drop all this stuff, and curse out my only friend. She had yet again tried to hook me up. Regina sent a man to my home disguised as a pizza delivery guy who had gotten the wrong address. We spoke for about five minutes, and when he asked to come into my home, I knew something was up. He confessed, and I nearly pulled off his face when I slammed the door.

Idealistically, I became a social worker with the noble idea that I could make a difference in a child's life. Realistically, I'm beginning to believe that I signed up to be the hall monitor of social corruption and apathy. It seems like I have made more of an impact on deforestation with the amount of paperwork involved than any real contribution to humanity. But yet I journey.

I slither my side close to the building, angle my badge against the locked "Staff Only" door, and wait for the loud click and release. I use my elbow to pull the door open wide enough to stick the front of my shoe in and then swing the door out wide enough for my body and its temporary appendages to make it through.

I walk past the empty security post, still unsure of the purpose since the guards start later and leave earlier than the employees of the building. My supervisor explained that the security officers receive pay from different funds than social workers, even though we are all county workers. The mental stamina needed to decode federal funding and regulation is too great, so I just nodded my head and agreed with him.

I turn onto my hall, bumping everything up and shifting everything to secure it for the last leg of my journey.

Making my way past the closed office doors, I feel a sense of pride. I really did it. I made it out of that dusty ass town with dirty attitudes, and I am never going back.

I hear the muted sound of a ringing phone as I pass Regina's office. I have not been employed here long, but even I know that Regina is never early and rarely on time. For this reason, I bring her an iced coffee. The temperature won't really matter by the time that she gets here.

Regina is the kind of woman I had dreamed of becoming: smart, sophisticated, fashionable. She always has a story about where she has been and who had been there with her. My life until now consisted of lonely nights in the backroom of the motel that I managed and school.

The ringing continues, and I notice that the sound is not coming from Regina's office. It is coming from mine.

"Dammit," I mutter. "Who's calling this early?"

I quickly rebalance my stuff and waddle faster toward the door. It would be easy to let the phone ring and then allow voicemail to pick it up. Of course, nothing about my life is ever easy. Although voicemail is set up on my phone, I cannot access it. The woman who had the office and job before me had apparently come with the building, but no one in the tech department could figure out how to override her password. I needed an entirely new extension, which, of course, takes time.

I contacted several people last week but didn't get a chance to speak with them. As usual, it was a serious case in which people with pertinent information went ghost.

I rush to my door, still gripping the duo of coffee, a multitude of folders, an overstuffed satchel, and a laptop that I had to pack up and drag from my car to the building, up the elevator, and down the hall. Curse my need to overachieve. I shouldn't have taken all of this home. Who works for free? Me.

I push at the petulant doorknob and bust through the door with my backside.

I drop my satchel on the floor, slide the files onto my desk, and then place the coffee on top of a stack of papers.

I yank up the phone just as the curled cord tugs at the drink carrier. The coffee crashes to the floor and onto the tops of my new pumps.

"Crap!" I yell with the receiver against my ear.

"Uh. Hello," the smooth voice on the line coughs out, obviously covering a chuckle. "Is everything alright?"

I hold onto the phone and begin cleaning up the mess.

"My apologies. I'm Nailah James, and I just wasted my only incentive to get up in the morning," I sigh and start straightening the mess. "Coffee is everywhere."

"Nailah," he smoothed out my name like spreading cool butter on hot bread.

He sounded familiar, but I couldn't place his voice.

"This is Dr. Tyriq Lewis. How have you been?" he asks as though we chatted every morning over coffee.

"Alright." I stretch out the word. Maybe he would give me some more information.

"You have no clue who I am, do you?" he asks. "You do a great job of puncturing my pride, as you put it."

It couldn't be. My heart pattered at the pace of hummingbird wings.

"Lew?" I question.

"Yes. Tyriq Lewis, general physician," he responds briskly. "You called and left a message for me to get in touch with you about a patient."

It had been a few weeks since I left him sleeping in the hospital waiting area. Never in the history of my life had I ever put a man to sleep, and we both had our clothes on. In general, I keep my distance from people, but there is something about Lew, and I felt it that day in the gallery, and even stronger at the hospital. I didn't feel like a knot of anxiety around him. The only thing about Dr. Lewis that made me uncomfortable was the fact that I was so comfortable with him.

"Yes." I scroll through cases in my mind to remember why I needed to speak with him.

"Thank you for calling," I say. "I literally tripped through the door two seconds ago. I need to grab the case file. Would you mind if I put you on hold for a quick minute?"

"Not at all," he answered. "You seem to do that well anyway."

"Um... alright," I reply. "Thank you."

The frustration in his voice catches me off guard.

His words stung. I had thought about him over the weeks, especially at night, but I had never imagined that I actually hurt his feelings.

I push the hold button and scramble through the folders in my satchel and the unbound ones on my desk.

Unsure why fate hates me, I take a deep breath and return to the call after I find the folder.

"I am researching information about a patient of yours-" I flip through my notes and locate the child's name. "Jordan Ames. How was he during his recent appointments?"

"Alright," he spoke again, not sounding at all like the funny guy I had met at the gallery or the concerned man who held me like I was his hope at the hospital.

I put the call on speaker so that I can organize my information and listen.

I ask questions and jot down notes as the doctor's cool and melodic voice fills the room. I imagine him all calm and seductive behind his desk.

"I mostly work with the private care of athletes, but I partner with a group that offers underinsured children medical services. They refer people to me, and I help the child with little or no cost to the family. He is one of those patients."

He just gets better the more that I learn about him.

"I usually work with Ms. Williams. Are you filling in for her today?" Dr. Tyriq asked.

Regina walks into my office before I answer.

She looks at my soppy mess of paper towels on the floor and shakes her head.

"No. She retired," I tell him.

"Are you her permanent replacement, or is this a pop-up and disappear type of thing?" the doctor returns.

Regina twists her head in the direction of the phone in a snap. A devious grin spreads across her painted lips, and I see the words scrolling across her forehead.

"Who is that?" she mouths.

I shake my head to quell any ideas that she may have and respond to Dr. Lewis.

"Not that it should matter to you, but I plan to stick around for a while," I reply. "Will that be a problem, Dr. Lewis?"

"Hopefully, you'll hang around long enough for me to get to know you, Nailah James," he confirms. "It took two months just to get two names."

Regina's eyes dart open and widen.

"Ask him out," she whispers energetically.

"Well, thank you, Dr. Lewis," I respond, hurrying to get him off the phone. "I will give you a call if I have any further questions."

I push a button to end the call.

"No, Regina. Stop it. Not him."

"Fine." Regina places her hands in the air as if she is surrendering. "At least tell me what's wrong with him."

"He's too fine."

Regina scratches at her eyebrow. "Now I have heard it all."

"My dad was that kind of man." I frown. "Smooth, popular, handsome, and I know how falling for someone like him ends. I have read the book and seen the Lifetime special on sexy men and heartbreak."

"Relax. You know that guys can be for fun, too." Regina's eyes light up with excitement. "Come with me to get a massage or something today."

I shake my head and straighten up my desk.

"I could never afford the places that you visit, Regina. Besides, you already bought me those dresses and heels. We got our nails and toes done, too."

"It's not a big deal, Nailah. I'll pay for it. I even get a discount because I post about them on social media," Regina offered.

I stop and look my friend in the eyes.

"I don't want any charity." I break the words down into syllables so that she can really understand. "I can do it on my own after I settle up a few things this month."

When I was a little girl, my grandmother worked as a house manager for a family in an upscale community. In return, the family convinced the principal to overlook the fact that I didn't live in the zone assigned to the ritzy school so that I could get an education in a better area. I learned a lot there, but I also remember the pity in their eyes. I didn't have as much as the other children.

"You won't let me buy you stuff, you won't let me hook you up with men," Regina pouted. "You're no fun."

"Look, Regina, I know you have these extra funds. I don't question why you can have expensive things and work here, but I am making a life for myself," I lecture. "The way that I grew up, nothing was for free. You get, and you have to give. Right now, I have nothing to give you."

"That right there," Regina pointed out.

I look at the files on my desk.

"That's what you have to give right there, Nai," she reiterates.

"What?"

"Your honesty. That's what I love about you. You say what you mean and mean what you say. No BS. I know it's simple, but it's a rare find," she explains before raising the cup to her lips.

"I appreciate you looking out for me. For real, you don't have to pay for my friendship," I tell her.

Living with a group of women and constantly being around men on the prowl, I learned to read people fast, judge their level of threat, and figure out how much I could allow them in. I recognized Regina as a person I could trust right off. But maybe I'd given her too much access to my life and feelings. Telling her that I secretly wanted a makeover and a boyfriend when we went for drinks one night has had her constantly shoving men in my direction and buying me stuff.

I think about the incredible chocolate man who had fought so hard to get to know me. Lew was too enticing, too flashy. I can't say that those types of guys have always liked me, but I have never liked them. On the other hand, Dr. Tyriq Lewis seemed to have a heart, the one thing that the flashy guys I knew often lacked.

"Alright." She places her hands in surrender mode again. "But we are still going shopping again for some slacks that don't look like clown pants."

I set a record for how far my eyes can roll.

When I pull up to the school where Jordan attends, I meet the lingering eyes of a custodian first.

My mother left me with my father when I was four. My father left me with his girlfriend, Dolly, when I was ten. Dolly left me at a diner when I was sixteen. Where I lived has changed over the years, but not the way that men look at me. I've been hiding under sheet-like shirts and balloon-like pants for years, and I know that it's time for a change.

All schools have the same disinfectant and wet glue smell to me. I check in at the front and wait for the counselor. I stand and check my phone as a small woman sashays to the front.

She is dressed like a model for a teacher-recruiting campaign, complete with a button-down shirt and coordinating cardigan.

Her bright, deep golden eyes and haphazard smile say that there is a little more to the woman than one might expect.

"Hello," she greets. "I'm Mali Summers, the lead counselor. Let me show you a private area where you can meet the student."

As we click-clack down the hall together, I had worn the low-heeled pumps and pencil skirt from Regina. One of the coaches nearly broke his neck, watching the two of us.

"I know that you probably get this a lot, but-" Mali Summers begins.

I hold up a hand.

"I look like the lady that won the Street Model Contest, Jubilee Monae," I finish for her. "It's amazing to me that she is considered plus-sized at a mere size ten."

"Right. And those fashion industry judges were so shocked at the response that they got from men," she said pointedly. "My cousin was obsessed with Jubilee. He never watched a reality show in his life until he saw her. Every week after, he was there with me or texting me about it."

"Your cousin sounds like a smart man."

"Most of the time, he is. ," Mali commented. "It was strange how industry people made such a big deal about her size, and she looked like a regular woman to me."

"I remember the episode when she ate the garlic bread, and the other models acted like she had lost her mind."

"People act like it's a crime to enjoy food. I love a good meal." Mali added.

Not that anyone would be able to tell. Her petite frame has some shape to it, but she is thin and has a waist that I would kill for.

"Me too, and right now, I'm missing some good food," I tell her honestly. "I want some smothered pork chops, candy yams, cabbage, and cornbread. Then I can top it all off with some Italian Wedding Cake made from scratch."

"Yes, you are my kind of girl," she adds.

"I haven't been able to find a place in the city that serves that stuff and my only friend does not eat any meat," I explain.

"There are a couple still around. I take lunch in a few," she says. "How about I show you my favorite spot after you meet with Jordan?"

"That would be great," I tell Mali.

CHAPTER SEVEN

Nailah

The sun warms my shoulder as I make my way into the oversized clinic that takes up most of the complex.

A quick change in temperature when I step through the door sends goosebumps spiking down my arms. Rich people sure know how to keep a place cold. In Texas, it takes a long dollar to keep a room at *sweater* temperature.

I cannot get rid of Dr. Tyriq Lewis. After interviewing him over the phone about a child last week, I received a call from the police department requesting the pickup of a left-behind child at his actual location.

The modernly decorated office looks both expensive and inviting. The empty waiting area, adorned with paintings and plastic plants, looks well taken care of and maintained. It definitely doesn't look like the type of place where a parent would walk away and leave their daughter.

"Hello," I say to the uninterested clerk behind the desk.

"We're closed," the stout older woman with a snatched bun sprinkled with gray hair explained.

She picked up a file and moved to an area with large cabinets in the back dismissively.

"I'm Nailah James with Child Protective Services. I'm here to see Dr. Lewis," I speak loudly, hoping to gain her attention. This is my last call of the day, and I do not want to be here all night.

I hear a filing cabinet close before the woman makes her way back to the front.

"Nailah James, is it?" she asked, looking me over. She seemed to be making a decision about me.

"You surely don't look like the last social worker we worked with," she added with narrowed eyes.

Suddenly feeling insecure, I straighten my black, curve-hugging dress. At Regina's request, I had gotten a few more flattering outfits. My dress today is tight enough to show off but roomy enough to allow me to move. It is low enough to display some cleavage but has enough material to keep my secrets. My nails were manicured, and my toes were pedicured to perfection. I went with the white tips this time, and the black peep-toe heels make them stand out even more. I even added a little eye makeup and extra curls to my bobbed, shoulder-length hair.

"I started a few months ago. I believe we spoke over the phone once before," I explained. "Mrs. Williams retired."

I handed her my badge that indicated my status as a social worker, and the suspicious woman nodded.

"Alright," she approves, then hands me back my badge.

"You can come on back."

A small dark girl with four ponytails sat on the examining table, her face wet and eyes puffy.

There is a pause when I enter, a moment for the emaciated child to register if I am someone she recognizes.

Her big amber-gold eyes widen and push out more tears. I'm not her mom, and right now, I'm sure that's the only person she is hoping will walk through the door.

"This is her," the assistant said. "She's been crying for about an hour now."

I walk over to the small girl.

She turns away.

"What's your name?" I lay my palm on her shoulder.

Her sobs answer me. The only move she makes is with her eyes.

"It's Tia," the assistant answers. "She hasn't said anything for a while."

"Thank you."

The assistant caught my subtle message and made her exit.

"I'm Miss James," I speak to her softly. "Tia, will you talk to me?"

Moments pass, and she doesn't respond.

"I want to help you find your mom," I inject as much sweetness into my words as I can

With tears streaming down her face, Tia turns to look in my direction but remains silent.

"That's why I'm here. My job is to make sure that you are safe until we find your mommy," I repeat, hopefully reassuring her that she can trust me.

She looks at me with round, red-rimmed eyes. Those startled, uniquely colored amber eyes are full of hurt but sweet enough to soften the soul of the devil himself.

"How about you read with me?" I pull a book from my briefcase and take a seat on the edge of the table.

"You have to stop crying to hear the story. Alright?" I bait.

Tia nodded and unexpectedly crawled quickly onto my lap.

I smile at her.

"Mommy reads like this," she whispers, gazing at my face before turning away shyly.

I nod and begin reading.

She appears clean. I eye her face, neck, and arms for bruises or marks as I read the short, colorful story about a squirrel who gets lost in the woods without any family. The other creatures in the woods began to help him and become his new family.

By the time I complete the story, her tears are complete as well.

"I like it," Tia displays a bashful smile.

She begins tugging and turning to previous pages.

"Do you like stories?" I ask her.

"Yes." She nods, sitting straight but not leaving my lap.

"Is it alright if I ask you a few questions, Tia?"

She nods slowly.

"What's your mommy's name?" I question.

"Mommy," she replies as though the answer is obvious.

"Do other people call her something else?" I ask with a chuckle.

"Nanna calls her Misty."

"Really?" I asked, trying to get her full attention. She looks up from her place nestled in my arms, and I continue. "I had a friend named Misty that I haven't seen in a long time."

There is a hint of a real smile on her. Hope seemed to chisel away at the corners of her mouth. I continue.

"Maybe your mommy might be the friend I'm looking for. Do you know where she likes to go?" I ask, gaining more of the girl's interest.

"We go a lot of places all the time," she answers. "We go to Nanna's house and the store and Joe's house."

Just as I open my mouth to ask about Nanna and Joe, the door swings open, and Dr. Lewis, the familiar statuesque man the color of steamed hot chocolate, rushes in, a clipboard in hand and white coat billowing from his swift movement.

The woman from the front desk stepped in behind him.

"Sorry to keep you waiting," he stated evenly while still staring down at his clipboard. "It's been a crazy day."

He hurriedly scribbles something on the trapped sheet of paper. He passes the clipboard back to the older woman before looking at me for the first time.

His eyes find mine, and I rediscover how deep and earnest they are.

The doctor's silence provides a new opportunity for me to feel self-conscious.

I help Tia out of my lap, stand up, and straighten my dress again.

"You look amazing, Nailah." He smiles. The doctor's almond-shaped eyes turn the curves of my body down one side and up the other, a smirk garnishing his face. His gaze is so sensual that I have to check to make sure I still have clothes on. "I knew that you had a body under."

"Lew," I cut him off and dart my eyes over to the child sitting next to me. I am not sure how he planned to finish that sentence, but it probably was not appropriate for four-year-old ears.

I know that a man enjoys what he sees, and Dr. Lewis is no different from the other men I have encountered, in that respect at least. His tall, lengthy, muscled body and pretty boy face bring different elements to the equation, though.

The doctor brandishes an embarrassed yet charming smile. "Tia has been crying for a long while. It's amazing that you got her to calm down."

"I've always been good with kids," I smile over at the young girl. "I lived in a group home of sorts as a kid."

Living with Dolly and Sugar after my father left, I had to watch random kids all the time. Dolly and Sugar's place, or Sugar Doll's to the locals, was a place for women with no home, but not officially a state group home.

"Well, Ms. Nailah James," Dr. Tyriq extended his hand. "Thank you for putting those awesome skills to use."

His warm hand encircles mine in a shake, and pleasure radiates through me just like every time before.

Quickly, he places his other hand on top of mine. His honest smile and engaging eyes make me want to capture them on camera just to look at them when I need a happy feeling.

"Please, call me Nailah," I didn't want to look away.

"Well then, Na-i-lah," the mesmerizing doctor lengthened my name. "I wish that we were meeting again under different circumstances."

I remove my hand from his. It had grown accustomed to the warmth and comfort he provided.

I pull out my notepad and clear my throat.

"Unfortunately, these issues occur far too often," My voice is tight. It is of the utmost importance that I gather my melted brain back together and be professional.

"The city is so lucky to have someone as beautiful as you to make it a better place," he adds, layering on another level of sweetness.

I must admit that he is enchanting. I stand still and let the tenderness of his words fall on me. The sound of his smooth voice lulled my attention completely away from Tia and my original purpose for even coming to his office.

"Thank you," I answer. After so many years of non-existent praise, his compliments are like a spring shower to the dry soil of my spirit.

Before he can say anything else, I get straight to business.

"What information can you give me about Tia?"

My eyes sweep across the doctor's sleek skin to his plump pecan-colored lips encased by a midnight black goatee. I have always liked a man with a little facial hair, and Dr. Lewis wears his distinctively.

"There's not very much information to give," he shoves his hands into his pockets.

Thoughts of pecan pie dance through my head. I fight the urge to lick his lips by running my tongue across my own.

His eyes follow my tongue.

"Any information is better than no information," the words tumble out. "Whatever you have, I'll take."

My eyes grow large at the double meaning of my words.

"I didn't mean it like," I sputter to explain, but stop.

An inviting smile invades the doctor's face, and he winked.

Looking toward his hard-soled shoes, I let my head fall between my thumb and forefinger. *How embarrassing.*

"Any information that you may have could be helpful," I dismiss thoughts of him giving me his goods in a bedroom setting.

"How about we head to my office and speak privately for a few minutes? I'll have Aunt Pat come and sit with Tia," he suggests.

I glance over at Tia, who is rereading the book we read earlier.

"Sure," I agreed hesitantly.

Turning to Tia, I place a hand on her arm to explain.

"I need to talk to the doctor a little bit, Tia, and I'll be right back."

I turn my attention back to the doctor.

"Follow me," he said, and I do.

Dr. Tyriq Lewis's office is smoother than that of the doctor himself.

Stevie Wonder's 'Ribbon in the Sky' floats from the computer on his desk, filling the air and calming the nerves flip-flopping through my body.

Plaques of all kinds and pictures of all sorts displaying him with athletes, local celebrities, and family fill the sandy-beach-colored walls. No pictures of a girlfriend or kids that could be his. This makes me smile.

In an alternate universe, where the bolder, sexier Nailah exists, she would take this opportunity to push everything off the desk, fling a naked Dr. Lewis on top of it, and ride that stallion until every part of her body throbbed in a pleasurable ache.

I shake away the vision and refocus on my mission.

The doctor moves behind his desk and takes a seat before turning off the music.

"Sorry about that," he apologizes. "I always keep my music going. It's my escape."

He looks at me as though trying to determine if I am real.

"I understand," I say, taking a seat in one of the matching chairs in front of his desk. "I'm a Stevie fan myself."

"Really?" His left eyebrow moves up into an arch as he questions. "You don't look old enough to know what I know about Stevie."

"What? 'Sir Duke' and 'Isn't She Lovely' are two of my favorite songs," I emphasize. "Don't get me going on 'For Once in My Life,'" I say, getting excited.

"So, you know a little something." A hint of surprise sprinkled his words.

"Music was my lifeline when I was younger," I explain. "And I'm twenty-eight."

"I would have pegged you as a pop princess around about twenty-five," he smirks. "There's a neo-soul concert coming up soon. Why don't you check it out with me? I'd love to go with someone who appreciates the music."

I looked down at my notepad to avoid his mind-changing eyes.

Any certified sane woman would follow him to the ends of the earth if he asked.

Unfortunately for him, I am not one of those women.

"I think we should probably talk about Tia," I sigh.

He nods, the smile sliding from his face.

"I can't believe a woman would just walk away from her child without a second thought." Tyriq sits forward. "Family is really important to me."

"Having people to love is important in general," I respond. "How is your mother?"

"She's doing well. She's home, and my pops have been home to take care of her."

"How's your ex?" I asked.

"Still married."

"And you're not?" I lift an eyebrow.

"Not at all." His answer is swift and precise.

"Why not?" I have to question. He looked too good not to have a woman hiding somewhere.

"That's an answer I'll give you over breakfast," Dr. Lewis winks before leaning back in his chair.

His cologne wafts near, warming the spot between my thighs.

I fight the urge to sniff and stare at him by doodling the date on my empty notepad.

"How do you like the job so far?" he asks.

"Some of the situations that I come in contact with are tough," I answer. I slide my left leg over my right to alleviate some of the sensations happening in between them.

I had never seen anyone like him in Brook Bonnet or the college town next to it where I lived later. Beautiful would be too generic of a word to describe the sensuousness that seemed to seep from his very existence.

"I can only imagine." Dr. Lewis temples his fingers and looks more like a kingpin than a general doctor. Even though the plaques on his walls boast degrees and specialties, his movements let me know that the street in him isn't too far away. "You have a very tough job."

"True, but there is nothing that I would rather do."

"I bet your man must worry about you all the time," his eyes lock in on me.

My heart thrums at his words. I like the intention of his attention.

"My man doesn't worry about me at all," When I look back at him, I notice that his brightness fades a little.

"Not that anyone holds that title in my life," I add.

"A woman as lovely as you should have someone looking out for her. Especially with crazy stalkers on the loose," slips from his incredible lips. The desire that flickers in his eyes tells me that he wants to be the one who looks out, over and after my body.

"Someday, someone may apply for that position. Until then, I can take care of myself," I say with a smile.

"So, you're taking applications?"

His words shock the senses in my lady parts like a bolt of electricity. Well-sculpted arms peek through the doctor's white jacket and shirt. I remember how well his pants fit around his solid legs and trim waist. Tyriq Lewis could easily blaze the cover of any magazine or add seduction to any cologne ad.

In what world does a suave city guy like him date a country girl like me?

"Do I remind you of an ex-lover or a kid that stole your cookies or something?" His face firms as he folds his arms across his desk.

"What?" I question. "No."

He shakes his head.

"Every attempt I make to get closer sends you running in the opposite direction."

I chuckle at the memory of me actually running out of the museum the first time that I met Tyriq Lewis.

The stress in the air lightens some. He seems to remember that day, too.

"I am a little taken aback, Dr. Lewis. You're so…" I pause and try to gather coherent words to explain my thoughts. "You're a very good-looking and successful man."

"I thought that would work in my favor," his chuckle is light and airy.

"It's not a bad thing, Dr. Lewis," I answer but do not elaborate.

"Call me Lew or Tyriq," he replies, the baritone in his voice like a massaging vibration. "I want to take you out to dinner tonight."

"I don't know if that is appropriate." There must be some regulation or rule against this. I can't date him. I can't be involved with anyone.

"You're not investigating me, so I don't see a problem," Tyriq said surely.

I sit up a little taller in the chair. He makes a convincing point.

"How about we finish our talk about Tia for a bit, and then we can talk about any personal matters a little later?"

"I'm going to hold you to that," he counters while nearly smiling me out of my senses.

"So, Dr. Lewis, why would a woman, Misty specifically, leave her child with you?" I question.

"Before today, I didn't know anything about this woman," the doctor answered. "And she didn't say much to me before she disappeared to the restroom."

I notice the thickness of his hands and how round and full each digit is. Meaty.

My breasts feel fuller with the wonder of how much he can hold and the pleasure that those hands may be able to bring. I bet other parts of him were just as thick and solid.

"Did she say anything unusual or do anything strange? Do you have any records on the girl?" I ask.

"No. She is a first-time patient. Supposedly, a member of the basketball team referred her, but no one knew her. My Aunt Pat got a copy of the mother's I.D., but it turned out to be fake. The information belongs to an elderly Hispanic woman who lives twenty miles from here. The phone numbers that she listed don't work." he answered.

His thoroughness in finding out more about the patient is a quick turn-on.

I wonder how thorough he is in other aspects of life.

I take a deep breath and work on focusing.

"She's been in my office for six hours; we've tried everything, and Aunt Pat is pretty strict about closing time," he said, flashing his pearly white teeth.

I swallow hard and jot down random words on my notepad as I suddenly feel like a groupie in front of her superstar crush.

"Well, if you could have someone make a copy of that information, I'd at least have a starting place," I say with a smile.

I stand to leave.

"Is there anything that you would like to add?" I ask.

The doctor stood as well and moved effortlessly around his desk to stand near me.

"Yes," he said, closing some of the gap between us. "But only if the business part is over."

"You're kind of close," I observed aloud. I do not object to his closeness, but it certainly makes it difficult to focus on the matter at hand.

"I don't want to make you uncomfortable, Nailah," he says in that voice, through those lips, with those eyes that make me want to fall right into his arms.

"You don't," I declare, deciding to take advantage of the opportunity to be close to him. How often do moments like this come around? For me, never. If there were ever a moment, minute, or day to seize, this is it.

Seize the day, Nailah.

"I believe in getting what I want," Tyriq explains.

"So, whether I like you or not is irrelevant?" I grin before shaking away my schoolgirl reserves and sliding into the sweet feelings overtaking me. Toying with the doctor and creating a few moments to focus on tonight is worth it.

There is a twinkle in his eye when he speaks this time. "Not irrelevant, just obvious."

"Really?" I questioned, scratching at my palm before crossing my arms to add space.

He rests his hand on my hip as though it belongs there, and I drop my arms.

His eyes say more than his lips need to.

"I want to see you tonight."

"I have to drive Tia to the intake center and then to a shelter. That could take a while," the answer formed and floated from my mouth without the full participation of my brain because all I could concentrate on was his lips.

The doctor nodded and then slid his substantially sized hand across my hip and around my waist.

I shiver as tingles of desire follow the movement of his hand against my body.

"Can I?" he breathes in a low tone that instantly saturates my girl parts.

I nod, the words lost somewhere between my need to touch him and my desire to lick those lips.

He wants me, and I want to know how his tongue tastes.

Tyriq moves forward.

I close my eyes slightly and lift my mouth toward his.

Our lips brush together, and I feel my insides melting and folding on themselves. This man is dangerous.

His tongue sweeps across my lips, and I part for him.

"Doctor!" his assistant yells through the door.

An abrupt knock follows, startling me to my senses.

I hop out of Tyriq's arms and across the room with the quickness of a gold medal sprinter and lose a shoe in the process.

My toe slams into the thick wooden base of the office chair as I attempt to escape.

"Danggit!" I cry out.

I double over at the throbbing pain.

The doctor let loose a chuckle that caused his whole body to move.

"That's not funny," I gave a harsh whisper as I hopped around on one foot.

"Are you alright?" he asked, moving closer to me.

He helped me into the chair that assaulted me.

"Let me look at that," Tyriq asks as he slips closer to me.

Most people have stories of their mother kissing their *ouchie* or their dad singing songs to their *boo-boo*. My mother, Mosel James, did no such kissing, and the only songs that my father, Curtis 'Slick' Green, knew involved James Brown. I cannot remember a time that someone took the time to check on me.

Tyriq gently takes my foot into the warmth of his hands.

I look at him, amazed by his tenderness.

The realization washes over me that a man who barely knew me showed more compassion toward me than my own father had.

"Can you wiggle it?" he asks.

I move my toe.

"I'm fine," I swallow back emotion. "Thank you."

My heart pounding, I try to recover from him.

The office door creaks open.

"Tyriq," I hear his Aunt Pat call.

Still holding onto my foot, the doctor gives it one last look over.

"We need to get things wrapped up," his aunt continues while stepping into the office. "Closing time."

"Alright," Tyriq directs his answer to his assistant, but his eyes never leave me.

When his aunt doesn't leave, Tyriq addresses her.

"I promise we'll be out of here in less than five," Tyriq tells her.

With a wink in my direction, he is up and back behind his desk.

"As you should," his aunt relays as she shuts the door.

"How about we continue this tonight after you handle things at work?" he suggests, scribbling his number on the back of his card.

I take the card and look at the back. There are ten digits there instead of just seven. Back in Brook Bonnet, area codes were not required.

"It doesn't matter the time," he states.

"I wouldn't want you to get the wrong idea about me," I explain, but he is so close to me that my words trail into whispers.

"I know what I like," he countered while watching me.

I take a step back at those words and that look.

"So why is it that I'm calling you tonight, Lew?" I ask with as much gruff as I can muster. "I don't do full physicals on the first date."

The doctor rounds the corners of his mouth with a smile.

This doctor is captivating. Everything about him sets my temperature to scorch. His daring but delightful eyes, his masculine but mindful presence, and his strong but soothing voice make me mush on the inside.

"Well, Miss Nailah James, as long as I get to see you again, a consultation will suit me just fine," he responds while sweeping the side of my face with his fingers.

I clear my throat.

"I think we should get back to Tia before your Aunt turns off all the lights," I remind him.

Reluctantly, I turn to exit.

"You're probably right," he sighs.

Together, we walk back to the examining room.

My feet stop me before I can enter.

Tyriq placed a calming hand on my back.

"Are you alright?" he asks.

I smile wearily.

"This is just the hardest part of my job."

He nods.

I walk into the room, and Tia smiles again. I wonder how long she will continue to smile. Today is the first day of a life with no one.

CHAPTER EIGHT

Tyriq

Nailah James put a hex on my head the moment I saw her in the art gallery. I pull car number two into garage number three and smile at the compound that I have built for myself.

My home is everything that I wanted and more. Not a thing out of place, not a smudge or a stain in the midst. It would be perfect, and it would be the epitome of a home if there were a family, my family, to live in it.

It is amazing what time can do to your perspective on life. For a long while, I had not even considered settling down. Life was given to me so that I can live it. My philosophy then was that the only way to live was untethered, unrestricted, and without limits. I have lived here for nearly two years now. Alone. An empty home is like an egg with no yoke, shallow.

I loosen my tie, flop onto the leather sofa, push the button to recline, and lose myself in thoughts of the lovely woman who locked lips with me. The lovely woman has plagued my dreams every night. In my mind, her soft hands massage spots across my body as her lips massage my mouth, and I palm her perfect backside. Her underwear come off with ease, leaving her glory unleashed and available for me to dive in and penetrate.

The constant buzzing from the intercom interrupts my dream before I can get to the best part. I push the button on the security system remote that opens the gate and another to unlock the door for my brother to enter.

"Damn man, you had me waiting out there forever," the usually calm Terrence huffs.

He enters the room with a case of beer, his shoulder-length locks loose around his face. "What happened, bro?"

"Sorry about that. I passed out on this sofa, man," I explain.

Terrence takes a seat and passes me a beer from the case.

"You alright?" His left eyebrow lifts to emphasize his concern. "I thought the old Tyriq had resurfaced, and you had some freak in here."

I chuckle at the thought.

"That ain't my style no more, T, you know that. Besides, I don't bring freaks to my home."

"I noticed that you've been more settled lately," he assesses carefully.

"Settled?" I question. Why would he choose that word? "I wouldn't say all of that."

"Man, back in the day, you'd have a different woman every week. No, every day, and a wild ass story about every one of them."

"I wasn't that bad," I contest.

"Then you bought this big ass house," he adds, surveying the surroundings. "And when you cut off all the ladies in your life, I knew you had lost all of your mind."

"The house is an investment," I defend. "I have a – different perspective- since mom's accident. I don't know, and it made me think about life a little differently."

Terrence takes a swig of his beer and nods. He knew about the meaning of life, love, and loss. Always the mature and calm one, he had gotten married at twenty-three to his high school sweetheart. She died a year later, and he has been single since.

"I feel ya," he said.

I love all of my brothers, but Terrence has always been my confidant, my partner in crime.

"Well, I guess for old time's sake, I do have a new story."

"Do tell." He sits forward.

"She's not a random girl. She's a social worker."

He frowns. "Like Mrs. Williams?"

"No, not like Mrs. Williams," I answer. "I mean, she has Mrs. Williams' old job, but Nailah is pinup material. Like JET Beauty of the Week, sexy under those huge clothes. I would have sworn that she was trying to hide it on purpose until I saw her."

I shiver at the thought of her in that dress.

"There's my brother," he laughs. "The old Tyriq is back."

"The first time I met her, she was going after this dude like she was a boxer. Then at the hospital, she was on some Yoda shit and had me spilling my feelings to her and shit about mom. It was crazy," I explain. "She's amazing. Smart, funny, caring, fine-"

"It's like that?"

"Shoot me if it ain't," I say with my hands up. "That's not even the best part. Aunt Pat had been trying to get this little girl to calm down and talk to her for hours. No luck. Nailah comes. Boom. The girl is in Nailah's lap telling stories."

"Nothing like the she-witches you usually date, huh?" Terrence adds in his usual sarcastic tone.

"Hey," I was slightly offended, but not much.

"I figure they have bad attitudes because they're hungry," Terrence concludes.

"Whatever, man." I shake my head and continue. "So, I get her cornered. I'm putting out my Edris bedroom eyes. She's feeling me; I'm waiting to feel her. I go in for the kiss and-"

"And?"

"And Aunt Pat comes knocking at the door."

"Brother, are you serious?" He laughs. "Your own aunty blocked you."

"Nailah gets all scared and is jumping around the room like a caught fish. It was over."

"Still, that's the shit I'm talking about. Stuff like that just doesn't happen to me." He shrugs. "I haven't been interested in a while."

"She still hasn't called me, so I guess she wasn't feeling me like I thought she was."

"What? A woman didn't jump on the chance to date Tyriq Lewis? Dr. Lew, millionaire extraordinaire," he jokes.

"It's not like that, man," I counter.

"Did you get her number?"

"Didn't think I would need it." I shrug. "I gave her mine."

"Good luck with that." Terrence takes another swig of his beer, and his disappointment deepens.

"Good luck with what?" Tyson asked, entering. "The gate and door were already open," he adds.

"Tyriq gave a woman his personal number, and she hasn't called him."

"In three days," I finish.

"Damn, bro, are you losing your touch?" Tyson's face contorts. "Ladies used to line up, and you just knock 'em down."

"You make it sound so bad," I respond. Did I really treat women like bowling pins before? I have been with many women, and each of them was special in their own way, not like bowling pins, but more like marbles: both beautiful to look at and fun to play with.

"You know where she works. Call her office," Terrence suggests.

"I don't want to be her stalker. She actually had a guy that bugged her out a little, so I'm taking it slow," I explain.

"But you would be calling to check on the case, and then you can slip in a date offer or something."

"Yeah, already offered that," I remind them.

"And she said no?" Terrence put down his beer.

"That's one for the history books," Tyson added, propping his sneaker-clad foot on my coffee table.

"She didn't exactly say no, just not yes," I say, trying to clean up my admission and change the subject. I had already told them more about Nailah than I cared to share. "How's the shop?"

My brothers and I own an auto care company with locations throughout Texas and southern Oklahoma. We provide auto repair, towing, and auto parts. Terrence oversees the day-to-day business and even works at our downtown Dallas location. Tyson travels to various locations for quality assurance.

"It's straight," Terrence answers. "We need to consider opening a second location of the Touchless Car Wash and expanding the towing options."

This wasn't an official meeting, but I needed to talk about something else.

"So business is good?"

"Not as good as all this," Tyson said, referencing my home. "But you know how we do."

"Being a doctor to the stars pays well."

"Speaking of stars, do either of you want to hang out with me at the Professional Athletic Association gala tomorrow?"

"Got a date," Tyson responds.

"What's new?"

"Sure," Terrence agrees. "I'm not doing anything anyway."

I make my way to the bedroom after my brothers leave and check my phone the entire way. Why hasn't she called me yet?

Shit. I approach women. Women approach me. They chase me. We meet our mutual needs. The end. Nailah is putting a kink in the process.

I slide into bed and then hear a buzz on the intercom from the front gate. Tyson is always leaving something. Even as kids, we always had to stop everything to go back and get whatever Tyson left.

"Hello." the small, familiar voice whispered.

"Briana?"

"Tyriq. Let me in, please," she whimpers over broken breaths.

There are only a handful of times that I'd heard the confident and assured woman I'd known since my freshman year of college sound like that, so I hit the buzzer to let her in and unlock the door.

I notice her eye first. Swollen. Bruised. Bloody. Her lips look the same, each one of them tugged in a different direction as if someone were pulling them with hooks.

She had always been a gorgeous woman. Her khaki-colored skin was smoother than whipped butter. Now, speckled with blood, bruises, and cuts, it appeared ragged and tired.

She stood there inside my front door, waiting.

I brought my first aid kit with me. I knew that if she had made a special trip to my house, then there had to be something wrong, and the something wrong was usually her husband's temper.

"Come over here and sit on the sofa," I say without much tenderness.

The first time I saw her beat up, I didn't curse, and I didn't yell. As if on autopilot, I walked to my closet and pulled out my .45. Briana attacked my back amid broken sobs. The way she attempted to keep me from walking out of the door that day checked me right back into reality. After registering her screams as "Don't hurt him," I realized she hadn't been trying to keep me out of trouble or keep me from doing something as stupid as throwing my life away. She was attacking me to protect him. She had fallen on her knees, spread her body across the floor in front of my door, and held onto my legs to keep me in the house that day so that I wouldn't shoot the man who had beaten her.

Now, when I see her fresh, recovering, and scarred bruises, I don't feel angry. I don't feel pity, either. I gave her an out, but she refused me.

"I didn't have anywhere else to go," she says as I begin wiping and bandaging cuts. "He was- I should have-"

She stopped and started her words like a teenager learning how to drive a stick shift car.

"Are you going back to him?" I ask her evenly, uninterested in the cause, as though there is a just cause for all of this.

I touch her wrists and ribs and check her arms, neck, and head. Nothing seemed sprained or broken.

"It'll be worse if I leave him, Lew," she whispers.

I don't want to argue with her, and I don't have the energy to try and convince her, again, that she is valuable and that her life is worth something beyond misery. *How could it be worse if you weren't there?* I didn't ask. I had asked her to leave him, begged her to stay with me. I even proposed. None of it mattered. Despite that, she stood at my door.

"Let me at least take pictures this time."

"Why?" she snaps as she snatches her wrist away from me.

"Calm down." I place a hand on her knee. "When he kills you, I want there to be some evidence that he had done this before."

"He won't- he wouldn't do anything like that," she said, looking away from me.

"Because he told you he wouldn't?" I snap.

She stands quickly and moves to the door. "I didn't come here for your judgment," she says.

"Only for my help, only for what you need, and now you're leaving, as usual," I snarl.

It had been this way between us for a long time now. She had married a ball player, the man without a blown knee, who wasn't in rehab when graduation rolled around, who didn't have an additional year of undergrad and countless years of medical school. She always found her way back to me, back to my bed, back in my head for something.

The tears move like rivers from her eyes, and I pull her close to calmly pat places that I hope are not bruised.

"Go to the guest room. Take a bath. I will pour you something from the bar," I tell her once the tears slow.

CHAPTER NINE

Nailah

D r. Tyriq Lewis and his tantalizing body have weighed heavily on my mind the last few days, but I refuse to call him. Dr. Lewis is the kind of handsome that makes a girl lose her mind and herself. I cannot get lost in some guy right now. Like Humpty Dumpty after his fall off the wall, I am just now gathering up my pieces and getting myself back together again.

Being around Tyriq makes self-control nonexistent. His presence pushes my hormones over the edge.

Like a mouse moving a mountain, I push the\\ thoughts of Tyriq out of my mind.

The phone on my desk rings.

"Hello?"

"I really want to keep her." There is no hello or bother with small talk. Debora got straight to the gut of it. "I want to keep little sweet Tia, but I can't."

"Your husband got the job?" I let my head fall onto my free hand.

"Yep. We have fourteen days before we need to be in Atlanta. The company is helping with relocation costs and all."

"I'm excited for your new opportunity but sad to see you go."

Debora had quickly become my go-to temporary foster home. The children are going to be saddened to lose her.

"I know you really care about this young one. You have a good heart, but we can't stay here, and we can't take sweet Tia with us."

Memories of watching my mother handcuffed, led away, and never seen again filter into my mind. Flashes of my father driving away when I was ten and Dolly walking away flip through my brain. It is never an easy thing when loved ones leave.

"We really like her," Debora adds. "I'm sure you can find someone to take her."

"Maybe," I sigh. "Thank you, Debora, for all that you and your family have done."

We discussed allowing Tia to stay with them until the very last minute before the family must leave and end the call.

"Are you trying to meet the rats and roaches? You know that they invade this place after five pm, right?" Regina jokes while walking into my office.

"What do you have planned for tonight? A friend of mine canceled on me at the last minute, and I have an extra ticket to the Professional Athletic Association Gala."

"Oh, hell no, I fell for it once. You go ahead and enjoy." I shuffle through some of the papers.

"Let it go, Nailah. It was just a trench coat."

"Who wears a trench coat in July? Not happening."

"No games, I promise." Regina put her hand over her heart as if she were saying the pledge. "Plus, you don't have one good reason not to go tonight."

"One, I love my condo. Two, I've been thinking about my crockpot chicken tetrazzini all day. Three, unless I can go in yoga pants with my hair in a ponytail, I have nothing to wear."

"First of all, I said one. Secondly, you're just making up excuses, Nailah." Regina rolls her neck and narrows her eyes, ready to pop out with more reasons for me to attend her event.

"Honestly, I do not have anything fancy to wear." I layer on an extra hint of woe to my voice and round my eyes. "I don't go out?"

"You have to start somewhere. I know I have something in my closet that can show off that fabulous body of yours. You have to come with me," Regina pleads.

I step out of the black limo and into the sparkling lights of the towering hotel. Wearing Regina's tight red dress makes me push my chest out a little further and up a little higher. Yes, *the girls* are on display tonight, and the looks I receive from people milling about the lobby confirm that my dress selection is the right one. Regina styled my hair and did a stellar makeup job. I make each step on purpose, as if everyone can hear the Beyoncé theme music rotating through my brain.

The grand ballroom is filled with men of every color and caliber. Pro athletes, owners, trainers, lawyers, and doctors saturate the room like a man mecca. I have never seen anything so spectacular. The men are dipped in gold, and the women in the place are ready to dig.

"You look awesome, Nailah," Regina says. "And you can have that dress. After tonight, I just wouldn't even do it justice."

A waiter walks by with a champagne tray, and I pick up a flute.

"Thanks," I say. "This place is kind of overwhelming. Everybody and everything in here screams rich."

"Well, you better whisper to the one screaming the loudest because I didn't order a ride home."

"Regina!"

"Regina, nothing. Did you think I came here for the food? I'm looking for some meat, but not the kind on a plate."

"Regina, you are so nasty."

"And I plan to show one of these men just how nasty I can be."

I should have known better.

The ladies I knew when I was a child never talked about nasty in a good way. The sweet part of life, the kind experiences were the conversation starters and what the ladies longed for. It was what I longed for.

Before we find our table, men find us, and not just any men. Naeem Matthews and Jermaine Timmons stroll up to us, looking like water fountains in the desert. If Naeem wasn't married, I may have even been a little thirsty. Jermaine is still single, and Regina is ready to drink.

"Regina." Jermaine smiled as he leaned in to hug her. "I thought that was you."

"It's nice to see you, Jermaine," Regina responds before greeting the other lanky athlete. "And you too, Naeem."

"Jermaine, Naeem, this is Nailah."

Recognition lit in Naeem's eyes as they roam over me.

"I've met you before, right?" he questions. "I never forget a face, and definitely not a beautiful one."

Regina and I swapped glances. I am sure she is wondering why I did not mention meeting Naeem before.

"We spoke briefly at an art gallery."

"Yes. We have a friend in common, Lew?" Naeem asks while stepping closer to me.

An awkward moment passes between Naeem and I. He's married, so I don't have as much to say to him as Regina apparently has to say to Jermaine.

"Well, it was nice to see you again, Naeem."

"Let's head to our table, ladies," Jermaine announces.

I look over at Regina, who detaches herself from her date to whisper in my ear, "Surprise!"

I blink a few times because it is the only way I can keep from screaming expletives. I count backward from ten, turn my fabulous heels in the opposite direction of the group, and walk away.

"Excuse us for just a few moments, gentlemen," I hear Regina say.

I make it into the hallway of the stunning event center before she catches up to me.

"Nailah, wait."

I should keep walking, but I don't. She had tricked me again, and that hurt.

I whirl around to face the woman that I thought was my friend.

"Please don't be upset with me, Nailah."

"Do I look like a whore to you?" I ask.

"Of course not, but this is a premium opportunity." Regina took my shoulders in her hands. "We are about to eat dinner with Jermaine Timmons and Naeem Matthews, multi-million-dollar, award-winning athletes."

"I do not care about any of that. Regular guys are assholes, and rich guys are whole assess. I came to have fun with you, not some arbitrary guy."

Regina jerked her hands away from me as though I had stung her.

"You better be glad that I like you. You are in a place full of sexy, successful men looking like a supermodel, and you're trying to hang out with me?"

"Naeem is married. What the hell am I supposed to do with that?"

"Get. His. Money." Regina claps.

I roll my eyes.

"For real, Nailah. His wife knows the game. They have an understanding. Jermaine explained the entire thing to me over the phone. As long as he doesn't parade it in her face, she's alright with him seeing other women."

"I don't care about their crazy ass marriage, it's a no for me."

"Nailah, please just have a seat with the man. I will make sure you get a ride home. I need this," Regina pleads.

Naeem and Jermaine were still standing when we entered the crowded ballroom, but guests were beginning to take their seats. I've faked my way through worse things before. I know how much Regina wants to snag a rich man, so I will play along for as long as I can.

"Why don't we have a seat?" Jermaine gives a lopsided grin as he slips his arm through Regina's extended elbow.

Naeem placed his large hand on the small of my back with a familiarity that we do not have.

I sidestep, effectively adding some space between us.

"Hands to yourself."

Naeem laughs as his eyes rove down my backside and up my front.

"Alright," he agrees. "I like a challenge."

"I'm not playing. I don't care who you are."

This only served to make Naeem laugh more.

"Calm down," he said. "We'll see how you feel when the night is over."

Just as I am about to curse Naeem out for placing his arm around me again, a camera flash fires off, and a small man in a tan vest appears.

Several more clicks go off in rapid succession as Naeem charges forward.

"Get back!" the previously smiling Naeem growled in the quivering photographer's face. "No pictures."

The man cowered and moved away quickly.

"You got rules?" I mumble, but Naeem isn't paying attention.

"He must be new or some shit. They know better," he grumbles before pulling out my chair at an eight-person table in the front of the ballroom.

"I'm out here trying not to embarrass my BM, and the damn vultures attack."

"Your BM?" I ask, looking between Regina and Naeem for clarification. She had come up for air.

"Baby Momma," she explains before getting lost in Jermaine again.

I frown.

"I know you have a wife, Naeem, and I honestly feel uncomfortable being here with you."

"We're honest though. My BM gives me freedom," he assures. "How do you think we've stayed together for so long? It's not because I only sleep with her."

Naeem doubles over in laughter, clapping his hands and nearly choking, but he finds it so funny.

I could have been eating chicken tetrazzini right now.

I turn away from the nimrod Naeem and my fawning friend to look for any normal person in the wide room.

When I see him, I instantly want to crawl under the table and then climb his sexy ass.

CHAPTER TEN

Tyriq

I was really hyped about going to the gala, winning an award, and what it could do for my practice at first, but when I heard the names of other honorees, I just wanted to get the night over with.

"There are a lot of prominent people here," Terrence notices. "The shop is doing pretty well, but if I can get a contract to tow for the arena-"

He rubbed his hands together.

"The right people are here for that tonight."

"And the wrong ones, too," he adds. "I didn't come dressed to scrap, so I hope you and Naeem worked through your shit."

"As long as he isn't abusing anyone, I don't have a problem with him."

"Cool." Terrence nods. "There's table number three up front."

I sigh.

"Of course, it would be right next to Naeem and Jermaine." They are seated at table number two with a host of people. Briana is nowhere in sight, but another woman is next to him. I was hoping not to see Briana, but this is much, much worse.

"He's still picking top-notch women, I see," Terrence added, rubbing salt into the wound.

"That's Nailah."

"Who?"

"The woman from the hospital. The social worker. The one who came to my office. The kiss."

"That's her?" Terrence's eyes round. "Damn. She had on a sheet the last time I saw her. She got those titties sitting nicely tonight."

"Quit looking at her." I push at his arm even though I know that Terrence is only stating the obvious.

Nailah looks gorgeous.

"I would if I could, brother, but damn."

I knew exactly what Terrence meant. Nailah looks almost like a different woman, and it pisses me off that Naeem may have had something to do with it.

My brother and I approach their table.

Naeem stands, and I fight the urge to punch his bitch ass back into his seat.

"Lew. What's up, man?"

He reaches out, and we clap hands before I lean in.

"If you harm her, I will lay you out," I speak so that Nailah cannot hear, but I make sure to get my point across.

"This ain't college homeboy, and we both know that I always win in the end anyway."

I step back.

"You don't want to test that theory tonight." I nod toward the woman that I could not stop seeing in my mind or in person. "Have a good night."

Terrence and I take our seats.

"Forget what I said before. I got your back if you want to whoop his ass right quick. You look like you do."

It is rare that my gentle and giant brother ever resorted to violence. He kept his emotions in check most of the time, but I see the fighter in him surface a little.

"He won't try anything in public. He has his reputation to keep."

Chapter Eleven

Nailah

Mega mogul Reginald Strong took the stage and began the ceremony. It was a good thing that the event was starting because Tyriq looked like he was ready to rip Naeem apart.

I take in a deep breath and look over to his table. I had thought of the doctor only as this square definition of perfection, but tonight, I can see that there may be more to him. He may even be able to handle a woman like me. A woman with a past.

Several awards were given out, and Lew doesn't notice me once. Every time I look his way, he and his brother laugh, or a vulture-looking woman at that table does everything in her power to get his attention.

I had really messed up. I really, really should have been with Lew.

I return my attention to the table of people with resignation to sleep in the bed I've made.

"Isn't the table setting beautiful?" Regina is wearing a bright smile, but I know her well enough to understand that this is code for 'perk the hell up and enjoy what is in front of you.'

"Yes, very glittery and such."

I give a good try at trying to like the people around the table. I really put in some effort, but they make it nearly impossible. Regina had set aside all her moral turpitude and flirted shamelessly with Jermaine, who seemed to puff out his chest a little more with each one of her displays. Naeem droned on endlessly about himself, and luckily, several people had found that interesting.

Waiters move seamlessly through the room with trays of food and drinks like trails of colored light that flicker and disappear.

No one notices their faces, and I wonder what the nameless people must say about these snoods when they return to the kitchen.

I am the only one at my table so far to say 'Thank you' when a petite Spanish woman places a plate in front of me. Naeem is so busy animatedly telling a story about himself that he doesn't notice the server dodging around him, attempting to place his plate.

"Hey, she's trying to feed you," I interrupt his story.

Naeem's eyes narrow as he looks from me to the employee holding a plate and then back to me.

Seconds tick by as everyone seated at the table ceases movement in order to watch our exchange.

The suddenly nervous server puts the plate down, and Naeem doesn't acknowledge the woman's efforts, and that pisses me off more.

"A thank you would be nice. Your plate did not magically appear from floating hands," I snap.

I hear Regina clear her throat.

Naeem looks over to the retreating woman and throws out a half-hearted "Thanks."

I shake my head and resume my normal task. Others at the table stare until Naeem speaks.

"You heard the lady, don't be rude. Say thank you."

Guests around the table echo and mumble sentiments of thanks as the servers move their large trays onto other tables.

"My grandmother would like you," Naeem finally spoke about someone other than himself.

"Are you calling me old?" I fumble the silverware under my fingers.

He laughs, and tensions ease around the table.

"No. She was all about manners. She believed in yes sir, no sir, and thank you."

I give him half of a grin.

"That's how I was raised. Take your manners with you everywhere you go."

The smooth and slick-suited Reginald Strong returns to the microphone and effectively interrupts the most enjoyable moment I have had the entire night.

"Now, we would like to honor our physicians," the gray topped man bellowed from the stage in front of us. "Medical professionals, would you please rise?"

Tyriq and several people sitting at his table stand. Thunderous applause, hollers, and whistles fill the room.

"While all these medical professionals have been an asset, there is one man who has helped a couple of you guys out of some pretty sticky situations. Dr. Lew, come on up here. Tonight, we honor you with the 'fixer' award."

Tyriq takes the stage swiftly, smiling as many of the players stand to their feet.

My heart flutters at the sight of him standing there looking delectable in his custom-fit suit.

"Wow," Lew says looking at the small trophy and then around the room. Finally, his eyes lock with mine.

"Thank you. It feels good to be acknowledged," he adds extra stress to the last word. I had obviously pissed him off.

I feel Naeem lean closer to me.

"My award is bigger," he whispers.

Naeem clapped along with the rest of the crowd when Lew exited the stage.

"Dr. Lew deserves that award." Jermaine nods as the applause dies down. "He's hooked a brother up a couple of times. Gunshots, scrape ups, shit, and infections too."

The host is back to present the next award, so I don't respond, but my mind can't keep quiet.

Maybe Lew isn't straight-laced. What Jermaine described is punishable by jail time. Maybe Lew isn't too good for me. Maybe he could understand my past.

Naeem is done with his food, and a player being awarded for their charitable efforts is on stage, occupying the attention of our table mates, so he scoots closer to me.

"I want to put you on this plate right now," his words are supposed to be sexy, but he has a wife. No matter what he or Regina says, I can't move past that.

To put some space between us, I stand up to clap as the player leaves the stage.

The pinch on my ass is light and quick, but I feel it.

"Get ready. I'm about to get all that tonight," Naeem had the nerve to say.

I turn, pick up my clutch, and push up my chair.

"Where are you going?" the low growl in Naeem's voice matches the darkening of his eyes.

"I'm going wherever you're not." I don't bother to stop and answer him. I would not stay a second longer.

Naeem clamps a strong grip on my forearm.

Shooting around to face him, I stalk closer to him.

"I know three ways to cut a man and clean out the insides. Touch me again, and you'll know, too."

My words are just loud enough for him to hear. My daddy didn't teach me a lot of things, but he did teach me how to hunt.

I snatch away from the vile man and shoot through the ballroom with lightning speed.

The hallway is not very crowded, and I am glad that Naeem or Regina do not follow. Naeem would get more than his feelings hurt, and Regina and I probably wouldn't be able to work together again.

"Nailah, wait."

I hear the only voice that would possibly make me stop. The way that he said my name made me stand still to wait for further instructions.

"You sure know how to make an exit," Lew said as he jogged up to me.

"Well, I-"

I begin to explain, but he interrupts.

"Are you alright? Did he hurt you?" his eyes race over and around me.

"I'm fine. It was just a little pinch and grab."

I'm not sure what compels me to tell him the truth, but I am sure that murder flashed in Lew's eyes.

In seconds, the fit and fine man is trotting away from me toward the ballroom.

I hop out of my heels and chase after him. Lew could not run into that ballroom and fight on the same night that he won the Fixer Award. He has a reputation.

"Lew, wait. I'm fine," I call out to him.

I get close enough to grab his jacket before he interrupts the program that is still in progress.

"Don't do it. I have survived worse." I hope that my words calm him.

He turned to face me, and I knew that they hadn't helped at all.

"You shouldn't have to survive any of it." I almost jumped back at the intensity in his eyes.

"And you shouldn't go to jail looking that damn fine. I'd rather be with you anyway," I tell him definitively.

His eyes soften then, but the tension in his shoulders is still there. His fists are still clenched.

I need to get him away. He is too good of a guy to get in any trouble over me.

Just then, Lew's brother, the one I saw him with at the hospital, appeared. The large man with locks, who looks like he can stop a train with his stare alone, glanced between us with assessing silence. He has smart eyes, and maybe he will speak some sense into him.

Lew nodded toward the brooding giant without a word.

His huge brother nods back and blinks a few times.

Lew turns and moves toward the door.

I wasn't expecting them to have some psychic connection and shit.

"Lew, if you leave right now, I'll go with you. Anywhere you want to go and do anything you want to do."

This stopped him in his tracks. He stepped so close to me that I nearly toppled backward.

"For real? Anything?" His eyes are narrowed slits of steel. "And you won't do any of your disappearing acts?"

His forceful stance and penetrating eyes have me so turned on I forget words.

"Yes. I promise to follow through," I assure him. "You can walk in that ballroom and beat Naeem's ass, or you walk out of that front door, and we figure a different way to use that energy."

My throat constricts when I feel his breath against my ear.

"Are you ready for me, princess?" he hums.

I touch him first, just a hand against his chest. I have no other choice. I am drawn to this man, and I am tired of fighting it tonight.

"I told you that I'm no princess," I remind him with equal parts sweet and sass mixed into my voice.

The valet pulls around the most expensive-looking sports car that I have ever seen in my life. The chrome color is so clean that I can see my gorgeous reflection. Today, I know that I look damn good. Always have. I got it from my daddy, but I tried to hide it because of my momma.

Lew slides open the car door, and it moves into the air like a bat wing before he helps me in.

We don't leave immediately. Lew pulls out his phone and sends a text.

"Telling your admirer goodbye?" I joke.

Tyriq chuckles.

"Jealous?" I roll my eyes.

"I'm just thanking my brother and letting him know that I'm alright. I don't want him to worry."

"Oh," I say and become very curious about who else he may feel obligated to. "No girlfriend or 'BM' to report to?"

"BM?" he frowns.

"Baby, momma."

"No kids, remember?" he winces. "BM sounds disrespectful."

He pulled away from the swanky hotel.

"It is. I'd fight any man that called me that."

"Mental note to self: Don't piss off Nailah," Tyriq laughs.

"I couldn't imagine you acting that way with a woman in your life."

Tyriq shakes his head.

"My mom, Aunt Pat, and cousin are the only women in my life right now, and they were never down for disrespect." He shudders. "Answering to those three ladies is enough."

"I'm sure it is." I agree, even though I don't know what it is like to have an involved family. I don't know what it is like to have a mother worry you because of her love or an aunt who makes sure that you stay on the right track at all costs.

"So, how is it that a woman as beautiful as yourself has no man and no children?"

"Well, aren't you direct?" I comment, shifting my body in the nice leather seat to stare at the city lights whizzing by.

I think about my answer. I think about my life situations. Living with my dad, living with Dolly and Sugar, and living on my own were all too deep and complex for a first encounter. They were all a part of why I chose to be single.

"I grew up in a small town, and boys avoided my thickness and brown skin like the plague."

"I think that you are beautiful."

When I lived in Brook Bonnet, boys my age didn't come after me for a variety of reasons. Since I had grown woman curves at twelve, it was grown men who were willing to give up their left nut just to get a whiff of me. 'Fresh meat,' they would notice. I keep that to myself.

"For the last year, it's been me, myself, and I. No guy," I answer and watch the look of disbelief spread across his face.

"Wow," he said. "What about sex?"

"Straight for the gut," I comment as I piece together a suitable answer.

"I knew women who would lose themselves over sex, and although I like it, it doesn't control my life." *Only my thoughts when I'm around him.*

"Do you have to be in love before you go there?" he asks while weaving the electric fast car through traffic.

"Love? Not really," I scoff. "In mutual respect, in mutual admiration, in mutual commitment, yes."

"So, do you believe in love?" he probed, lightly asking an extremely heavy question.

I look over at his sculpted face and bright eyes and imagine that love might be possible for a man like him.

"It depends on the day that you ask me. I do definitely believe that it can exist," I answer.

"But not for you?" he inferred.

I shrug. My answer to that question is too sad to speak out loud. Given the choice between being in love and misery behind a man with good sex and being sexless and single, single will win every time.

"What about you?" I ask. "Why are you unattached?"

Lew reviews me with contemplative eyes before returning his gaze to the blurring freeway.

"How about I take you to my favorite place in the world first? Then I'll tell you about my sad love story."

"Sure," I say, enjoying the exhilaration of the movement.

I'm surprised when he pulls up to a brightly-lit twenty-four-hour donut shop.

CHAPTER TWELVE

Tyriq

Nailah James makes me lose all common sense. When I saw her run out of the ballroom, I knew that I was about to beat the shit out of Naeem in front of people who relied on me to take care of them. I knew that he had done something to her. The first reason that he still has functional legs is that I checked on Nailah before dropping fists into his face. She stopped me from receiving a murder charge tonight. The amazing part is that she was concerned for me. That shit turned me on more than he pissed me off.

I help Nailah out of my car. It looks just as out of place in this parking lot as we do walking into the small building in our evening wear, but being with her makes it all worthwhile.

I tuck Nailah's hand into mine as we head into the sweet-smelling donut shop.

"Hey, Tyriq!"

"What's up?" I lean over the counter and hug the cashier with my free arm. "Miss Tasha, this is Nailah. Nailah, this is the best donut maker in the world."

"Nice to meet you." Nailah gives her a genuine smile and extends her hand.

Tasha pulls her in for a hug, and Nailah falls right against her.

I could have never brought Briana here and gotten the same gleeful reaction.

"Good to meet you too, honey." She plops a hand onto her hip. "And that smile you put on Dr. T's face."

I get a box of colorful donuts along with two coffees and bring them to the table.

Nailah, who had taken her seat while I ordered, was bent over, pulling those naughty heels from her feet.

"Sorry, my dogs are barking." A country twang eased out in her words as she removed the shoes.

The rise and fall of her round breasts are hypnotizing. I understand why she often locked those weapons of mass distraction away under a pile of loose clothing.

I should have taken Nailah to my home and licked those melon-sized delights until she was as breathless as I felt. I can tell that she isn't ready. She's still guarded and choosing her words carefully with me. When I get her under me, I need her mind clear and every inhibition removed.

"So, this is your favorite place in the world?"

Nailah leans back in the chair, effectively removing her beautiful bounty from view.

"Yep." I give an enthusiastic smile. "I am certain that this spot is the only reason I made it through my residency at the hospital. Sugary sweets and tons of creamy coffee."

She takes a bite of a cream-filled strawberry-covered donut, and I can't remove my eyes.

"Oh yes, this is good." She slides her tongue across her lips.

My body twitches in response.

"I completely understand how this place could be a place that anyone would love," Nailah continues, oblivious to the firestorm she sparked on the inside of me.

She licks a bit of filling from her thumb, and I consider spreading her legs on the table.

Fuck it, Ms. Tasha knows me. I would pay her well to walk away and lock the door behind her for an hour.

"So why are you single?" Nailah asks.

Her words douse my fiery thoughts of wild table sex and a body-licking contest, but it takes me a second to refocus.

"Hello," she sings the word while waving her hand in the air. "You still have to answer. Giving me a sugar-gasm didn't make me forget the question."

"A sugar-gasm, huh?" I repeat, because- damn. Nailah had my mind gone.

"Answer the question." She licks at a sugar-frosted finger.

I turn away.

"You have to put that donut down if you want me to speak intelligently," I explain.

She laughs and drops the sweet onto a napkin.

I clear my throat.

"It's simple really. I fell in love with a woman in college, and she fell in love with a guy being drafted by the NBA. I didn't find out until I was watching the draft with my entire family and saw her kissing him on TV live for the nation."

"That's cold-blooded," Nailah grimaces. "You haven't been a monk or something since then, have you?"

I shake my head.

"Hell no. It was school, work, and then my clinic. I was focused. Women have been for fun."

Nailah leans her back against the wooden chair before turning her head slightly.

"So, this, you and me, the goal is fun?" I see the light in her eye; it seems like fun is what she wants.

Every moment that I have shared with her has been interesting. I need more from Nailah, but I don't want to scare her away.

"I'm not sure what this is or will be. Things in my life and priorities have shifted a little since the last time I was involved with a woman."

"I can understand that. I started college later in life and just finished my Master's degree in sociology before moving here."

"Congrats."

"I was set squarely on working and graduating. Now that I have the job I needed, in the city I wanted, I can relax a little."

"You said that you were from a small town. Do you have any family here?"

"It's just me. Both of my parents passed away before I was a teenager. I lived in a group home until I was sixteen after that."

I lean across the small table to lift her fallen chin.

"I'm here now, and I plan to be around as long as you allow me. Beauty and strength are a powerful combination. No lie, I'm drawn to you."

She lifts her cheek in a half grin.

"I'm slightly fond of you too." Nailah places her hand to her mouth. "Is it Lew or Tyriq? I've heard both."

People had been calling me Lew for so long that I just went along with it, but the name from Nailah sounded out of place.

"Tyriq is my name. I prefer it," I explain. "Lew is a basketball thing. People thought my name was too hard. Really, they thought it was too black, so coaches made everyone use my last name, Lewis, which was shortened into Lew."

"You played college ball?"

She sipped on the coffee.

"Yep. The crowd used to chant 'skip to my Lew' when I shook off players."

She laughed as I did a mock stutter move in my chair.

We keep the conversation lighter after that. We laugh about her confession to loving all things crochet and my addiction to Nintendo products. We debate the merits of affirmative action and the sadness in student loans. We discuss celebrities falling from grace and the impact of U.S. reliance on foreign goods.

I was enjoying her so much that I even pulled out my impression of Eddie Murphy. Anything to see her face light up and hear her musical laugh.

Around three in the morning, the coffee isn't enough to keep her awake any longer, and her head and my eyelids begin to droop. I don't want this night to end. I don't want to stop talking to someone who gets me, who likes me, who wants me. I don't want to leave her presence.

"I hate to say it, but we should probably call it quits for the night."

Her eyes close a little when she yawns. "I'm so sleepy, I'm dizzy."

I help her up from the chair, and she leans on me. The rise and fall of her warm breast against my side instantly hardens me.

I look down at her smiling face and want to kiss her.

"Thank you." She gives me a goofy smile. "Can I just go home with you? I don't want to be alone tonight."

At a loss for words, I just nod. *Could life be any kinder?*

"I just want to sleep. No funny stuff," she adds.

"No funny stuff," I repeat. "I promise that we'll just have a serious sleep."

I am rewarded with another throaty giggle from her.

CHAPTER THIRTEEN

Tyriq

Nailah fell asleep during the ten-minute ride from the donut shop to my house. After I pull into the garage, I open the car door and gently pick her up. Her nipples brush across my chest, testing my resolve to be the perfect gentleman tonight. Her body has my full attention. To have it pressed against me at this time of morning complicated my concentration.

I lay her across my king-size bed and slide off her shoes.

"Do you want me to help you out of this dress?" I ask while eyeing the clingy material that covered the body that I craved.

Her eyes don't open, but Nailah expertly wiggles in the bed, slides the dress over her body, and exposes her plump bra-bound breasts and laced underwear.

My mouth goes dry. How can I survive a night next to her and not be inside her?

"You got that part then."

Peeling my eyes away from her, I slip into some pajama pants. I often sleep in the nude, but if there is any chance for survival tonight, it's best that there is at least some material between us.

I pull the covers back and climb into the king-size bed, ready to face the challenge of a lifetime. They should award medals of valor for this shit.

Nailah stirs, moving her body to face me.

Groggily, she wraps her arms around my neck and kisses my cheek.

Maybe the guest bedroom would have been a better option, but I'm selfish. I didn't know when she might disappear. Being with her felt like a dream, and I didn't want her to slip away.

I pull her closer.

"Thank you," Nailah sings sleepily, dragging out the word. "Thank you, thank you," she continues, adding a kiss with each expression of gratefulness.

"You're more than welcome."

I attempt to unhook her arms from my neck, but instead, she hooks my mouth with her lips.

I tear away from her kiss.

"You are literally making it hard for me to resist you right now," I hum. "I'm trying to stay noble here."

She gives me that sexy little giggle again.

I fight the urge to nip at her lips. One kiss won't be enough.

"I can feel you, Tyriq, and I like the way you feel on my stomach. I like how hard you are. I like how wet you make me feel."

Oh shit. I hold back my excitement and let her drive this time.

Taking my hand, Nailah guides it across her soft stomach and underneath the cloth covering her.

Her moist heat is too much for me to keep calm.

"Nailah," I moan. "I'm a strong man, but-"

"Just touch me, Tyriq."

"I don't know if I can do just that. I'm ready to jump inside of you right now."

Her response is to kiss me and slide her leg up the length of my arm, effectively putting my fingers at the core of her.

"What if I touch you too? Will that be enough?"

She rolls her hips beneath my hand.

"You're playing with fire, princess. I'm about to flip your ass over and make you flood."

I hear her breath hitch. Good.

I position myself between her legs so that my manhood spans the length of her wetness and onto her belly.

"I don't want a piece of you Nailah." I kiss her neck. "I don't ever half-ass anything, fucking included."

I circle a hand around both of her breasts and push against her.

"When we do this, I want it all. I want to fuck you all over this house and make you come so many times that you can't breathe."

Nailah's middle is pulsing so strong that I feel it through her panties and my pajamas. I imagine what that pulse will feel like around me and almost decide to find out.

"Are you ready for me, Nailah?"

"I- uh- not yet," she sputters.

I lean down and kiss her lips.

"Let me know when you want the full experience. Until then, let's get some sleep."

I fall into the spoon position with an ever-hard dick growing against her backside and will myself to go to sleep.

Nailah is snoring in seconds. I wanted her to be fully aware without restriction.

"Tyriq," I hear her whisper sexily. She's still in my arms, but I get the luxury of looking into her eyes.

Her face looks different in the morning, in my bed. Her lips were a little fuller, her skin a little brighter with the sunlight cascading against it. Like a sweet memory, you hold onto it to make life a little easier.

I smile at her, and she smiles back.

"Good morning, beautiful."

I pull her tighter, caressing every exposed portion of her skin. Her smooth arms, the column of her neck, and perfectly aligned cheekbones are fair game.

Nailah pulls back, and I unwrap her.

"You kept your promise."

My concentration falters as she explores my chest through soft, caressing touches.

I scoff at the surprise in her voice.

"There was no other option," I tell her with a wink.

When her fingers stop grazing my skin, I look up in time to see her soft face transition into a serious gaze.

"Are you real?" she asks.

The expectancy and uncertainty in her eyes cause me to make a move.

I sweep her body atop mine to show her how real I am and push full, thick morning wood against the middle of her.

Her moan is quiet but powerful, and I want to hear it again.

"So, you do like me?" Nailah asks, a playful grin dancing across her mouth.

"Yeah, just a little bit," I try to sound indifferent, but with my desire building for her by the millisecond, it comes out as a jerky whisper.

"Ain't nothing little about that 'like' down there," she laughs.

"Glad to get good reviews," I reply and watch the flicker of want in those eyes of hers.

"Thank you."

I kiss those pillow-like lips of hers.

Nailah hums after ending our connection.

I watch her fall off me and back against the bed.

Instantly, I feel a chill.

"I like you, Tyriq." She shakes her shoulders in a shimmy. I guess she feels the same currents shooting through her body as I do.

"Promise me it will always be this fun. We're just going to have fun, no matter what."

"I promise," I say and take advantage of her exposed belly.

She giggles when I kiss her skin.

I make a trail across her stomach to her breast, slide her bra to the side, palm one, and then capture the other in my mouth.

If this is payment for waiting last night, then I'll give her another night and wait for glory in the morning.

She moans and moves, wrapping her legs around me. I savor her broad-budded nipple and slip a finger between her wet folds.

Her body contracts against my finger, and I push in.

"You're so wet for me."

"Yes," she moans.

When the villainous alarm on her phone rings, I want to smash it.

"Tyriq," she whines. "I have to go."

"No, you don't," I tell her between kisses. "You can stay and make out with me all day."

"I can't miss work," she whimpers between breathy pants.

I growl and rollover.

"Sorry. I have to go to work." She doesn't move. She lays there with her hands over her face. "I'm sorry, Tyriq."

"You're really leaving me like this?" I ask, sitting on the edge of the bed.

She slides her leg over me to straddle my lap and look into my eyes.

"When we do this, Tyriq, we'll have time, and we'll do it right."

"Let's do this tonight. Come and see me as soon as work is over." I slip my arm around her waist.

"We'll see," she answers. "If you feel this good with clothes on, I don't know how I'm going to handle you naked."

I mentally prepare for what I am going to do to her body when I see her again.

I drop Nailah off at her friend Regina's apartment. She walks to a car that I'm not sure is safe to drive. She assures me that it, Lucy, gets the job done, but I don't feel any better about her driving that contraption anywhere.

She kisses me, promises to call, and I drive away.

I drive away from the powerful woman. The sorceress had the ability to hold my attention, cloud my mind, and fill me with desire at the drop of her hip. Never have I had to question, plead, or persist for a woman's attention and affection.

Chapter Fourteen

Tyriq

I made it to the airport on time to pick up my mother and father. My mother smiles when I spot her across the terminal. Every three or four steps, her flouncy vacation hat flaps against my father's shoulder as they make their way toward me. My father, weighed down by his bags and those belonging to my mother, doesn't look as joyous.

"Hey, son," he said, hurrying to put some of the luggage down. "Help me with some of these bags."

I helped my father put the bags away, and he helped my mother get into the car.

"How was the trip?" I ask after everyone is in the car.

"Oh, we had the greatest time!" My mother went on about the moon, the sky, and the palm trees in between.

I listen to it all until I hear the beginning keys to an old Gerald Levert song sound through the radio. A song about being in love, about wanting to make a woman yours, about giving her body what she needed. The song strikes a chord, and the words lift from inside me and out through my mouth, bringing my mother's monologue to a close.

I sing while smiling at my mother and even do a little dance.

"What's gotten into you son?"

"Or who has he gotten into?" my dad retorts.

"James. Don't be crass."

"That ain't what you said on the beach, woman."

"James!" my mother huffed.

Nailah had put a song in my heart, and at that moment, Gerald was singing my song. Singing the words that I wish I could say to Nailah.

"Are you ok, son?" my mother asked calmly.

I laugh.

"I'm fine," I answer. "Great."

"I see," she said with a questioning glance. "And why are you so great today?"

She gasped, I assume drawing her own conclusion about the source of my joy. "Did you finally call Sister Randolph's granddaughter like I been asking you to do?"

"No," I answer and take a deep breath before divulging the rest of the information to her. "I did meet someone."

My mother placed her hand over her heart and lifted her other hand to the sky.

"Prayers are answered. Yes, they are," she said with conviction. "You like her too, I can tell. I had a vision. I was supposed to have twelve grandbabies before I die, and I only got two."

"He just met the girl, Shirley. Damn. You're talking about grandbabies, and we don't even know who she is," my dad said loudly. "You sound like Pat."

To others, my mother and father seem like polar opposites. One look at my mother, who believed a woman should always be dressed for company, and my dad, who might maybe dress if there is a visitor, and anyone would wonder how they came to be together. My dad, a smoking, cursing, card-playing drinker, and my mom, leader of the deaconess board and sorority chapter president, fell in love over barbeque and music almost forty years ago at a friend's picnic. My dad says that she was the only woman that ever called him on his shit.

"Who is she?"

"She's a social worker I met at the art gallery," I smile at the thought of Nailah the first night that we met.

"Who are her people? Anyone we know?"

"She doesn't have any family," I reveal.

My mother reared back as if in shock.

"No family? Everyone has a family."

"She spent some time in a group home, but she hasn't really given me the details."

Concern crowded every feature on my mother's face.

"Don't worry, mom, once you meet her, you'll understand."

My mother, the queen of decorum and high priestess of heritage, is probably imagining Nailah as some street urchin with no manners or class.

"Well, bring her by soon. Any woman that has your nose wide open like that is someone I need to meet," my mother concedes.

I touch my nose.

"Alright, Mom. I'll bring her by. I promise."

I slam down a spade to cut the group of diamonds my brother Terrence led with.

My cousin and Spade's partner, Chad, stood up.

"One more book, and you're set!" he shouted above the music and TJ playing in the background. "Wave bye-bye to your points."

I look at my phone on the table. It has been my enemy tonight. It's giving me the silent treatment when I can't wait to hear it sing. Can't wait to hear her voice again.

Our family gatherings get loud, really loud, especially with a house full of men and children.

My brother Trystan and his wife, Crystal, have a toddler and a newborn who always seems to always be crying.

Terrence mumbled something.

"Man, shut that shit down," Chad laughed, throwing a Dorito at Terrence.

"Who's cursing?" Mali shouted from the sofa. She is putting a puzzle together with little Trystan right across from where we set up the card table.

"Put out before you get shut out!" I bark at Terrence and then look at my phone again.

This is ridiculous. Even after seven o'clock, Nailah hasn't called me. I knew in my brain that by six this evening, we would be sweating between some sheets. In the glory of the morning and her bright smile, I didn't get her number. Now, I am at her mercy when it comes to connecting.

In the history of my dating life, I had never had a woman not call me. Because Nailah disappeared, I should have asked for her number and references as well. How could I mess that up again? I was so confident that I had her, that she was so into me. If she felt half of what I felt, she would have called me at lunchtime.

"What's got you stressing over there, little brother?" Terrence asked.

"Nothing," I say and check my phone again.

"Nothing sure has a lot of your attention. Kind of like that woman did last night."

"Really?" Chad inquired, perking up. "You got a new smasher?"

"Just play the game," I huff.

Then, like a beacon reaching out into the darkness, my phone lit up, and music sounded.

I grab it quickly and answer.

"Hello?" I greet while moving away from the table.

Chad and Terrence grumble.

There is silence on the other end.

"Hello?" I say again, waiting to hear her voice. Waiting to put the sweet sounds with the sweet pictures that have been on repeat in my mind since I met her.

I look at the screen again. It's a real number, no eight hundred digits, but some random recording starts to play.

I hang up, disappointed.

"Man, you holding up Terrence's ass whipping!" Chad called out.

"Keep it PG over there!" Mali fussed.

"Get your head in the game, bro!" Terrence sounded off.

"Man, I'm winning. I'm in the game," I tell my brother.

"He's waiting on Na-i-lah to call," Aunt Pat spilled, making sure to accentuate the name.

The room went still. My brothers knew about her. My parents had heard of her. When Aunt Pat knew the name of a woman in anyone's life- when Aunt Pat made it a point to remember anyone's name and pronounce it correctly, this family took notice.

"Who the hell is Nailah?" Mali asked, her eyebrows twisted in my direction.

"Damn, Mali. Didn't you say keep it PG, no cursing?" Chad laughed.

"Some woman has my cousin's attention for real? I need to know about this," Mali responded with the attitude that the men in the family have learned to love and not to push, no matter how big we are.

"I don't know what she's talking about," I respond.

"Whose turn is it?" I ask, trying to get the attention back on the game.

"Naw, man. You got to tell it," Chad ordered as though it was law.

"Right," Trystan agreed, bouncing his daughter in his arms. "We haven't seen you excited about a girl since Briana in undergrad."

A collective groan rose from the group.

Trystan always knew how to say the wrong thing at the right time.

"Let's not go there," Terrence piped in, walking over and turning down the music.

"What are you all in here gossiping about?" my mother scanned the room as she scooted through the opening. She had been in the kitchen finishing up tonight's meal. It was her turn to serve. The next time when we gather at Aunt Pat's house, she'll do most of the food organizing. No matter where we ate, my mother always made the cakes.

"Nothing, Mom, everyone is getting all excited over nothing," I explain. "She hasn't even called me back."

Wrong words. I knew when they left my mouth that I should have held them hostage in my thoughts. My family came at me with questions in rapid succession like punches. Each one landed in the gut. The sad part was that I had yet to hear from the only person who could provide any answers about what would happen next.

"So, it is about a girl?" Mali tried to confirm. "And a Nailah? I know a Nailah."

"It's not any of your earthy soul sister, body oil friends," Chad chuckles. "You know Tyriq only goes for the supermodel kind."

"Is it the girl that you mentioned to me in the car?" my mom follows up.

"You told momma about her?" Trystan solicits in shock.

"He didn't tell me much," my mother spoke.

"Oh, so he didn't bother to mention that he ditched me last night to hang out with Nailah?" Terrence provoked.

"What?" Mali, my mother, and Aunt Pat shout in unison.

"I knew it!" my aunt exclaims like she has solved a leading mystery. "When she walked into the clinic, I knew Tyriq was a goner, and then I found them in his office."

"I thought we came here to play and eat. Right now, we're doing neither," I plead on deaf ears. There is no use in trying to get them to stop. Once Mali, Mom, and Aunt Pat start rolling, I might as well just step aside. With a cigar and whiskey in his hands, my father had already made his way to the porch earlier, and he was the only one who could reign in the terror squad.

"Hush, boy," my mother chides. "I want to hear more about this lady with no family that has you ditching yours."

Aunt Pat stands up as silence falls over the room. Even the little ones team up and agree to remain quiet just so my aunt can embarrass me more.

"It was right before closing, right as I was ready to finish up the filing," her serious eyes and calm voice made it seem like events from my failed love life were from a top-secret mission. "This gorgeous woman walks in dressed to the nines. I thought she was one of those hot-tailed church girls who stop by for 'medical advice' after hours. Then I looked at her, and guess which model she looks exactly like?"

"Don't tell me it's Jubilee. Does she look like Jubilee?" Mali shouts.

"Hold up, this is not Wheel of Fortune!" I protest to my non-listening family.

"Is she the thick one with the big ol'-" Chad is interrupted by Mali's glare before he can finish. "Big ol' personality is what I was about to say. Damn, Mali."

"Yes. That one," Aunt Pat continues. "And get this, she's a social worker."

Their heads swivel in my direction at once.

"Weren't you going to go into social work, Tyriq?" Trystan asks the obvious question. All those years in the law books had left his social skills lacking.

"Yea. Until he found out how much money they made," Chad answers instead of me.

"Wrong," I throw in as if anyone would even care.

"I know her. I swear, I know her," Mali chirps. "She's gorgeous."

Mali sprouts up from the floor like a flower while shaking her hands in the air like tambourines.

"Yes. There will finally be more women in the house!" Mali says.

"Family!" I holler, trying to get everyone's attention. "Those of you who claim to love me, there is nothing to get excited over. I really thought Nailah looked nice and spoke well, but nothing-"

Before I can finish my sentence, my phone lights up, and music begins to play.

I look at the number splattered on the screen and instantly know that it is her.

"Answer it," Mali shouts.

I move my hand to pick up the phone, but Chad beats me to the punch.

"Hello?" he answers and sprints away from the table with my phone.

I take off after him and nearly catch him before he slips into the bathroom. I hear the lock on the knob turn.

The combination of chuckles from the living room and hearing him talk to the woman I had been fantasizing about all day made me want to rip the door off the hinges.

"This is his cousin Chad," I hear him say.

I jiggled the knob while pushing my shoulder into the door.

"What's your name?" he asks her.

"Open the door!" I yell and push my shoulder against it harder.

That gets the attention of the others. With six boys, things often got torn apart when we were nice to each other. With frustration and adrenaline involved, it is given that redecorating will occur.

"Ya'll better not break anything in this house!" my mom yells.

"Na-i-lah," Chad sounded the syllables. "That's pretty. I heard that you're pretty, too."

"Chad, open the door! I'm serious!" I yell.

"For real. I'm finer than a mutha-fucka over here. I look a whole lot better than my cousin if that's what you want to know," Chad continues on the phone.

"I'm about to break this shit down, asshole!" I hit the door again.

"Open the door, Chad!" Aunt Pat yells. She doesn't move from her seat on the sofa in the living room, but her message is extremely clear.

"I have to go now. Tyriq is throwing a tantrum because I took his phone," Chad says as he unlocks and opens the door.

I punch him in the arm, the one not holding my phone, with all my might, but he only laughs.

"How old are you?" I yank back my phone and then punch him again.

"Nailah?" I question, hoping she's still there.

"Yes," she answered, and my body felt at ease.

"Sorry about my cousin. Sometimes, he acts like he's sixteen instead of twenty-nine."

"He was sweet. No harm, Lew," she chuckles.

"Didn't we already discuss this? What's my name?"

I hear her breathing and wish that we were in the same air right now, that I could feel her breath against my neck or on my chest, and I could make her breathe harder.

"How did you receive a degree, and you don't know your name?"

"I want to hear you say it."

I want to be as close to her as her phone is. I'm jealous that some inanimate object gets to feel the warmth of her skin.

"Tyriq."

My name on her lips is so sensual that I want to crawl through the phone and kiss her.

"I like the way you say that. Promise you won't say it any other way."

"I promise," she answers.

"What are your plans for tonight?"

When I walked into the front room, my family jumped back into playing games as though they hadn't been straining to hear my conversation.

I threw out a wave and headed out the door as Nailah explained that she was hanging out at home.

"You ditching me again?" Terrence yelled toward my back.

I hop into the car, switch to my hands-free mode, and head home.

Chapter Fifteen

Nailah

Tyriq and I talk and then talk some more. Four hours pass, but it feels like thirty minutes.

He tells me about his family and how they meet some Fridays for games and the second Sunday each month for dinner.

"So, Chad is the prankster?" I question.

"Yeah, and the noise talker and the lady slayer. He's wild, but he's family, so I gotta love him. He's also smart as hell. He develops games for computers and systems."

"He has a lot of titles."

"Believe me, he earned them all," he grumbles.

"What about your mom?"

"My mom is the president of her sorority chapter, a deaconess board member, and helps several nonprofit organizations. She's always trying to get me to come to this event or that."

Respect and jealously curdle up a little on the inside of me. He has a family. He has support. He has love and gives it just the same.

"That must be nice," I say truthfully.

"And what is that?"

"Having a family that loves you and loving them back," I answer.

I twist on the sofa a little bit and stretch my little throw blanket to cover my bare toes.

In every aspect of my life, I have been searching for family, for people who will answer the phone when I call, call when they fall, and not fall short of loving me.

"I think it's cool that someone cares if you made it through the day. Family is important. Everyone doesn't have relatives to chat with, to laugh with, and to love on."

"My family isn't perfect," he laughs.

"It doesn't matter. They're your people. I've been alone for a long time."

"So why be alone tonight?" he questioned. "Come hang out with me."

I look over at the clock. It was 11:23 p.m. I liked Tyriq, but seeing him too much too soon will only make this feeling stronger.

"Sorry, doctor, no house calls tonight. I have early plans tomorrow," I explain, but leave the details to his imagination.

"I'll personally get you wherever you need to be, whenever you need to be there," he reasoned. "I kept my promise last night, and you should keep yours from this morning."

I don't say anything. I think about all the things that we could do.

"What's your address?" he asked. "I'll come get you."

"I know where you are," I reply.

"Call me before you leave. I don't trust your car, Lucy, like you do."

Tyriq had been appalled by Lucy, so I didn't dare show him where I lived. Although my condo neighborhood is nice and well-maintained, I can't say the same for the surrounding community. My hood is alive, not contained in neat little packages like the suburban area Tyriq lives in. At every time of the day, helicopters are hovering, music is playing, and sirens are blaring. Life is happening. No one seemed to fit into a perfect mold, and I love it.

The scenery, as I drive, doesn't change drastically all at once, but slowly and significantly. The farther I drive, the more trees I see, the better the sidewalks look, bike lanes appear, and street lights switch to street lamps. The closer I get to Tyriq's home, the roads become smoother, the stores become brighter, and the landscaped areas become neater. The people where I live probably come here to properly manicure the lawns.

Tyriq's home is majestic and imperial. I pull my little, much-loved Lexus up the drive to stop at his closed gate and feel small. Like his home would come to life at any second and swallow me up. I can't even fathom how much this place must have cost him, but what I make is sufficient for me. Sufficient enough for me to maintain my condo and car. Sufficient enough for me to shop for clothing and food without worry and purchase gas without concern, but never this kind of lifestyle.

I wait for Tyriq to open the gate, and I drive in.

I turn off the car, grab my overnight bag, and step out.

Tyriq appears at the front door. His long muscular legs are covered by a pair of cotton pajama pants that hang low below his waist and give a preview of muscles that shouldn't be uncovered on the second date. His bare chest, chiseled arms, and defined abs that flex with each breath, cause me to lose mine.

Fun friend. He is a fun friend. Just have fun, Nailah.

"You made it," he acknowledges, taking my bag and walking me in.

"Yes, and you don't have on any clothes," I observe.

He serves me a devilish grin. He is shirtless on purpose.

"You're not fighting fair."

Tyriq folds his arm around my waist and pulls me close to him. He takes my lips with his, then slides his warm tongue between them.

"Every time I'm near you, I feel like you're not fighting fair either."

He let go of me, and I looked at him in all of his gorgeousness.

"I've got movies set up in the media room," he explained, pulling me through the massive home.

"This house is amazing, Tyriq," I say, sitting on the leather loveseat after the tour. "I didn't really get a chance to look around this morning."

The mounted projector did a countdown before illuminating the full wall screen.

"Thank you, but I can't take much credit for the looks. My mom and a decorator did most of this. I just live here."

"It's kind of a large space for just you, isn't it?" I ask, wondering why a young, untethered man would buy a five-bedroom house with way too many bathrooms.

"I thought I should start laying a foundation," he answered placing a bowl of popcorn and a pack of candy on the table. "One day, I hope to have children. Got to have space for that."

"So, you plan on adopting these kids, or is a concubine involved?"

"I want to have a wife first, then as many kids as she'll give me," he answered, watching my eyes. "What about you?"

"No. I can honestly say that I don't want a wife," I joke hoping to ease some of my nervousness.

"How do you feel about marriage and kids?" he asked quickly before busying himself with movie cases.

"I thought we talked about this already," I deflect. "Men usually avoid this subject at all costs."

He looked up then.

"Are you calling me a girl?" he asked with a chuckle. "Baby, I'll show you that I'm all man."

"That I can see."

"I've just been thinking about my future more."

"You're still young though."

"I'm not talking about having kids tomorrow. Women are too scandalous."

I let loose breath that I didn't even know I was holding. Having children worried me. What if I ended up like my mother?

"Men are just as dirty though. One woman is never enough." I smile.

"But women hear what they want to hear," he insisted. "When I was honest about only being physical, they were always trying to make it into more. Snooping through my phone, popping up at my clinic, at church."

"Do they pop up at your house too? Do I need to get my stun gun ready?" I tease.

Tyriq's laughter makes me smile too.

"No worries, Nailah. First of all, I never let those other ladies know where I live. Second, I have a security gate that my brother doesn't even have the code to."

"You never know, though. When a woman feels wronged, anything is possible," I explain. "There's probably a coalition of women ready to jump over your security gate in ninja suits and take me out right now."

"Ninja suits?" he questioned with a hearty rumbling laugh. "Who do you think I dated, the karate kid?"

I chuckled, but his face straightened.

"What kind of man do you think I am, Nailah?"

"The worst kind of man there is."

"Is that right?" he questioned with a lifted eyebrow. "Explain."

"You seem like the kind of man that women feel safe with," I explain, with more feeling than I expected. "The kind that reminds a girl that all men aren't bad, that makes you feel like dreams do come true when in reality you're just a nice guy with a high sex drive and not a future husband."

"Damn," he says leaning back. "Let me borrow your term. That's cold-blooded."

Tyriq contracts his chest as he pretends to pull a knife from his heart area.

"What's so bad about being a nice guy who just wants sex?" he asks.

He doesn't get it.

"You don't act like the villain," I say, feeling like I'm on a discussion panel. I needed to switch the topic. I'd rather talk about anything but love and relationships.

I turn to face him, sliding my knee up on top of the plush sofa cushion.

"Some ladies don't realize that no one is ALL bad or ALL good. Good guys can do bad things," I explain.

I remember several so-called respectable men who frequented my foster home often enough to notice when I grew an inch.

"To some women, you're the guy that just hasn't realized that he wants to settle down yet. Buried in many girls is this hope that you'll transform into that one-woman man and love them forever."

"I'm not that guy, but I feel what you're saying." He nods after taking a sip of his beer.

"Are you speaking from experience?" Tyriq asks.

I shake my head.

"I've never been in love before. I can't lose if I never play the game."

"True." He leans his beer toward me in agreement.

"Besides, I've always seen men for what they are."

"And what is that?" His eyebrows move together this time when he speaks.

"A means to a pleasurable end."

Tyriq doesn't say anything and a slight fear that I may have spoken too freely creeps in. The man had been nothing but kind to me, but I kept bringing up the sleazy men that I knew in the past.

"I'm going to start calling you Ice Blade," he said with a sly smile. "Cold and sharp all at once."

I turn the words over in my mind.

"Ice Blade? Damn, I sound gangster."

"You are. Nailah James, you are a danger to me."

I track his eyes while wondering if he is serious.

"Not hardly. I just tell it how I feel it. No false expectations here."

"So why are you here with me tonight?"

There is no laughter in his eyes, no smiling, and no playing.

"I like the way that we talk, and I hate talking on the phone, especially cell phones."

He pulls me close to him and kisses me dizzy.

I pull away with my mind made up. I am a grown woman, who knows what life is about. Tyriq may be nice, but his body is even better, and he has distracted me for far too long.

"What movie are we supposed to be watching?" I ask, changing the subject.

"The first in our 90's Black Film Series," he explains. "I can't believe you have so much music knowledge and haven't seen Boyz in the Hood."

"Music is personal, and you don't have to stop life to enjoy it. I could listen to my headphones while doing my chores and let it take me to some far-off place."

"I hate that life was so difficult for you."

Tyriq pulls me into his arms.

"I promise you that our time together won't be. While you're with me, no difficulty," he rhymed.

"I don't need anyone to take care of me, Tyriq." I am somewhat offended. "I've managed on my own for a long time," I explain.

"But I'm here now," he replies kissing my cheek.

I drop the issue. He's here now, but what about next week, next month, or next year? Where will he be on the bad days, when work is annoying when money is funny when Lucy has one of her frequent breakdowns? Gallivanting the globe, living his good time life with whatever wife he's dreaming about tonight? Somewhere, but not with me.

Tyriq is just like chocolate when I am on a diet. I crave it, need it until I get a piece. I just need to get a little piece, a nice treat, and then I can focus again. I'll get a piece of Tyriq tonight and move on with my life tomorrow.

"I like the way you kiss."

"I'm awesome at whatever I do."

Tyriq quickly diverted his eyes from the screen to my face.

"Is that so?"

"Decidedly so."

His eyes follow my hand as I move it up and down to trace the stacked abs calling out to me through his shirt.

"You sure this is what you want?" He licks those lips.

"Definitely."

"I can't do the start and stop Blade. It's alright if you just want to chill."

"I want all of you, Tyriq."

He nods as though making an important decision, and I gulp.

Like a focused hunter, he moves toward me and I recline further back until my back is against the plush leather and his body is above mine.

"I've been waiting for you, Nailah."

He takes my mouth while pressing his hard erection against my thigh. Sensations travel to my brain. All rational thought and worry must exit the building, pleasure is performing a hostile takeover.

"Here. I. Am," I pant between kisses.

No other words are required as Tyriq pulls off my shirt and moves my pants away. "Yes."

He guides his tongue through my mouth like he has a map.

His hands are everywhere. Thick and full, he slid them up and down my front, touching my nipples, up and down my back, squeezing my ass, and then *there*.

"Oh. Oooh. Ty-ooo," I try to call out his name, but just coo out sounds of pleasure.

"Yeah," he nips at my lip. "Say it just like that."

Tyriq slides his hand beneath my underwear to rub two fingers against my throbbing core, and I nearly crawl backward off the sofa.

"Always running." He pulled my waist closer to him again. "Right here."

"Ty- Ty- Oooh," I call out again.

In the process of me trying to stutter out his name, Tyriq had pulled off any material covering my lower half and replaced his fingers with his face.

"Damn," he groaned against my flesh. "You taste good too."

I twist with every lick of his tongue against my center. My body betrays me and lightning bolts of pleasure fire across my body and burst in my brain. No feeling compares to Tyriq.

"I need you," I whine. "I can't take it."

He looked up then, and I knew that this was payback.

With a devilish grin covering his glistening mouth, he shook his head, "I got you."

He promptly returned to working my core.

I move my body against his face as if this may be the last orgasm I'm allowed in life. I can't stop pushing against him.

Tyriq continues lapping his tongue over my clit and then presses two fingers into me.

"Ty-" his name catches in my throat as he curls those fingers in and out of me.

My entire sex life flashes before my eyes. It's over. I'm dying.

Possessed, I grind against him without regard for his wellbeing or ability to breathe. I can't control any of it. Nothing, just feeling.

His big hands cover my waist and press my body harder against his face.

He feels so good.

Squawks and squeaks erupt from somewhere deep in my soul, and I can't figure out which wild animal has taken root inside of me.

"Tyriq!" I screech, clawing into his shoulders as my body quakes and the world shakes.

I explode against his tongue among shooting stars, fireworks, and then a light floaty bliss.

CHAPTER SIXTEEN

Tyriq

Nailah was so sensitive to my touch that she literally passed out. I had never had a woman lose consciousness under my tongue before, and I wanted to do it over and over again, but I needed to feel the inside of her first.

"Am I alive?" she whispers against my neck.

I feel like a superhero as I carry her limp and delicious body to my bedroom.

"I wasn't expecting that to happen," she nuzzles into my chest. "Sorry."

"Don't apologize. That was beautiful." I catch her eyes. "I want to see it again."

She shakes her head as I lay her down on the bed.

"That's never happened to me before. I couldn't – damn." She closed her eyes. "I still feel the aftershocks."

My body is harder than concrete, but I wait for her.

"I'm ready."

Nailah spreads her bare legs for me, and I debate between tasting her again and diving into her core.

I cover myself with a condom and then lean down to kiss her lips.

Her tight, wet opening is like heaven to push into.

"Oooh. Shit," I stutter out the words.

I pulled back before entering again just to make sure that I really felt what I did.

I shudder as she takes me in, only to buck against me as I slide back out. We repeat. Push, pull, in and out.

"You feel good. So good, Nailah."

"Tyriq!" she shrieked as the sounds of her sloshy opening spurred me to move faster.

When she clamps her slick muscles around me and begins milking out pleasure, I let go. Restraint is nonexistent.

"You needed this?"

"Yes!" she wails while clawing at my chest.

"Tell me," I pump into her.

"I need it, Tyriq!" she yells and spasms around me.

Wildly, I propel into her again, plunging in deep and grinding one last time before losing all sense of reality.

"Oh shit, baby! Nailah!" I yell into the air, and I release everything into the condom between us.

I can't breathe, just pant. I collapsed across the bed as satisfaction trickled across my body.

Nailah rolls into my arms and kisses my chest.

"You can have anything that you want from this day forward."

She laughs before snuggling in closer, but I mean it.

CHAPTER SEVENTEEN

Nailah

He makes my body feel like I'm flying through clouds of cotton candy and sliding down a strawberry licorice rainbow. Like warm marshmallows, gooey.

He wraps me in his arms and kisses me until I fall asleep. Kisses across my neck. Kisses against my back. Circles over my breast. Traces my thighs. This man literally praised my entire body.

Throughout the night, he held me.

Feelings of being safe and protected, commonly not associated with my life, inch up in my gut. Grateful is the only word that I can think of. Thankful that I can be here in the same space with him. A man who opens doors for me, a man who pays for meals for me, a man who makes me feel comfortable enough to be just me. If tonight is just tonight, I am glad to have spent it with him.

I slide away from the comfort of his embrace and tiptoe out of the room. I grab my overnight bag, shower in the guest restroom, and get dressed in a pair of jeans and a T-shirt. I had already stayed longer than expected in bed with Tyriq.

In the past, spending the night with a man wasn't an option. We did what we did and went our separate ways. Being wrapped up in Tyriq all night is another new experience to add to the list of what he's provided for me in such a short time.

In the clear, I tip-toe to the door. I feel his presence before I hear him and get a head rush from the smell of his cologne before I see him.

Three steps away from my exit, I'm caught.

"Leaving without a goodbye?" Tyriq questions with the same sarcastic tone that he used the night we met at the art gallery.

The situation was him in a pair of boxer briefs, his magic muscles moving with every step that he took in my direction. I reconsidered the hour-long trip ahead I'd make alone. How could I leave him and all of that behind?

"Tyriq, hi," I smile.

He stops in front of me, standing so close that I can feel the heat rising off him, or is it me that's hot?

"You were sleeping so peacefully. I didn't want to bother you," I lie, hoping that he doesn't point out the obvious.

"Blade," he said, shortening the nickname he gave, had given and g me against him. "You're never a bother, especially after last night."

I take advantage of kissing him. This may be the last time.

"I'm glad you had fun," I replied honestly.

"You need me to take you anywhere?" he asked, stepping back to look at me.

"You took me all the places I needed to go last night," I jest. "I got it from here."

"Alright," he said and opened the door for me. "My schedule is open. We can hang out all day if you want."

I sigh, considering the option, but I need to do what I need to do. Tyriq is best in small doses. If any, at all. Like Dolly used to say, 'Too much of a good thing isn't always good for you.'

"I have to head out," I say and kiss him once more goodbye.

Like a kid longing to play outside on a rainy day, Tyriq stood in the door watching.

I hop into Lucy and turn the ignition. Nothing happens.

"Come on, girl, not today," I coax.

I smile and wave at Tyriq.

Hopefully, he'll go inside and leave me and Lucy to our routines. She may have performance anxiety.

I turn the key in the ignition several more times to no avail.

I hit the steering wheel.

Tyriq stood at the driver's side door in his pajama pants, knocking on my window.

Lucy's window doesn't roll down anymore, so I open the door, scooting Tyriq back some.

"You need some help?" he offered.

"She's just a little testy this morning," I say, turning the key once again. "Can you give me a jump?"

Tyriq smirked. His mouth turned up into a sneaky smile.

"No nasty. Not jump my bones. I need a battery boost."

He laughed with his whole face. His ears moved, nose twitched, forehead wrinkled.

"How about you just let me take you where you need to go?" he suggests. "We can get Lucy fixed up later."

"Are you sure it's not a problem?" I ask.

"None whatsoever. I got you," he affirmed, helping me out of the car. "I just need to shower and dress, and we can head out."

The elation beaming on his face makes me giggle, a side effect of being with him. I can't think of a time when someone was happy to help me.

I watch Tyriq undress when we make it to his bedroom.

I wasn't sure why my resolve was being tested. I had been running away from heartbreak at all costs, only to trip right into it.

I am captivated by every part of him when he enters the bedroom from his shower.

His face brightened with a sly grin.

"We can stay in if you like," he suggests unwrapping his towel.

Deep breaths are necessary. I take in air slowly and release it as I graze my eyes over the length of his body.

I could give myself a nice birthday present, but I had to stay focused on my mission.

"You promised that you would get me where I needed to be when I needed to be there."

"I did, didn't I?" he said, sliding into his clothes.

"Yes, you did," I muse and cross the room to him. "After you help me do what I need, maybe I can help you with what you want."

Tyriq pulled around to the front of his home in an elegant four-door Mercedes, a totally different car than the one I was introduced to last night. I have trouble taking care of one car, and he's maintaining two. He pops open the sunroof as I hop into the passenger side.

"This is nice." I wiggle against the leather seats and eye all of the buttons and screens protruding from the dash.

"So where are we going?" he switched on the navigation system.

I give him the address, and the system chimes in acceptance before Tyriq pulls off.

The radio filled the comfortable silence between us as he drove. Peace, it feels like. The tree-lined road felt like a place skillfully crafted as the definition of calm.

He drives his sedan almost like he drives his sports car. His sturdiness, the sureness that he possessed as he moved the car as though it was a part of himself, gave me confidence that we would arrive safely at our destination.

"You drive fast."

"I got you," he says, giving my leg a rub.

His touch shoots a spark of desire through me, and I smile in his direction before finding the beauty in the blurring trees shading the sky as we zoom by.

My thoughts wandered through last night to the grinding and stroking section. I can still feel traces of his hands sliding over me. I shiver at the memory.

"You cold?" He rubs his large hand against my shoulder.

"I'm fine."

"You sure?" He lowered the blasting air to a steady stream. "You're quiet. Is something on your mind?"

"No." I smile, taking a leisurely glance at him.

"I hope that's not the only word you plan on saying to me today." Tyriq jokes.

"No," I answer again.

When I hear the intro to one of my favorite songs, I yelp.

"I love this song!" I exclaim, turning up the radio.

I imagine that being in love, if it were possible for me, would be like the song Anthony Hamilton sang. Each word had been engrained in my brain as the definition of what the undefinable condition would entail. So, company be damned, that was my jam. I lifted my voice in tribute to the soul singer's creativity and ability to make the intangible, untouchable real.

Tyriq surprisingly sang the words to the chorus with me, and we enjoyed our own version of car karaoke.

We belted like we were internationally known singers.

For verse two, I turn to look at Tyriq, mainly to see if he knows those words, too. When our eyes meet, I feel a sense of knowing that moment was more than a look. It was a portal opening due to rare and unforeseen circumstances that will allow me the privilege to view life like those with a solid, whole heart.

The tips of my fingers scrape over my palm.

He sang right along with me until the song ended.

"I see you know a little something about Mr. Hamilton," I acknowledge.

"Why yes. Yes, I do." He smiles. "I wasn't lying when I told you that music was my thing."

The bubbles of joy that fill my insides float out as laughter, and I feel like I can rise along with them straight through the roof and into the open sky.

Tyriq placed his arm around the back of the seat.

"For a woman who has never been in love, you sure know a lot of love songs," he laughed.

"The best love songs come from a place of pain, and I know pain very well."

"Joy and pain," he commented.

"It's like sunshine and rain," I add, referring to an Al Green song my dad used to play when I was younger.

Tyriq's mouth moved into a straight line.

"My mother told me once that in life, you got to take the good with the bad. You have to find that person that makes you feel good enough to want to hold onto them through the bad." He took his eyes off the road quickly and glanced at me. "Loving someone can have more good moments than bad, you know."

"I'll take that into consideration," I answer.

He turns off from the freeway into the land that time forgot and eventually down a small-unpaved road to a clearing and then a cemetery.

"A cemetery," he acknowledges.

"Yep," I answer and pull out the map of the land and the location of my mother's plot. "My mom is here."

I unbuckle my seat belt and look ahead at the trees.

"I feel the closest to her today," I explain. "I'll be right back."

Tyriq took my hand and kissed it.

"Take your time. I'll be here," he said.

"Thank you."

I walk over to the site and tell her about my life after her. Tell her about life with my dad, then life with Dolly and Sugar.

CHAPTER EIGHTEEN

Tyriq

While Nailah sat at the gravesite, I cleared my schedule. Divine intervention allowed her to stay with me, but my goal was to keep her happy and hanging out with me as long as I could.

"Tyriq. Where are you?" Trystan questioned before even saying hello.

"Sorry. A friend of mine had car troubles, and I offered to help."

"So, you haven't heard?" he asked. "Naeem was arrested."

"Arrested? What happened?"

"Briana was picked up about a mile from the team hotel wandering the street bruised with no shoes on," he explained. "Naeem had already caught a flight out of the city back to Dallas, but they picked him up here."

"What about her kids?" I ask. "She was just at my house a couple of nights ago for medical care."

"I thought you had stopped seeing her in college."

Even though he can't see me through the phone, I shake my head.

"When Naeem was traded to Dallas, she found me and apologized," I explain.

No one had known about her and me reviving a version of our failed relationship, especially Trystan. He was likely to blurt out anything at any moment.

"And you fell for it?" he admonished. "That girl has been nothing but drama since you met her."

"I thought she had changed."

"It's been alleged that the fight was prompted by a cheating rumor. A couple of names were floated out there, and yours was one of them." Trystan continued. "If you were sleeping with a married woman and her husband beats her because of it, it can be bad for...."

"Why do you automatically assume I was sleeping with her?" I cut him off. "She's still a friend."

"Save that shit for these women who fawn all over you. If you were talking to her, then you were fucking her."

"I didn't have anything to do with her and Naeem's fight if that's what you're getting to," I make clear.

"I believe that," he said. "The info popped up in a search alert that I set for your name. The blogger listed several possibilities with your name closer to the end of the list. We need to be ready if or when the press starts sniffing this way. Past lovers who live in the same city are primary suspects."

"I wouldn't call her my secret lover. Briana and I played around for a couple of months. She didn't want to leave Naeem, so I called it off. We haven't been together in almost two years."

"That's all I need for now," he spoke dryly. "I can compose a statement from this just in case."

"Thanks."

My finger is near the screen so I can end the call when I hear him call out.

"Hey! Tyriq, don't go trying to be a superhero either," he warned. "The police will figure this mess out. The more you snoop around it, the more they will assume you are involved."

"I'm good. She's made her decision about where she wants to be. If I help her, it will be medically only."

After ending my call with Trystan, I am ready for something more pleasant, ready to be involved with someone that I don't have to hide. I don't want to hide Nailah. I'm ready to take this girl all over the world, she had me feeling so right last night.

I have never had a woman be so intuitive about my body. It's like she was reading an instruction manual on how to blow my mind.

I don't know where Briana is, and I hope she is alright, but my experience with Nailah scarily trumps any emotion I have ever felt for any other woman.

I walk over to Nailah, kneeling near her mother's grave.

I place a hand on her shoulder, and she looks up at me. There are tears there. I instinctively wipe them before I squat down beside her and cloak her in my arms.

"It'll be alright," I whisper in her ear.

We sit there like that for a few minutes, her crying, me rocking, the wind blowing. Then there are no tears and her head is against my chest.

"I'm ready now," she spoke softly.

Inside the car, I prepared myself to tell her the news about Naeem. I need to know that she isn't the person they were fighting about. I need to hear her say that she isn't involved with Naeem at all.

"How about we stop for lunch?" I ask her.

At the diner, the waitress swishes over to our booth with a smile, and after we order, she disappears.

"What's wrong?" Nailah asked. "You seem distracted."

I take her hand into mine.

"Naeem was arrested this morning."

"Are you serious?" she gasped, pulling her hand from mine to cover her mouth. "What happened?"

Before I could answer, Nailah pulled out her phone and quickly typed in a few words. Her eyes grew larger at what I assumed was confirmation of what I told her.

"This article says that Briana had multiple broken and bruised ribs, contusions, and bruises," she said, her eyes darting back and forth across the device quickly. "Damn."

"I know that you and he-" I begin before she cut me off.

"It wasn't like that," she asserted. "Regina knows Jermaine. It was the first time that I had met Naeem and it wasn't very pleasant."

"Really?" I question, glad that they had not been involved for real. Glad that they had no real connection like she and I do.

"Everything about him just rubbed me the wrong way."

"Did I rub you the right way?" I ask not wanting to talk about Naeem anymore. I know I won't shed a tear for him.

She could have projected images of last night onto the wall her eyes beam so brightly.

"You already know," she answers with a smile, putting her phone away.

"The way you snuck out this morning, I thought that I'd done something wrong."

I almost let it hurt my feelings that she was trying to get away without saying goodbye, but I realized that she probably thought that it was what I wanted.

"I was not sneaking. I was being considerate of your sleeping habits."

"I'll buy the consonants, B and S, as long as you promise not to do that again," I tell her. "You don't have to play me like some piece you picked up in a bar."

"I don't want there to be any confusion," she replied, sounding less sure than before. "We're just friends, right?"

"And friends can say goodbye to each other," I explain. "Friends can be there for one another."

I feel the words coming out of my face, but they are wrong. She isn't just a friend. I've been in enough empty situations to recognize one of substance.

I take her hand and know that it is more, but I don't want to scare her.

"Alright. Deal," she agrees. "If I choose to spend the night with you again. I will make sure to say goodbye in the morning."

I don't like the way she used the word 'if.' She makes it sound so indefinite, something I am not willing to accept.

The waitress brings our plates but lingers this time.

"Umm. Excuse me," she says before I can un-swaddle the fork and knife from the thick paper napkin.

She sways slowly.

"I was just wondering. Just if- Are you Tyriq Lewis from the University of Southern Texas?"

I lift my cheek and give her sort of a half grin.

There aren't many people that I run into daily who remember my glory days, who remember when I would and could run the court with the best. For that I am glad. There were a lot of NBA players that came out of school the year that I would have. I was in the company of greats, and because of that, when the excitement of finding me yet still alive wears away, the inevitable question is hurled at me like a ball during a chest pass on the court; 'So what happened to you?'

"I am," I say looking up at the grinning waitress. "Tyriq Lewis."

I extend my hand and she shakes it vigorously.

"Skip to my Lew! I knew it!" she says with tenacity. "My brother used to watch every game on the only TV that we had in the house. Will you take a picture with me?"

I look to Nailah. This is a rare occurrence, and I don't want to take a picture, but my Nailah is smiling, enjoying the recognition, so I unfold from the table and stand near the giggling lady.

"Would you take the picture?" she asks Nailah.

"Sure," she says, jumping up and taking the camera from the anxious woman.

Nailah counts to three, and I pose with the waitress.

"Now take one of me and my lady here," I ask of the waitress.

I hand her my phone, and Nailah pops under my arm for a picture.

"Hold on," the waitress says, snapping another picture of Nailah and me with her phone.

"Thank you," I say, taking my phone back.

The waitress flitted away after the picture, most likely posting the event on some social media site.

The food is decent, and we eat without event.

After paying the bill, I am not ready for the day to end, for our time together to be over. It's weird that doing nothing with Nailah had been more fun than the expensive date nights I had concocted in the past.

I order milkshakes to delay her departure a little longer.

"If you could ask me anything, what would you want to know?" I ask. The key to any woman is knowing more about her. Nailah doesn't give me a lot of information freely. Maybe if I give her access to me, she'll grant me more access to her.

"I heard that you 'fix' a lot of things for the players. Is Naeem one of the players that you help?" she asks without hesitation.

"That's the question that you want to ask?" I shrug. "I give you the VIP pass to my life. I'm an open book right now, and you ask about Naeem?"

"Correction. I want to know about you and what you do for players. You can tell a lot about a person from the company that they keep."

"I've helped out a few players here and there. I am kind of a concierge of medical treatment. I support clients with whatever they need, and they pay me well."

I downplay my help. Truthfully, I had saved the lives and careers of professional athletes from Houston to Oklahoma City by keeping incidents under wraps.

"How did you start doing the 'fixing'?" she asked inquisitively.

What I do is not technically illegal. Not anymore, anyway. Not since I have my own fully equipped office. I rarely have to take any clients to the hospital. The hospital requires documentation and reporting. Private practice, not so much. Still, I don't want to broadcast things that may look unfavorable to some of my first patients.

"Why do you want to know?" I laugh in the guise of a joke. "You work for the morning news?"

I examine her body language. I don't need someone writing a tell-all book, or selling the story to the National Enquirer or something.

She shrugs her shoulders.

"I was just wondering. Is it something that you set out to do? I had never heard of it before."

Her answer eased my automatic suspicion that she was working an angle to net a new cash flow. She isn't Briana, but she is the first female in a long time that I've shared a significant amount of time with. Others had not made it to the question and answer portion of the evening.

"Jermaine Timmons, Naeem, and I all played college basketball together. They called us 'The Amigos.' Everyone knew we were going to take it all in the championship our junior year until I made a move left and my knee went right. It was over for me." I recall. Basketball had been my life, where all my dreams resided.

"How long were you out?"

"Forever. It ended my career before I ever had one," I explain.

"The good thing is that I had already switched my major from social work to sports medicine, so when I changed it again to general medical studies, I already had some classes that fit."

Nailah nods her head. "You figured out how much social workers make, huh?"

I cover my face and my shameful grin behind my hand.

"Sorry, the pay scale was a problem." I catch her eyes again after dropping my hand. "The fixing part came along when I was in my residency. It was a way to make some extra money without getting another job."

"I hear that. Back in the day, I had my hotel job, did event security, and braided hair on the side." She shook her head. "It was crazy."

Nailah's resourcefulness is amazing and I take a moment to admire her stirring eyes.

"Who was your first client?" she asks, leaning her smiling face into her hand.

I can't remember Briana ever being this interested in me or my life. Every time we were together, it was always about her. It's about her wants, her needs, her goals, her dreams, never me, never us. I enjoy that Nailah listens to me.

"Jermaine," I chuckle thinking about my one-time friend. "He was always a knucklehead, and when he came to play pro ball in Dallas, he was in need of 'off the record' medical help on the regular."

Wild isn't enough of a word to define the young Jermaine that I ran the court with back in the day, and even less of a word in comparison to the man that he became as a professional basketball player.

"The first time he showed up slinking through the E.R., where I was working the night shift, with a jacket covering his bloodied clothes, I knew his presence in Dallas was going to be an adventurous one. I just didn't know how lucrative it would be," I explain.

She nods and smiles.

"Some of his teammates started paying me to help them out too. In cash, a lot of it," I tell her, thinking about the ten thousand dollars J handed me that night. "I paid off my debt, opened my own practice, and here we sit," I explain as though it were that simple. Being a smart guy who paid attention in class, and prayer helped me through some of the intricate procedures I performed in an empty room of the hospital with only a nurse or two who needed some extra change to help.

"I didn't know the three of you had that much history," Nailah commented, sipping on her drink.

"All the better," I answer. "Part of being a fixer is that most people don't know who I fix stuff for."

"I don't have many friends," she admits. "Regina and I became close while she trained me. You traveled the country, practiced, and lived with these guys for years. Do you miss that?"

I take a second to think about that.

"I never needed any more brothers. I already had three by birth and two cousin-brothers who may as well have lived in the same home as me. Going to college was a welcomed break from my sometimes-intrusive family. I didn't suspect that being on a team with Jermaine and Naeem would bring about more brothers and more family in a sense."

When I walked onto the court on the first day of training, I was an instant hit because my skills were recognizable. Handling the ball came easily, and since everyone wanted to be associated with the best, most of the players gravitated toward me. All except Naeem. Jermaine and he had shared the spotlight in their small town, and he wasn't looking for a three-way split. I couldn't see envy and greediness then, but thinking back on his actions rather than his words, I realized that it was always there.

Nailah sips more of her milkshake through a straw and I momentarily lose focus. It's time to taste those lips again.

"Continue."

"We hung tight. We practiced together, trained together, and studied together, but it was never about supporting each other. For Naeem, it was about figuring out what I was doing so that he could do it better. It was about figuring out my secrets, my moves, my actions, what made me great so that he could emulate or destroy it."

"What makes you think that?"

"We didn't have a lot of money back then, and I remember this guy, De Juan, who was at a sneaker store hooking me up. He wasn't so good with the ladies, so we worked out a system. He would come hang out with me and the guys on the weekend, and I told them that they should hang out with my friend De Juan, whatever girls I didn't want. Whenever he and a girl hit it off, I got a new pair of shoes. Since I have the gift of gab, and I'm just a little irresistible, I had a new pair of kicks every few weeks."

She frowns.

"That's kind of sleazy."

"To a college student with no money, it seemed like a good idea. It definitely changed my view on what a girl would do in the hope of being with a rising star. Women aren't nearly as unpredictable as most men think."

Except for Nailah. I can't figure her out.

"I knew too many women like that," she agrees. "Whatever happened to your hook-up?"

"I made the mistake of telling Naeem about the hookup. A week later, I went to the store and found out De Juan had been fired. A few years later, I ran into him at a different location and he told me that Naeem had gotten him fired when he couldn't give the same deal."

"What makes you think that he won't do anything to mess up your hook-up now?"

"We both have too much to lose. I know more about both those men than they ever would want the general public to know."

"Still, you should be careful."

"Why, because you'd miss me too much if I got caught and sent away?"

The light sound of her laughter brings a smile to my face.

"Negative," she says with a snap. "I just don't think that pretty face would last too long behind bars."

"So, you like my face?"

She rolls those gorgeous eyes of hers.

"Honestly, I don't do all of the crazy things that I used to do for players that would get me in trouble. I provide private services and coordinate with other medical providers to maintain player care. Players don't have to find a doctor wherever they travel, I can meet them there or get someone there to support them. That's why I got the Fixer award this year."

"That makes me feel better," she sighs. "I really did not want to be disappointed on my birthday."

I take a moment to stare at the woman that I spent the night with. I had seen every crevice of her body and entered her with multiple body parts, but she had never mentioned a birthday.

"Why didn't you tell me it was your birthday?"

"For what?" she shrugs. "It's just another day. I'm just another year older."

I don't know whether to be offended or not at the fact that she didn't feel that I was important enough to share this information with.

"I thought we were friends Nai," I say taking her hand. "I want to know things about you. Whatever you are willing to share."

"We're cool Tyriq, but I am under no illusion that this is a forever type of thing. I didn't want to get too personal or for things to get too awkward. You are under no obligation to hang out with me because it is the anniversary of the day I shot out of my mother's vagina."

I can only smile and shake my head.

"Damn Ice Blade. Sliced again."

CHAPTER NINETEEN

Nailah

A real live giggle escapes me, and I clasp my hand over my mouth so quickly that I scare Tyriq.

"What?" he slides each finger away from my face. "What's up?"

His eyes are hypnotic, and I almost forget what he asked.

"Giggling?" I slip a fingernail between my teeth.

Sitting in Tyriq's media room after an evening exploring the mall, shopping in stores that I had never known existed, the laughs rolled out of me so regularly that my stomach hurt.

"The funniest part was when the sales lady walked into the wall because she couldn't stop looking back at you," I laugh. "I can't believe the effect that you have on women."

He smiled that bright, hypnotizing smile. The one that could make both my heart and traffic stop. That smile is what scares me. The power it contains to render me useless.

"But for some reason, you're immune, Blade," he replies. I can tell that he meant it in a lighthearted manner, but truth and heaviness laced the statement.

"Who said that I was immune?" I question. "I'm still here with you right now."

He moves in closer to me and hovers near my mouth.

"I wish that you would have let me buy more for you."

I am drawn into his eyes and wait to feel his lips.

"You did- did enough," I stutter, trying to take reign of my speech. His nearness distracts me.

Tyriq licked the seam of my mouth.

"Not enough. I'm ready to spoil you."

He takes my mouth before I can reply. I fall against him.

I don't want him to spoil me. I don't want to be swept in the tide of his interest only to be left floundering when he takes his affection away, and the drought occurs.

Tyriq slides his hand around my waist and presses my body down onto the sofa under his.

"You feel so right. I just need to touch you all of the time," he mutters.

I believe him. In the mall, he grabbed my hand. When we walked, his arm resided around my waist. In the car, his fingers grazed my thigh the entire ride. When I spoke, he watched my mouth as though it were the most appetizing entree he had ever witnessed.

The need to touch him swirled around on the inside of me, but I kept those feelings at bay as much as possible.

Being in his arms was like floating through stars, but he didn't need to know that.

I tugged at my bottom lip with my teeth, keeping my kind words there. He doesn't need to hear from me how sexy he is, how great of a lover he is. Tyriq knows those things. He doesn't need to know how much he affects me.

"Damn, Nailah," he said, removing the warmth of his body away from mine by scooting to the other section of the sofa.

I instantly felt the draft, coolness from the loss of his touch.

"What is it?" I scoot closer to him.

"I'm usually pretty secure when dealing with women, but-" he paused. "Are you interested in me? Are you enjoying our time together?"

"Yes!" I nearly shout, surprising myself.

He laughs a little.

"You seem like you're holding back." Tension fell from his face, and concern replaced it. "Do I make you uncomfortable?"

Yes, you do make me uncomfortable, is what I think about saying. He makes feelings crawl through each pore of my body, even though I had been trying for so long to keep my emotions swaddled and buried.

"No. I just don't believe in inflating the ego. So, if you're waiting on me to sing your praises, please be aware that I don't even own a hymnal."

Dawning a sarcastic grin, he shakes his head.

"Ouch." He holds his hand to his chest. "It amazes me how you can be so hard." Tyriq encloses my face in the palms of his hands. "Then you have this sweetness that appears from nowhere."

I shrug. "I am who I am. Take it or leave it."

Tyriq searches my eyes again before he releases my face and smirks.

"I saw you with the little girl in my office, the way you were gentle and nurtured her," he explains. "You were even concerned about me fighting and my career."

Tyriq moves his arm around my side and encloses me in a hug. I breathe in his sexy scent and fall languid against him. There is zero possibility to control my steely façade when I'm in his arms.

"What happened? Why is that same nurturing spirit unavailable to me?" Tyriq's words are slow and spoken with concern. "Even if you don't care about my feelings, I want to know about yours. I want to know about who you are in every aspect."

It was as though he were speaking an entirely different language. The words coming out of his mouth register with me piece by piece. Where I came from, people already knew my background. They knew that I was the left behind child of that lady who talked to herself and the guy with the pretty hair. They knew I had lived in the whorehouse. Those who didn't know didn't care.

"My mother was mentally ill," I confide. "I didn't know it then, but looking back, I can tell."

I watch his expression. He is neutral, non-judgmental, waiting for more.

"I remember the day that she left me like it just happened. I remember her fussing and cussing the whole way as we trekked down the street to the grocery store. Daddy had the car. Momma was pissed because there was no food in the house, and Daddy was out in the streets yet again."

Squeezing my eyes shut, I focus on the rhythmic caress of Tyriq's hand against my arm. I had not spoken about that day in years, but it was time.

"Momma grabbed a cart, and the festivities began. She spoke the entire time that we were in the store, but never to me."

I take a deep breath.

"It was just the two of us. Momma kept mumbling while we walked down each aisle about how much she was tired of being alone. She didn't put one item in the cart. Momma's mumbling got louder on the second trip through each aisle. Still no groceries in the cart. By our fourth trip through the aisles, momma's mumbles were growing into yells, and the clerks began to notice. On trip number six, a manager slowly approached us and asked her to leave the store. She kept walking like she didn't hear him. On trip eight, the police asked her to leave the premises. Momma made a hard left onto aisle seven on trip number nine. The cops were done playing games and cornered her. She ranted about how much she hated being a mother and my father always breaking her heart."

The rest of the words get caught in my throat. It's hard to tell.

At the brush of Tyriq's thumb across my cheek, I open my eyes.

"We can talk about it another time."

His gentle eyes meet mine, and I make my decision.

"When they attempted to handcuff my momma, little petite Mosel James became a bucking bronco. I tried to go to her. I wanted to understand her. It didn't make sense to me. Why was she crying? I needed to know why the tears wouldn't leave my eyes, why her sadness was seeping into me. I needed her to love me, to hold me, to say that she wanted me. To say she wouldn't be crazy anymore. I needed her to be there."

Tears slip from my eyes then, and I rush to remove them.

Tyriq pulls me closer to him.

"So, your mother was taken away," he concluded. "She didn't really leave you."

"She didn't come back when she was free either," I add. "And talking about this does nothing to change that."

"What about your father?" he asked.

"He's gone too," I respond, but I move closer to him. "Wouldn't you like to talk about something more interesting?"

He smirked as he watched me stroke his arm.

"Changing the subject?"

I reach out to touch his face.

"Maybe," I quip. "Either way, it benefits you."

Sex is easier. Rehashing the past is too difficult.

He licks his lips before taking a cursory glance up and down my body.

"Alright. I'll let you get away with it for now," he speaks huskily.

Pressing his lips against mine, I allow myself to fall into the pleasure of Tyriq.

I groan when he pulls away.

"You can be mean if you need to; I still see the sweet in you. I know that it comes from a place of honesty. Just don't lie to me. Ever. Don't do that to me."

"Alright. Truth only," I tell him and kiss him back.

I wake up in the darkness of the night in his bed and in his arms to the sound of a buzzing bell.

"Tyriq?" I call out, pushing up and out of his arms.

The strange buzzing bell sounds again.

Tyriq sat up groggily and looked at me.

"Someone is here," I say.

When the buzzer sounds again, he looks at the clock and then his phone.

"No one called." He got up from the bed, displaying his nakedness.

I am grateful for a creation of such perfection and for allowing me to partake in such an excellent specimen.

My eyes glaze over his body as he slides into a pair of shorts and walks over to an intercom.

"Who is it?" he asked after pressing a button.

There was a crackling sound before a small female voice sounded through.

"Tyriq. I need someone to talk to," the woman said.

My eyebrows lifted.

Tyriq turned to face me.

"It's Naeem's wife, Briana," he explains.

"Why would she come here?" I ask.

He paused for a second before pressing another button.

"I've treated her since they have been in Dallas. Their issues never kept office hours." He shrugs. "I'll make it quick."

Tyriq slips on a shirt and house shoes before kissing my cheek and exiting the room.

CHAPTER TWENTY

Tyriq

She doesn't look hurt when I open the door wide enough to view her. There aren't any tears or visible bruises. She had always been good at hiding things. I don't see anything that requires medical attention, and that's the only reason that she would be here.

A frown covered her once-beautiful face. Over the years, plastic surgery needed to repair her nose and cheek had changed her look.

"Lew, stop playing and let me in," she demands while pushing at the door.

"Briana," I stop her. "You cannot come here. You cannot stay here."

The frown did not leave her face from before and only deepened at my words.

"What are you talking about?" she waves her hand dismissively in the air. "What is wrong with you? Have you not seen the news?"

She moves forward again, but I don't budge.

"As a matter of fact, I have seen the news. That's more of a reason for you to get into your car and go home."

"If I wanted to be at home, I would be there. I am divorcing Naeem. It's over."

Briana reaches out a hand and slides a finger up the side of my neck. I stop her.

"I'm glad that you are finally moving on. That's good for you and your children."

"It's good for us. We can be together now. I have my bags in the car."

I look around outside and notice that the expensive SUV is void of people. It shouldn't bother me, but it does.

"Where are your kids?"

The nearly permanent frown is apparent again.

"With my mother," she shakes her head. "What's going on?"

"I'm not your consolation prize, Briana. Hell, I'm not even going to be your doctor anymore. You shouldn't be here."

Her face scrunches as she squints.

"What are you talking about? This has always been the plan. Since Naeem and I moved to Dallas, I was supposed to come back to you."

"That was the plan two years ago when I actually thought that you were leaving him when I thought that you loved me. When was the last time that we even talked? You didn't even call me back when my mother was in the hospital."

"You bought a whole house just to be with me. This big ass house was supposed to be for us, me, you, and my kids. If you don't want me, then why do you still live here?"

"I have to live somewhere," I grunt and run a hand down my face. "None of this is important. You turned down the house and promptly began ignoring me."

"Naeem and I were trying to make it work," she whines. "I'm ready now. Can't I just come in? My marriage is over."

"I'm glad you finally realize that you deserve better, but it is not with me."

She looks up at me like she wants to cry, but she doesn't.

"I'll give you a call," she says.

"I won't answer."

She turned to walk away, and I knew the exact moment that she spotted Nailah's car.

"Who the hell is here, Lew?" she yells.

"Go home, Briana."

The venomous scowl that she shoots at me is evidence that she will be back, but she makes her way to her car and drives off.

Nailah is sitting on the side of the bed, sliding on a pair of pants when I enter the room.

"You're back," she greets, her voice flat and emotionless. "I thought one of the little ninja suit women captured you."

"Ninjas? What?" I ask. "Where are you going?"

I dive into the bed on top of her and fold my arms around her lush body.

She squiggles but laughs as I roll about the bed with her tucked against me.

"I'm going away from here. I don't need my tires slashed by one of your ninja-suited psycho groupies."

She stops wiggling, and I stop rolling. My mission is complete, and her pants are now on the ground.

"No need to leave. Everything is taken care of."

She shakes her head, but the dreamy look is there.

"Famous last words," Nailah quips. "Do you know how many people get killed in Lifetime movies after someone says that? The numbers are staggering."

I brush the back of my knuckles against the side of her face, amazed by her charm.

"I'm not going to let anything happen to you, Nailah. You are the one that I want here with me."

"Yeah? Show me?" she teases.

CHAPTER TWENTY-ONE

Tyriq

"Where is your food?" Nailah asks as she enters my bedroom.

Nailah was awake. Fully awake and moving around the room in my t-shirt and a pair of socks that she had yanked from my drawer. Strangely, the shirt fit similarly to the one she was wearing when I saw her at the hospital. Loose and baggy.

"Why? Are you trying to cook for a brother?"

She flounces into the bed with a jar of peanut butter and a spoon.

"If you had some food, maybe. The only thing that's not expired in your kitchen is peanut butter," she snaps. "To be a baller, you sure live broke."

"I don't have time to shop."

"Hire someone."

"I'm not that guy."

"But you have three cars and this huge house." Nailah then dips the spoon into the entire jar of peanut butter and pulls out a big glob.

"Are you really about to eat that?" I am somewhat mortified but turned on. If she can work that much peanut butter in her mouth and throat, then the possibilities of what she can do with me are endless.

"Hell yeah. Peanut butter spoons are the best." She slides the upside-down spoon containing a glob of peanut butter over her tongue.

With precision, she licks the entire spoon spotlessly. I have to blink a few times before adjusting my dick.

"I agree, the way you eat peanut butter spoons is the best."

She laughs and licks at the spoon again.

"Come here," I summon. "I think I see some peanut butter."

She looks across her chest and legs.

By the time she finishes asking where she dropped the peanut butter, my face is between her thighs, licking her like she is on a spoon.

Nailah found some creative uses for the peanut butter that later required us to shower.

I was ordering real food when Nailah asked about a picture of me with the basketball and cheer squad from college. It is the annual photo from my sophomore team. The players and coaches are lined up in three rows. The cheerleaders pose in front of the players. Each member has their name listed across their chest.

"That's you, isn't it?" She points to my younger self in the back row.

"Did my name printed at the top give me away?" I chuckle.

She looks over the picture again.

"Hey, there's a cheerleader here named Misti. Could it be the same Misti as Tia's mom?"

Looking at the picture, I shrug. "I don't know. We weren't that cool. There were a lot of cheerleaders around then, but I didn't know much about them. I'll ask my cousin. He hung out with her a couple of times when he came to the campus."

"Well, it might be a lead. It's more information than I have now. I had to place the little girl in a group home. I really want to find a parent or relative for her."

We settle down in the theater room to continue our nineties movie binge. Nailah makes herself comfortable between my legs as I recline on the huge sofa.

"I'm mad." Nailah crosses her arms. She didn't look mad, but I questioned her anyway.

"What's up?"

"I didn't realize that you had three movies queued up to just start automatically without even a credit roll. Every time I think a movie is over, another one starts, and I'm locked in." She narrows her eyes at me. "You did that on purpose?"

"Maybe. Maybe not." I shrug. "You are free to leave at any time."

I cover her body with my arms and pull her against my chest.

She giggles, and those irresistible dimples pop out.

"Lucy is all patched up for the moment. You can roll out as soon as you like," I remind her, but secretly hope that she decides to stay.

She turns her head to face mine and I lick at her lips. She parts them for me, and we press our lips together for what seems like the hundredth time.

She shakes her head when we part. "That kiss keeps me captive."

I gasp.

"Blade, did you just give me kind words?"

Nailah shoves at me playfully.

"By the way, where did you get those mechanic skills?" she asks. "Not everyone can bring Lucy back to life like that and so quickly."

"Well you know how I do," I pretend to pop my nonexistent collar at her compliment and cackle like a cartoon pimp.

She swats a playful hand at my chest.

"For real. I want to know."

I take her wrist and kiss her hand.

"My dad. He's into aviation mechanics but restores classic cars, too. My brothers and I actually own several repair shops. My brother Tyson travels across North Texas and Houston to manage them. My cousin, Cairo, owns a car dealership. I've always been around tools and car parts. Also, based on the knowledge of my kinship, you need a new car."

Every conversation is a chance to learn about Nailah. I want to know everything about her. I want to be able to recite facts and stories about her like a Wikipedia page with references listed.

One thing I have learned is that Nailah has a stellar *diva gaze*—a silent look that makes me feel as tall as an ant.

She stares at me, her *diva gaze* fully activated, and I wish I could retract my statement.

"I cannot get rid of Lucy."

She folds her arms.

"You don't have to scrap her. You can drive something else," I reasoned.

Nailah tilts her head to the side, regarding me as though I am clearly a mental patient before she rolls her eyes.

"It's just a suggestion," I retreat from my previous suggestion. "I'm sure with some more work, Lucy will be running like new again. Why is that car so important to you?"

That's when all the tough falls from her body, and a flicker of sadness crosses her eyes.

"Tell me about Lucy." Obviously, the car is special to her, and I want to be just as significant in her life. It's a shame that I am slightly jealous of a beat-up old car.

Without a sound, Nailah slides a hand against the front of my pants before puckering up the side of my neck.

"Are you trying to distract me?" I get the distinct feeling that she is swerving a conversation about her past.

"No," she says with a nibble against my ear.

Flipping over the band of my basketball shorts, Nailah wraps her hand around my cock.

"You're avoiding the question," I moan.

"What question?" She leans down and suckles at the tip of my manhood. The sight is breathtaking. I grab onto the cushion of the couch and attempt small breaths. I was right about her mouth abilities.

"Shit." I have had head before, but it was mostly the obligatory kind, the *I-need-a-bill-paid* or *You-did-me-so-I'll-kinda-do-you* type.

Nailah is doing this for fun. I can tell by her enthusiasm.

On all fours, she flattens her tongue to lick the length of me before flicking it across the tip.

"You want to talk about the car?" she asks my dick before looking up at me. Her brow lifts. "He said no. What about you?"

"What car?" The two words combine in one breath.

I cry out her name when she takes all of me into her mouth with one swoop.

Nailah spirals her tongue around me while managing an up-and-down motion that nearly brings tears to my eyes.

"Get that shit, Blade." She moved her head faster. No hands, just the warmth of her moist mouth against my skin, sucking and pulling.

I alternate between watching her work and watching the ceiling for the heavens to open up.

The sight of her bouncing breast and the jiggle of her ass war for a spot was the second-best thing about this experience.

I get a handful of both.

"Nai-lah. I'm about to," I try to warn her. Words are difficult. She keeps sucking like she wanted to do it for days like I was the candy treat she had finally gotten to have.

"Baby," the plea falls on deaf ears.

I pull away from her mouth, scramble to put on a condom, flip Nailah over, and drive into her with a hunger so raw I nearly frighten myself.

The pull of her mouth is something to behold, but being enveloped between the folds of her is beyond glory.

"Oh shit. Damn, Blade."

I go wild, thrusting and pounding into her body with a need so great it overtakes my existence.

She serves it all back to me, every push is met with a pull of her juicy core.

"I'm- Ty- Oh- oooh." Her body contracts and pulsates a ring of pleasure around me.

I lose it. Screaming expletives in a guttural roar that probably shook the walls, I release everything in me amid a flurry of bright lights bouncing across my eyes. Nailah made me see sunshine inside a windowless room.

"Tell me something," I whisper against her neck.

We were lying in bed after leaving the theater room. There was no use in attempting to watch a movie after what had happened. I needed sleep and a moment to rethink what I have been doing with my dick all of these years because it should have been in Nailah James a long time ago.

Sprawled out next to me, Nailah lazily tracks her fingers across my bare body in a hypnotic rhythm.

"Tell you something like what?" she speaks into my chest.

"Why won't you let go of Lucy? What does the car mean to you?"

She huffs out a breathy chuckle.

"You don't give up, do you?" she asks.

"I thought you figured that out."

I kiss her forehead and slide a lazy hand along her belly to calm her increased heartbeat.

"Just talk to me, Blade. I want to know everything about you," I coax.

Nailah adjusts her body and pushes closer to me. When she looks into my eyes, I see the weariness buried in her eyes. It is not easy for her to tell.

Before speaking, Nailah looks away.

"Lucy was a gift from my foster mother, Dolly," she stops her words there, and I am disappointed that she doesn't feel safe enough to tell me the story in its entirety.

"That was a nice gift," I compliment, hoping that it will encourage her to keep talking.

Nailah looks up at me again.

I press my lips against her forehead.

"Just talk to me."

Her breath tickles my skin as she presses an ear against my chest and wraps her arms around me.

"Lucy was her car," she continues. "It was the last thing that she gave to me before she walked away, never to be seen again."

Damn, it was not a nice gift then.

"I was sixteen and Lucy was my home, income, friend, and family."

Because of the wobble in her voice, I pull her nearer.

"Dolly took me to a diner for lunch and told me that she couldn't keep me any longer. She gave me the keys to her car and some money, walked out of the door, and took a cab somewhere unknown."

"What did you do after that? I was smart at sixteen, but faced with the same situation, I'm not sure my outcome would have been the same.

"She gave me the contact information of her great-aunt in Oklahoma City. I went there, worked, and sublet a tiny apartment until I was eighteen. Then I moved to Augusta, Georgia because my mom once told me that she had family there. No luck. After that, I went to Houston to try and find my foster mom. No luck there, either. Everywhere that I moved, I went to school and worked."

"How did you get to Dallas?" I would lay in bed and listen to her until she had explained the last twenty-eight years of her life. Being wrapped up with her in our little world is better than anything offered outside of my four walls.

"My mom always talked about living in the big city. Dallas was a magical place when I was a kid. She talked about it like dreams came true in the city," she takes a slow breath. "When I finished school, I went back to our little town to find her. I found out that they had transferred her to a facility right outside of Dallas where she later died. Settling here in DFW just seemed like the right thing to do."

A few lone soldier tears fall from her eyes. She touches her face as though crying is something foreign to her.

"It is the right thing to do and I'm going to keep your mean ass right here in Dallas too."

Nailah chuckles.

"You got me laughing, horny, and crying. I am truly crazy over you."

I shoot off a brilliant, full-tooth smile at her compliment.

"Thank you, and I hope you know that I am crazy about you, too," I tell her honestly, wiping a stray tear away. I'm here for you."

"For the moment." She rolls her eyes and her body away from me simultaneously.

Before I could pull her close, the bell from the front gate chimed.

Nailah scurried up, shedding sheets and blankets magician-style. The material never seemed to touch her skin.

"Where are you going?" I gently tackle her back to the bed and take her mouth again.

The bell continues to chime, but I ignore it. Fuck whoever it is. They don't even understand what I have in my bed right now.

"Don't you want to get that?" she asks when I let go of her tongue.

"Naw. Not really." I eye her body and slide a hand down to her core. "I'm trying to get that."

The chimes ring again.

"You should answer that." She scoots away from me.

I stand, too, and draw her into my arms.

"I'll answer, but that just means you have to stay with me longer."

Releasing Nailah, I move to the front gate monitor, click the touchscreen panel to switch on the video, and see Chad.

"Damn." I already know what he wants. "It's my cousin, Chad."

Nailah nods.

I push the button to speak to him at the gate.

"What do you want asshole?" I greet.

"Is that any way to speak to the man who saved you on the Sabbath?"

"Saved me from what?" I ask.

"Open the gate, or there will be hell to pay."

Chad removes a phone from his pocket and slides his finger across the screen to accept a call.

He then holds the phone up to the camera.

"Open the gate, Tyriq!" my mother's voice booms through the speaker. "We came to check on you."

I turn back to look at Nailah but notice that she is missing.

A second later, she stumbles out of the restroom, and I see her sliding into her clothing.

Ignoring my cousin, I call out to Nailah.

"Wait, not again. Can I get you to sit still for a minute?"

This girl is harder to hold onto than lottery winnings.

Nailah is working double-time to find all her clothing and dress.

"I don't want to be in the way," she huffs, sweeping her hand under my bed while on all fours. "Have you seen my bra?"

"How can you be in the way if I invited you and keep asking you to stay? Just chill. You can meet my family."

She stopped moving for a long second, turned her head, and glared at me.

It hit me like a bag of nickels where I had messed up.

"No. I didn't mean the 'meet my family' big relationship thing. You are here, and he is here. It's hello and then goodbye."

The bell chimes again.

Nailah stands and continues pulling on her clothing.

Chad doesn't budge from the camera, and Nailah looks like she can't leave fast enough.

"Just wait here in the bedroom. I'll get rid of him."

This slows her dressing pace to a stop, and I let out a sigh of relief.

"I don't want to sit around waiting all day," she huffs.

"You don't have to. Give me five minutes. I'll have him out, and then I'll be in you."

The bell chimes again, and I tell Nailah with a kiss how much I need her to stay.

Her eyes are glossy when I step away.

"You better be glad that I like you." She smiles and takes a seat on the bed.

I push the button to open the gate.

"I'll be right back," I promise.

"You owe me."

CHAPTER TWENTY-TWO

Nailah

When I walked into the front room, his cousin Chad was standing there with his arms folded while Tyriq spoke on speakerphone with an angry woman. I peeked around the corner but didn't step all the way out.

"You had us worried when you didn't show up or pick up your phone, son," the voice on the line rang through.

"I'm fine. I just needed a break," Tyriq answers.

I had never had a family that worried about me, but I can imagine what his family must be thinking.

"Oh no," another voice rang through. "You can't take a break from God. What if He took a break and forgot to give you breath?"

I chuckle at Chad, mocking the phrase word for word as the woman on the phone speaks to them.

"Aunt Pat, Mom, I love you both. I am fine. I'll talk to you later."

Tyriq hangs up the phone.

"So why did you really stay home?" Chad asks while putting his phone away.

"The door is this way." Tyriq guides Chad toward the door.

In a flash, his cousin does a spin move like an NBA star and is sprinting in my direction. He stops right in front of me.

"Damn!" he yells, dragging out the word as long as his stare over my body. "You were hiding her, cuz?"

"Hello." I reach out a hand. "I'm Nailah."

"The Nailah?" He looks between me and Tyriq. "Oh shit! I'd lose my religion over her, too."

Tyriq grabs his cousin by the arm with a force I had never seen before and moves him toward the door. Chad even looks surprised.

"My bad, Ty," he laughs as Tyriq ousts him.

"Goodbye, Chad."

Tyriq gives me a sheepish grin. "I apologize for my cousin." He drops his eyes as he moves toward me. "My family can be a little-"

"A lot-" I correct.

"A lot overbearing," he finishes. "It's all in love."

He wraps those tree trunk arms around me, and I melt against his body. Nearly floating, I forget all about the crazy people related to the sexy man holding me as we magically end up in his bed naked again.

After two rounds of bouncing across the sheets, I am in a spot that is becoming more and more familiar. My back was pressed against the hard plank of Tyriq and lost in his massive hold while he rained kisses across my neck. It was my new favorite location.

"There's this group named the Foreign Exchange that I really like," I half-whisper in a haze of bliss.

"Yeah. What about them?" he mutters between pecks.

"They sing this song about taking off your blues like you can take off your shoes," I breathe. "I feel like that when I am with you. You make me feel like a love song like I can take off my worries and leave them at the door."

When I feel the swift coolness of Tyriq's absence, I know that I messed up. I shouldn't have been so open. Already, I have messed up the only little piece of paradise in my life.

"Come closer, babe," I hear him say.

I turn to see him sitting at the foot of the bed and slide down near him.

"I just want you to know that what you just said," he kisses my cheek, "that's the sweetest shit that I have ever heard in my life. I used to deal with women who were always wanting more, just trying to get as much as I could give until there was no more left of me."

He picks up a long velvet box that is tucked near his muscular thigh.

"Thank you for liking me for just me. Thank you for being honest about your feelings. Most of all, thank you for being here with me. Happy Birthday."

Tyriq opened the box, and I nearly fell off the bed. Inside is a gorgeous gold link bracelet with a circle tag that says "Sharp and Sweet" in italicized letters. Bright diamonds outline the custom tag, and I instantly know that it is expensive.

"I got it made while you were shopping this weekend."

I pick up the heavy piece of jewelry.

"Tyriq, this is too much."

He takes the bracelet from my fingers and clasps it around my wrist.

"Not really. It's only the beginning."

CHAPTER TWENTY-THREE

Nailah

I make it to my office on time, ready to work and ready to get Tyriq off my mind.

"Good Morning, Mrs. Lewis," Regina chirped, flittering into my office. "How was your weekend with Dr. Tyriq?"

"Magical," I smile. "And if you would have brought your ass to work Friday, I could have told you about our fun Thursday night after the gala too."

"Girl, you don't even have to say a word. That face is speaking universally. That's the *he put it down* smile. I swear you floated up about six inches off the ground."

I laugh at my friend.

"It was a nice time," I relent. I did not want to enjoy him as much as I had, but some trouble is worth getting into.

"This bracelet you're rocking says that it was more than that. He must be feeling something mutual for you."

"It was just a little birthday present." The crazy giggle that is only spurred by conversations about Tyriq or the man himself pops out.

"So, when are you seeing him again?" Regina asks as she gets comfortable in my office chair.

"Not anytime soon," I respond. "This weekend, I lived my birthday fairytale wish. I got a great souvenir from the land of make-believe, and now it's back to reality."

"What? Rewind that right quick." Regina spun her finger around in the air like she was rewinding a tape.

"I'm not trying to get caught all up in feelings," I explain. "It's easier to end things on a high note. We had fun. Life goes on."

"Sorry, I have a hard time understanding crazy."

My cell phone rings and Tyriq's name pops up on the screen.

I slide my finger across the screen to end the call.

Regina's eyes bloom into wide saucers.

"Girl, are you crazy?" she yells as she fumbles over my desk to the phone. "Hello. Hello-" she taps the screen before dropping it back onto my desk. "So yes, you are crazy. Feelings or none, you can't dismiss a man ready to give you gifts and make you feel magical."

Regina took a close look at the bracelet again.

"I'd use the fourteen-karat gold to mend my broken heart."

I gently move my arm from Regina's clutches.

"You heard about Naeem, I'm sure," I begin changing the subject.

Regina doesn't get it. I'm not trying to be that woman who does anything for something shiny or the chick chasing some man in a love-dumb state. No. I got my physical needs met, my girly fantasies brought to life, and I had some fun. That's it.

"I heard about Naeem," Regina answers. "That bastard Jermaine wasn't about shit. I ended up meeting one of the conditioning coaches, Myles. He could go on and on for miles. Girl, he-"

"Regina, focus," I interject.

"I was at Myle's house when the news broke Saturday, and he wasn't even fazed. He said Naeem beat his wife regularly for fun. The dude was disloyal and slept with a couple of players' girlfriends. He said that the team lost a player because he slept with the boy's momma and teased him about it. 'Arrogant asshole' was how he described him."

"Damn, and you were pushing me to go out with him," I snap.

"I was pushing you to use him as a gateway to other successful men. How do you think I even got the tickets to go to the gala?" she asked but answered her own question. "Flunky on the B team."

I shake my head.

"I also saw several posts of you and Naeem floating around the internet this weekend. People are speculating that you were the reason for the blow-up with his wife."

"What?" I scrunch my face. "Who would even think that? We weren't even together an entire night."

Just then, a man in a green jumpsuit knocked on my open door.

"I have a delivery for a Ms. James."

"That's me," I say as the guy brings the most gorgeous bouquet of flowers to my desk and sits them down.

I skim through the multicolored blooms and the card from Tyriq before dumping it in the trash.

"Nailah! What did the flowers do to you? These are beautiful and expensive."

"You can have them," I tell her. "I'm trying to forget him as soon as possible. I told you already. I'm done. He was good. It was fun, now back to real life."

I am grateful for our weekend, for the glimpse of the good life, but that's not my reality.

"At least hang out with him for a few. He seems like a pretty decent guy," Regina adds.

"No guy is a good guy if you get to know him. I would rather he remain a sweet memory than a sour aftertaste."

Regina threw her hands in the air.

"You can't know that he is going to dog you. He may be the guy that is meant to be with you."

"I checked thoroughly this weekend. He has a penis. Therefore, he has the potential to hurt me."

"Damn, you should come with a defrost button. You are so cold sometimes."

"Tyriq said the same thing. He even gave me the nickname Ice Blade."

"Wait." Regina presses her fingers against the bridge of her nose as if gathering strength to continue the conversation with me. "So, you got a nickname and jewelry and spent the weekend? Sounds serious."

"I think your office phone is ringing, Regina. You should go check."

"I forwarded all my calls to my cell," she said, raising her phone. "Now what?"

Regina left after I gave her the flowers Tyriq had sent. I forward all my calls to my cell, which is something I hadn't known about previously, and head out to clear a few cases.

I pull into the school parking lot, excited that the day is moving quickly. Tyriq left me a voicemail explaining how much fun he had this weekend, that he was looking forward to a repeat, and that he would be out of town for a week with the basketball team.

I know I'm doing the right thing. He's not the relationship type.

Good sex and love are two different things. I knew too many men and women who got the two confused. Tyriq has the power to make me pass out with his tongue. I know for sure that he would do detrimental damage to my heart.

I walk into the elementary school with *a caring, professional* smile. I'm hoping to help someone today and take my mind off Tyriq.

After giving the clerk my badge, I am directed to the counselor's office, where Mali greets me.

"Hey, Nailah. Are we having lunch today?" she asks.

"Most definitely."

"The student is back this way." She led me to a small office in the back where a small boy around the age of seven sat, and I began to work my magic.

Once the interview is over, an assistant helps the student back to class.

I find Mali in her office.

"I'm finished," I say before noticing the Senegalese dance mask on her desk.

I walk forward and look at the intricately carved art, wanting to touch it but remembering my manners.

"This is beautiful."

"Thank you. I have three pieces from this guy."

"Really? I'm looking to get some more artwork for my condo."

"He's holding a private showing next Wednesday. I would love the company of a fellow enthusiast," she invites.

She handed me an invitation. It is being held at a gallery different from the one where I met Tyriq.

"That would be great, Mali. You don't know how much this made my day."

"Let's go then."

"Sure," I agree, ready to mix and mingle in the city.

CHAPTER TWENTY-FOUR

Tyriq

When I stepped off the plane and back into the city, the only place that I wanted to be was inside Nailah. While I was out of town, we texted and held short conversations. I wrote it off as her not liking to speak much over the phone, but when she declined to meet me at my home for a revamp of our weekend together, I knew that she was giving me the brush-off.

"It's your go," Chad prompts.

I let a card float haphazardly to the table and then looked at what remained in my hand. They all blur together. Sitting with my brother and cousins for a Friday game night, they have received the brunt of my hurt feelings.

"You done with Nailah's fine ass yet?" Chad asks.

"Or is it Briana on your mind?" Trystan suggests.

I shoot daggers over at Trystan.

"This is family. Attorney-client privilege doesn't count in Aunt Pat's house."

"She still asks for medical help, here and there," I divulge, but leave it at that. "There's nothing going on. I'm done with Briana."

"I asked about Nailah," Chad restates.

"She's not your type."

"Cousin, I'm offended." He places a hand over his heart like I have truly wounded him. "All women are my type. And the woman standing in your house that Sunday was top-of-the-line fine."

"Not happening," I tell Chad in a stronger voice.

"You don't think that I could get her?" the challenging gleam in his eyes pissed me off more than his words. Chad likes games so much that he makes them, but Nailah is not to be toyed with.

"She's off limits," I growl.

I nod up at Mali, the cousin I adore when she enters.

"What are y'all in here talking about?" Mali asks.

"Stuff not meant for girls," Chad shoots back.

Mali dismisses him.

"Whatever." She looks over in my direction. "Guess who I saw the other day."

From the singsong tone of her voice, there is only one guess.

"Nailah?" Chad answers for me. "Did she ask about me?"

I got up from the table, and before I could strike, Chad hopped up from the chair and was across the room.

"I was just playing," he chuckles.

I advance around the table, and Chad does some weird backward hop-skip shuffle to get away.

"Calm down, cuzo!" Chad shouts. "My bad."

I look him in the eye.

"Keep her name out of your mouth."

He nods in concession, and I turn away.

"So those nice round breasts are fair game as long as I don't say her name, right?"

I lunge at him, nearly throwing the card table over.

Terrence holds the table down. "Ya'll trippin' tonight."

"Ignore his childish ass Tyriq," Mali states grabbing my arm. "He knows better than to mess with your girl. Let's talk in the hall."

I take a deep breath and follow Mali into the hall. Is she my girl? She doesn't seem to think so.

"This again," Terrence calls out. "You're breaking up the game for a woman that ain't even here?"

Mali chuckles at Terrence's outburst as we settle against a wall in the hallway.

"You said something about not getting an opportunity to see Nailah. I may have some intel about where she'll be next Wednesday," Mali entices.

"That's what I'm talking about," I give her a high five. "Spill it."

"Now, cousin," she drawls.

The tilt of her head and the lift of her eyebrow are clues that this information about Nailah that she may share must come with an exclusive season pass for her into my business.

"First," she places a finger in the air, "tell me what you did to make her ignore you."

I lift one hand like I am saying the pledge and place the other on top of the air over a pretend stack of Bibles.

"On my honor, I did nothing wrong," I respond. "She randomly answers my texts and calls. When she does answer, she keeps the call short. If she were anyone else, I would-"

"I already know your record. I have stepped over the bodies left in your wake."

Suspicion fills her narrowed eyes.

"That was a long time ago." I shrug. "Plus, I apologized about your line sister and her cousin."

"But not about her sister." She reminds me as she darts a finger into my chest.

I brush her hand away.

"That is ancient history now."

"Anyway," Mali rolls her eyes," there's this nice bag, which my little educator salary can't afford."

I guess her price has doubled. Full access to my relationship and a purse. Damn.

"Send me the link," I sigh. "Do you want me to ship it to your apartment or Aunt Pat's?"

Mali's smile is nearly blinding once I agree. All traces of anger have fled.

"My mom's house, thank you!" she beamed. "And I invited Nailah to the Pan African art show next Wednesday."

"And she agreed?" the simplicity amazes me. "You just asked her to hang out, and she said yes without a problem?"

"Yep," Mali grins. "She's cool people."

"How would you know?"

"We've been to lunch twice."

"She doesn't know that I'm your cousin?"

"Nope."

"I need you to do a little intel for me."

"That's going to cost more than a bag," she smiles.

I was more than nervous about my plan. Mali had agreed to help, but when I didn't see Nailah, I began to worry.

"I'll get her here," Mali reassures.

She better, or I was going to reroute all the loot she bartered.

"When are you going to have this girl over so we can meet her the right way?" my mother asks.

Mali conveniently left out that both of our mothers would be attending. When Aunt Pat and my mother strolled in wearing their Sunday best, I almost lost it. There was no way that my plan could work with my mother and aunt hovering around, asking questions, and judging her.

"She's a little skittish, Mom, and I don't want to scare her away."

I give my mom a heads-up.

"If she doesn't know what a good catch you are-"

I stop her mid-sentence. I rarely, if ever, dare to interrupt my mother, but when it comes to Nailah, nothing that I do is normal.

"Mom, she's been through a lot in her life. People haven't always been the best to her. Please be on your best behavior."

Shirley Lewis's neck rolls back so far that I think it might detach.

"Son," she says, placing a hand on my shoulder. "I'm grown, and I'm gonna do me. If your little girlfriend can't handle that, then she's not the one."

My mother walks away, still grumbling about who she is and her level of grown.

I rub a hand across my face, but I really want to put it around Mali's neck. If I hadn't scared Nailah away before, my family surely would.

I find Mali outside on the phone, ending her conversation.

"Come on anyway, girl. I'm still here, and you should come unwind after such a long day."

She pauses.

I want to take the phone and scream through it for Nailah to come here now, but I don't. I take a deep breath and pace.

Mali ends the call.

"She had a late visit and went home," Mali reports. "She's going to get changed and head this way."

For that feat alone, Mali is the best cousin in the world. She got Nailah to answer the phone more than once, leave her home after work, and come to an event. All my earlier animosity is replaced with respect.

"Thanks for having my back." I squeeze her in a bear hug.

"I can't breathe," Mali chokes out before I release her. "Shit, you acting like it's Christmas morning, and you got a brand-new bike. Calm down."

"Not possible." I rub my hands together and do a joyful two-step on the sidewalk to the beat of my own song. "Nailah is coming. Nailah is coming."

I don't care that Mali is cracking up over my dance moves or that some of the stupid people are gawking and pointing. If they couldn't tell by my song, Nailah is coming, and that is something to dance about.

CHAPTER TWENTY-FIVE

Nailah

In Brook Bonnet, there weren't many opportunities to get dressed, so I am glad Mali asked me to attend the art show. It's crazy that I have made more friends here in a few months than I made in Book Bonnet during my total existence.

I slip into my new high heels, which cost more than my cell phone bill, and notice how well my dress makes my best body parts pop out a little more. Regina had been kind enough to go shopping with me at lunch to find a few outfits for my foray into the art scene.

This is what my move from Brook Bonnet is about: making connections with people and building a base of friends, not men. Men are trouble, and I'd had enough trouble in my life to last a lifetime.

The posh and gentrified downtown building is illuminated by old-style street lamps, giving the area a European vibe. I feel like a sophisticated girl in the movies.

Before I can enter the imposing building, my cell phone rings.

Since it could be Mali again, I answer without looking at the screen.

"Sunshine," he says. "Sunshine, are you there? It's me, your daddy."

"Daddy?" Levies break in my mind, and a flood of questions and thoughts barrel through with haste. "Where are you? What are you doing? How did you get this number?" I say all in one breath.

"I just got back to Brook Bonnet, and a friend told me you were looking around for me," he answered.

I don't have anything to say. Words escape me. What do I say to the man who left me? The man who decided I wasn't good enough to be his daughter, who drove my mother insane, who didn't visit, write, or call until now.

"Um. I'm busy at the moment," I respond slowly before ending the call. No goodbye or talk to you later because there is nothing else to say. My mother is dead, and my father is alive.

I take a deep breath. He will not shake my cool today. He will not mess up this opportunity for me to hang out with like-minded people and build the peer relationships I missed out on as a kid.

The interior is stunning. Art and sculpture consume the walls and ceilings. Like before, people touch, talk, and smile in small, well-dressed groups. Laughter jumps across the room like a grasshopper in spring, and I follow the reverberations of joy. A live band is playing somewhere, and I slip into the groove.

A few steps in, I consider spinning on my heels and running out of the room.

"Nailah," Mali said, standing close to me. "You made it!"

I can only look past her to the man I had been avoiding since I met him.

Mali followed my gaze to Tyriq, entangled in a conversation with several older women. I only recognize his Aunt Patricia in the pack.

"Why don't I introduce you to my cousin, Tyriq?" Mali extends, guiding me in his direction before I can respond.

I can't move. He's dressed up, but I remember what he looks like with nothing on. I instantly want to hop on his hose and get wetter.

"I don't- I can't go over there."

Mali examines me like a mother would.

"What's wrong?" she asks.

I take a deep breath and try to regain my composure. 'Never let them see you sweat' Dolly would say.

I look at Mali, and I know the smile that I try to scratch out is hideous.

"Nailah, really, are you alright?" the concern in her face deepens.

"He's just a tiny bit breathtaking," I whisper, staring off in his direction.

"So, I've heard." She wrinkles her nose. "He's my cousin, so I don't really get it."

I take a steadying breath.

"Are you going to make it?" she asks.

"Yes."

I walk with her, trying to move my eyes away from his. I push back the real smile straining against my mouth when his eyes brighten in my direction.

My heart hadn't known how much it missed him until it was near his again and able to beat in the same space.

Tyriq places an empty shot glass on a waiter's tray and picks up another. Was he nervous? Could he possibly be nervous about me?

His Aunt Pat and the pack stopped speaking and turned in my direction.

"Everybody, this is Nailah," Mali introduces. "She's a social worker. I met her when she came to the school for a case concerning one of my students."

"Hello," I say, but my eyes barely leave his, only glancing away at the woman.

"This is my mother, Patricia," Mali introduces starting at the right. "This is her sister, my Aunt Shirley. Tyriq is Aunt Shirley's son. Sister Thompson and Sister King are members of the church we attend."

I nod.

"Nice to meet you." The feeling of five sets of eyes tracing me is extremely unnerving. I am glad that I took the extra time on my makeup and dress.

They all respond with a similar greeting and smile. All except Tyriq.

Then, there is silence and weird glances ping-ponging across the group of women like a silent tournament of expressions.

I don't know what to say.

"That's a nice painting over there," Mali said pointing to the wall across the room. "Didn't you say your colors were brown and gold?"

"Huh?" It takes a second for it to register what Mali is doing. "Oh, yes. Brown and gold."

I actually hadn't picked out a color scheme, but that didn't matter.

"Let's go check it out right now," Mali insists quickly and happily.

Mali and I walk away from the group, and I breathe a sigh of relief. My feet stop near a series of paintings on the other side of the room.

"Tyriq has been my cousin all of my life," she says, looking back at the man who had permeated every aspect of my mind for the last few days and now my social outlets as well. "I have never seen him freeze up like that."

I refuse to look at him again.

"Are you alright? Both of y'all look shell-shocked." Her bright eyes fill with worry. "Will Tyriq being my cousin be a problem?"

I sigh. I like hanging out with Mali.

"No," is what I answer. "It won't be a problem as long as I know when he will be around."

The haphazard grin that dawns on Mali's face is almost enough to make me happy about attending tonight's art showcase.

"I grew up with boys," Mali prattles. "I don't know how to do the friend thing so much with girls. I pledged in college, but we all live so far apart now. Anyway, I like our association so far, and I would hate if my cousin got in the way of that."

"I just wasn't ready to see him," I reply fighting the urge to look around the room for him.

"Why not?" she questions.

I shrug. I had already given her more information about my feelings for Tyriq than I should have.

I twist the bracelet on my arm, the one that he had given to me. I hadn't even taken it off to shower. Sharp and sweet. He was all sweet when it came to me.

"I'm not looking for anything serious, and I think that's what he wants," I explain. "I'm trying to keep him as a buddy, or friends with benefits."

She let out a sigh.

"Let him down easily. He's only gone the serious route once before, and it ended badly."

Mali's face soured like I had just broken up with her.

"You're talking about the girl who chose an NBA player over him?"

Her eyebrows shoot up, and she does a weird wobble with her head as though she is unsure of what she has heard and seen.

"He told you about that?"

I shrug. "Yeah." Tyriq and I covered a range of topics during our time together. If we weren't screwing, we were laughing and talking.

Mali nods. "Just be honest with him. If you don't want to be with him, just rip the bandage off, don't drag him along."

"Gotcha," I agree.

I turn my attention to the series of three large wrapped canvas paintings that Mali had mentioned originally to steer us away from the group. Music from a four-piece Jazz band adds to the ambience, that I finally get the chance to notice. There is even a small dance floor in front of the quartet with couples dancing. I allow myself the vision of being wrapped in Tyriq's arms gliding across the tile for only a second, and then return my thoughts and focus to the art. No use daydreaming about things that should not be.

The first of the realistic paintings is of a curvaceous, gold-dressed woman standing in a man's hands. The descriptively painted muscled man, dressed only in black slacks, is holding her up as she reaches for the sun. A grayish-blue moon is painted in his pocket.

The next painting is of the same couple sitting on top of a blue world. The gold-dressed woman is wrapped in his arms as they hold the moon and sun together.

The last painting is of the same couple holding the sun and moon but sharing the world with a child.

"This is beautiful," I say to Mali.

"Funny," a sharply dressed man in a suit and bowtie added as he approached us. "I was thinking the same thing about you."

The gentleman extended his hand for me to shake.

"I'm Lawrence," he spoke in a mellow voice.

"Nice to meet you, Lawrence. I'm Nailah."

"Hi, Lawrence," Mali cut in. She turns to me. "Lawrence and I went to high school together. He's now a money manager for entertainers and athletes, but still also does my mother's taxes."

Mali doesn't seem quite as pleased to have Lawrence join our group and even cuts her eyes in the direction of her mother and their hen group.

The man seems nice enough. He is handsome and well-dressed but nothing like Tyriq.

"So, as I was saying, Nailah," Mali spoke, ignoring Lawrence, who was still present. "I really like this series."

"The tones are beautiful," I agree.

Lawrence reviews the painting with us.

"I like the message," Mali adds. "It's rare to find a man to support the dreams of his woman."

"Women only have to aspire to do things because today's man is sorry," Lawrence comments before taking a sip of his drink. "If a man is taking care of his business properly, which includes his wife and child, then a woman should basically want to please her man and family, not try to be the man."

Mali turned her neck toward Lawrence with a quick precision that required no explanation. He had touched a nerve.

I take a sip of wine and step out of the line of fire.

"So, you're saying that the only goal that a woman should have is to take care of her man and children?" Mali questions.

"If a man is doing what he is supposed to do, a woman shouldn't have to do anything other than be a woman," Lawrence digs all the way into his point.

That struck a nerve with me.

"What an insecure chauvinistic thing to say. A woman should have her own identity outside of her man and family."

"Why?" Lawrence asks with a smirk.

Did he just smirk at me?

"So, when he leaves, she can still fend for herself," I conclude.

"Thank you," he says reaching out for a handshake.

"I wasn't trying to prove your point."

"But you did. If a man is faithful, if a man is taking care of his family, and stays where he is supposed to, why can't the woman be all about family?"

Did he just bust out the 'woman's place is in the home' cliché?

"How can the modern woman be supportive, if she has no concept of what her man is going through or no experience to teach these kids, she dedicates her life to?" I question.

"I'm not saying that a woman isn't capable, but as a man, I would take such good care of her that she wouldn't want or need a thing."

I allow him to take my hand this time. He's charming. He has some cute lines, but sparks don't fly. My skin didn't tingle like when I was with Tyriq.

"If I were your man, you wouldn't want for a thing," Lawrence smugly pontificates.

I blink a few times, not because I'm not flattered, but because I feel his presence before I hear his voice.

"Luckily, she already has a man to take care of that," Tyriq informs him.

I smile at Lawrence and remove my hand.

"Hey baby," Tyriq kisses the back of my neck while sliding his arms around my front.

"Uh. Um. Hi?" I respond, not exactly sure of what I should say. Tyriq is not my man, but the fury of tingles and excitement invading me proved that my body feels otherwise.

"Are you going to introduce me?" Tyriq's question is more of a request.

"No introductions needed my man. I know who you are." Lawrence reaches out his hand for a handshake. "Tyriq Lewis. I used to watch you play ball."

"Thanks, man."

"I'm Lawrence," he adds.

"Nice to meet you." Tyriq nods but leaves Lawrence's hand hanging.

Tyriq effectively steers me away from the paintings and toward a sculpture that has fewer eyes looking at it.

Although Mali doesn't seem to like Lawrence much, she walks away with him.

"It's good to see you." His tone and eyebrows don't match his words. Annoyance coats each syllable.

"Nice to see you too," I smile because it really is. I had tried to forget how fine he was.

"Is it?" he asks. "Are you really glad to see me?"

I meet his gaze and move in closer to him. My heart beats wildly and the only thing that I want to do is kiss him. Being hurt didn't matter; it would be worth it to feel those lips again.

"Yes," I answer honestly. "I am really glad to see you."

"Then why stay away so long?"

I place a hand on his hard chest and suddenly regret it. I want to touch more of him. I want to feel more of him.

"We had fun. It was a weekend. That's all," I say.

The hardening of his jaw tells me that it meant more to him.

He touches the bracelet on my wrist.

"You can say what you want. I felt you, I heard you moan. I know the truth."

And suddenly, I feel that he can see straight through me. I scramble to come up with a rebuttal.

"Seems like everybody knows what's good for me lately," I retort.

"If life keeps reminding you of the same lessons, maybe you should listen."

I don't say anything. I just looked at his amazing mouth.

"Come dance with me," he requests.

I nod and fall in step with him. We move through the gallery and I notice all the couples. It feels nice to be one of them, a part of a duo this time.

People smile in our direction. Could they possibly feel what I felt about other couples? Could they possibly see how in awe of this man I am?

We stop in front of the four-piece band, and I fall into his warmth. He feels like the sky and I am a star nestled against him. He feels like my perfect place.

"You hear the music?" his voice is low and tender against my ear.

I didn't at first. I had been listening to his heart, the deep rhythmic pattern that reminded me of the way he stroked into me the last time that we were together.

"Listen."

I do, and then look up at him once I recognize the familiar melody.

"Ribbon in the Sky, by Stevie Wonder," I name.

"Yep. The song playing during our first date."

"That was not a date. I was working," I bat at his shoulder.

"That was the first time that I got to taste you."

My cheeks burn, and I lick my lips remembering the taste of his kiss.

"You may think that we met by coincidence, but I know that it was more than a random chance. I was meant to know you, Nailah."

That did it. All the resistance that I had stored up washed away with the dampness he generated in my core.

"So, you just want me to swoon right here?" I try to minimize his effect on me, but he knows.

"I prefer it be in my bed."

He spins me in a dance move and then pulls my backside close against him.

I lean into his body.

"I missed you," Tyriq spoke into my neck before kissing it.

It was like his kiss was truth serum because it compelled me to tell the truth.

"I missed you too."

"Prove it." He spins me around to face him. "Do something about it and come home with me tonight."

He pulled me close to him and proceeded to kiss me like I was his. It was like he had missed me for months and not just days. His cool, minty mouth sends currents of fire coursing through my skin. The room, the people, and the earth melt away. He is the sky and space is on the other side of my eyelids.

He releases me as quickly as he sets me ablaze.

"Tyriq, I... I just-" A stammer is the best that my brain is able to give because my heart is winning the struggle, and I can't quite spit out a dismissal.

"Hold on to your answer for just a little while longer, Blade. Walk with me first."

Tyriq leads me further into the gallery to a corner where there is a painting covered by a black sheet. Bold letters printed on a slip of paper stuck to the sheet spell out 'sold.'

Tyriq reaches for the sheet and then looks over to me.

"You dare me?"

"To unveil someone's paid-for painting?" I question with a crook of my neck. "You fine, but I didn't bring the right shoes to box in. You'll have to handle that fight on your own."

He laughs and pulls the sheet down anyway.

"I bought the painting," he says, scanning my face before he adds, "for you."

I gasp. I have to move closer to it. I look to Tyriq, then go back to the painting again.

It is a remake of the Ernie Barnes painting that we saw the night we met. This strong woman in red is not wearing a dress but a red T-shirt and jeans. Her features are like mine.

I run a finger over her face since he's paid for it and all.

"How did you?" Complete sentences escape me as I stare in wonderment at the art.

"I used the picture that we took at the diner," he explains." I have a friend who has a friend who knew a painter who got the work done quickly."

I examine the picture more. In the original painting of *My Miss America* by Barnes, the woman was carrying the bags alone. In the recreation, the woman is holding only one bag, and an unknown arm takes the other.

I am awestruck.

"I know that you feel like you're in this alone, Nailah, but let me in. Let me carry some of whatever is weighing you down. I'm here, and as long as you let me, I'll stay."

His words are spoken softly, but they hit my chest like baseballs.

"I don't- I can't- the words. Shit," I can only stammer out incoherent thoughts.

He slides a calming hand around my waist, and I am in his arms again.

Tyriq kisses my forehead as we stare at the painting together.

Finally, I ask, "You think I am worth all of this?"

He looks down at me. "Baby, I'd do anything for you. You're worth this and much more."

"Thank you," I whisper and press a kiss against his arm.

"You can thank me at home." He nips at my ear before sliding his hand around my behind. "I can't take much more of your fine ass in this dress. I actually kind of miss the baggy clothes right now. At least I could stay in a room with you without having pornographic thoughts."

I laugh.

"Alright, Dr. Freaky, I will go home with you."

Tyriq steps away from me.

"For real? I won?" He gives me a skeptical once over. "You're really going to come home with me. Tonight? To my house? And stay?"

"Yes, for real. We can spend the whole night together. I'll even eat peanut butter out of a jar for breakfast because I know your ass ain't bought groceries."

He licks his lips.

"I already know what I'm going to eat." He grabs my hand. "Let's go then."

Tyriq is pulling me through the throng of people before I can say another word.

"Wait," I tug at his arm. "Don't you want to see the rest of the artwork? I at least need to say goodbye to Mali."

With a hand on the exit door, he looks at me. Worry replaced the joyful expression he held only a few seconds ago.

"Nailah, don't leave me." His eyes are wide and round, and it nearly breaks my heart that I made him feel that way. He had been nothing but wonderful to me, and I had caused him to be so anxious.

I can tell that Tyriq is a confident man, and my actions made him feel unsure.

I place a quick peck on his lips.

"I promise that I will meet you right back here. I just want to tell Mali thanks for forcing me to come out, and let her know that I am leaving with you."

"Alright. We'll find her quicker if we split," he says pulling out his phone. "Whoever finds her first, send a text."

"Cool." I stick my hand out, and he places his hand on top of mine like we are a team about to head out on a mission.

"Ready," he starts.

"Break," We say together, and the giggle monster strikes me again.

With pep, I set off to find the wonderful friend who had helped me come to find such joy.

Before I can find Mali, I spot Tyriq's family. His mother and aunt are standing with the other churchwomen gathered around a painting.

Their backs are to me, but I hear them speaking.

"Tyriq can do so much better than that thing he had switchin' her hips up and through here," one woman in the group commented.

My phone buzzed in my hand.

"I thought so too. The girl didn't come from anything, so I figured she was plotting to get something. That's why I sent Lawrence after her," Patricia, Tyriq's aunt, explained.

The ladies nodded, their faces fixed in staunch agreement as Pat continued.

"Lawrence is well off," Patricia dawns a proud gleam. "I figured he could throw her off Tyriq's scent. She met my nephew in a gallery, so this is the perfect place for her to scoot under another victim."

The ladies provide a three-part harmony version of "Uh huh."

"Don't worry," I say, stepping between the women. I had heard enough. "Your precious son and nephew are safe from my clutches."

The church members have the decency to look away, but Aunt Pat just purses her lips and looks me up and down.

Tyriq walked up with Mali then.

Concern darkened his eyes, as he stepped closer to me.

I place a hand in the air to stop him.

"Good, you are all here." I look at Tyriq's family and friends in the group. "For the record, I am good with what I have and don't need Tyriq or his money to survive."

"I know." Tyriq steps forward again, but I halt him with my glare. "What's wrong?"

"Ask your aunt why you need to lose my number."

I turn on my heels and storm out of the gallery.

Same story, but in a different town. They don't even know who I am and already assume that I am not good enough for him. If they ever knew the truth, if they ever knew half of what people in Brook Bonnet believed about me, a relationship with Tyriq would not work. He loves his family, and his family loves him. With the basic knowledge of who I am, the women who raised him do not like me. Knowing more about me wouldn't make things better. Tyriq and I could never exist in peace amid that kind of turmoil.

I take the windy walk across the street to my piece of sanity parked parallel to the building. Lucy, with all her imperfections, had always been there for me. She didn't care who had left me or kept me. She didn't care where I came from or where I was going.

"Nailah!" Tyriq calls my name, yelling it like a crazy person, but I don't stop. He should be embarrassed like I was. I hope he gets a ticket for disturbing the peace.

I can't face what I have to turn away. He can't be mine.

Tyriq makes it to Lucy at the same time as I do and blocks the door.

"Talk to me. What's wrong?" he asks.

"Just move!" I shout louder than expected, the hurt elevating my frustration on several levels.

He doesn't move.

"I can't fix what I don't understand Nailah. We were just alright. We were just fine. What happened?"

"Apparently your whole family thinks that I am a gold-digging whore who's not good enough for you," I lay out bluntly. The quicker we can get this over with, the quicker I can get over him.

Fire shot from his eyes, "Aunt Pat said that?"

"Basically, but in her *saintly* speak."

Tyriq scrubbed a hand across his face.

"Please tell me what happened exactly," he sighs.

I hear the frustration in his words.

Good, he should be as frustrated as I am.

"I went to find Mali but found Aunt Pat telling the saintly slayer squad that she tried to pawn me off on Lawrence. Obviously, my broke ass will screw anyone with money and a smile."

Tyriq blinked a few times as I waited for a response.

Silence invaded the seconds between my words and the lift of his lips into a smile.

He started laughing. He laughed so hard that he had to hold his stomach as a few tears slid from his eyes.

I frowned.

"That shit is not funny, Tyriq," I said, but I smiled at him anyway.

"Saintly slayer squad?" he reigns in his laughter long enough to speak. "Blade, I love those people in there. They are my family, but they don't choose who I date. I want you, and they can't change that."

I allow him to move closer and take me into his arms.

Tyriq strokes a hand over my shoulder.

"They think I'm after you for the wrong reasons, and I wasn't even chasing you," I remind him.

"Exactly," he states, his eyes firm and his jaw set. "They don't know us. They don't know you, Nailah. I can go set them straight right now if you want."

I shake my head.

"Do you believe that I'm using you? I mean, you keep buying me things and dangling your money in front of me." I need to know. He has to know that I would never be like that.

A lazy grin slides over his lips, and I am anxious to hear his answer.

"I like to do things for you Nailah, and I won't apologize for that." He catches my eyes with his. "The night of the gala, you were in a room full of millionaires and influential people, but you walked out with me. You chose me then, you chose me tonight, and I choose you now."

I fall into his arms and feel his sigh of relief.

CHAPTER TWENTY-SIX

Nailah

I wake up in his arms, wrapped up in the bliss of him.

Gently, I slide away from his embrace. If I wake him, he might take me all over again. Every single time that I moved last night, he moved and found his way inside of me.

My body can't take any more of him.

I glance over at his carved chest and sigh. No, I want it all, all that he is willing to give. He has more than replenished the well since my dry spell.

I move through the house in his T-shirt only and into the kitchen. He had been the perfect gentleman last night for all of five minutes. As soon as he understood that I wanted him and that I was willing to let my body be his playground, all calm was over. He ripped my poor zipper apart.

So here I am again, in his shirt, scrounging through his kitchen for food. Each cabinet and drawer that I opened revealed more about how little time he spent in the kitchen. This time, even the peanut butter is gone. I find a few bags of sample coffee and a filter this time. They look like they came from a hotel.

I found his spotless coffee maker and dumped in the ingredients. I press the button to begin the brew while I hunt for cups.

All the cups look brand new as if they came with the home, and he forgot that they were there.

I hear his footsteps on the hardwood floors before I see him wearing only pajama bottoms.

"Good morning," I smile.

"Good morning," he replies before giving me a kiss on the lips. "I thought I lost you. Every time I close my eyes, I pray that you don't disappear."

I want to tell him that nothing lasts forever, but instead, I change the subject.

"I thought we talked about these bare cupboards you have. It's like a wilderness in your refrigerator."

"My bad, I order meals mostly," he replies as he pours a cup of coffee.

"I wanted to make you breakfast, but the only two things that I could find that matched were coffee filters and coffee."

"So that means you're cooking tomorrow?" he asks, leaning against the countertop. His eyes leer above the cup.

I mimic his pose and pull a cup to my lips.

"Is that your way of inviting me to stay another night?" I ask mocking his serious tone.

"Well," he gives a goofy grin. "Just to make sure that I give you a fair assessment. I need to sample your cooking skills."

I laugh at him. He did a lot of sampling of my body last night.

"If we're keeping score," I add, "then there are a few recalculations I need to make in reference to the state of your kitchen."

I move in closer to him.

Tyriq puts his coffee down and lifts me up onto the counter.

He slides my legs open with ease, pushing his body in between them. My brain clouds and floats off into a Tyriq-induced haze.

"I can't keep my hands off of you," his words rumble into my neck while he rocks against my core.

My hands caress the hard surface of him.

"You're going to make me late for work," he says between kisses.

I accept his affection, relieved by the appreciation.

"I have to go home and get ready myself," I explain.

"My last appointment begins at 2:30." He steps back. "What time do you leave work?"

"Not until after five."

"How about this?" he suggests between kisses. "I pick you up, we swing by your place and get whatever you need, and you stay with me. I'll take you to work in the morning."

I stop my affection and then lean back to look him in the eyes. Is he serious?

His eyes dart over my face, reading the worry lines that automatically appear. His shoulders tense and his mouth flattens into a straight line.

This is all too soon, all too domestic.

"If I'm moving too fast, if this is-"

I quiet him with a kiss.

"I'm honored that you want to spend time with me, Tyriq," I explain. "I've been long overdue for a little happiness."

He still looks concerned.

"How about I meet you here at seven?" I suggest to ease some of the tension. "There's no need for you to go out of your way for me. I have a car. I can drive."

He almost smiles, and then his eyes narrow as his mouth straightens into a line again.

"Why all the mystery about where you live? Are you hiding bodies for someone or something?" he questions.

Tyriq is the kind of man to come after me if I walk away, and I need to be able to walk away from Tyriq in one piece when the time is right.

"Do you have to see my home to see me?" I counter. "I haven't been here long, and my place is nothing like yours."

I kiss his full lips while sliding my hand down the front of his pants to cup him and massage his warm thick muscle.

Tyriq moans into my mouth.

"You win," he breathes into my neck before planting a kiss there and rocking against my palm. "Just call me when you are on your way. I worry about you and Lucy."

"No worries, man. I got this."

I really don't, these foreign feelings are out of my control.

CHAPTER TWENTY-SEVEN

Tyriq

For two straight weeks, I had gotten Nailah to spend the night multiple times. Then an opportunity to travel with the team came up and I wish I would have stayed home. Traveling with the team had been fun and exciting, but this time, I had something to miss, someone to look forward to being home with.

Sitting in a booth at the hotel restaurant, I press a finger to my phone to expand a picture of Nailah's hand. The goofy grin that I cannot hide reminds me how much she has come to mean to me in such a short time. Each day that I am with her makes me look forward to the next day.

If Chad were around, he would tell me that my game is slipping, but I don't care. My girl sent me a picture of four fingers, and I cannot stop smiling like an idiot.

Because the team manager asked me to sub for a doctor during an away game, Nailah and I had been texting. I sent her a request because, after two days without her, I desperately wanted to see her face.

Me: Send me a picture.

Nailah: Of what?

Me: Of you.

Nailah: Which part?

Me: Surprise me.

A few seconds later, I received a picture of her left hand. Since she is right-handed, I assume that taking a picture of her left hand was the easiest thing to do. I am sure that she is joking. If I have learned nothing else about Nailah, I have learned that she is a fan of sarcasm. The picture of her smooth hand and perfectly manicured hands is thought-provoking. It is also a confirmation of what I have been thinking for the last two weeks since we left the art gallery.

I type back:

Me: Perfect picture. Thank you for the notice.

Nailah: What notice? Just a pic of a body part.

Me: Message received. Your ring finger is missing something.

I can see when she reads the message and three little dots pop up at the bottom of my phone screen, but then they go away.

I laugh. She wasn't expecting that.

Me: Every part of you is beautiful. Great picture, new mission.

I close out the message app. Nailah will read it, and I know she'll think about my words, but she won't respond. Blade uses sweet words sparingly and never in a text.

I'm surprised when I get a notification of a new message. She replies with hearts and kissy face emojis. Another step in the right direction. One day, I am going to get that girl to love me.

I put my phone away.

Ready for some time in my room, I head to the small back hall with two elevators stashed away from the lobby.

There aren't many people around, and I am glad for the solitude.

"You must like passed around pussy?" a voice says from behind me.

I am not a violent man, but when I turn to see Jermaine walking up, my only thought is to kick in his front teeth. He had better not be talking about Nailah.

"You want to say that shit again?" I don't know what his problem is, but I have time to solve it today.

"I heard you swept up Naeem's girl from the gala."

Jermaine had always been Naeem's lackey. I don't know why I thought adulthood would change that.

"Naeem can't lose a girlfriend because Naeem has a wife." I step closer to him and fight my urge to slam him into the ground.

Jermaine slides one hand into the other.

"Briana said that she was going back to you, Lew, and then you pop up on a blog with his push-piece in some whack-ass diner pics."

Without thinking, I yank Jermaine by his collar and feel the steam building inside of me.

"Say some slick shit about Nailah again, and it won't end well for you." I jam my forearm against his neck as I push his back against the wall. "You will respect her."

Then I see it in his eyes, a gleam. He wants me to hit him. He wants me to beat his dumb ass and lose my connection and income from the team.

I release him. Losing my temper wouldn't play out well for me in the long run. Regardless of what he said, I would be going home to Nailah.

Jermaine stumbles down with a low cackle and places his hands up in surrender mode.

"I'm just breaking down the visuals for you. You were good people, so I'm warning you. Stay away from Briana. Naeem is out on bail and looking for your woman swiping ass."

I chuckle at that.

"He wants to fight men now? Shit, that muthafucka ain't looking hard enough, or did his probation officer tell his punk ass no? Don't forget, I know where your skeletons are buried too."

The elevator dings then and the doors slide open. A gaggle of rambunctious youth spring into the hallway followed by the slow steps of adults.

Jermaine falls away with the group, exiting the elevator with only a lift of his lip to acknowledge my response.

As much as I like Nailah, there is still a hell of a lot that I don't know about her. I can't pinpoint what she's hiding, but secrets have never worked in my favor. Regardless of how much I like her, I still have questions.

CHAPTER TWENTY-EIGHT

Tyriq

I arrive at the airport around noon feeling exhausted and ready to see Nailah. When she agreed to pick me up from my flight like a normal girlfriend, I had to pause and look at the phone to make sure I had heard correctly. Progress.

Cameras, and not Nailah, are there to greet me once I reach the airport lobby. I had noticed the growing group of people as I walked but figured that some football player or country singer must have been in the area. That they were looking for me never once crossed my mind.

The clustered group descended upon me with camera clicks and questions all at once.

"Lew, did you win her back?" one man shouts.

"Lew, what made you beat up Jermaine?" Another man shoves a video camera in my face as he walks backward.

"Who is the mystery woman that you cheated on Briana with?"

"How do you feel about being the first infamous male side-piece?"

The cameras were my first clue, but when I saw Trystan, I knew that something was wrong. He is wearing a look similar to the one my father wore on report card day when we were younger. Disappointment.

Trystan holds up four fingers in the air, his arm raised high enough for me to notice. This had been our signal for years. When we couldn't speak and something was wrong, flash the four.

With the huddle following and shouting questions, I rush toward Trystan and through the doors. We jump into the luxury SUV parked in the fire lane, and I throw my carry-on bag into the backseat.

"What the fuck is going on?" I inquire breathlessly.

Trystan punches me in the arm before pulling off.

"I told you to stay the hell away from that girl. My exact words were, 'Don't try to save her'."

"Who? Briana?" I question.

He nods. "Who else?"

"I didn't do anything. The only time I've seen her has been at functions and when she needs a doctor."

"That's not what the tabloids are saying. It hit the blogs this morning that you are the reason that Naeem and Briana broke up. TMZ has been running a story that Jermaine is hiding Briana, you flew to the game to find her and then threatened him when you didn't get access to her."

"That's bull shit." I slam his dashboard, but really wish I had whipped Jermaine's ass.

"They have a video of you stringing Jermain up against the wall."

A nauseous feeling swam over me, as I realized who had picked me up from the airport.

"Where is Nailah? Why isn't she here?" I swear, if I lose her over someone else's dumb shit, I'm releasing my entire arsenal of dirt on every player.

Sitting in the front seat, I power up my phone and sit back in amazement at the number of notifications that ding and vibrate.

I scroll through the millions of texts from family, business partners, and even church members, but there are none from Nailah.

Electric nervousness clamps down in my gut. Nailah has a hair trigger flight button. My slightest misstep can send her off in the other direction.

"Would you really have wanted her out there in all of that mess?" Trystan asks.

I shake my head and dial Nailah's cell number. It goes straight to voicemail.

I care about Nailah and her safety. I would never want to put her in danger, but I am itching to see her. I need to know that she is alright, that we are alright.

"What worries me more than anything is that she might have believed this craziness. I don't want anything to do with Briana. I was helping her for a while, but that's it. I thought she was a friend, but we're less than that."

"I don't think Nailah thought that you were with her. You've got a pretty special woman." Trystan looks over to me. "Don't mess this up."

I look down at my phone. If only I could get Nailah to pay attention to her phone. She was damn near impossible to get a hold of sometimes and never cared about text response time.

"I'm trying to hang in there with her," I explain, "but she doesn't make it easy."

"She handled herself well as far as I know. Mali contacted me, but that was after Nailah had called her about the video. I knew it could possibly be a hectic situation, so I advised her not to come."

Hearing that makes my shoulders relax and my chest expands with pride. I feel like my heart grows a size or some shit. Nailah had been looking out for me. She had gotten in touch with my cousin to get in touch with my lawyer/brother.

When Nailah's number floats across my cell phone screen, I want to sing with the tones.

"Meet me at my house," I demand. I need to see her eyes and feel her body to make sure she understands. There is only her.

"Well hello to you too," her soft chuckle relaxes me. "I'm out with Mali right now getting a pedicure."

I could listen to the sweet tingle of her voice all day, but I'd rather have her with me.

"Ditch her and come kick it with me."

"I heard that!" Mali shouts in the background. "You can't have my friend today."

Nailah's musical laughter rings through the line.

"Tell that hater Mali to quiet down," I smile into the phone. "Come see your man. You know you want to."

"I was wondering when that ego was going to pop back in," Nailah sucks at her teeth.

"Yep, and you like my big ego."

"Maybe, but I really want to catch up on our shows. You better not watch any without me. I'll be right there as soon as my nails are dry." Her words are comical, but then she pauses before continuing in a more serious tone. "Are you alright?"

"Are you?" I counter.

"I'm fine. A few bloggers have put together that I was at the gala with Naeem and at the diner with you, but nothing like the frenzy surrounding you and that video."

I never meant for any of this to affect Nailah.

"I only went there to work. This trip had nothing to do with Briana."

Silence invaded the line and nothing around me mattered.

The hum from the cars around us disappeared. Trystan's constant tap against the steering wheel faded away.

"Tyriq, you've been straightforward with me from the beginning. I've been around enough cheating men to know the difference. I believe you."

I release a sigh of relief.

"See you in a few?"

"Of course," she agrees, making my day ten times better.

We end our call, and I settle back against the chair.

"Now that you can focus," Trystan starts. "How do you want to play this?"

"I got a message from the team. I'll have to give a statement. You'll need to be there of course. I am a consultant, not an actual employee of the team. Sometimes, I contract with the arena for events when they are short of the required on-hand medical staff. This time, I was filling in for a team doctor that was out."

The team and arena all seem less important now. The extra income was nice when I needed it, but now my side hustles were taking me away from Nailah and causing problems that spilled over into my everyday life.

"Send me your consultant contract and I'll review it just in case."

"I will, but I'm alright. My private medical service is good without the team, and you know that the shops are great. I wish it had been Naeem's sorry ass there instead of Jermaine, but other than that-"

I let the words trail off. I'm not sure how to explain that basketball didn't matter so much anymore.

Being a team doctor and working with players was a way for me to still feel involved in sports on a professional level. It felt like I was keeping my dream alive, which was everyone's dream, really. My parents had been so proud of me on the court. My brothers and cousins were always at the games rooting for me, and ready to run with me in the streets. When I hurt my knee, everything changed. All of it. The girls didn't look at me the same, and neither did my family. My parents always looked worried, like hurting my knee was the end of my life. My brothers just pitied me, and that hurt too. None of that mattered to Nailah. To her, I was just a cocky guy with a smile who didn't let her run away.

"How did it happen anyway?" his voice is low as he looks over to me. "What set you off?"

I meet his concerned gaze.

"Jermaine said some foul shit about Nailah. He doesn't even know her. I really think that he was trying to figure out if I was sleeping with Briana or had plans with her."

"Are you?"

"How many times do I have to say that I'm over her?"

Trystan glances at me, but my answer will not change.

"I've been done. Maybe because Briana left me publicly, I wanted to prove that I could still have her. We did the undercover thing for a while and I thought I would get that feeling of accomplishment. In some twisted way I wanted to prove that even though I busted my knee and didn't have an NBA contract, I could give her everything that Naeem could and more. I wanted to win." I shake my head. "That's not love. That's not a reason to be with someone."

"I'm glad to hear it. I'm glad someone helped you see the truth."

CHAPTER TWENTY-NINE

Nailah

After a sleepless night, I was totally taken off guard when a video of Tyriq about to rip off Jermain's neck popped up on social media at three in the morning. I had clicked through the various blog reports and commentary on several different outlets. By the time TMZ reported it, I'd gotten in touch with Mali and heard back from Trystan. I knew that whatever they were reporting wasn't true, and the story was quickly squashed by team reps who confirmed their invitation for Dr. Lewis to travel with them.

After the long morning trudge to my office, I was totally ready to jump out of my skin when I found a very calm Briana Matthews sitting in my desk chair. I thought about the empty security desk I had passed on my way in.

"Good morning, Nailah." Her head lifts as she leans back in the chair.

Folders cascade from my arm to my crowded desk as I sat my satchel in front of it.

"What do you want?" I ask, quelling my anxiousness and slipping a hand into my purse to wrap around my pepper spray.

Dressed in a tight black V-neck shirt, tights, and tennis shoes, she looked like a modern homemaker out for a morning jog. However, the devious look in her glare revealed otherwise.

"Tyriq, but you seem to have his attention for the moment." Briana stood and tipped a folder over with her long nail.

Paper floated to the floor like snow flurries, and I contemplated the age-old question: if an evil person screams in an empty building and there is no one around to hear it, did it really happen?

"That sounds like a personal problem," I retort taking a cleansing breath.

She steps closer to me a sneer dawns her face.

"Oh yeah. It's going to get real personal," she threatened. "When I'm ready for Tyriq, you better not be in my way."

I eye the thin woman up and down, and frown.

"You look like a grown woman. If you want him sweetie," I usher my hand across the air, "go for it. Unless he doesn't want you, I can't help you with that."

Briana doesn't back down, just smirks.

"We'll see. Sometimes feelings change and people disappear." She tilts her head almost identically to a possessed child in a scary movie.

Briana moves toward the door but turns to face me again before exiting.

"You're from Brook Bonnet, right?" She places a finger to her chin as if the information recently popped into her mind. "Isn't that the place where the big prostitute ranch got raided? The whole city is known for its whores." She blinked a few times. "What do you want to be known for?"

It was like a punch to the chest, but I pushed back the terrorizing panic clamping down on me and motioned toward the door again. She may be bluffing. She may not know anything about my past, but what if she did?

I activated my tough girl shield before rebutting.

"Don't you have a husband to bail out or a new doctor to find? How are your ribs?" I ask with a roll of my neck.

A wince of pain flashed across Briana's face and disappeared.

"I left your friend Regina's badge and door key on your desk. Make sure that she gets it, will you? Tell her that Jermain says hello."

With those parting words, Briana left my office and I was left to wander through a myriad of questions. What did Briana Matthews know about my life in Brook Bonnet? Should I walk away from Tyriq before my past caught up to me?

After the thirty-minute expressive discussion with Regina about how Jermain Timmons came to her home to seduce her but ended up swiping her badge, my cell phone rang. I had hoped that the day would get better, but the familiar number on the screen indicated that another 'h' word would be more accurate to describe it. Horrible. Since I was already in a foul mood, I decided to answer.

"Hey. Sunshine?" the harsh rasp of his voice held notes of eagerness and surprise. "This your daddy."

"Hello. How can I help you?" the stiff formal words are easier to release than my pent-up emotions.

"How can I-" he mumbles the confusing words to himself as if to understand them better. "This your daddy. Curtis. I don't need help. I called to talk to you."

I waited for him to say something else. Did he need my permission to say what was on his mind? He certainly didn't need my permission to walk away.

"Can I see you? I got some things that I want to talk about, some things to tell you."

"I'm at work right now, and really, after all of this time, I'm glad to know that you are alive, but I don't need or want a relationship with you. Please stop calling."

Ending the call doesn't end the ache that I feel in my chest or the weariness that I feel in my body. I was glad that I had taken off half of the day to pick up Tyriq.

When I was ten, we took the long drive to the ranch, all the way to Sugar Dolls together. I had been there before because that's where he picked up Dolly and dropped her off. That day, Dolly walked out, took me by the hand, and my father drove away.

Weeks went by without phone calls from my father or sightings of Briana, and I was beginning to think that everything was going to work out alright. I had been in Tyriq's bed four out of seven nights for at least three weeks, and he was trying to convince me that I needed to spend more time in his home.

His media room had become my second favorite place. It's where we caught up on all of the movies my childhood prevented me from seeing and all of the love that my life prevented me from having. Sofas, sitcoms, and sex became our routine. I had even finagled a few reality television shows in our lineup as well. Through an extension of Tyriq's interest, I had become infatuated with the model Jubilee. Once we binge-watched her debut in the televised model competition, we settled into her weekly spinoff, which documented her troubled past and promising future.

I plop down on the sofa next to Tyriq with a bowl of popcorn.

He grabs a handful before I can even fold my feet up.

"Greedy much?" I comment.

"Survival. I have to take some before you drown it in hot sauce," Tyriq retorts before popping a kernel into his mouth.

"Don't hate on me and my hot sauce."

"But on popcorn?" he scrunches his nose.

"Yep, just how my momma used to make it." I kiss his wrinkled nose.

He shakes his head as I change to Jubilee's show.

"First Mali, and now you. I can't believe I'm watching reality television with you."

"Isn't she the reason that you wanted to get with me in the first place?" I tease. "I thought that you liked Jubilee."

"I like Nailah James." He puckers a loud sloppy kiss on my cheek with extra gusto. I swat at him.

"Good, because Nailah James is watching Jubilee in the Night," I tell him as though this is my house and my television, and I really run something. "Pass me my purse so I can get my hot sauce. Who doesn't have hot sauce in their kitchen?"

"Oh, shots fired!" Tyriq pokes me in the tummy, and I giggle and squirm like a kid.

"If you make me drop this popcorn-" I warn.

"You'll go make some more." Tyriq kisses my lips before I can hit him with a comeback.

"There is no more," I remind him once he lets my lips go. "There is nothing in your desert of a kitchen."

I still haven't felt comfortable enough to grocery shop for him, and I know that is what he is waiting for.

"You can always go out and get a few things. I can send you some money or give you my card."

I roll my eyes. He is still trying to give me money.

"What is that look about? The money or the food? I stopped trying to buy you things, didn't I? I take out you every night, don't I?"

"True." I shrug. "I'm used to cooking. I don't mind cooking for you whenever I spend time here."

"And how often will that be?"

I narrow my eyes at the sneaky man. He will find a way to bring up our relationship goals in any conversation.

"I just want to know, so that I can stock up on the essentials," he explains.

"Shh. My show is on. We've been waiting this whole damn season for her to find her father and they are finally about to reveal him."

I divert the conversation and my attention as quickly as possible.

On the screen, Jubilee enters a restaurant as dramatic music flourishes in the background. The camera zooms in on Jubilee's face as she walks to a booth.

"This is so cheesy." Tyriq pops another piece of popcorn into his mouth.

"You love it," I quip.

"I love you," he shoots back.

And just like that, he took all of the air out of my lungs. Just like that, I can't breathe.

I look over at Tyriq's smug grin as he exaggerates, chomping on his popcorn.

"Don't look over here, you're missing your show," he winks.

I turned my head back to the television, but not because he told me to. I don't want to talk about love. I cannot talk about love. I refuse to have the conversation.

When I look at the screen, I have to look twice. Then I pause the screen.

"What in the hell?" I screech in horror.

I step closer and run my fingers over the smooth surface of the image.

"What's wrong?" Tyriq is up and off the couch next to me. "What is it?"

The thick wavy hair that he wore platted into two braids on his head was the same. Even his dark green eyes look similar. Only the skin that used to be super smooth has changed and is now wrinkled.

"That's my daddy," I point. "The man on the screen right there, Jubilee's father, that's the man that left me in Brook Bonnet eighteen years ago."

CHAPTER THIRTY

Tyriq

She was leaving. I am not sure how it happened. One minute, I was rubbing her shoulders, wondering how a father that she told me was no longer alive was suddenly walking across a television screen, and the next, she was walking out of the door. Shocked is an understatement, but I kept that feeling tucked behind the concern that I felt for the bewildered-looking Nailah.

Earlier that night, when I thought she was all right, I asked her.

"What really happened, Nailah? Why do you believe that the man on television is your father?"

We were in the bed. She had already stripped down to her nightly uniform of a T-shirt and small boy short underwear. Tonight's t-shirt ensemble featured a Christmas theme with big gold script letters that read 'She Sleighs.' Nailah quickly tied a bow in front of the silk scarf wrapped around her hair. By all accounts, it seemed that we would be in for the night.

My question changed that.

"Why does it matter?" she sighed.

"It's your father." I try to keep the frustration out of my voice.

"He used to be my father. He walked away from me."

It is never easy to get Nailah to talk about the past, and I did not have the energy to pull information from her in a clever way. I was tired of playing games with her in order to figure out who the hell she was.

"Damn, it would be nice to have one regular conversation about your life."

Each missile of a word served to explode the fantasy of a regular night with my girl further apart.

In normal Nailah fashion, she did not say a word. She got up from the spot in the bed that now slightly dipped in the form of her and began sweeping the floor for her shoes.

"I'm sorry that I'm not all emotionally ready to talk about a guy that I haven't seen in years and left me stranded with no parents," she fusses.

I watch her huff across the room mumbling things and trying to find her belongings.

"Nailah, you don't have to leave, but I am not going to apologize for wanting to know more about you."

Nailah was sliding her feet into a pair of ballet flats in the dark.

"You know that I grew up in foster care. You know he left me. What else is there to know?" she yelled.

I took a deep breath and used at least two of the techniques I saw on social media to avoid yelling back at her.

"Did you know that he was alive?" I ask.

"It doesn't matter." Nailah stands and grabs her bag from the closet.

So yes, she knew. Nailah had known that her father was somewhere in the world alive but led me to believe that he was dead. She had lied to me, but I cared about her. I had to shake that shit off.

She walked out of the room to the front door and I followed.

"It does matter because it means that you lied to me. It means that after all we have shared, you are keeping things from me."

Nailah spun around on her heels so fast that I almost bumped into her.

"Tyriq, you know more about me than any one person outside of my hometown. You know that my middle name is Le'Mae. I like to crochet, and I hate people who touch cake with their hands when they serve it at parties. You know who I am right now, that I like you and enjoy spending time with you. Nothing else matters."

I slide a hand across my face.

"Let's not do this tonight. It's been a long day." I pull her into my arms. "We can talk about it when you come home tomorrow."

I can feel both of Nailah's eyes widen against my chest. She doesn't jerk away and run like I expected. She calmly lifted her head and took two steps back.

"I didn't mean- shit," I begin explaining, but she lifts her hand. I could have kicked my own ass for that slip-up. Relationship words can send Nailah running on a good day.

"It's ok. I need to go. I'm not what you need Tyriq. You need someone who requires less glue, someone that doesn't need to be held together. You deserve someone better, someone that you don't have to fix. I'm sorry."

I let her walk away because I don't know what to say, and I may somewhat believe her.

CHAPTER THIRTY-ONE

Nailah

I kick the tire twice and walk to my trunk. Two tires flat. Zero spare tires are available.

"Lucy," I say to my beloved car. "You let me down today."

I sigh and walk around to sit in the front seat, reevaluating my entire adult existence. Just when I had been doing so well, life happened.

There is no one to call.

No more Tyriq. I had thoroughly messed that up.

After narrowly surviving an entire weekend without him, I had successfully made it to work two days before I missed our morning donut runs. I had made it through three nights before I had to break down and touch myself to thoughts of him, and four days before, I knew with complete certainty that I was a dumb ass. My father had cheated me out of a happy childhood, and I had used him as an excuse to cheat myself out of happiness as an adult.

I thought Tyriq would call me, at least. No flowers came to my office. Neither Regina nor Mali invited me anywhere. Mali did not even mention Tyriq when she texted me on Tuesday. Obviously, he had not said anything to her about our spat or possible break up.

I miss him, his laugh, his criticism of my food choices, and that phenomenon of a tongue. I need to apologize. I need to be more open. He would understand, maybe.

It's nine in the morning, and he has patients, but I call him anyway. Maybe he will forgive me. Maybe he will at least be my friend even if I have messed up the option for us to be more.

My call goes straight to voicemail.

He was always complaining about my lack of calling him, and then when I did, voicemail. Maybe he was blocking my call?

I looked at the name of the street where I pulled over and searched for the nearest tow company with my phone.

Fifteen minutes later, the Brother's T towing service pulled up. A lion-colored man with intricately maintained locs exits the driver's side of the truck looking like he could be a daytime soap opera star if it weren't for the overalls. I instantly recognize him as the man from the gala, Tyriq's brother, Terrence. A bold-bodied guy who favored both Tyriq and Terrence exited the passenger side.

I get out of the car and greet the two masculine men. These brothers need their own calendar. There is a swagger about them that can't be explained. Manliness just exudes from the brothers at all times.

"You need some help with your car?" Terrence, the lion-looking one, asks.

"Yes. My front tires are flat and falling apart." I look back at my tire tread lining the street.

"No problem, we'll get it hooked up and over to the shop for you," the other brother explained. "I'm Tyson and this is my brother Terrence."

"I'm Nailah," I say.

The two smile and I'm sure that Terrence already knew my name, but I stay quiet. No need to get my feelings hurt today. I had not been formally introduced to his brothers, and since the status of my relationship is unknown, it's best to not bring up Tyriq.

I stand back and let the two men get to work.

The Brother's T Tow is not an average shop. The building took up a whole block and not only offered tow services, but car maintenance, car detail, and an auto supply shop. Next to the shop and store is a drive-through automatic car wash that the brothers own as well.

The simple waiting room is nice and clean, more than I can say for the many garages that Lucy and I have frequented. I pay for a soda from the vending machine and sit back to watch the news on the flat-screen television.

Tyson stepped into the waiting area thirty minutes later with a grease towel in his hand.

"It's finished," he said before asking the question that most others think. "You ever consider investing in a new car?"

"Lucy, the Lexus is a classic," I answer. "Can't get rid of her. We have a ride-or-die type of thang going on."

"If you say so." The shake of his head lets me know that he doesn't get it. No one ever gave me anything. My daddy didn't even give me his last name.

I walk with him to the counter to pay.

"You should bring her here sometime, so she doesn't die on you sooner than you want," he suggests.

He pushes some buttons on the screen and a receipt prints.

I look through my purse for my wallet.

"How much do I owe you?" I ask, but Tyson shakes his head.

"Nothing."

"Quit playing. Two brand new tires and a tow all for free?"

That is unreal.

Before he answers, Tyriq emerges from the back of the shop and I swear that my heart must have stopped beating.

Tyriq, dressed in slacks and a button-down, causes my breathing to pause as well. Every damn time. He hasn't gotten any less breathtaking with time.

"I didn't say it was free," Tyson said quietly. "Big brother got it already. And you have four new tires."

Tyriq walks over to me and kisses my cheek as Terrence enters the room.

"Hey, Nai." His face is solemn and he's looking me over like I'm a wounded animal he found in the forest. "Are you alright, babe?"

I want to be alright. Shock stole my mind for a second.

"I'm good. Your brothers took excellent care of me," I say, unsure of what else to say and how this works.

"Thank you, guys," I say looking at each of them. "I won't even hold it against you that you snitched on me."

Terrence laughs a little.

"I know my brother wouldn't be happy if I came across his lady somewhere and didn't let him know," he explained.

"His lady?" I question and look to Tyriq who cleared his throat and turned his attention to his brother.

"Thanks, bro," he said bumping fists with Terrence and then Tyson. "We'll be back for Lucy later," Tyriq told the two before putting his arm around my waist and escorting me to his SUV.

Being in his arms again is pure joy. I inhale his scent as we walk side by side like nothing has ever gone wrong.

The SUV ride is smooth and quiet; nothing like the jitteriness of Lucy, or the exhilaration felt flying through the streets in Tyriq's sports car. The leather seats are soft enough to sleep on. Every air vent opens and closes, and mysterious smoke doesn't appear from the hood after the left turns.

"I'm surprised to see you," I say light heartedly.

Tyriq says nothing and just keeps driving.

His face is tight like someone had stitched it that way. I know that I walked away from him, but it is good to see him. He came to help me.

"You alright?" I ask.

"Yep."

"Thank you for the tires. Lucy needed some new shoes," I laugh hoping he will join in.

"You're welcome," his response is bland and lacking feeling, not like him at all.

Tyriq talks about his thoughts and feelings more than any man that I have experienced in life.

I look out of the window. Obviously, this is not the chatting time.

Ever attentive, Tyriq opens the door to the restaurant and ushers me in. The look in his eyes is so reserved. I miss the light in his eyes and the happiness in his voice from our previous time together.

The hostess smiles a little too much at Tyriq for my liking when she sits us in a spacious booth near the back of the restaurant.

She takes our drink order before swiping her hand across his shoulder.

"Let me know if there is anything that you may need," she winks in his direction.

"Yes, Elizabeth. We will let you know if we need anything else," I emphasize the 'we' with a flare of my nostrils.

She turns away quickly to leave.

Tyriq smiled.

"Finally, something made you smile. Even if it is me getting snappy with that leprechaun of a hostess," I say. "What is she, like twelve?"

Tyriq looks over to the hostess, standing still, grinning.

"I'd give her nineteen," he guesses.

"You better not give her anything."

My statement only serves to increase the size of his smile.

Another waitress brings over our drinks and takes our order. This one is much less flirty.

"So, you're jealous, Miss James?" he teases.

"No comment." I pick up my tea from the table.

"Why is that? Is it that difficult for you to say it? To tell me that you want us to be together exclusively?"

I mis-swallow my drink. How can he just throw that out there?

"See, every time I mention an 'us' you tense up," Tyriq observed.

"Why didn't you call me today when you had car trouble?"

"Why would I?" I shrug.

I didn't know the right answer, but I had said the wrong thing. The scowl on his face made me wish that I could pluck the words out of the air and stick them in my pocket like I hadn't said them.

"What I mean is-" I rephrase. "All that you would be able to do is what I did, call a tow truck."

Tyriq rubbed his hand over his mouth and looked off to the side before speaking.

"This is that moment then?"

"What moment? You've had me confused since we left the shop."

He takes a deep breath.

"We either go forward together or this is it."

His distressed eyes meet mine, and I feel an ache in my chest.

"I thought that we may have had something," he says slowly.

My world begins to spin. A wave of emotion rushes against any logical control that I have. He's leaving me too. I know it. I can feel it. He said it. That gut-wrenching feeling that captured my body when they took my mother away comes back like it had never left.

"What?" I whisper. I think I am the only one to hear the word.

I feel dizzy. Oceans of worry wave through and roll into the hurt. We are breaking up.

"Either we do this for real- no more running and no more hiding- or we end it now."

Tyriq is serious. He had given me heaven and was going to take it away.

Without thinking, I move from my side of the booth to sit next to him, to be near him while I still can.

"If you want this to be over," I start, but the words are clogged in my throat. Stuck. I was stuck, and he wasn't. Tyriq was going to leave me just like everyone else had.

"That's not what I said," he interjected.

I jump a little at the force of his words. This was the closest to anger that I had seen.

The tears come from a place that I cannot describe. I guess they had been saved up somewhere from something that happened in my past because I dare not cry over a man.

"Don't cry. I can't-" Tyriq grunted as he pulled me into his arms. "I'm here, Nailah."

Still, complete words are lost in the pit of me. What can I say to make him stay? How can I make this right?

"I wake up thinking about you, Nailah. I go to sleep wanting you. I need to know that you're okay every day," he spoke at a slow deliberate pace. "When I laugh, I think about telling you. When I'm pissed, to calm down, I think about holding you."

Tyriq sighed, looked out of the window, at the table, and finally, my face again.

"If you don't get those kind of feelings, then-"

I swipe at my eyes. His words push down some of my stirring worry.

"It wasn't just physical for me Tyriq," I find myself saying. "I wish you could hear inside my brain sometimes to know how I really feel about you," I admit. This man makes me feel all kinds of amazing and I don't know what to do about it.

"You could just tell me, or better yet, show me," he suggests.

"I did. We had sex like every other night," I whisper.

"Not just sex Nai," he says. "Call me sometime before dark, invite me to meet your friends. Tell me about your past. Tell me about your dad. Talk about the future, and show me where you live for the start."

I take a deep breath.

"Is that what you want, Tyriq?" I feel the beginning of a headache.

"It's about what you want. You feel it or you don't."

"Tyriq, I have been taking care of myself, by myself for a long time."

By any scale, I was failing this test. Every word that came out of my mouth led us farther apart.

"And is that the way you always want it?" his gruff question reminds me of when we first met. I was so sad then, lonely. Being with Tyriq changed all of that.

"I didn't want to assume that because we were sleeping together, I was your woman," I clarify. "I keep my distance, keep us distant, so that when it's time for you to leave, when it's time for you to walk away, you won't take my heart with you."

Tyriq bows his head and closes his eyes as if praying for strength before he speaks.

"Nailah, I don't arbitrarily invite women to spend nights in my home, let them eat all of my peanut butter and desecrate my popcorn."

"So, there are other women?" I ask.

"You are it. You are the only one, numero uno," he claims. "You're the woman, my one woman. I went to war with my aunt, gave my mom a warning about hurting your feelings, and damn near cursed out Mali over you. Naeem and Jermain both almost got dealt with. I will tear up this muthafucking world for you, girl."

I let his statement sit still for a second and let the gravity of his proclamation fall on me.

His eyes are as intense as I have ever seen them, and I know in my gut that he means every last word.

I scoot closer into his embrace, and offer him the only thing that I have to give; an explanation.

"I called you first," I tell him. "You're the first person I called, but it went straight to voicemail."

His eyes narrow down at me and I feel like I am in trouble before he finally speaks.

"Give me your phone."

"Why?" I ask.

The look on his face is not one that I like. I want him to stay a part of my life and to keep doing what he's been doing. I want him to keep making me feel weightless and free, so I hand over my phone.

"What are you doing?" I ask.

"Adding my office number and Aunt Pat's cell," he explained. "If you need me, you got me."

I'm not sure how to feel about that. I'm not sure how to feel about 'having him,' but I smile.

"If for some reason, you can't find me, then call Terrence," he continues while adding another number. "I don't want you sitting on the side of the road somewhere alone."

He hands my phone back to me and we sit in silence for a bit. I guess he said all that he needed to say, the next move was on me.

"My family broke me, my friends left me, and I've never had a real relationship before," I make clear. "I can't take any more heartbreak in my life Tyriq."

"How are you so sure that I will hurt you? Why do you assume the worst of me?"

He never met my father. He never saw what love did to my mother. He's unaware of the longing that women I knew felt for men who were heartless carcasses.

"The men I've met and known are the worst kind of candy-covered evil," I try to explain. "They were poison on a plate that women gobbled down willingly because they thought that they were supposed to. Like the only experience in life was the pain and pleasure of a man and nothing else mattered."

He rubbed a soothing hand down my shoulder as I remembered the ladies that I lived with.

"It seemed like pain was this foregone conclusion, covered up by snippets of pleasure," I tell him. "I don't want to live like that, running crazy behind a man, and I can't just go throwing my heart around."

With the caress of my cheek, I try not to melt in his arms.

"I'm not asking you to throw your heart around, but at least give me the option of earning it." His eyes dart across my face before he continues. "You give me a peek of you, of the real carefree, human feeling Nai, and then you drop the curtain on her before I can get a good look, and it's back to Ice Blade."

There is truth in his words. There are parts of me, of my life that he should never see.

This shell, this body heals quickly, I don't know if my heart can recover from another blow.

"What do you want from me Tyriq? We were already spending every weekend together?" I ask, unsure of what to do next. "I'm not seeing anyone else."

He looks at me.

Disbelief and concern cloud his eyes when he takes my face into his hands.

"I want you to let me in. I want to be your best friend, your lover, your confidant, your provider, your support-"

"I don't know how to do that, Tyriq. As my guy, you have to be patient with me if I don't get it right."

He nodded, letting my face fall and I wanted to feel him again.

"And you have to know that I take care of what I care about," he explained. "Please don't run, but I feel like you are mine already like you belong with me."

Belong? What does it mean to belong with someone? I had belonged to my mother. I had belonged to my father. Neither one of them worked out so well.

I scoot back to my side of the booth and sit quietly. He had given me a lot to think about.

I thank the server when our food is delivered and we eat in peace, my mind whirring around all the words we had spoken.

Tyriq pays for our meals and we hop in his SUV.

The inside of the car provides the much-needed privacy I am hoping for, and I lean over and kiss him with all the hope that I have inside of me. I hope that he is true, that he won't hurt me, and that one day I could truly belong to him fully and in every way.

I hum a little after letting go of his tongue, and he is quiet. Unusually quiet again and watching my eyes.

"What's up?" I ask, breaking the silence.

"Come with me to family game night tonight," he insists.

I shake my head no before I can say the words or even think about them. Families ask questions. Families have expectations. Families like his want to know about the past and have plans for the future.

"Here we go again," he says, frustration creeping back into his voice.

"Today has been hectic," I whine. "I just want to get my car, go home, and get out of these clothes. I want to relax. Plus, you know that your people do not like me."

"Mali will be there. Terrence and Tyson will be there, and they like you. Trystan made me promise not to mess this up with you and Chad asks me about you every time I see him," Tyriq counters. "I can even help you get out of those clothes."

"How about we skip game night and I take them off right now?" I respond placing my hand on the part of him that makes me so grateful to be a woman.

I push my mouth against his still holding on to that patented piece of pleasure. Tyriq palms my breast like a basketball, and he is ready to go full court.

Unexpectedly he snatches his lips away from mine and moves his member away from me.

"Nope," he says. "I want to see you tonight."

"Tyriq." I try to slip my hand back over him, but he pushes it away.

"You almost got me that time," he says. "I'm on to your little devious *distract him with desire* strategy."

He puts the car in reverse, and I sigh.

"I'm going to help you relax," he explains. "Tonight will be good. I promise."

Stepping out of Tyriq's SUV is like stepping out of a chariot. Those on the lot know we have arrived. Even in his casual business clothes, he looks like a superstar, ready to run the world with a smile that can transform terrorists.

The valet in front of the resort-sized massage palace opened and closed my door, but Tyriq was there to place his arm around my waist as soon as my feet touched the ground.

He ushers me through the door swiftly and sweetly as warm greetings from staff shower him like he is a second cousin they haven't seen since childhood.

"Hello Dr. Lewis, we have one of your favorite rooms set up for you," the female attendant dressed in a tan uniform explained while leading us down a long hall corridor.

"A massage Tyriq? Really?"

"Damn, Blade. Can I spoil you a little?"

"How much spoiling? This place looks expensive."

"When you're with me, Nailah, you're with me, and I got you," he says as though he is explaining it to a six-year-old. "The price is for me to figure out."

His words remind me of a saying that Sugar had, 'Every pussy has a price that any penis will pay. You decide the entry fee.'

Questions fire through my mind machine gun style: is this part of my entry fee? Is he doing this because he thinks it's required in order for him to sleep with me? Would it be worse if I told him that it doesn't cost anything to be with me? Would that mean that I'm free? Who would want a free woman?

"You don't have to do any of this," I finally say.

"And that's why I enjoy doing it," he replied kissing my neck.

I move so that I can look him in the eye.

"I just need you, Tyriq. Being with you is awesome enough."

Gently his fingers trace the side of my cheek.

"I know this is not what you're used to, but every time I see the awe on your face it makes me want to do it all over again."

I thread my fingers through his and nod in understanding.

"Thank you," I say.

"We better get undressed before the masseuse arrives," he tells me.

I take off my clothes and wrap a large towel around me while Tyriq does the same.

"I told you I would get you out of those clothes," he jokes.

I fall asleep during my massage. One minute, Tyriq is talking about this place being one of his favorites and the next there is nothing but the floaty feeling of pleasure.

When I awake, Tyriq is fully dressed and sitting on the sofa with his cell phone in hand.

I sit up, feeling refreshed, as Tyriq ends a call.

"How long was I out?" I ask.

"The masseuse left about fifteen minutes ago if that's what you're wondering," he explains.

"Sorry," I apologize.

Tyriq wrapped his large arms around me.

"It's alright, I had a few phone calls to make anyway."

I lay my head against his chest and relish the warmth of him.

"So, you got to get out of your clothes, you got to relax, and we're about to get your car," he lists.

"You don't play fair."

"But I'll see you tonight," he insists.

I catch his eyes and see his sincerity, his desire for me to be there with him and meet his family. He has never made me feel less than comfortable anywhere that I have been with him, so I agree.

"Tell me the time and place and I'll be there," I concede before he kisses me.

I see Lucy on a lift when we pull into The Brother's T Auto Care Shop and I look at Tyriq.

"I thought my car was done before I left," I say anxious to know the reason for it being in the air again.

"Stay calm," he said as he parked in a spot near the front. "Tyson told me about the shape of your car, and I told him to go ahead and fix whatever problems it has."

I look at Tyriq like he has two heads.

"Why would you do that without even talking to me about it?" I nearly scream. How dare he make a decision about what is mine?

My confusion transfers to Tyriq.

"It's a surprise," he justifies. "I want you to be safe when you're driving. If something happened to you-"

"Regardless of what you believe Tyriq, I have taken care of myself pretty damn well for years without your assistance and I can continue to do so," I argue.

Tyriq pulls my face closer to his and wraps his lips around mine. Kissing away the words that I had left and preventing any others from forming.

"You can fuss all you want," he says after releasing me. "I can't let you drive around the city to random places, knowing that your car is about to disintegrate."

His words are gentle but strong, but the word 'let' sticks out like a thumb on a hand. I am my own woman. He didn't have to let me do anything.

"Tyriq, you have to talk to me about this stuff," I protest. "Lucy is mine. I just don't let anybody work on her."

There is more emotion in my voice than I meant to display. He doesn't understand what Lucy means to me.

"My brothers are certified mechanics and specialize in foreign cars," he responds logically.

Yes. Lucy breaks often. Yes, she should be fixed. Yes, it is nice that he helped, but I can do this. I don't need him to do it for me.

I sigh, knowing that he has more stubbornness than I have the energy to go against.

"How long will it take until she's finished?" I ask.

"Depending on parts. Tyson said at least two weeks."

"Two weeks?! Tyriq, this is crazy!" I yell frustrated all over again. "What am I supposed to do without a car, when my job depends on it?"

"Who said you wouldn't have a car?" He winks.

"You can't just do these things. Take my things without talking to me." I place my hands over my face and take deep breaths. I want to scream and cry and yell and run. I want to grab my keys, drive off the lift, and keep rolling, but I sit and breathe. I tell him my problem.

"Car rental is not within my budget for the month," I explained to him.

"Relax," he said. "It's taken care of."

Tyriq exits the car and comes to open my door, but I don't move. I can't.

"Hey," he says slow and kind. "I want you to be safe Nailah and since I'm in a position to help you with that, let me."

"You should have at least asked," I reiterate but with less zeal.

"Nai, I already knew you wouldn't accept my help," he insists.

Tyriq is right. If he would have asked, I would have said no.

"Stay right here," he says excitedly before running into the shop.

He returns quickly.

"So, what's up?" I ask.

"Just wait." Tyriq is smiling so hard that I think his face might break.

Before I can utter any hesitation, Terrence pulls up from behind the shop in a new model Lexus, black with tinted windows and a sunroof.

"Tyriq, you didn't." I shoot him a scowl.

"I didn't buy it," he explained trying to ward off any attacks. "My cousin owns a dealership and you can use it until your car is ready."

"This is too much," I say. "Is this model even out yet? I can't accept this."

"Nai," he says pulling me close to him. "Calm down. It would ease my mind to know that you are safe when you are driving. No strings. You can erase my number from your phone today, and you can still use this car."

I look at him and look at the car and something shifts in my soul. He is totally for real. I know that regardless of the length of our time together this man has my back in a way that the people who gave birth to me would not.

Emotion wells up and before I can catch them, tears appear and cascade down my cheeks.

"Wait, don't do that," he says hugging me tightly.

"Thank you," I blubber between sighs and tears.

He wraps his arms around me, and I let my head fall against his chest. I'm sure this wasn't the reaction that he was expecting.

I sniffle and pull myself together.

Tyriq snags some tissue from his car and hands them to me.

"What's wrong?" Tyson asked walking up from the garage.

"Sorry," I say to the men who had helped me through this day. "I didn't mean for that to happen."

I have not cried like this since I was a little girl before the day at my mother's grave.

"It's alright," Tyriq added.

"I'll have your car ready as quickly as possible," Terrence reassured stepping toward me.

"Yeah," Tyson added. "And if you need to see her, just drop by."

I laugh through the tears gathering against my eyelids. I wipe them as quickly as I can.

"No one has ever been this nice to me before," I explain.

"Well get used to it," Terrence suggests. "This is how we do it in the Lewis family."

"You get all of us, not just that donkey head," Tyson added.

With those words, I smile.

"Thank you so much."

Terrence handed the keys over to me.

"Don't have so much fun joyriding that you don't make it to game night, Nailah," Tyson added before leaving.

"I'll be there," I answer.

"If you need us, call us," Terrence added before walking away as well.

"I have to go check on the clinic and do a couple of things. I'll text you my mom's address."

I clear my throat and suggest something different.

"Why don't I just text you my address, and you can pick me up whenever you get finished?"

"I like that even better," he said moving closer to me and letting his arms fall into place around my waist.

"You have to promise me one thing first."

"And what is that?"

"When you see my place, you won't go out and try to buy me a new one."

He laughed from a good place in his gut.

"I promise," he agrees.

CHAPTER THIRTY-TWO

Tyriq

"I like how you decorated the place," I comment, trying to ignore the fact that Nailah answered the door in a black lace panty set.

I walk with Nailah through her small condo, enjoying the view of every step she takes. African masks, jazzy paintings, and candles fill every space of her spot. The smooth sound of the singer, Joe, floats through the house, and the swirl of her intoxicating perfume and enticing candles make me reconsider leaving the quaint and sexy compound.

I strolled into the compact living room to view the painting I had given her. It hangs over a plush black sofa and fits in well with the décor. The red tile on top of a small black end table is the exact color of the woman's dress.

"The painting looks nice there," I compliment.

"I know. Thank you again."

Nailah plugs her phone into a charger and places it on the end table.

"Anytime."

"Be ready in ten," Nailah promises as she scampers toward the stairs.

I take hold of her waist before she can make her ascent.

"Are you going to let me get ready?" Her smile makes me pull her closer and hold her tighter.

I answer with a kiss. Nailah's body falls limp against my chest while I grow harder.

I slide my hand across the waistband of the perfect-fitting underwear, moving them further away from what they were meant to protect.

"No, Tyriq," Nailah admonished, pulling out of the kiss and playfully pushing me away, but my hunger for her wouldn't allow me to let go.

I attack the flesh on her neck as she lifts her arms to push me away.

"I thought we were going to your parents' house," she whined.

I pull her body into mine and move my hardness against her.

"I can't go to my parents' house like this," I explain.

She hummed in pleasure when I let my tongue take a trip around her nipple.

"What about family game night? You never miss it."

"I want to play some games and make a family with you right now," I respond.

Nailah's body goes stone-slab straight, and she jerks away from me.

I give a haughty laugh, trying to cover up the self-shocking admission.

"Sorry," I pull her into me.

"We're taking it step by step, right?"

"It's because I'm horny, Blade," I explain. "You and this fine-ass body are doing something to my sanity."

I kiss her lips, knowing what came from mine is a lie. Given the chance to put a baby in Nailah right now, I would. I love her. Everything that I have ever wanted, I knew from the start, besides Briana, of course.

"I'm going to get dressed so you won't be tempted any longer," Nailah announces.

"That won't help any," I say. "I can't un-see all that beauty or booty."

Nailah rolls her eyes.

Before she can escape up the stairs, her cell phone rings. Every part of Nailah bounces as she crosses the room, and I pop her ass.

"Keep playing," I warn.

"I'm just getting my phone," she giggles, but I know that extra pop in her step is for me.

The grin drops from her face when she looks at the still-vibrating device.

I notice her slide her finger across the screen to end the call.

She drops the phone to the table and heads towards the stairs, but her bounce is missing.

"Who was that?" Who had made her lose the joy in her step that quickly? Who the hell else mattered enough for her to be sad about them?

"Nailah, talk to me."

She turns her uncovered body toward me. Everything about her is exposed, and she looks uncomfortable. It probably had nothing to do with the fact that she was nearly naked.

"It was just my father," she sighs. "He's been calling since the show aired and leaving messages. He wants me to call him back, but-"

She shakes her head.

"Maybe you should talk to him," I encourage gently.

Nailah slides a hand across the front of my already bulging jeans and begins stroking me through the material.

I slip my hand down the front of her belly and then further down with a finger between to massage her center.

She whimpers in my ear, and I lose it.

With one tug, I snap the lace covering from her body. In seconds, my pants and boxers are at my ankles.

I heft Nailah up and around me. I push into her, and we fall against the wall, both heaving and moaning with the bliss of being connected.

"Damn," I moan. It feels good to be inside of her. It had been too long.

She kisses my mouth like it is her given mission, looping her tongue and sucking mine.

Her legs wrap around my waist as I slam my body into hers. There is nothing soft about our movements, no pretense, just raw lust colliding and joining over and over again.

"Stop distracting me, dammit," I growl while driving into her warmth.

"Oooh..." Nailah whimpers. "You need to stop asking questions," she huffs out between moans.

"Answer the question." I pound into her.

She grinds harder against me, and we race to make the other lose control. Someone had to give in. Someone had to let go.

Her arms secure around my neck, and Nailah grates up and down with an intensity that demands every inch of me.

I thrust into her like the survival of my life depended on her satisfaction. I can't imagine surviving without her, without this, without us.

Her body contracting around my length as I glided in and out felt amazing.

"Damn, I missed you!" Nailah yells as she rolls her body one last time. Those rare, kind words renew my exhilaration and driving push.

Nailah's back bowed, and her body strained still. I felt a shudder erupt through her core as she screeched out an ear-piercing shriek and then a soul-cleansing sigh.

She falls forward against me.

With another push, I thunder out a yell of bliss as I fall over the edge and explode into her for the first time with nothing between us.

Connected, I shuffle us over to the sofa and sit with her on top of me.

Once my heartbeat stops racing and I can breathe, I lean back and lift Nailah's chin.

"My bad, Blade. I'm sorry, baby."

"For what?" she asks, her beautiful eyes rounding.

"It's my job to protect you."

She rears back. "From what? You got something that I need to know about?"

"No. We discussed this. I'm clean," I laugh. "I don't want to put you in a situation that you're not ready for."

She smiles before kissing my neck.

"We'll be fine." She waved a hand across the air, dismissing my worry.

She kissed my cheek and stood.

Nailah moved toward the stairs gracefully but stopped before taking them.

When she bites at her lip, I can tell that she is struggling with something internally, so I don't prompt her to speak or ask any other questions.

"I don't want to talk to my dad or see him. At one time, I thought that I wanted a relationship with him," She shakes her head, "but I don't. The state never officially took custody of me. My dad took me to his girlfriend Dolly's house one day. Dolly had a girlfriend named Sugar, and both women were very kind to me. They took care of me, but he shouldn't have left me there. He had his chance to love me, and he left me."

I nod and accept her explanation. I have questions, but I understand her vulnerable gesture.

"However you want to handle things with your father, I will support you."

At that moment, I felt closer to her than I did while inside of her.

"I just want him to leave me alone. I don't want to see him. He has another daughter now, anyway. I just want to move forward."

Walking up to my parents' home with Nailah feels like the most natural thing in the world. I hold onto her waist with an overwhelming sense of luck and pride. She looks damn good tonight. Before we make it to the door, I have to get more of her. I swept her into my arms, kissed the lips that haunted my dreams last night, and taunted me the entire car ride. Her tongue twisted and intertwined with mine, so she felt it, too. Our connection is stronger today than last night, and we're closer now than an hour ago. I know without a doubt that she is the one for me.

"Give the girl her face back, Tyriq," Mali shouted from the door.

Nailah literally leaped out of my arms and let go of my kiss. I was glad she didn't trip again.

"Mali, you're more like your mother than you think." Both of them know how to mess up a good time.

"You take that shit back!" she snapped.

"Never. I mean that fam," I reply as Nailah and I walk into the house.

"Whatever." Mali flips me the middle finger before turning to Nailah. "I'm glad my cousin finally found some manners and brought you by to officially meet us."

Mali pulled her in for a hug.

"Don't be too mad at him. I gave him a little trouble," she replied.

Mali took Nailah away before I could blink twice.

"Where are ya'll going?" I ask, following behind the two.

"Shoo!" Mali exclaimed, flicking her wrist. The guys are in the dining room!"

That was my not-so-subtle cue to disappear while the council, my mom, Mali, and Aunt Pat convened.

I give Nailah one last look before heading to the dining room.

Terrence, Tyson, Cairo, and Chad are clinking dominoes against the table when I step in. My dad, who heads the table, is sitting sipping his patented clear glass of brown liquor.

"Hey, Pops," I say, hugging him before sitting next to Cairo at the eight-person table.

"I thought you were bringing your lady along with you," he questioned.

"Mali got to her already," Cairo responded before I could.

"You know it," I confirmed with a laugh. "Nailah's in there with the council now."

"Make sure my Lexus comes back in one piece, cousin," Cairo added.

"I'm good for it," I tell him. "If Nailah likes it, I'll buy it for her."

"I need to meet this woman," Cairo mentioned before slamming down a domino. "She must have pixie dust in her p-"

"Hey," I cut Cairo off. "Keep my girl and those words out of your mouth."

"That's a boat!" Chad called out as he dropped a domino on the table with emphasis. "Count them up, cousin!"

"You didn't win," Terrence scoffed, adding points to the piece of paper where he had recorded his score.

"Tyriq, all I can say is don't let those ladies in the kitchen know how much you like her. Your momma will be putting in reservations for the church and reception hall," Chad warned.

I laugh, but with Nailah, the possibilities are endless.

"When did you know it was that time with mom?" I ask before stares and glares shot across the room at me.

Chad stopped his domino midair.

"I'm just asking," I explain, and the game resumes.

"Don't scare me like that," Chad added.

My dad grunted before finishing his drink.

"I knew Shirley was it when I showed her who I was, faults and all, and she was still there. She kept helping me become better than I was the day before."

I take his words into consideration.

"That's deep pops," I nod. With Nailah, it wasn't about her making me a better person but us enjoying each other. She enhanced my life.

"They don't make women like that anymore, Unc," Chad chimed in, unconvinced. "These new types of chicks are 'pay for play.' They look like they have something going for themselves when, in reality, benefactor funds buy everything they have. I'm nobody's come up."

"I hear that, cousin," Terrence added. "The women that come through the shop are all about what I can do for them. They look at me differently when they find out I'm not just the guy twisting the wrench, but I own the place and several others."

"There are still some good ones around," Pops said. "Just be patient."

"That's fifteen!" Cairo shouted as the game continued.

"What was up with your girl crying today at the garage?" Tyson asked.

"She won't really get into it, but her childhood was certainly jacked up. She spent a lot of time in a group home." I took another swig of the beer I had picked up and looked at the people who had enriched my life. Without these men, I would not be where I am. "I believe that the kindness overwhelmed her."

Terrence nodded.

"Every family isn't like ours," Tyson added.

"Boom! Give me twenty five!" Chad exclaimed, slamming the domino.

"That's game," Terrence said sourly.

CHAPTER THIRTY-THREE

Nailah

Mali ushered me over to a breakfast nook, babbling away about something that happened at work. The pounding in my ears and churning in my stomach blocked out all other noises. I am meeting Tyriq's mother, Tyriq's super religious, uber-connected, perfect-in-his-eyes mom. It hadn't mattered so much when I met her before because we hadn't labeled what we had. Since I was officially in girlfriend territory, things were different.

"Hi, Mrs. Lewis. It's nice to see you again."

It is also nice to see her dazzling open kitchen. The large, cream-and-gray modern space features clear-faced, lighted cabinets, stainless steel appliances, and marble countertops.

Mrs. Lewis places a bowl of batter on the matching marble top kitchen island and wipes her hands against the frilly red and white apron tied around her waist.

"Good to see you." She nods with a lift of her cheek. "Do me a favor, please."

She moved toward me, and I wobbled a step back, clutching my watery palms. It's not like the woman had the plague or something. The mere fact that she had given birth to and raised four men and managed to look like the actress Lynn Whitfield had me in awe of her.

"Tyriq bought me this gadget." Her forehead creases. "It's a speaker with no wires, and I can't seem to make my phone work with the thing."

Mrs. Lewis twisted the small black box with blue flashing lights between her maroon-painted nails. "Will you hook it up and turn on some music for me?"

Was this a peace offering? Could she have had Mali or one of her sons do that?

My smile is weak when I look around at the busybodies in the kitchen. Mali had the oven open. Mali's mom, Patricia, worked on some meat in a cast iron skillet on the stove.

"I would really appreciate it," she coaxes. "I can't get those boys to focus long enough to help me out."

"Sure thing." I take her small, flat phone. "Is there anything in particular that you want to listen to?"

"Music doesn't come with the phone? I thought it came with all of that." Her eyebrows furrow as she goes back to mixing.

"There's an app for that, I'll add it."

I added a music app and turned on some Frankie Beverly and Maze.

"Alright!" Mrs. Lewis popped a swaying hand into the air and snapped her fingers. She swings her hips to the beat. "What you know about that young one?"

I chuckle a bit and relax my shoulders. Tyriq had asked me something similar. "I was raised on it."

Patricia and Mali worked silently around us, back and forth between the stove, oven, and sink, not saying a word like they had planned it that way.

"Tyriq said that you had a difficult childhood," Mrs. Lewis commented as she poured the batter from her bowl between two baking pans. "Hold that."

I wrap my fingers around one of the pans to steady it as she pours.

"Things were rough. I lived in a foster home once my parents disappeared. Before my father left, he used to drive me around our small town and play music as loud as it could go."

After I get the bad part out of the way, tension loosens in my neck. Even though it was years ago, speaking about my family is not always easy.

I change the subject as I ease onto the stool. There are plenty of things that people should know about me beyond the fact that I am orphaned.

"Is that German Chocolate Cake you're making?"

His mother scoots the two tins into her sparkling oven.

"It sure is." The corners of her mouth turn up as she steps back to the island.

Mrs. Lewis brushes a comforting hand across my shoulder

"Great. I love any cake with pecans."

"You have to taste my Italian Wedding Cake then," she offers.

I lift my feet onto the stool bar and lean my elbows against the marble top.

"That's my favorite cake of all time. My grandmother always made an Italian Wedding Cake for me and never skimped on frosting and the pecans."

"My kind of girl." Her wisp of a smile dissolved my remaining anxiety. "Did she leave you with a recipe?"

"She passed away when I was seven, and I never got to learn her process."

I remember my grandmother smelling like frosting and feeling like love. Every hug and word was comfort. All the sweetness in my life died with her.

"How about you let me make one for your birthday? I can even show you the steps."

"Really? My birthday already passed, but I would still like to learn."

"Next week, I'll show you when you come to game night."

I don't know what to say to that. Mrs. Lewis invited me to come back.

Mrs. Lewis nods toward her sister, Patricia. Both Mali and Patricia step over to the counter.

I try to keep my face straight. It was Tyriq's family. He loves them. He needs them.

"Nailah, I want to apologize for the things that I said that night. I shouldn't have judged you without even knowing you. I took it too far. It is very clear that you will be a part of Tyriq's life from now on, and I want us to get along."

I look into the faces of the women staring back at me and wonder if Tyriq had something to do with this or Mali. Did he really think that I would be a part of his life going forward? Would these women ever really accept me?

"Thank you for that. I want you all to know that I care about Tyriq as a person, not for what he can give me. I made it through hell and lived to tell it because of my determination, not because anyone anywhere did it for me. Mooching is not my style."

The ladies all nod, and I hope we have come to an understanding.

"I will do everything in my power to make sure that Tyriq is happy," I explain.

"Well, I have never seen him happier," his mother added. "I am glad that he found you."

I excuse myself to the restroom when a text message alert sounds from my phone.

The number is blocked, but I am clear about who the message is from.

There is a link to an article about a raid on Sugar Dolls. The message warned me to leave Tyriq, or everyone would know who I was.

CHAPTER THIRTY-FOUR

Tyriq

I walk into the living room, and she's there. Nailah is holding my niece and rocking her like she is her own.

"That baby looks good on you," my mother says, shuffling into the room and drying her hands on the apron she has used since I was short enough to tug at it. "I can't believe she's so taken with you."

"She's not the only one," I chime, rubbing my niece's head.

I try to pick up the baby, but she turns her body away from me, snuggling closer into Nailah's chest.

I wish that I could rub against Nailah's breast right now, too.

"It's like that now, niece? How easy they turn."

Everyone laughs when the baby gurgles up a smile and leans closer.

When I look at Nailah, I see my future.

I look to my father and mother, who are looking at me. I can only assume that they see the way I look at her.

"You're so beautiful." I place a kiss on her cheek and take a seat at the card table. Maybe some space will get my thoughts to change.

Nailah smiles as the baby makes gurgly sounds and grabs her chest.

"Kids just like me," Nailah explains.

"Means you have a good spirit," my mother adds. "Food is almost done."

Crystal walks in, holding a tray of deviled eggs.

"Thanks for holding the baby for me, Nailah." She places down the tray of eggs and picks the baby up.

Even with the baby out of Nailah's arms, it didn't change what I felt when I saw her holding her.

"Where the cards at cousin?" I holler at Chad. "You ready to lose your dignity in a game of spades?"

It was after dinner, and although I was ready to take Nailah home and slip between her thighs, I was enjoying the interaction with her and my family.

"Really? Is that a challenge, I hear?" Chad replies. "You really want to get embarrassed in front of your girl like that?"

Chad turns to Nailah, who has joined me at the card table.

"I'm sorry I have to do this to your guy, but he asked for it." Chad pulls a pack of cards from his pocket and sits them down on the table.

"Not if I'm playing," Nailah adds. "I hope those words tasted good coming up 'cause you're about to swallow them."

"Let's get it going!" Cairo added, taking a seat at the table.

Chad is pouting ten minutes into the game because Nailah and I are winning.

"Boom!" she lays out a spade.

"This is ridiculous," Chad mumbles as his face crumbles.

Nailah scoots the cards across the table and into her hand.

"That's my girl," I chuckle.

"I thought social workers were supposed to be all sweet, mousy, and kind. You, Nailah, were a hustler in another life," Chad grunted.

Nailah cut her eyes in Chad's direction and only smirked as she reviewed her cards.

My dad sauntered over with a glass of Hennessey and an unlit cigar.

"I'm walking out to the porch," he offered. "If any of you want to head that way."

No smoking was allowed in the house, so my father always took a trip to the porch to light up whatever he was smoking.

"Is that the Montecristo line of cigars? I bet it is the Montecristo number two," Nailah asks my father while repositioning the cards in her hand.

Pops nods and turns the cigar around in his hand so that the label is facing my curious woman.

"Good eye," my father lifted both the cigar and an eyebrow in Nailah's direction.

"I thought so," she grinned. "I recognized the label. That's an excellent brand. That's a wise pairing with the Hennessy VSOP you have."

Nailah's eyes brighten as she looks away from the cards to my father again.

"Oh, and if you like the Montecristo, the Macanudo Café is a great choice, too. It's really smooth and light."

"Hot damn, that's what I'm talking about," my father smiled so hard it looked like his ears were trying to steal his lips. "I've been trying a few things. You know I have to switch it up a little."

My dad is the king of not switching things up. Last year, I gifted him a cigar-of-the-month club membership, and I never saw him with anything else.

I see the warmth in his eyes, so I don't call him out.

"You follow cigars?" Pops asks Nailah. "How'd you guess what I was drinking and smoking without even looking. That's a real skill."

She gave an innocent smile.

"I grew up in a small town where liquor and tobacco were a source of entertainment." She shrugs off. "I can tell most liquors by the smell."

"You're serious?" Chad jerked his thumb toward me. "How did you end up with my square-ass cousin?"

"End up with him?" She gave a subtle wink in my direction, a dreamy haze in her eyes. "Tyriq is my happy beginning."

Imitating a person vomiting, Chad makes a gagging noise.

"I still believe you were a hustler. How many clubs did you run? Did you have cops on the payroll?"

Nailah spluttered out a hearty laugh.

"Dude, you're funny," she fans her cards. "I just happen to be very knowledgeable about liquor and cigars."

"That's what a kingpin would say."

Nailah shakes her head. "I used to collect the cigar boxes and labels I found. They looked so expensive to me as a kid. I still love the smell of a good cigar to this day."

"If you don't mind stepping outside with an old man, I keep a few Cohiba's and Davidoff's tucked away."

Nailah's eyes light up.

"If you have the Cohiba Behike, Tyriq may be out of luck," she grins, standing up from the table.

"You just about to walk away with my Pops like that?" I question throwing down the cards.

Terrence had entered the room at some point. "Now you know what it feels like. We haven't finished a game since you met her," he chimes in.

CHAPTER THIRTY-FIVE

Nailah

My lips didn't touch the air until after my back touched the door. Tyriq kept them covered with his mouth as he walked me backward to my condo entrance.

Breaking away from his kiss, I gasped for the breaths of the oxygen I had been deprived of.

"I have to open the door," my plea changes nothing.

His magnetized hands roam over the bottom half of my body, pulling me nearer to him.

"I'll take you right here at this door and make your neighbors know my name," Tyriq jokes amid neck nibbles and continuous caresses.

Somehow, with minimal brain power, I managed to get the door open. We nearly fall through, and I barely get the door closed when Tyriq begins yanking off anything covering my body.

Without bothering to take off my new, non-ripped underwear, Tyriq hoists me against the wall, pushes the fabric to the side, and enters me.

I quiver at the intensity of his moan as he moves in and out of me.

"I needed to feel you, baby," he growls into my ear.

Sex had never been a necessity before. Beyond a nice self-massage or vibrating toy, I had deadened those wants and feelings a long time ago. Tyriq had not only given my desire a new life; he had sent it into attack mode.

"Yes," I moan and begin to work my hips against the length of him.

There is not a solitary joyful feeling in the world that I can compare to the overwhelming satisfaction of being connected to Tyriq.

He pumps into me, penetrating my gushing core.

"More!" I yelp.

I claw against his skin with hopes of gripping some of my sanity, trying to keep myself in one piece. He is going to shatter me in the best way, and holding myself together seems impossible.

My toes curl through the crushing waves of passion, rowing through my entirety with each pulsing push from his hips.

There is no safe place for me to touch, no piece of him that I can feel and return a sense of balance to myself. I clench his thick arms, scrape at his hard chest, and pull against his muscled back before cinching my legs tighter around his waist to let the powerful movement of his thighs glide into me.

Wild and rapid thrusts take the place of his smooth, teasing ones, and I lose track of physical time and space. Unsure of what dimension I belong to, I cry out to him.

Tyriq responds with a series of grunts. His force increases as he rears away, only to wedge his piece back into me over and over. I feel like he is either going to split me in half or reorganize my organs. Either way, I would happily gather together any lost body parts just to feel him like this at any time.

"Got damn, you got me addicted!" he stuttered hoarsely between persistent pushes in and out of me.

"All yours!" the feral cry rips from my throat as Tyriq grips my hips to press me impossibly closer to him. How much deeper could he go?

"Is this for me, Blade?" he grunts.

"Yes. All you," my whimper comes out between bouncing against Tyriq and over the sound of our skin slapping together.

I hold onto his flexing arms as tension mounts in me, and I can barely keep a grip on reality.

"Ty- I can't-." I let go and succumbed to the bliss. The release, the fall into indescribable pleasure, is magnificent.

"Oooh," I drag out the word through the rolls of ecstasy cascading within my body.

"All mine!" he growls before crashing into me a few more times and filling me with a release of his own.

"This is the best damn place under the sun," he pants into my neck. "Shit. You are the sun, and this is my fucking sunshine."

CHAPTER THIRTY-SIX

Tyriq

The sound of someone pounding at the door woke me up out of a near-comatose state. With Nailah still pressed against me and my eyes narrowly parted, I search the foreign room for any indication of time. Through my pleasure-induced haze, I find the glaring red numbers of a small alarm clock stashed away on a dresser. It had only been about fifteen minutes since I lost control again and let loose inside of Nailah. I have to get my shit together. In thirty-plus years, I had not ever been as careless with sex as I was with her. I had never gone raw with Briana or anyone else. Only Nailah. Just Nailah. Something about her made me want to protect and keep her forever—the forever kind of forever.

I look down at the beautiful woman and kiss her neck.

Nailah stirs some.

The banging at the door starts again. Who would be at Nailah's door after dark?

A loud clanging sound snaps me awake.

I hop up and slide into my pants.

Nailah pops up from the bed, the confusion of sleep and the situation apparent on her face.

"Are you expecting someone?" I ask, ready to war with any dude that thought he might have a chance.

"No one comes to my home, and definitely not after midnight," she begins slipping on her clothes.

"I'll get the door," she says, swiftly leaving the room and hopping down the stairs.

I am at her heels.

Before she can open the door, I jam a hand against it to keep it closed.

"Step back. I got it."

Nailah twists her face up at me.

"I know how to answer the door, Tyriq." The roll of her eyes is usually a turn-on, but not his time and not when her safety matters.

"Do you want to argue or let me be your man right now?"

The banging sounds again.

Nailah steps back. "Fine."

I yank open the door and then duck.

A flurry of photos stab at my face and body as I use a culmination of my athletic abilities to dodge them.

"The hell?" I swerve the large corner of a glossy color print.

Several scenarios had played through my mind in the moments before opening the door. I was ready to whoop the snot out of any fool who stepped up, including Nailah's father. No man was about to cause my girl any grief. I was unprepared for what stood on the other side of the door.

"You want this ugly bitch?" Briana yells.

Speaking doesn't slow down her antics. Briana continues to make a stack of color photos rain against me like Chinese stars in a fight movie.

Flickering to the ground, photos of Nailah and me during our adventures today and some weeks ago cover the pathway.

"Calm down, Briana. What the hell is wrong with you?"

I step outside through the storm of photos and close the door.

"I left my husband for you!" Briana yells as she finally runs out of photos.

"Get out of here with that. You left your husband for you," I counter.

Looking just as determined as ever, she doesn't back down.

"You lied to me." With her hands open, Briana pushes at my chest.

"Leave. We were over damn near two years ago."

"No." She tussled away.

"How did you get Nailah's address?" I asked. I hadn't even known where she lived.

"I had you followed by a private investigator!" Briana yells, alternating between jabbing her fingers into my chest and pushing at me.

I blinked to make sure that I heard her right. She had a private investigator follow me like I was her man.

"We are not together, Briana. You being here isn't healthy." I want to shake her, but stuff one hand against the other.

"Is everything alright?" I hear the front door shut.

I turn back to see Nailah walking toward the unnecessary and embarrassing fiasco.

The bright light on the back of her phone is shining, and Nailah does not seem rattled at all; she is even recording.

On the other hand, Briana goes off.

"Get your raggedy ass back in your little shoebox house because if you step in mine again, I will step in your ass," Briana warns, taking steps toward Nailah.

"Say hi to the camera first," Nailah teases. "Now all your fans can see how mean and desperate you are. Tyriq said he doesn't want you, but you're still out here begging."

With a steady arm, I intercept Briana's flying lunge to get at Nailah like I was taking a charge in a championship game.

"Let's go!" I bark at Briana.

"You are temporary, hoe! He built that house for me and my kids!" Briana yells.

I have to open the door with one hand and shove her wild ass into the car.

"Go to your home and to your kids," I remind her.

Against my hopes, Nailah had come closer and continued to record. That only kept Briana hostile.

Nailah is smiling and doing some sort of happy dance with her tongue out.

"I will hurt that bitch!" Briana screams. "I will kill you, dead hoe."

"Go home," I tell her again.

"Get rid of her fat ass, or I will, Tyriq!" Briana threatens too calmly for me not to believe her. Her cool voice and blank eyes shake me more than her words and antics. When she slams the car door and drives away, I know that this will not be the end.

Nailah makes it back into the house before I do, but not quick enough to lock me out.

"Wait!" I slid a leg into her closing front door and squeezed my body through to slip in.

"You can take your lying ass home too!" Nailah is all attitude.

"I don't want Briana. I don't know why her crazy ass came over here."

"I agree. Briana is crazy, and now she knows where I live. I don't want those kinds of problems, Tyriq. You and her have splashed my life across blogs and social media. You wanted her for years. How long will it be before you leave me to run back to her?"

I have not perfected hiding my thoughts, and my face shows all the shock I feel as Nailah continues speaking.

"You never said that she was the one that left you for an NBA player, but I figured it out. Bloggers have been putting you two together since her whole divorce started. Women don't do all this crazy shit for no reason," she fusses. "You must think I'm dumb."

I swipe a hand across my face and push out a breath. "I think that you're beautiful. I'm not trying to play you. Briana chose Naeem over me again years ago, and I was done. Over the last year, any time that he beat her ass, I patched her up."

Nailah stepped forward, and I could see her jaw ticking as she worked the back of her mouth.

"You mean the house that you bought for her and you had me all up in?" she asks through gritted teeth.

"I mean the house I bought to show her I am just as rich as Naeem. The house that she has never lived in."

Cautiously, I slide a hand down Nailah's arm. "Listen, Nai, that woman did not want me until someone worth having did. She wasn't worried about me until I found something real. She wants to push us apart. Are you going to let her do that to us, or are you going to pack some stuff and come with me before her crazy ass comes back or sends someone for you?"

What hurts me more than anything is that she does not even consider leaving with me. I had just made love to her raw, given her all of me, and she didn't even give me a three-second pause and think.

"Get out, Tyriq!" The sheer volume of her voice is a newer experience than her anger is for me, but I don't let it phase me.

I walked away and jogged up the stairs to her bedroom.

CHAPTER THIRTY-SEVEN

Nailah

Home is supposed to be a sacred place. In all of my couch surfing and city hopping, no one place had ever felt like it was mine. No place had ever felt like home until I moved into my condo. Tyriq and his little tag-along troll were working to disrupt that feeling.

Tyriq opens and closes my dresser drawers like he owns them.

"What the hell?" I yell. "Put my stuff back!"

"I'm not arguing with you, Blade," he huffs while stuffing a handful of t-shirts in the beach bag he had grabbed from my closet. "She threatened your life, and I take that seriously. Until I know you're safe, you are staying with me."

He is just as crazy as his ex is. Tyriq is big mad, but I don't give a damn. He can't tell me what to do or where to live. Briana threatened me and then showed up at my house to do it in person. She had already gotten into my office once. What other kind of foolery was she capable of? She could spread information that would end my relationship with Tyriq and my career.

"I'm not letting her run me out of my house. I will cut that bitch." Physically, Briana did not scare me. I grew up scrapping with girls, but I worried about what would happen to Tyriq, how his family would feel, and what would happen to them for being associated with a woman like me.

Tyriq stopped for a second.

"Nailah, if I don't believe anything else in this world, I believe that you would end Briana without a second thought. But I love your mean ass, and I will wrap you up and carry you out of here to keep you alive and from catching homicide charges."

Tyriq went back to picking up clothing, but I had to think about what he had just said.

"Tyriq?"

"I'm not playing with you, Blade. As a matter of fact, we can leave all this shit here. I'll buy you whatever you need."

Tyriq chucks the bag to the ground and heads toward me with determination in his eyes.

"Do you love me?" I ask.

My words end his trek. "What?"

Confusion twists his face, and I take a moment to recap.

"When you said that you love me. Is that true?"

"Hell yeah, I love you. I am in love with you, Nailah. I mean it. Come stay with me so I know that you're safe."

I nod.

It had been years since anyone had meant those words to me. I believed him.

"I'll go."

CHAPTER THIRTY-EIGHT

Tyriq

I stare at the woman that I professed my love to. In the morning light, she looks as beautiful as ever, but sitting at the small breakfast table in my kitchen, I wonder about her meal decisions.

"Butter and sugar?" I ask. "Why would you do that?" I had heard people talk about it, but I had never witnessed it with my very own two eyes.

Of course, Nailah uses her two eyes to roll at me.

"Grits with butter and sugar is the bomb." She smiles after a spoonful and gives a shimmy.

"Yeah, an abomination," I frown. "Salt and pepper, that's it. That's all you need."

Nailah shakes her head, "No," wholeheartedly. After staying with me for two days, she finally broke down and went grocery shopping. It was the first time I saw her doing things the way she would if we lived together.

"These sugar grits gave me all this ass that you like to grip onto, so quit talking about my meals."

"Touché. I do like to grip that ass." I slide a hand under the table to get a quick rub of her.

"Tyriq, it's time for you to leave. Don't you have an early appointment?"

I finish the egg whites and wheat toast Nailah had prepared for me, lean over to kiss her lips, and then pick up the to-go mug of green tea she had placed on the counter.

She asks, "Are you coming back for lunch? What time will you be back for dinner?" while walking me to the door.

I notice she doesn't refer to my place as home, and I want her to. After two days of Nailah being with me, I am certain that I want her to stay and that I would never let anyone harm her.

"I have a short day today," I explain. I have one follow-up and then a business meeting."

"The one with the arena owner, Mr. Strong?"

"Yep. If I can secure that towing contract with the arena, it would mean a huge revenue increase to Brother's T Auto."

"Well, I'm rooting for you, boo," she says, kissing my cheek. "My boss was okay with me taking another day to recover from my mysterious stomach virus, so I'll be here whenever you make it back."

I try not to lie to Nailah and tell her the truth whenever possible.

Besides Tyson leaving something anywhere that he stays for more than ten minutes, he has always been the sophisticated one. That's why he handles the business side mostly and makes sure that everything is running smoothly with our finances. Every once in a while, during the peak season of our auto care company, Tyson will fire up a tow and put in some hours at the shop. I was more surprised that he helped Nailah with Lucy than that Nailah's beloved car had a mishap.

"Hey, brother." We give each other a one-handed pat on the back. "Thank you for doing this with me."

In addition to being a financial whiz, Tyson had connections to the best investigators. He had studied to be a forensic accountant, so he knew people from college and his few years in the regular workforce.

"No problem. When you told me it was for the sweet little lady I met at the shop, I was more than happy to help."

"She's really special to me," I add.

"I can see. Anyone can tell."

"I'm trying to hold onto her. Trystan is already working on the restraining order for Briana. He's using the video that Nailah recorded as evidence," I explain.

Tyson frowns.

"You know that's going to come with some media backlash, right? Everyone already thought you two were an item."

"As long as she keeps away from me and mine, I don't care what the blogs say." I shake my head. "She's the one who had a show and a high-profile life."

Concern fills Tyson's dark eyes as he lifts his hand to chastise.

"Don't let it affect your business, though."

We order cups of coffee before continuing the conversation.

"Everything is on track so far. I chose to end my consulting contract with the team, but I will work with the arena as needed, even if it includes some basketball games."

"Seems like everything is coming together then."

I nod.

The waitress returns with our cups of coffee. Both Tyson and I thank her.

"That's why this is so important. The phone calls to Nailah have increased enough to affect my sleep."

Before we finish the conversation, a slender, hay-colored man with a thick crop of wavy black hair steps through the door.

"He actually made it," I mumble while standing.

He heads toward me and my brother.

Tyson steps away to sit at another table.

"Curtis Green?" I extend my hand when he nods.

"You the fella that's after my girl?" His eyebrow lifted, and his head tilted as he spread his legs and gripped his hands in a gangster stance.

I grin. Under normal circumstances, meeting a woman's father is a special occasion, but with the way that Nailah felt about Curtis, the outcome wouldn't matter much.

"I'm the man who loves a wonderful woman who happens to be your daughter."

We take a seat in the hardback red chairs around the rickety table.

"So, what is it that you want to talk about?" he asks. "I figured this wasn't no social call, and since I don't see Nailah anywhere, it ain't the reunion I asked for either."

Even with his appearances on television, Nailah's father had not been easy to contact, but Tyson had made it happen. He started with the number that Nailah had stored for him in her phone. That number turned out to be a landline belonging to a woman who lived in Greenville, TX.

"The question is, what do you want from her?" I redirect.

He is quiet for a moment, probably sizing me up. I have never been a thug, but I would do whatever I had to for Nailah.

"I never said that I wanted anything," he counters.

"Let's be honest here, Mr. Green." I lean forward. "You haven't contacted your daughter in over a decade, and then you pop up on a reality show and suddenly can't go another day without Nailah. There is a piece missing from the puzzle, and we need to put it all together before we leave here today."

He doesn't say anything; he just leans back and crosses his left leg over his right.

"Today's meeting can benefit the both of us," I explain. "Discontinue all contact with my lady; do what you've been doing for years wherever you have been doing it, and we can negotiate a price. I have my accountant with me, ready to make an offer."

I nod toward Tyson, who nods back.

Curtis Green wrinkles his face like a pack of fresh-fed elephants had slopped their way through.

"I don't want any money." A slow smile dawns on his face as he moves forward with a gleam in his eye. "I see that Nailah learned a trick or two from the ladies who took care of her. She caught herself a big fish."

I'm not entirely sure what any of that means, but I don't let him know how clueless I am about the majority of Nailah's past.

"What do you want then?"

"I want my girls to have their own money. I don't want them having to depend on no jokers like you," he spoke like a proud father who had always had his children's best interests at heart. "Jubilee got her own show now. The producers say if the two girls meet up, it can bring in a lot of views. The more viewers, the more opportunities for the girls to make money. Nailah is just as pretty as Jubilee, maybe even prettier, so I know she can make a lot of money that way, too."

Nailah's father reminded me of a pimp, but I keep that comment to myself. Maybe he is the old mack that Nailah mimics.

"And then you can benefit from the both of them, huh? Nailah is already independent. Did you even bother to think about what she wants?"

"Did you?" he chuckles. "I bet money that Nailah ain't send you here."

Curtis stands then.

"I need to see my daughter, and no matter what I have to do, I'll get her to see me."

I stand as well and move toward him. Tyson must have caught the drift because I see him on his feet in my peripheral.

"Keep your money schemes to yourself. Nailah doesn't want any of that. And I swear if you even make her frown, I will fuck you up on sight, father or not."

Curtis looks between Tyson and me and straightens his shirt.

"You've made your point." His face is flat and neutral. "She can reach me at Tea Cake's number when she changes her mind."

Curtis Green leaves the small café just as smoothly as he had strolled in.

"How'd it go?" Tyson asks.

I shrug. "He'll back off for a bit, but not for long. No money for now."

"Let's go handle shop business then."

CHAPTER THIRTY-NINE

Nailah

"I should have known that he wouldn't be ready." Terrence shook his head and followed me into the living room.

It was a week after I had bunked up with Tyriq, and things were still going well.

"Sorry. I don't go into the office until noon today, so I was at home."

Although Tyriq had initiated the in-the-shower and out-of-the-shower romp rounds we enjoyed, once he got all dressed up in his suit, he looked so good that my mouth required that I lick him. The licks led to him shedding the suit and sliding into me.

"He's almost ready." I give a sheepish smile.

Terrence and Tyriq were one step closer to securing the tow account for the arena and had a final meeting to review the numbers.

Since meeting Terrence, I had yet to see him smile. Tall and mellow, he did not dress like he had millions of dollars stashed away, but Tyriq assured me that his brother was nearly as wealthy as he was.

We sit, and I turn on one of my favorite sports commentary morning shows.

"You watch Taking Sides?" he asks.

"Every day. I don't always catch the games, but I always catch his commentary."

"MJ, Kobe, or Lebron?" Terrence asks with narrowed eyes.

"LeBron, of course," I respond adamantly.

"Oh, lil' sis, we need to talk."

Terrence shook his head and schooled me like I was indeed his little sister until it was time for him and Tyriq to leave.

Tyriq stepped out, fresh and fly, and I had to look at him twice.

He smiles and moves closer to me.

"I know that look." He nibbled at my ear. "Terrence can handle this with Trystan and Tyson if-"

I place a hand against his chest and take in a deep breath.

"Hey, you're ditching me again? You set this whole meeting up," Terrence cut in. "Can you two stop humping for one minute?"

Terrence walks away toward the door, and Tyriq pulls me in for one last hug.

"Let's go now!" Terrence demands when he finally turns to see Tyriq snuggled into me.

Tyriq laughs but lets me go, and I walk the brothers to the door.

When I pull up to the small aged home, I tamp down my excitement. Because of the picture I had found in Tyriq's home, I could look up the college cheer team and their names. Once I found out that the name of Tia's possible mother was Misty Trenton, I did some more research to find that she had been locked up for possession of drugs and, indeed, had given birth to a daughter named Tia Grant.

Stepping out of the car, I grin and am proud of my super sleuth work. When I knock on the door, a small brown woman with oak bark eyes answers.

"Hello, are you Jenny Trenton?" I ask. "I'm Nailah James, and I spoke with you over the phone about Tia Grant."

"Yes." She gave a warm smile. "Come in."

Her home is a picture of tidiness. She had a crocheted afghan on the back of the sofa, and she invited me to sit.

"I love your blanket." I touch the intricate stitches of the colorful yarn.

"Thank you. I made this one for Tia when she was born." She gazes at the blanket as though she can still see her granddaughter.

When Jenny looked back at me, the smile in her eyes faded, and she looked worn.

"Can you tell me about your daughter and Tia?"

She nods.

"Misty has always had a wild, defiant streak. She got into drugs and partying in college. When I got the call from the hospital that she had overdosed, I had no idea all of the things that had been going on with her." Her eyes drift to the ground as she rubs her palms across her thighs. "I brought Misty home and worked extra jobs to pay for rehab. She got clean. A year or so later, she met a nice young man, and he proposed."

She releases a pained sigh and closes her eyes.

"It sounds like she was on the right track," I encourage her to continue.

"She was. I am not sure if it was the pressure of moving out and starting a new life or the stress of planning a wedding, but something changed, and she wasn't the same anymore. Her moods were erratic. She was missing work and disappearing for days at a time. One day, she came home and told me she was pregnant and that she wanted to get clean. Her fiancé understood and stood by her until Tia was born."

Wrapping her arms around herself, the older woman gives me a half smile as her gaze catches mine.

"Why would he stay through the drug use and leave when the child is born?"

Jenny visibly swallows before frowning.

"Her fiancé was a very Caucasian fellow, as pale as they come. When Tia was born, there were no signs of him in her at all. He said that he could have stayed to help her recover, but he would not be able to raise a child that was supposed to be his but came from another man."

My heart breaks for little Tia. She did not ask to be born into any of this.

"How did you lose contact with her? Do you know who or where Tia's father is?"

Without a word, the embattled grandmother walked over to her bookshelf and returned with a black leather Bible. She spoke as she flipped through the pages.

"Misty stayed home after she had the baby. She worked hard at staying sober and working her new job until she saved up enough money to get a new apartment. She did well for two years. Then Tia started asking for a daddy and walked up to strange men who called them daddy. It bothered Misty because she loves Tia."

She looked up from her Bible. Then, she wanted me to understand that her child was not a monster and that Tia was loved.

I nod.

"Most mothers do the best that they can."

"She really tried. Last year, Misty lost her job. When I asked her about moving back in with me, she said that she could handle it. Six months ago, I noticed that things about her had changed, and Tia didn't look clean."

She blinks back a tear and clears her throat.

"They had been living in a car," Jenny continues, her voice strained. "She had tried to give Tia to her father, who is a famous game designer, but he wouldn't take her. I got Misty to come home with me one night, but they were gone the next morning. I didn't know where either of them were until you called."

I reach out to place a hand against hers.

"Tia was with a wonderful family in foster care, but they have moved out of state. She is in a group shelter now, so I was adamant about finding a family member."

"Thank you," Jenny sniffles, plucks a picture from the Bible, and places it in my hand. "This is the man that Misty says is Tia's father."

Staying professional in any situation is not as easy as it looks. I try to hold my face together and mute my expressions when I see a familiar smiling face plastered next to the pecan-colored woman named Misty.

CHAPTER FORTY

Tyriq

"So, you mean to tell me that your deranged ex-woman hunted her down, showed up on her doorstep to threaten her life, and she is still with you?"

I nod.

"That's some playa shit right there." Chad claps his hand against mine before we snap. One of the many handshakes we had perfected over the years. "I knew we were related somehow."

Terrence shook his head.

"You need to make sure that Nailah is safe from Briana and pick one, bro. Briana or Nailah."

"I vote for Nailah," Trystan added.

"Because you want a babysitter," Chad chimed in.

"Damn straight. I'm trying to get my wife back, and Crystal trusts Nailah with the babies."

"First off, there is no vote. Nailah is it, end of story," I state. "Second, you just need to hire a nanny because I plan to give her my own kids to worry about."

I love being with Nailah, and even though I hated being in that situation with Briana, it brought us closer.

"As a matter of fact, I hear the gate opening right now."

"You gave her the code?" Terrence asked in amazement. "I don't even have the code."

Chad shook his head. "Man, I can't believe we grew up in the same city right now. The way you're acting."

I chuckle at my cousin, taking back his earlier compliment. He can feel whatever he wants about me, but I plan to do whatever it takes to keep Nailah coming home to me.

"I had to grow up at some point," I rebut. "Nailah makes me feel ready for more."

"I hope so. Mom had her helping with the children's church and the bake sale on Sunday. Dad's been talking cigars and cognac with her," Terrence pointed a finger. "Don't let her get too comfortable if you don't plan to do right by her."

My eyebrows row together because I am unsure who I am looking at now.

"Whose brother are you? Hers or mine?" I question.

"I don't want to see her get hurt. She has some good basketball insight. I find that talent important in a family member."

"You got anything to add, Chad?" My family had never cared one way or the other about who I dated or even if I dated. Now, with Nailah, everyone has an opinion.

He shrugs.

"She fine as hell, so if you're going by who's rack-"

"Nailah. Hi, you're here," I cut into Chad's inappropriate description.

"Hey," she said, walking into the living room. "I didn't know you were having a guy's night."

Over the past two weeks, I woke up to Nailah's sweet face and went to sleep looking at the same. I had watched her cook, clean, pay bills, dress, and then, more importantly, undress. I had gotten the privilege of seeing every piece of her in every way imaginable and in other ways that some could not imagine. When her left eyebrow lifts slightly, her top lip folds over the bottom, and she starts blinking those long lashes like she is fanning a pharaoh, I know that something is weighing on her mind. The last time that I saw her make that face was when she was trying to figure out why a random auto-draft from her banking account had occurred and threw off her perceived bank balance.

Whatever the problem, if it causes her to make the *where-the-hell-did-my-money-go* face, then it must be terrible.

Nailah looked around the room as I stood to hug her.

My brothers and cousin waved and said hello in chorus.

"Hi, fellas. It's good to see you all." The words skate out of her lips as normal, but her face is stuck in worry mode.

"I'll be right back," I tell my family before placing a hand in the center of Nailah's back and guiding her to my bedroom.

"Again?" I hear Terrence fuss as I leave. "Did he really just walk out on me again for real?"

When we reached the bedroom, I shut the door and kissed her mouth. I needed to figure out her issue, but I could not do that while my mind focused on the taste of her lips.

I pull away first and almost decide to undress her when the frown returns.

"Nailah, what's going on with you?" I ask.

Her head drops, and the more she fidgets with her nails, the more unnerved I become. Several scenarios flash through my mind. The first is that she had done something wrong. Had she cheated on me? Had Nailah done something with another man and now had a guilty conscience? My gut dropped at the thought. Could karma be that harsh? I had finally given my heart to someone, and now she was about to smash it.

"Nailah, talk to me," I encourage.

When she looked at me, I knew that she had not done anything shady but was playing tug of war with another decision in her mind.

"I need to tell you something, and I am not sure if I can. I think it's important that you know because you should know, and it involves your family and their futures. I believe families should stay together, and fathers need to be a part of their lives. Children should know their parents, and little girls should have their daddy, and-"

Nailah continued to ramble about family, but the blood rushed to my ears and prevented me from hearing more.

What the hell? I had joked with Nailah and even my brother about giving her a baby, but shit. Standing there watching the woman rattle on nonsensically about family and remembering a few of our reckless nights, I figure that I must have slipped a baby in her.

The room is a little wobbly, but an overwhelming sense of pride settles over me, and I jerk the woman that I love into my arms for a hug.

"I'm going to be a daddy?" I question while hugging her tight to me.

The shriek of terror that escapes Nailah is nearly deafening as she scrambles out of my arms.

"Shit, no!" she yells. "I'm not having any kids."

Now I was confused, frustrated, and low-key hurt that she looked so terrified at the thought of having my baby.

"Nailah, spit it out. What the hell is going on?" I boomed.

"Chad is! It's Chad!" she nearly yelled.

"You fucked Chad?" I yell. I am going to kill him!

Before I can make it out of my bedroom, Nailah is on my back.

"No. Tia is Chad's. Tia that was left at your clinic, her mom's name is Misty, and Tia is Chad's daughter."

I feel the rage draining from my body as I turn to look at Nailah.

"I was nervous about telling Chad, and I know that I'm not supposed to tell you because the information is confidential. I just know how important family is, and Tia reminds me of myself. I want her to win. I want her to get her father and be a part of this beautiful family. The family that I never got to experience," she says.

"That trick around here lying again?" Chad yelled as he walked into the room.

He was angry. My playful cousin wore a scowl so deep that it looked like his face would crack.

"What are you doing back here?" I ask.

"We heard yelling and played rock-paper-scissors to see who would check on y'all. I wasn't sure if it was the good or the bad kind of screaming. I lost," he explained.

"Chad." Nailah approached him cautiously. "Tia's grandmother seemed pretty sure that you were the father."

Chad shook his head.

"She had a fiancé. I found that shit out around the time she stole my damn wallet, shoes, and Ninja Blender. He called me a few days later once he found my wallet in their apartment. He explained that she had begun using drugs and doing strange things. That baby ain't mine. She already tried to leave her with me once."

I was shocked still.

"You knew it was possible for you to have a kid running around here, and you didn't bother to check? That little girl sitting with strangers could be yours, and you left her with a crackhead?"

My brain was having a difficult time processing the crazy notion that my childish cousin possibly had a child that he was refusing to claim.

"I stay protected. I ain't ever had a slip-up, and definitely wouldn't have one with a random chick."

I throw my hands in the air.

"Of course, Tia can't be yours then because condoms are fail-proof," I respond.

"Chad," Nailah cut in. "Her fiancé was white, and Tia is just as brown as you are. She has eyes like Mali and your mom. Would you at least be interested in a DNA test? At least we can rule out the possibility."

I look between my mute cousin and Nailah.

"Hell yeah, he's interested," I answer for him.

"Fuck that! She's not mine," Chad responds. "I'm not about to even entertain that shit."

"For real? You know what-" I stop and turn completely toward Nailah, excluding him from the conversation. "A DNA test tells us if she's related to me. If she's my family, I'll take her."

I feel Chad step toward me, his chest bumping into my arm. At six feet six inches, I am four inches taller than he is and much more muscular.

"You about to the take the word of this-"

I spin around to glower at Chad, effectively cutting off his words.

"You don't want to go there," I interject before he could call Nailah out of her name.

Chad pinched at his nose before looking me up and down.

"That pussy got you tripping, fam," he said. "You out here ditching your brothers about losing your job and taking her word over family. You were trying to marry a bitch that was already married and had dissed you on national television. I'd beat your ass, but you're already a joke."

I step closer to my cousin.

"You the joke, muthafucka. Quit running around here acting like you're twelve. Just because you make kid games don't mean you got to be one." I point at him. "Your dumb ass got a whole possible child that you let get lost in the system. You a chump for not even trying to step up and find out the truth."

I knew that Terrence and Trystan entered the room at some point because I felt Terrence separating the two of us.

"Let's go, Chad," Trystan says, walking him out.

"What the hell is going on?" Terrence asks.

CHAPTER FORTY-ONE

Nailah

"Say thank you," Regina demands as she points her sharp teal nail at me.

Walking through the Galleria mall with Regina had been more difficult than I thought. Nearly every male's head turns, and every eye follows when we pass by. Regina is amazingly gorgeous, and she knows it. To make matters worse, because of Jubilee's popularity and our resemblance to each other, both of us were getting catcalls and grins.

"Why would I thank you?" I ask, but then I get sidetracked by a store display. "Oooh. Let's go in here."

Back in Brook Bonnet, there was a ten-store strip mall for shopping and that's all. In Dallas, there were so many places with stores that every time we went shopping, I foud something new.

"Lingerie? Naughty girl," Regina chides. "This is why you should thank me."

I walk over to a black lace number.

"Why? Are you buying this nightie for me?" I ask.

"Nope," Regina scrunched her face. "You should be buying me gifts for taking you to the Gala that brought you and Tyriq together. Of course, I want to be your Maid of Honor and Godmother to the first baby."

"It's not even that serious."

"Didn't his momma add you to her weekly prayer line conference calls?"

"Yes, but she prays for everyone."

"I didn't even know your heathen ass knew how to pray," She laughed. "Did you or did you not send his father Cohiba cigars and a bottle of Remy Martin 1738?"

"They were on sale," I refute. "He was so kind to me the first time I visited."

"Of course," Regina continues. "So, the fact that you have a bag of baby clothes in your hand for his niece is just a coincidence?"

"Clearly, I cannot pass up a good sale, Regina, and the clothes are just so itty bitty and cute."

Regina shook her head. "Just admit that you're gone over this man and his family."

"Maybe I'm not," I add. "Maybe I want to explore new possibilities."

"What?" Regina, who is constantly flitting about, stops cold to stare at me.

I shrug.

"You're always talking about all of the ballers that you meet." I hang up the nightie. "He's the first guy that I have really dated since I got here. Maybe I should test the waters a little more?"

"Test the water?" Regina shuffles close to me and places a hand on my forehead as though she is checking my temperature. "Girl, the well is dry, the pool has been drained, and drought-like conditions lie ahead for snatching up a good man," Regina warns. "Besides, you aren't me."

"What do you mean by that?" I ask, feeling slightly offended.

"I didn't mean it that way. I'm not talking about your looks," Regina clears up. "You know you look good. I don't do ugly friends. I mean that you are a good person, and you deserve some happiness for once."

"Thank you," I tell my friend. Happy is a foreign concept that I hoped to be more acquainted with.

When my phone vibrated, and I fished it out of my purse, I knew for certain that my dream of happiness with Tyriq would never come true.

"Damn," swiping through the photos make my stomach drop.

CHAPTER FORTY-TWO

Tyriq

Aunt Pat called a family meeting. It was actually more of a family intervention. Trystan had let it slip that Chad was possibly denying a child that belonged to him. Tyson was out of town again checking on the Houston branch, but the rest of the crew, the brothers, plus Mali and Cairo, were gathered in the family room of my aunt's house.

"I'm going to tell all of you just like I told Trystan's flipping lips," Chad glares at each one of us as he speaks, "I met Misty after one of Tyriq's college games. We hooked up a couple of times over the years. The last time I saw her was nearly five years ago."

"And Tia is four," I interject.

"Just because the timeline works out doesn't mean that it was me." Chad shakes his head. "Anyway, I ran into her at a club. I noticed that she was acting wild that night, but I figured that she was a little drunk. We had fun, and the next morning, she was gone along with half of the valuable stuff in my apartment and my wallet."

Aunt Pat holds onto her cross as she grunts a sigh of disapproval.

"I thought that I raised you better than that, Chad." Aunt Pat closed her eyes as though the sight of her son made her head hurt. "You should remember how hard it was for me raising you alone. I know you are enjoying your life, but if there is even a remote possibility that this little girl is yours, then we need to find out through a test."

"That's what I'm saying. It's not possible," Chad responds with a shake of his head.

I hear my mother begin to weigh in, but a random text from an unknown number steals my attention.

Tapping the screen, I opened the message to a picture of Nailah that had to be at least a decade old. Her hair is much shorter in the picture than it is now, with stacked and layered curls. Her face is slimmer in the picture but rounder. Her eyes are hollow and even slightly sunken. She doesn't look like the beautiful woman that I hold every night, but I have never seen a flattering mugshot.

Suddenly, all the phones in the room are vibrating, singing, or dinging. One by one, my family members find their communication devices, and their faces drop. The words that accompany the picture request that we turn the television to a specific channel to find out more.

My mother gasps. "Did you know about this?"

I shake my head, "No. Nailah never mentioned going to jail before, and I never asked her specifically about it."

"Well, I guess we should turn on the TV," my father imparts. "The text says to watch at six o'clock. That's two minutes away."

Aunt Pat narrows her eyes in Chad's direction.

"And that doesn't mean that I'm done with you, Chad," she huffs. "You are getting tested with this child even if I have to swab you myself while you sleep."

Cairo turns on the large flat screen and changes the channel.

Quickly, I forward the picture to Nailah.

> **Me:** *What the hell? Call me.*

> **Nailah:** *I'm sorry. I should have told you.*

> **Me:** *Call me.*

My phone rings, and I step out of the family room and into the kitchen.

"What is this mugshot about, Nailah?"

Silence. Her answer doesn't come quickly enough for me.

"How did you forget to mention that you were arrested? Who the hell found this, and why didn't you tell me?"

"I'm sorry, Tyriq," she sniffled, and ended the call.

"Tyriq, get in here!" my mother yells.

When I walk into the room, I have to blink twice to make sure that I am seeing the screen correctly.

"They are just running the teaser now," my mother stated. "They'll play the interview after the break."

"Who was that man sitting with Briana?" Trystan asked.

"I've seen him before," Aunt Pat interrupts. "He's been on the show Jubilee in the Night. That's Jubilee's father."

My chest tightens, Briana teaming up with Curtis was pure havoc.

"He's Nailah's father, too," I explained. "Until the show aired, Nailah thought that he had died."

"This is bad," Mali grumbled close to me. "This is really bad."

"What could this be about? And how does she have a mug shot?" my mother asked.

My eyes are glued to the television screen, watching the flickering commercial scenes change. I just stood there, waiting for the firing squad to return and hail bullets into my love life.

"I don't know. I called her, and she apologized. That's all I know."

The entertainment news show returns with a small woman sitting in a soft armchair across from Briana and Curtis.

"Hello, I'm Trinity Taylor, and this is your sip for the day, where we give you all the hottest tea with receipts on your favorite celebrities and entertainers."

Trinity smiled brightly as the camera panned from her face to Briana and Curtis sitting in identical armchairs.

"Today, we have Briana Matthews and Curtis Green. Let's pour right in. Recently, Briana, you've been in the news for your impending divorce to Naeem Matthews," the reporter states with giddy excitement. "And Mr. Green-"

"Call me Curtis," he interrupted.

"Curtis, you're the father of the international supermodel Jubilee."

He nods while looking directly into the camera with an eagle-proud smile.

"What do you and Briana Matthews have in common?" the reporter asks.

Curtis Green clears his throat, leans forward, and pokes out his chest for extra dramatic effect. He and Briana are a perfect match.

"Most people don't know this, but I have another daughter."

The interviewer nods. "Alright."

"I got a job on an oil rig out of the city," Curtis continued. "My daughter's mother was locked away, and I had to leave her with the only people I knew that would take her in."

Curtis clears his throat again.

"Who did you leave her with?" Trinity asks, leaning her head to the side with mock concern.

"They were in the business." The last few words of his statement are mute. Curtis looked at the camera and then back at the host. "Can I say that?"

Trinity gives a slight chuckle.

"No. We'll edit." She smiles. "So, who did you leave her with again?"

"Well, they were prostitutes," he says with a nod.

My mother gasps.

Aunt Pat raises her cross to the air, "Oh, Lord."

The men look at me.

I close my eyes to distance myself from the train wreck happening before me. I need to know, but I can't look.

On television, Trinity continues her corrects Curtis before continuing her questioning.

"They're called sex workers, and I'm sorry that you had to do that. Leaving your daughter must have been very difficult for you."

I open my eyes then. I didn't care if it was hard for him or not. I only cared about Nailah.

"How does this relate to Mrs. Matthews here?" the interviewer continued.

"I can answer that," Briana piped in. "His daughter, Nailah, not only went after my husband but turned around to use the man that had helped me through the abuse."

I winced. I physically felt the venom in Briana's words and how they were intended to hurt the woman that I cared about so deeply.

"And I'm really sorry about that," Curtis piped in. "When I saw what happened, I reached out to apologize to Mrs. Matthews. Nailah didn't have a momma. I was gone, and all she had was those night ladies to look up to."

"Your daughter was even arrested for being a sex worker, correct?" Trinity asks.

Curtis nods before they splatter Nailah's mug shot across the screen.

"I think we've seen enough," I hear my mother's voice, but it is distant.

Suddenly, the screen goes black, and everyone is facing me.

"It's alright, son. We'll get through this together," my father says.

"Yeah," Chad adds. "That's fucked up what her father did."

Aunt Pat doesn't even bother to chastise Chad for the curse. "I wasn't too sure about her at first, but once I got to know her, I realized that she is just as sweet as she wanna be and got a good praying spirit."

I look over to Mali, who is tapping the screen of her cell phone and probably texting my new ex-girlfriend.

Chad was right. I was brainless over Nailah, and I was embarrassed on national television in front of my family again.

CHAPTER FORTY-THREE

Nailah

Nothing feels right, nothing tastes right, and I don't want to move. I don't want to do anything but lay still in my sadness. I fell for it. I fell for him. There was never a verifiable scenario in my entire life that worked out for someone in love. Never. Not one. I wasn't any different.

The day after the crazy interview aired, my supervisor called me into the office and fired me for lying on my job application. When I explained that I had the record expunged and that a third party ran a background check before they hired me and found nothing, they threw a morality clause at me. I was sixteen when they raided Dolly's home. The police arrested everyone in the house for the same thing- prostitution. I just lived there.

Tyriq had completely shut me out. He didn't change the gate code or locks on the house. He just never came home. Every day, I sat there waiting for him to walk through the door, jumping at every sound that resembled a gate, car, or door. He left my texts as 'read' with no response. My phone calls went straight to voicemail, and I felt like a piece of me broke with each unanswered communication.

Regina came by, required that I wash my ass, and took me to meet Mali at a spa for a massage, manicure and pedicure. She knows the owner of the shop and gets a discount for posting her visits on social media sites. We get the VIP treatment, along with a private room and three attendants for our services.

There were times in my life when I didn't know if there would be food or lights, a sane parent in the home, or a police raid. Sitting next to two women who uplifted and supported me was almost overwhelming. Through the bullshit and lies, Regina and Mali were still there, trying to make me smile.

"What is that look about?" Regina waggles her finger across the air. "This is a got damn happy zone. Fix your face."

"Right now," Mali chimed in. "No crying. We are happy, we are healthy, and we are whole. Say it with me."

Mali had been sending me affirmations daily, and if I didn't appreciate her trying to look out for me, I would bop her in the head.

I swallowed back the lump in my throat that threatened to release tears.

"I've cried more this week than I have in years," I explained while swiping at my face.

"I hate that. Get it out. I swear, he may be my cousin, but I will fight him about you." Mali sat forward in her chair like a fed-up mother who was about to grab a switch. "You are not about to shed another tear over his tantrum-throwing toddler ass today."

"I'm not crying about him," I chuckle. "It's about this."

I point between myself, Mali, and Regina.

"Nailah, I told you I'm not into that freaky shit," Regina warned.

"Everybody don't want you, Regina. I'm happy to be here with you ladies. Because of where I lived and who I lived with, I didn't have many friends. Girls assumed I wanted their dusty boyfriends, and guys assumed I was easy to get with. Everybody in town already knew I was the daughter of a pimp and a crazy woman that lived at the hoe-house."

Regina rested a hand on my arm.

"I wish you would have told me. No matter what happened, I'm here for you."

Mali agrees.

The women providing our manicures nod at us as they get up and gather their things.

"Thank you." I smile at the woman and pull a cash to tip from my robe. We had started with massages.

"Sit still to dry," one woman imparts in heavily accented English.

"I appreciate you not judging me. I worked hard to leave that town, get a degree, and help people," I explain. "I kept myself in the background and stayed away from relationships because I didn't want to be associated with my past."

"But none of that changed it," Mali said kindly. "Ignoring it or running from situations don't change what they are."

"I know that now," I smile. "And now that it's out there, I feel freer. It's like a weight has been lifted."

Before I can divulge more about my past, a soft knock on the door interrupts my confessional.

"You have a visitor," one of the workers announces while grinning as she steps in.

The door opens wider, and I am at a loss for words.

It is like looking into a mirror. I could tell that we looked alike when she was on TV, but seeing her standing in front of me, I didn't know what to say. I scratch at my palm.

"Hello, Nailah," Jubilee's eyes sweep the floor.

"Oh, hell no," Mali leaped out of her chair in attack mode. "Your raggedy daddy has already done enough."

"I'm sorry. I'm not here for that, I promise. I want to speak to Nailah, that's all." she says.

"Your father made that a problem," Regina adds.

"I had nothing to do with hopping on air to talk about her, I promise. I didn't know that he would do that, Nailah," she said to me around Regina and Mali who were acting as my bodyguards. "He told me about you and who he left you with when I met him. I made sure that editing removed anything referring to Sugar Dolls and what happened."

"It's alright, ladies," I say. "This is a part of facing my past."

Jubilee took a seat on one of the free nail tech stools.

"Don't try no slick shit," Regina pointed a finger at her.

Jubilee raised her hands in mock surrender. "I come in peace."

"Why are you here?" I asked.

"I want you to know that I was not a part of the scheme that Curtis had to get us both on reality television and build a Kardashian-like empire. Once I found him, we talked about family. I told him that I wanted to meet you. He said that you wouldn't talk to him and that your boyfriend threatened him to stay away."

I look at Mali for confirmation, but she only shrugs her shoulders.

"After I saw the interview, Curtis explained that he wanted to get you a reality show as well and that if sex worked for other girls, it could work for you, too."

"But nowhere in his genius plan did he even ask if I wanted a reality show," I counter.

"That's exactly what I said. Television life isn't for everyone, and you have to be a certain kind of person to just throw all of your dirty laundry in the air for the whole world to see and comment on. He shouldn't have put your business out there like that, and if you didn't want to meet with him or me, he should have respected that."

I should probably assume that she is evil like my father. I should probably run in the opposite direction, but something about Jubilee made me waddle my wet toes over to her and hug her neck.

"Thank you," I say. "I appreciate you stopping by to explain that."

"I wanted to meet you so bad," her shaky voice revealed her nervousness, and I feel her tears hit my shoulder.

"Okay, I'm here," I tell her, "and I'm glad you're here."

I scoot back to my chair.

Jubilee wipes her eyes.

"Good. I wasn't sure how this would turn out. I stalked your social media page, and I saw the post about you being at this spa. So here I am hoping that you accept me because I really want to know you, and I really hope that we can be close because I don't have anyone else, and the father that I just found is an asshole." Jubilee rambles.

"It's ok," I interject. "I'm still pissed at Curtis, but none of this is your fault. I'm glad you found me, and I'm glad at least one good thing can come from this."

I had stopped watching her show the night that my father debuted, but I'm glad she's interested in building a sister bond with me .

"Thank you." Jubilee walked over to hug me this time. "Curtis promised to introduce us, and when he finally admitted that you wouldn't speak to him and that your boyfriend had made it clear that you did not want a relationship with him-"

"That part," I interrupt her. "Are you saying that your father met with some man who threatened him if he didn't leave me alone?"

"Not some man, your man." Jubilee looks certain. "I saw on the blogs that you're dating this guy that used to play basketball with Jermaine Timmons and that crazy ass Naeem."

"Yeah, that sounds right."

Jubilee pulled out her phone.

"Curtis and I went to meet him at a café off in nowhere. Curtis was the only one who went in. I waited in the car when we didn't see any women in the diner."

Jubilee slides her finger across her phone and then pushes it near my face.

"I didn't know what was about to go down, so I snapped a picture of the two in a restaurant with my phone."

I looked at the picture on the screen, see Tyriq sitting across the table from my father, and knew without a shadow of a doubt that it was time to leave. I had done too much, caused him too much embarrassment.

***

Over the years, I had perfected the art of packing my clothes in a pinch. With the help of Regina, Mali, and Jubilee, it took less than an hour to put everything that I had brought to Tyriq's home in a bag. The ladies helped me get all my belongings back into my condo with only a few disgruntled comments. Then Regina made a store run for all things that involved sugar and an alcohol percentage greater than five.

By the time she returned, Mali and I were laughing with Jubilee as though we were all old friends.

"Let's get this party started!" Regina yelled as she walked through the door, holding a bottle of something potent and bags of junk.

Jubilee laughed.

"I like you guys already. Thank you for letting me crash your girl's day," she smiled. "I wasn't trying to cause a problem between you and your man. I wanted to meet you."

Regina hands everyone a glass, opens the bottle, and makes her rounds pouring.

"Stop apologizing. It's alright. It was time for me to come back home anyway. I was only staying with Tyriq temporarily, because of Briana. Now that everything is out in the open, Briana has nothing to hold over my head. Tyriq has no reason to keep me in his house.

Quiet invades the room, and the ladies look between each other and then back to me.

"What?" I ask.

"I know my cousin is messed up for ignoring you, but I really hope you two work it out," Mali speaks after taking a long sip.

Both Regina and Jubilee let out a deep breath.

"You too?" Regina adds. "I didn't want to say anything because I was trying to have your back, Nailah, but damn girl, he is a good guy. Give him some time to process the information. I think he'll come around."

"I know that I'm biased as hell because he's my cousin. Keep trying to talk to him about it; don't give up."

I look at the freaking traitors around me and wonder when their loyalty disappeared.

"You need to tell him that," I fuss. "I've been blowing up his damn phone and waiting in his damn home alone for a week now."

Jubilee, who I was just beginning to like, chimed in.

"My mom kept me away from Curtis for a long time because she was worried about his motives," she added. "Because of my daddy issues, I've chosen the wrong man over and over again. Don't lose a great guy because of a horrible one."

The tears come so quickly that I'm not able to stop them. I collapsed into an ugly cry.

"Oh shit, we broke her," Regina acknowledged.

Through my watery eyes, I saw her move from the loveseat to comfort me.

"I can't be with him," I blubbered through deep sobs and hitched breath.

Regina picks up my glass and inspects it while Mali speaks.

"Nailah, what are you talking about, honey?"

"Did one of y'all put something in her drink? She sounds drugged," Regina added.

I take a deep breath, try to reign in some of my crazy so that I can stop scaring my friends and start from the beginning.

"My past keeps running into my future, and I can't do that to Tyriq. I know he won't take me back." I shake my head. "I embarrassed him. I kept the truth from him. Everyone knows my secret. How would he ever be able to go anywhere with me? I can't keep pulling him down into my mess."

"I disagree, but the more important issue is you," Regina says, patting my hand.

"Yeah," Mali adds. "Were you hurt while you lived with them?"

I looked them both in the eye to let them know that their profession was not mine.

"I didn't have to take any clients. I just lived there," I explain.

Mali released a burst of air. "Good. I didn't know where this story was going."

"I was their housekeeper, bartender, cook, and secretary. That's how I know so much about cigars and alcohol. I served while men waited their turn or relaxed after. I never ever took a client."

All three women nod.

"We got your back," Regina assures. "I admired you before, but you are my hero now."

"Yes," Mali agreed. "I am your friend first, so if you and Tyriq don't work out, I will still be here to pop bottles and eat good food with you."

I give a watery grin.

"And if you don't mind, I would like to be there with you when you talk to Curtis," Jubilee adds.

"Thank you," I choke out. Streams of tears cloud my eyes as the women all move in to embrace me at once.

I have never been this surrounded by love.

Regina is the first to release me. I notice her dabbing at her eyes as she sniffles.

"Enough of this mushy mess. What are you about to tell Dr. Lewis because I refuse to let you break up with him over some bullshit?" Regina asks.

Both she and Mali picked up the bottle and refilled the glasses.

"I agree with Regina," Jubilee adds, grabbing the bottle.

"Smart girl." Regina lifts her glass to my sister as Jubilee continues her explanation.

"Good love is hard to find, and that man was ready to fight for you in that café. I wish I had someone who cared about me like that."

I shrug my shoulders.

"Love is a fleeting emotion, a feeling just like hot or cold. He may have loved me once, but-"

"Not for my cousin. This man has said those words to all of two women before." Mali plopped her hands on her hips as she lifted from the couch. "First was Sheila Tompkins because she snuck him into the house and let him get it. The second was Briana."

Hearing Briana's name makes me scowl.

Mali waves her hand across the air.

"Don't even worry about her. Once Tyriq makes up his mind about something, you don't have anything to worry about. He'll be back after he mends his ego."

"What if he's made up his mind about leaving me?" I caution. "He won't even acknowledge me now. After fighting so hard to be with me, he won't even say a word to me."

Mali continued like I hadn't said a word.

"And I saw how he was looking at you when you were holding that baby. He ain't ever looked at a woman like that. Never."

"How do you feel about him? If you care about him for real, then you need to be honest with him and fight for your love."

"I think-" I pause and accept the flutters. "I know that I love him too."

CHAPTER FORTY-FOUR

Nailah

When I get to The Brother's T to return the car, the urge to cry hits me all over again. I have never been messed up over a man.

Although I had turned down the volume on my phone, the device began to vibrate loudly in my bag.

My head pounded, my heart ached, and I was alone still. Despite the pep talk from my girls, Tyriq was still a no-show, and it was time for me to move on. Regina had already started hinting about guys that she called placeholders.

I refused to answer. It was either Mali calling to talk shit about Briana, Regina calling to offer me a new man, or Jubilee calling to apologize more. I can't bring myself to speak with any of them.

No one had ever cared for me as much as Tyriq had except Dolly. She had given Lucy to me so I could leave Brook Bonnet.

Terrence is sitting on the sofa in his office, yelling at a basketball game when I enter.

Nearly forgetting my sadness, I rushed in to check the score. When my team scores a three-pointer, Terrence and I high-five.

"Hell yeah!" I shout. "I forgot the game was on."

"You can watch it with me if you want."

I rear back.

"You really want to be around me? You're not avoiding me like your brother?"

He looks a lot like Tyriq when he shakes his head.

"Not at all. Come sit. Just me and you, little sis."

We watch the game together and drink a beer. We didn't say much to each other, just sat on the sofa and chilled.

When the game is over, I hand him the keys to the Lexus.

"You know Tyriq bought this for you. He paid our cousin for it already. The car is yours, free and clear."

"Nah. I love Lucy," I tell him. "He can keep this one."

He laughed.

"I'll have him save it for you," Terrence winked.

It irritated me that no one believed that Tyriq and I were really finished.

"Not you, too?" I asked.

"I'm staying out of it." Terrence rubbed the back of his neck. "Even though I know this can't be the end of the road for you two."

"I don't know. I really feel like my past has scared him away."

"More like your mug shot." he joked.

I pushed his shoulder, but he didn't move at all.

"I'm just saying," he smiles. "You looked pretty rough."

"It's a mug shot, and it was a long time ago."

"Lucky for us all, you got better with time," Terrence added.

"Oh, but you didn't?" I jab back.

Terrence placed a hand over his heart.

"You hit me hard, sis."

The laughter floated away, and silence settled. I took a moment to bask in the beauty of the sky around us.

"What happened back then?" Terrence asks.

I think back to that day, to that time, when I had never felt so alone. Standing there with Terrence, who felt like the brother I never had, I knew it was time to tell my truth to someone.

"By some miracle, one of the star football players decided that he wanted to date me or at least hang out with me at the house. It was called Sugar Dolls, and it was a huge ranch-style house with six bedrooms set away on the edge of town," I say. "One day, after about a month of him coming over to the house and kissing me, he invited me to come to his house. When I got there, he wasn't alone."

I stopped because this was the first time that I had spoken the story aloud since speaking to the police.

"Because of where I lived and who I lived with, they um-" I plucked at my nails and swallow back some of my emotion. "They all took advantage of me, stuffed a collection of one hundred dollars in my bra before throwing me in the back of someone's station wagon and dropping me off at Sugar Dolls."

"Shit," Terrence rubs a hand over his face. "You know any of those little fuckers' names? I got a few words or bullets for them."

I was not expecting that response from Terrence. When I was younger, everyone had assumed that I was the problem. I was the temptress. I was immoral. There was no accountability for the guys.

"I know who they are. Most of them are still there, but small-town life is different. Their parents still have power, and now so do most of them." I close my eyes to explain. "One of the boys involved even felt guilty enough to tell the coach what happened. Because they were headed to state for the playoffs, they wanted to keep everything under wraps."

"That's bullshit."

"You know Texas football is nothing to play with." I try to shrug off some of the returning hopelessness that I felt. "The police, even the ones who were frequent customers, raided the place, saying that we had been corrupting the community. They made sure to arrest me, too. I was told that if I wanted to walk away from the jail cell, I couldn't tell a soul about what happened."

He nods as though he understands, but how could he? I still have trouble believing that people would be so horrible.

"I was young, and I took a plea. None of the football players involved got in trouble, but everyone that I knew and loved went to jail because of me." I rub a hand down my neck. "Later on, I got my record expunged. There shouldn't have been any record of it. I'm not even sure how anyone got ahold of the information."

Terrence looks off into the sky before looking back at me.

"Thank you for sharing that with me." Terrence shoves one hand into the other and fists them. "I'm not going to lie, I want to go shoot every last one of the people involved, but I know that won't change shit."

I should have been mortified at his words, but it felt good to have someone on my side, to have people who cared about my well-being.

"Thank you for wanting to commit homicide on my behalf." I give a halfhearted chuckle. "I've been to trauma counseling, and I am at peace with that part of my life. I should have told Tyriq about all of this, but I didn't know how. I just wanted it to stay where it was. I wanted to have a fresh start without all of that, but I realized that no matter what, it is a part of me."

"I understand that." He gives a comforting glance. "My wife died when I was twenty-three. Part of the money that I used to start this place came from her life insurance. I haven't dated a woman in seven years."

My eyes nearly fall out of my face because I spread my eyelids so wide. Terrence was an attractive guy, and staying single that long had to be a feat.

"I've been thinking that it's time to live more." His shoulders slumped, and his sullen eyes drifted away. "Eventually, I'll have to let someone in so that I can get something out of this life. I want to move forward."

It must have been very hard for Terrence to lose the woman that he planned to spend the rest of his life with. Even though Tyriq was still living, I had lost him. We would never get to be together.

"We all have our things that we carry." I place a hand on his shoulder. "Any woman would be lucky to have you."

Terrence gave a quick smirk, the closest thing that I had seen to a smile since knowing him.

"Thank you for that, Nailah. It's going to be hard to put myself back out there, but you've inspired me."

"What? Me?" I point to myself. "How have I inspired you?"

"I can tell how much you care about my brother, and I also know that he had to fight to get you there. I see how good it is for the both of you."

"And how is that?"

"You finally get the care you deserve, and Tyriq gets the loyal companionship he needs. Anyone that would hold onto a car like Lucy has got to be dedicated."

"You got jokes?" I tap his shoulder with my fist.

"Nailah, I'm going to say something, and I don't want you to think that it's because Tyriq is my brother."

I roll my eyes the long way. I knew where the conversation was heading.

"Go for it." I accept that he will probably give a speech about my failed relationship, too.

"I can't be with the only woman that I loved for years." His foot taps against the concrete as he talks, and his eyes wander over the street. "You and Tyriq still have time to make this work. Think about it. I'll talk to my brother, and if he lets you walk away, then he's an idiot."

My eyes cloud with emotion, and I want to punch Terrence reminding me of his brother again.

"That's the problem. Tyriq is really smart and really great. Your entire family, even Chad, is awesome."

The tears rise in my eyes again. I didn't want to like them. I didn't want to care about Tyriq and his family. Caring is a burden. Caring requires vulnerability, which ultimately leads to hurt.

"As a family, we like you too." Terrence nods. "One thing my family does well is stick together."

When I had been at my best, my mother, my father, and my surrogate mother left me behind. Since this perfect family knew about my awful past life, they would leave me, too.

"I can't-" the words strain in my throat, and my eyes cloud. "What is it about this place that makes me cry?"

Terrence wrapped his arm around my shoulder, and I stiffly fell into the warmth of his bear hug.

"I can tell that you don't do this regularly," Terrence observes. In true Terrence style, his words are flat and unexcited.

"I'm glad that the lack of affection I received as a child brings you so much joy," I muffle into his bicep.

Terrence releases me.

"Don't be a stranger, Nailah," he adds. "I love Lucy too. I'll still help you take care of her."

Terrence pulls my car keys from his pocket and holds them out in his hand.

"I don't do handouts," I snapped, reaching for my worn keys.

Terrence shuts his hand in a flash and moves the keys out of my reach.

"Give me my keys," I say, trying to reach around the large lumberjack-built man.

Terrence tightened his face.

"I'm serious," he says. "If you need help, ask. I will be there."

"And like I said, I don't do charity."

"It wouldn't be that," Terrence responds while strategically keeping me from getting my keys. "I plan to charge you. Family rate, of course."

"Alright," I agree.

Terrence releases custody of my keys, and I stick my tongue out at him. It's childish, but it feels right.

"Be safe," Terrence adds as I get into the car.

CHAPTER FORTY-FIVE

Nailah

"I came by to see how your date with Dr. Eli went and for a wellness check. You know, to make sure that you ain't locked up in this house crying and about to hurt yourself."

I stutter my eye roll for a lasting effect and then loop them around for a second roll. Even though everyone hoped Tyriq and I could make amends, Regina had suggested a 'meantime for between times' friend. Eli was generally a good guy, and we had a nice date, but the sparks weren't there, and I didn't have the energy for any more of Regina's matchmaking tips.

"I'm fine, Regina."

She follows behind me as I trudge back to the sofa, still dressed in yesterday's pajamas.

"You don't look fine at all."

We have a seat on the sofa, and I turn off the television. There is no need to try to watch anything when Regina is around; she's always talking. I bet she even talks in her sleep.

A wave of nausea overtook my body, and I expelled everything that I hadn't let go of thirty minutes before into the bucket next to me.

"My stomach has been doing flips since Friday," I explain. "I haven't been able to keep anything down."

"It's Wednesday, Nailah. You need to go to a doctor. You've been sick way too long for it to be a stomach bug."

"Already went, and I'm not wasting my money for them to tell me that it's a part of pregnancy and give me some pills for nausea that don't work," I quip. "I'm jobless right now. Nausea will pass."

Regina blinks at me. Her mouth is open, but no words are exiting it.

"Did you just say-?" she stops mid-sentence like someone pushed the pause button on her brain as she was speaking.

Plucking a wet wipe from the pack, I wipe my face and then lean back. I tuck my feet beneath me and wrap the throw blanket around my shoulders.

"Yep." I drop my head back against the couch. "I am with child. Prego. Popped. Knocked up. I went to the women's clinic Monday."

The shift across Regina's face from surprise to anger is swift and undeniable.

"You knew yesterday?" her voice was louder than normal as she hopped up from my sofa.

I wince as Regina begins wearing a path across my floor while shooting irritated glares in my direction.

"I can't believe this. I thought we were better than that." She shook her head. "What did Tyriq say?"

"Nothing." I shrug. "He won't pick up the phone."

When Regina stops pacing and plops her hands onto her hips, I feel like a little kid in trouble.

"You're being that petty now?" Regina rolled her neck.

"I don't even want to be bothered with telling him." I am exasperated with all of it.

"Oh, now you're talking real crazy." She bounced down on the sofa next to me, like coming closer would make me change my words.

I give her the justification that I crafted between rounds of puking.

"It's still early. I don't need months of him looking at my belly." I watch her face to gauge her reaction. "Besides, we're not even talking right now."

Regina drops her head all the way back and then forward with a frustrated grunt of disapproval.

"Start talking to him them. It's not like you don't know where the hell he is," Regina blasted me with much gruff. "Shit, you got everybody's phone number, work location, and address. You better get to calling."

"And say what?" I ask. "The whore is carrying your child? Please. I don't need the headache, and I certainly don't need the heartache."

"But you do need the funds. Kids are expensive. I'm expensive by myself. Adding a little critter to my payroll would be devastating for my lifestyle."

"Everything isn't about money, Regina," I answer.

"Lies, you tell," she huffed.

Tears slip from my face one at a time.

Regina gives an exasperated groan when I double sniffle.

"Don't cry, my friend," Regina comforted. "Mali should be here any minute. She'll get in touch with Tyriq for you, and we'll tell him together."

She pats a cool hand on my back.

"You're right. I need to tell him." I let my head fall into my hands. The dizziness is overwhelming.

"Damn girl, you look bad."

The knock at the door stops my curse words.

Lifting my head feels like the task of climbing a mountain, so I let it wobble to the side as I fall against the armrest.

"Call Tyriq," I tell the figures standing in front of me.

Colors swirl through my vision, and my eyelids become barbells against my eyes.

"Do you hear me? Open your eyes, Nailah." The shadowy figure resembling Mali pushes her arms around me, and my body begins to jerk without my permission.

"I hear you. Do you hear me?" I feel like I'm screaming.

Mali doesn't seem to hear me.

Why did she turn down the lights?

"Nailah!" I hear her scream.

Total darkness surrounds me, and I finally feel like I am at rest.

CHAPTER FORTY-SIX

Nailah

Bright, blinding lights cause me to squint. I try to adjust my eyes against the intensity of the beams, and I see enough to notice the hospital bed and a manila-colored man.

"Miss James, nice to see you. How are you feeling?" the strange man in blue scrubs continues to wave objects in front of me.

"Bad." My mouth is dry. My voice is creaky. Even muttering hurts. "Real bad."

Tyriq stood in the corner, his arms folded and mouth tightened into a straight line.

Maybe it's because I haven't seen him in a long time. Maybe it's because he's so damn fine. I am not sure why an urge to smile blooms inside of me and spreads.

I remind myself that he's here as an obligation to his medical profession and snuff out my kindling joy.

"Your friend told me that you were complaining of stomach problems." Is that true?" the doctor asked.

Shifting my legs in the bed, I confirm my stomach issue.

The room began to shrink as Tyriq's gaze intensified. He steps closer to the bed and further from the corner.

"Do you mind if I check for anything abnormal?" the doctor asks.

I gave him a thumbs up. Tyriq had taken a wide-leg stance and watched me carefully as the doctor lifted my shirt.

"Tell me where or if you feel any pain."

The doctor pushes on my stomach, and as he moves lower, I wince.

"There?" he questions.

I nodded, looking over at Tyriq, whose eyes had narrowed.

I take a deep breath.

"Alright, let's get a sample and run a few tests," the doctor concluded before stepping out of the room.

I take a few long blinks before looking in his direction.

Tyriq and I were alone together for the first time in weeks, and words to explain what was happening in my world escaped my brain.

"Where's Mali?" I question.

"She had to go home," Tyriq said dismissively, still eyeing my stomach.

"Is there anything that you want to tell me?" Tyriq really looked me in the eye for the first time since I'd opened them.

"Yes. I called Mali so that we can get together at my condo and talk."

"Mali-" he stops his words to rub a hand over his trimmed goatee. "Nailah, we don't need a third party to have a conversation."

The room shrunk another size with his glare.

"You weren't taking my calls and didn't come home, so I-"

Frustration flashed in his eyes as he interrupted my explanation with a justification of his own.

"I was angry, Nailah. You intentionally kept important information from me. I needed some space and time to think about us. I should have called, but-"

"Can I have some water?" I return the favor of cutting into his words.

"I'll go grab you some ice chips if you tell me what's going on," he replied. "Mali says you won't take her calls now either. You missed the women's day service that my mom was hoping you would come to."

"We broke up." Speaking the truth prompted the eruption of a cavalcade of tears. "We're not together. What am I supposed to do?"

Tyriq softened his shoulders, his arms falling away from his chest. His hands caressed away my tears.

"I miss having you as a part of my life," he said quietly. "I hate seeing you like this, but I'm glad to see you."

I let his words wrap around me, snuggle me like a church mother's hug. They feel good until I remember why he missed me.

"You rejected me," I remind him.

"It wasn't about rejecting you, love. It was about determining if I could have a future with you."

We quieted the conversation as a nurse entered the room.

"Nailah James," the nurse read from a sheet of white labels as she stepped to the side of the bed. "I am here to get some samples from you."

She sat down her tray of vials, and as she whipped out a tunicate, she noticed Tyriq.

"Dr. Lewis?" Her eyes dart from side to side and then take the journey up and down his body. "It's been a while."

The confused look that invades Tyriq's face is priceless.

"Yes. Um-"

"Tyeisha," she inserted her name as she waved long lashes over her eyes. "I see you're doing well," she added, connecting the vial to the other end of the needle before my blood began to flow.

She moved seamlessly, almost robotically, as she continued her task but gave all her attention to Tyriq.

"Yes. I am," he responded.

"I haven't seen you around the E.R. on the weekend overnights anymore," she acknowledged, digging for information from Tyriq but switching vials.

"No more pick-up shifts for me," he said, sliding a finger down his collar and clearing his throat.

She finished drawing my blood, placed everything neatly in the tray, dropped her gloves in the medical waste bin, and walked over to Tyriq.

"Well, give me a hug, stranger," she directed. "Who knows when I'll see you again?"

Tyriq let out a nervous chuckle before giving her a side hug.

"Oh. I know Dr. Monroe is great," he encouraged

"There's no one like you, Dr. Lewis," she said with a wink before exiting.

"Guess you got to know her pretty well."

"It doesn't matter how well I knew her," he huffed.

"Because we're not together, right?" I respond quickly.

"No, because it's in the past. If I wanted her to be a part of my future, she would be."

I turned my head away so he couldn't see the hurt, can't see the water that won't stop leaking from my eyes today. It hurts too bad.

"How is it that your past doesn't matter, but you punished me for mine?"

"Because if you ask me about my past, I'll tell you exactly what's up. You don't have to ask other people about me."

Suddenly, my head hurt.

"Just leave Tyriq," I tell him, closing my eyes. "I'll be fine."

"Is that what you really want?" he asked.

Before I can answer, someone knocks at the door.

"Knock. Knock." Eli, a doctor I had met through Regina, peeked into the room before walking in. "I saw your name on the board, and I had to come check and see if it was you."

Eli takes a seat on the edge of the bed.

Although Regina had hopes of Tyriq and I reconciling, after another week of silence, she offered to hook me up with a 'meantime for between times' friend. We had gone out on one date and had a few conversations through instant messages. It was cool to know that despite all the horrible things being said about me, he was willing to listen and get to know me as a person.

"Hello," he said, turning back to Tyriq and then doing a double take. "Lew?" he questioned.

I feel like I'm in the middle of a train station with a superstar. Does everyone know him?

Eli got up from the bed and slapped hands with Tyriq before bumping chests.

"Man. How are you?" Eli asks. "I haven't seen you since rotations."

"I'm alright. What's been up with you?"

"Just trying to get on your level, man. Private Practice," Eli answered jovially. "Is Nailah family?"

Tyriq looked at me, then at Eli.

Because of all the drama that happened between Tyriq and me, one of the first things I did was break down my crazy situation.

"No. She's-"

"A family friend," I answer.

I see the anger radiating from Tyriq.

"Cool," Eli said before returning to my bedside.

"I know you had a little stomach bug the other day. How'd you end up here?" Eli asked.

"I'm just-" I look toward Tyriq, and the words won't come out. "I don't know."

"They're running some tests now."

"What kind?" Eli asked, standing and walking toward Tyriq

"Full panel, CBC, Blood Chemistry. You know the drill."

Eli nodded, then turned his attention back to me.

"Why didn't you call? You know I would have been right over," he asks with concern.

"He's been to your place?" Tyriq asked quickly, not hiding his surprise.

"I was a gentleman," Eli answered for me. "Stay calm. I know how protective you are over your family."

"Eli?" Mali questioned, entering the room. "I didn't know you were on duty tonight."

"You know him too?" Tyriq questioned, his look of offense unhidden.

"Well, when you left-" she started with conviction.

"Hey. I have to run," Eli interrupted when his phone sounded.

The lanky man leaned down to hug me.

"It was nice to see you again, Lew and Mali," Eli said with a smile, checking his cell phone. "I will be back to check on you later, Nailah."

"So, you knew about that dude?" Tyriq asked, stepping toward Mali.

"Don't come at me like that, Tyriq," Mali decreed, not backing down.

"I'm going to tell you just like I told Nailah, what goes on between you two is between you two. You want your girl? Get her. If you don't, get over it."

Tyriq puffed out like a blowfish, and I held back my laughter.

At that moment, I understood that Mali was more than just my friend. She was willing to go against her ever-loved cousin just for me.

"You're my family, and family is supposed to," Tyriq started, sounding like a preacher in the pulpit before the doctor interrupted.

"Ms. James, I have some good news and some other news."

"Let's hear it," Mali said, facing the doctor as fast as she could.

The doctor looked in my direction.

"It's alright. They're family," I say, smiling at Mali. Better for him to tell Tyriq than for me.

"Well, the good news is that we found out what is causing the nausea."

"Awesome," Tyriq added.

"Based on the urine exam, your pregnancy seems to be the source of the sickness. From the paperwork, you are probably about seven or eight weeks along."

Mali bounced up like a cartoon character and hugged me.

"I get a new mini cousin!" Mali exclaimed.

"Thank you, doctor," I say in an even tone.

"We're still waiting on the bloodwork, but I wanted to let you know what we have found so far. We'll keep you on the drip a little while longer, get you something to slow down the vomiting, and let you go home," the doctor said with a smile, but I just watched the expression on Tyriq's face.

He is too calm. Too cool. Too quiet.

"You'll need to schedule an appointment with an OB/GYN as soon as possible, and I recommend either staying with someone or having someone help you for the next two or three days so you can rest." The doctor smiled as though he hadn't dropped earth-shattering grenades in the room. "Any questions?"

"No," I answer, but I can only watch Tyriq.

"I'll have the nurse finish up your paperwork and prescriptions and get you ready for discharge."

The doctor exited.

"A new baby!" Mali danced.

"Is it mine?" Tyriq asked. He asked with very little volume, but it felt like he had uttered the words right against my ear.

"Did you really just ask that?" Mali responded, sounding offended for me, but I understand.

I knew he had issues with trust and that his words weren't about me but his pain.

I take a deep breath. "Yes, Tyriq. I haven't been with anyone else during our relationship or after."

He studies my face before nodding.

"If you want to do a paternity test in a few months, I am fine with it," I tell him. "I don't want you to have any doubts."

"I believe you," he said, walking toward my bed.

Before I can resist, he has me wrapped in his arms.

I hold onto him because I need that support. I hold onto him because I know that no matter what, he will never let me go.

He kisses my cheek.

"Mali, I know you're living the bachelorette life and all, but would you mind?" I begin before Tyriq cuts me off.

"You're going home with me."

"And what if I say no?" I wouldn't, but what if I did?

"Then I'll come home with you," he said with a look of resolve that let me know that he was serious.

"Just because I'm having a child doesn't mean that you get to treat me like one."

"You know that's not how I mean it," he explained. "I need to be sure that you and he are alright."

"He?" Mali and I say in unison.

"The last thing we need in this family is more boys," Mali stated. "Nailah, you're welcome any time at my home. You're family."

CHAPTER FORTY-SEVEN

Tyriq

I arrived home to two cars parked outside of my gate.

I park behind the last one.

"I'm going to see what's going on. You alright?" I ask Nailah, whom I can't seem to stop looking at.

She's having a baby, my baby. I'm going to be a father.

"I'm just tired," she responded, closing her eyes and leaning against the headrest.

I open the car door and walk down the path to the first car.

My mother and aunt are inside with Trystan. Mali is in a second car behind them.

"What are you all doing here?" I ask

Trystan rolls down the window.

"Trying to get in," my mother responded with much attitude. "You got this place locked up like a fortress. Open up the gate."

"Why are you here, Mom?" I ask, as though I don't already know.

"Mali told us about the baby causing Nailah some trouble. You know I had to check on her."

"I'm a doctor. I can take care of her," I explain.

"I know what you do, Tyriq, but you ain't a woman. She needs a momma right now," she quipped.

"Are you going to open this gate or what?" my aunt added from the back seat.

I walk past Mali's car, giving her the evil eye the entire time.

She shrugs.

I push 'open' on the gate remote and trail the two cars in front of mine.

"My mom and aunt are here," I tell Nailah.

She smiled but didn't open her eyes.

"It's alright," she says. "I know your family is excited for you."

"Correction," I say, looking over at her. "The family is happy for us. We're in this together."

She opens her eyes.

"I know that even if we aren't a couple, you will take care of our child."

"And you too, Nailah," I add. "Don't forget that part. This baby is a part of me, and you are too. Your life is directly connected to his."

I put the car in park and helped Nailah out.

I hear my family shutting car doors and shuffling to the front door.

"How do you feel about having company right now?" I ask Nailah.

"Do I have a choice?"

"Say the word, and I won't let them bother you." And I truly mean it, too. I will put every last one of them out of the front door if they bother her.

I don't want to ever see her like that again.

Nailah allowed her face to move in that upward motion into a smile. *Damn, she's beautiful.*

"I will go and say a few words, then head back to the guest room."

"Why the guest room?" I question. "We're about to..." I can't find the right words. "You know that you and I are having..."

Nailah placed her delicate hand subtly in the air, saving me from my nose dive into idiocy. It didn't occur to me that she would sleep anywhere but with me. We used to sleep together all the time.

"We're not together. This baby does not change that," she explains matter-of-factly, as though explaining weather patterns. It sounded like 'Yes, there was sunshine, and now it is raining' rather than the 'I'm not your girlfriend anymore stupid, stay the hell away from me' it should have sounded like.

I frowned but decided not to push the issue.

"How are you feeling, Nailah?" my mother said, extending her arms for a hug.

"I'm a lot better than I was," my soon-to-be baby mother responded, embracing my mother.

"Go lay down and rest," my mom explains with a pat on Nailah's back. "You don't have to worry, and we're going to make sure that you are taken care of."

Seated on my sofa, Mali is swiping and tapping her phone, and Trystan is rubbing his temples.

"We'll get you to feeling better in no time," Aunt Pat adds as she heads to the kitchen.

I guide Nailah to the guest bedroom across the hall from mine and drop her things in the closet.

"I'll head out and grab you some toiletries," I explain. "I'll have Mali pick you up a few outfits to lounge in until you feel well enough to get your clothes."

"I'm only staying here for the weekend," she said, twisting her lips and scooting under the thick blanket on the queen-size bed.

"And after that, who are you staying with?" I ask.

"Myself," she answered, her voice raising about two octaves. "I'm pregnant, not an invalid. I'll be here for the two days, and then I'm going back to my condo."

"You want to play ice princess like you don't need anyone, then go right ahead," I tell her, "but don't plan on locking me out of my child's life."

Nailah sighed.

"That's not what I intend to do," she explains, looking more tired than earlier before. "We have plenty of time to talk about the details, but I would never deny that opportunity to my, I mean, our child."

I nod.

"We'll talk later," I say calmly. "Get some rest, and use the intercom to let me know if you need anything."

When I enter the living room, my mom and aunt are waiting for me in a battle stance with folded arms and scrunched faces.

"What is this? An intervention or a coalition?" I ask, noticing everyone's tense body language.

"I can't believe you!" my mother huffs.

"What?" I ask.

"I can't believe that you left this poor child without a friend or any family in this world to tend to her!" she replies, poking me in the chest for emphasis. "I didn't raise my son to abandon his family."

"I didn't abandon her, Ma," I say, stepping out of range of her razor-sharp nails. "We broke up."

"No excuse!" Aunt Pat chimed in. "You should have been looking out for her."

"I know one thing," my mother quipped. "Nothing better happen to my grandbaby, or you'll have hell to pay."

"You ladies know me," I explain to the matriarchs.

"Yes, we do," Aunt Pat piped in sarcastically.

"And you should know that I take care of my business," I explain. "So be assured that I will take care of Nailah as well."

"And how do you plan to do that, son?" my mother asks with much bite. "You plan to change pampers via text message?"

"Nailah and I will work out the details."

"Do those details include a ring for the spring or how to be a part-time parent?"

"I'm not going to marry her just for the baby if that's what you're asking. I'm not Trystan."

"Leave me out of your mess," Trystan said, looking up for once. "I take care of mine. I did what I had to do."

We had never discussed why Crystal and he had gotten married, even though everyone assumed it had something to do with the baby born eight months after they were married.

"If that's how you get through the day," I respond to Trystan. "I will take care of her and my baby," I explain to my mom.

"Oh, you better," my mother concludes as she turns and follows my aunt into the kitchen.

"Welcome to the club," Trystan added once my mother and aunt were out of the room. His words said welcome, but his eyes said worry. 'Welcome to worry' is what he should have said.

"What club?" I ask, not really needing him to clarify but wanting to stop talking about this with all of the wrong people. Nailah holds the real answers that I need right now.

"The 'My feelings don't matter anymore, it's all about the kids' Club," he explains sarcastically.

"Right," I sigh before sitting down, as the weight of the day hit me as hard as the whack-a-mole game in an arcade.

I am going to be a father.

"I, for one, am excited!" Mali added with vigor. "I love Nailah, and I was scared you were going to be stupid enough to let her get away without making her a part of this family."

"No worries, dear cousin. She's not going anywhere if I can help it."

Nailah slept through Terrence's visit. Regina came by around the same time. That's when I knew that I was tired because I swear I saw Terrence checking her out. To my knowledge, he had not been interested in anyone since his wife passed away.

We chatted, drank, ate, and everyone said that they would either call or stop by the next day except for my mother. She settled into the guest room on the other side of the house.

There was no use trying to sleep. I hadn't slept much since we had been apart. When I walk into the room, Nailah is sprawled across the bed, covered in random spots, and with only one sock.

She groans softly and twists in the bed.

I kick off my shoes and plop down in the plush armchair in the corner.

I had pushed her away once, and now that I knew what it was like to be without her, I will not let her go.

CHAPTER FORTY-EIGHT

Nailah

When I open my eyes, I can tell that it is night. My stomach doesn't care, though. This baby is not playing fair. I scoot from the warm bed and feel an instant chill as I move to the attached bathroom as quickly as I can.

I heave and hurl into the porcelain bowl while praying for relief.

"Nai," I hear him first and then feel his body kneeling next to mine.

As best as I can, I motion for him to leave. Then, just as I had been doing for the last few days, but without an audience, I gag and cough up everything still left inside of my body.

"That's- ooh- Can I help?" Tyriq asks, sounding both uneasy and concerned as he smooths a hand across my back.

Feeling empty, I slump back into his arms.

"Just shoot me," I whine. I am not sure what level of hell I have descended to, but I cannot imagine ever feeling worse.

"No, Nailah," he gives me a soft chuckle. "You're going to be alright."

"This is the end," I wholeheartedly disagree with him.

Tyriq leaned me against the tub, lifted me up, and then scooped me into his arms.

I let my head fall against his warm, hard chest.

"I got you, Blade."

While in the bed, through the small, barely open slits of my eyelids, I see Tyriq walk back into the bathroom.

A few seconds later, the dip in the bed alerts me that Tyriq is next to me again.

"Look at me."

Slowly, I turned toward his voice and then felt the warm towel he soothed across my face.

I hum my thanks. I am so tired and cold and even scared that I muster up the last bit of strength that I have to speak.

"Stay with me," I whisper.

"Baby, I wasn't going anywhere," he says before sliding against me and pulling me into his arms. "I'm here."

CHAPTER FORTY-NINE

Tyriq

The morning smells of having my mother in my home find their way to the guest room where Nailah lay curled in my arms. I lift out of bed, drawn to the kitchen by the promise of mother's signature breakfast sandwich, an omelet full of ham, bacon, sausage, and veggies in between grilled cheese bread.

"So, you do love me?" I ask my mother as I enter the kitchen.

"You know it, baby," she answers before hugging me. "Good morning."

She slides her masterpiece meal onto a plate for me.

"Thanks," I answer, plopping down at the breakfast table near the window.

"I see Nailah finally got you some food in this house."

"Yes," I mumble between chewing. "She complained almost as much as you do about my eating out and not stocking the cabinets."

"Good," my mother huffs.

"She wanted to start cooking for me, so I let her drag me to the market. I think she bought one of everything, but she made sure that I had a balanced meal."

"She got some good seasoning, too," my mother adds. "That's how I know she was feeding you right. Besides the love pounds you've put on, she got the right ingredients and seasoning."

"Love pounds?" I lift an eyebrow before taking another bite of the sandwich.

My mother took a seat across from me at the table, a small cup of coffee in her grip.

"It happens to everyone when they fall in love. You're dating and eating out, comfortable eating in and not working out, and then staying in bed more, and those pounds catch up."

I shrug. "I do love her. Nailah is caring, funny, and smart, but-"

"But what?" the tone that my mother often took when I was a teenager and said something out of line popped out, and her eyes dared me to say something wrong about Nailah.

It seems that my family had forgotten that I am their actual relative.

"You've been crazy about the girl since you met her. Now that you found out about her past, there's a problem?"

"Her past isn't the problem. I know she didn't do what Briana suggested on live television, and I honestly wouldn't care if she had lived her life that way. It bothers me that she keeps hiding parts of herself from me."

I look at my mother, unsure of how she even lured this conversation out of me. The last thing that I wanted to do was sit and talk about my feelings.

"Do you think that she would do what Briana did?" my mother asks. "Do you think that she would betray you?"

I take a deep breath and shake my head.

"Would she randomly drop off the face of the earth and not say a word to me? Yes, but she's loyal to those that she cares about. I noticed that in her friendship with Regina. She has a heart and a conscience."

"Then what is it?"

I blink because my only answer is that I left her because I do not want her to leave me.

"Uhm, hmm." My mother stands and takes her cup to the sink. "If you love that girl, then act like it. She ain't perfect, but nobody is. You have to love her through it. Help her learn what having a dependable man in her life is like."

"I can't make her love me," I rebut.

My mother claims her chair again.

"You young people are so quick to throw stuff away. Everything is made microwave-quick and then disposed of even quicker. Good love ain't done quickly, and when you got it, don't throw it out."

I chew on the food and her words.

"You know, I love you boys."

I nodded, and she continued.

"I just hope that your father and I have given you an example of how important having a loving, stable family and home is," she said before pausing. "It hasn't always been easy."

"I got it, mom. I got Nailah."

"As you should." She scoots her way out of the kitchen.

"I'm a grown-ass man," I mumble before sucking at my teeth.

My mother pops her head back through the opening.

"You got something you need to say?"

"No, ma'am."

CHAPTER FIFTY

Nailah

Tyriq had been the perfect gentleman for the three nights and two days that I had been in his home. After the hell of the first night and the adventures of sleeping in a queen-sized bed with Tyriq's tall ass, I moved over to his room and the king-sized bed.

Miraculously, with the help of the nausea pills, some real sleep, and Mama Shirley's chicken broth, I felt much better after night two. It seemed like ages since I had slept next to him, and even though I was conscious, my body was too tired to be aroused. Last night, though, when Tyriq slid his fine self under the cover and whispered in my ear to check on how I was feeling, I was ready to break every chain and cross all the lines placed on our relationship.

My entire reason for bunking with Tyriq is the illness, so when he questioned my recovery, I did something that I was not totally proud of. I told him straight to his face that I was only feeling slightly better. I was originally reluctant to stay with him, but as with everything, Tyriq has changed my heart and mind over time.

"How are you doing?" Regina asked.

Since sitting up with my eyes open is a possibility now, Tyriq helped me move into the theater room when Regina came to visit.

"Better." I give a half smile.

"With the way that man is taking care of you, I bet that you are better."

Tyriq peeks back in then.

"My mom left a gallon of the ginger-honey-lemon tea that you liked. If I don't offer you some every few hours, she will descend upon the house again. You ready for more?"

"I wouldn't mind having her come back," I chuckle. "I'm good for now, though. Thank you."

Tyriq's mother, or Mama Shirley as she asked me to call her, had left the day before after making sure I was able to speak and had her number saved into my phone. She made me promise to call her if there was a problem or even if there wasn't.

"Are you ready to come back to work?" Regina asked. "The higher-ups asked about you. They can't reach you since you changed your number and have not responded to any emails."

"I haven't even looked at my laptop in a week," I answer honestly. "Why are they so interested in me now?"

Not one supervisor, direct or indirect, was interested in discussing the truth with me when the story broke. The bigwigs told me unceremoniously that I no longer had a place with the department.

Regina hands me a letter.

"Rumor is that a team of high-powered attorneys came in on your behalf and whipped out a dictionary of issues, including unlawful termination without due process, discrimination, and defamation of character."

"That's all news to me. I don't even have a lawyer." I slide a finger through the seal of the envelope to open it and then remove the contents. "Did you do this, Regina? I know that you've dated a ton of lawyers."

Emphatically, she shakes her head no. "This wasn't me at all, girl. I didn't even think about getting a lawyer. Plus, none of the lawyers that I've dated have enough influence with a state agency to make them reconsider a termination."

Scanning the letter, I gather words of an apology and an official offer to return.

"Wow," I wait for the excitement to come, or at least a flutter. None ever does. Weeks ago, I would have been jumping up and down to return, but now, knowing that I am developing a life, the thought of working long, stressful hours while driving through the city does not entice me as much.

"So, when are you coming back?" Regina bounces in the chair, her hands clapping together with glee.

I move my eyes from the letter to gaze at my friend.

Her bright smile falls in the same direction as her shoulders.

"You're not coming back, are you?"

I tug my bottom lip between my teeth before I speak.

"I don't have an option, really. I have to go back." I glance over the words in the letter again and sigh. "I have to take care of this baby, so I have to work."

"Maybe not. Have you spoken with Tyriq about it? He probably wouldn't mind you staying home."

Home? As in my condo? Where would home be for me?

I had not even considered asking Tyriq to support me financially while I took care of our baby. Even if he agreed, how would that work? Would we live together as friends and co-parents? Would he require that I marry him in exchange for him taking care of everything?

"Talk to him about it, Nailah. You have to let him know what you're thinking and feeling. Be open and honest, and if he says no, then I definitely have your back. Mali too. We'll make sure that little rugrat has the best of everything."

Rolling my eyes had become an automatic reaction to Regina. "Don't call my baby a rugrat."

"Water moccasin? Crumb snatcher, belly buster?"

"No," I chortle.

"Oh ok, we'll stick to It."

"How about Baby Bug?" I suggest. "I thought that I had a stomach bug when I found out that I was pregnant."

"Baby Bug." She nods her head from side to side as if weighing the name in her mind. "I kind of like it. In the meantime, we have to work out a fierce ass name for my new godchild."

"Of course, because that's the important part."

"Anyway, let me give you the tea, sis," Regina peps up in excitement.

"Pictures and video of Briana with Jermaine Timmons surfaced, and guess who was hunching her husband's best friend?"

"No!" my mouth drops. "How do you know? Why was she after Tyriq if she was with Jermaine?"

"Jermaine wasn't trying to wife her ass, that's why she was after Tyriq. Jermaine was trying to keep things at the night buddy level even after she agreed to leave Naeem. She thought her best shot at a husband was Tyriq."

"Shit. Was she trying to mess him over again?" The thought that someone would be so heartless is unfathomable to me.

"Good thing he was so into you that she didn't get the chance."

I wonder what Tyriq feels for me now? Shaking my head, I clear that line of thinking. I will just ask him later.

"How do you know all of this?" I ask again.

Picking at her nails, Regina looks away.

Instantly, alarms ring in my brain that something is wrong. During our friendship, she never looked nervous.

She took a deep breath and looked in my direction.

"My father is Reginald Strong."

"Shut up!" Slapping a hand to my chest in shock, I drag out the two words. "Your father is Reginald Strong, a real estate mogul who is a part owner of the basketball arena?"

I have so many questions for her. Why was she a social worker when her father has been a multi-millionaire a few times over?

The despair in her eyes cautions me to tread lightly and let her talk about it in her own way.

"That's him, dear old dad, the super mogul." Her downcast eyes and flat voice contradict the description she gives of her father.

"Do you two not get along?" I inquire.

"Something like that." She slides a hand through her silky hair. "I turn thirty in two months. By my thirtieth birthday, if I haven't found a suitable mate, one that is up to my father's standards, he is going to choose a man for me or discontinue his support."

If my eyes were not attached to my head, they would have fallen on the floor.

"Married? Wow. That's crazy. Will the queen of hooking people up get hooked up by her father? "

Her shoulders touch her ears in a shrug.

"I don't know. My father has these tests and challenges for men to pass to prove his worthiness. No one has succeeded yet."

"Do you even want to get married?" Regina is such a free spirit that it is hard to imagine her tied down.

"Of course I do. I just hoped that love would be involved, too. My parents were placed together because of their social circle, and it grew to love. My father feels that the same can happen for me."

"How do you feel?"

"I honestly don't know." She gives a half grin. "At least I know that if I have to survive on my own, that I can. It would be tough, but if I have to walk away from my father's fortune because he tries to throw some ancient asshole at me, then I will."

We are both quiet for a bit. Being poor and parentless caused me a lot of grief, but being rich with loving parents seems to be bothering Regina just as much.

"Enough of my rich girl sob stories. Whatever happens, I'm going to soldier this shit out and do what I have to do," the Regina that I am used to pops out. "Anyway, I know the security guard at the arena, and because of my father, they give me a little more information than they would the normal person. I politely asked him to alert me of any suspicious activity regarding Briana. He already had a story for me when I first spoke her name. Because she and Naeem treat everyone like crap, he's been waiting for the right person to ask for the info."

"See, that's why you have to be nice to people who work with your food and security," I point out.

"So, the upgraded cameras near the locker rooms and tunnels have color, audio, and video. He conveniently took a break while reviewing footage of a fight between Jermaine and Briana after a game. Briana had confronted Jermaine because, after a twelve-year relationship, he's been ignoring her ass too."

"Twelve years?"

"Apparently, she was doing all three men at some point in college and planned to ride off with whoever made it to the NBA first. Supposedly, she had real feelings for Jermaine, who knew her before the other two."

I can't believe my ears but listen as Regina continues.

"Jermaine burst her whole hope bubble, though. He knew that she was only staying with Naeem through the abuse because of the giant contract he had and was now trying to hop off the train because Naeem was being traded again at the end of the season and would make less than Jermaine, less than Tyriq."

"I haven't even heard about the trade on sports shows or anything."

"I know." Regina lifted her chin. "That's some top-secret shit, so I just sent a screen recording with audio to my friend who blogs, and boom, everyone knows Briana is lying and conniving. The show that she and your father went on is going to do a retraction and apology about that interview."

I'm not sure what to feel. My friend had done all of that for me?

Jumping up with a sudden burst of emotion, I wrap my arms around Regina's shoulders for the tightest, deepest bear hug that I can give.

"Thank you. Thank you. Thank you," I repeat.

"Alright," her mock annoyance apparent in her voice and the pat that she gives me on the back. "No need to get all sentimental. You know that I got you, girl."

So many things have happened in my life, but for the first time in a long while, I know that I am not fighting the battle alone.

CHAPTER FIFTY-ONE

Tyriq

I leave Nailah for about four hours to attend a meeting with the arena owners and my brothers. The Brother's T tow is taking over the towing needs of the arena and two businesses near the arena. With this addition to the company, we will be ahead of schedule with Terrence's five-year expansion plan.

"Well," Reginald Strong stands, "it has been an honor to meet such aspiring entrepreneurs as yourselves, especially you, Terrence."

Throughout the meeting, my older brother laid out a solid plan with financials and profit forecasts so well that I feel proud that we are related. The auto repair and car parts service had been his brainchild.

Tyson, my youngest brother, had put in many man-hours to help get the business off the ground. Trystan and I funded upgrades and expansions as our bank accounts grew, and Terrence came up with new ways to enhance the business. I had been mostly hands-off until now. After a chance meeting with Mr. Strong at the gala, where we discussed ways that we might be able to partner, I brought the idea to Terrence, and now we are signing on the dotted line.

"Thank you." Terrence gave a stiff nod of his head. "I appreciate the opportunity to work with you, sir."

Mr. Strong clasps my hand in a firm shake, then Trystan and Tyson's as well. He turned to Terrence but, along with the handshake, offered him an opportunity.

"You have a firm grip there, Terrence," the older gentleman acknowledges. "I need a fourth for an upcoming golf game. Would you mind humoring an old player with a game or two?"

Terrence looks at me with surprise. I don't believe it, either.

"Of course, Mr. Strong. I would love to," he answers, pumping the businessman's hand with vigor.

"Hello?" I call out, entering my home. Every time that I leave and come back, I wonder if she will be here. After nearly five days of staying with me, I noticed her strength had returned. For the last day and a half, I have been avoiding every opportunity to have a conversation with her. Nailah had given me notice on the day that she reentered my home that she would not be staying long.

"I'm in the kitchen."

I bite my lip at the sight of her bent over and pulling food from the oven. Shaking her hips, Nailah shimmies a roast onto the counter as she sings along to a Beyoncé song.

I want to wrap her up in a hug but slide my hands into my pockets instead.

"I'm glad that you're home. Do you have some time to talk?" Nailah asks as she ends the music.

Turning on my heels, I realize that I had stood there too long. I had given her too much time to discuss her exit plan with me.

"I need to go-"

I move toward the hallway.

"Tyriq. Please." Her touch is soft but sends a hard jolt through me.

The octave change at the end of her plea tugs at my heart, and I face her.

"How about we sit at the table?" Nailah slides her hand into mine without waiting for an answer.

"First, thank you for taking care of me this week. I appreciate it."

My nod is not as enthusiastic as it should be as I wait for the rest of what she has to say. The part that will hurt me.

"No matter what Nailah. I'm here for you."

"I also want to apologize for not being totally open with many of the things that happened in my past. We haven't spoken since the story dropped and-"

"Nailah," I interrupt, taking her hand into mine again. Waiting for her to give a departure date had me tense.

"I was offered my job back." The words are hasty and flat, and the lack of dimples and teeth confuses me. *Shouldn't she be happy about going back to work?*

"Crystal and Trystan put in some calls on your behalf once Mali told us that you were fired."

"They did that for me?" Her eyes flew open.

"Of course. He's a corporate lawyer and specializes in human resource cases, remember?"

Bobbing her head up and down, Nailah places a hand on her chest.

"I figured that someone did something. I never thought that it was your family." Her eyes finally land on my face. "I will have to thank him."

"You're not mad that we helped? I figured that you would freak out if we told you about the correspondence, but you are not upset?"

A timer on the stove beeps, and Nailah moves to turn it off.

"My reaction to the car thing was a tad bit intense." After moving the pan from the oven onto the stove, Nailah leans against the counter instead of returning to the table.

"I appreciate that you and your family look out for me." She twists her hands inside each other, and her eyes barely leave the floor.

"Talk to me. Tell me what's going on with you."

With two steps, I am in front of Nailah, giving her shoulder a reassuring rub, even though her demeanor makes me nervous as hell.

"I am not sure how to ask, but you told me that if I needed you, I could ask, and-"

"Blade-" I slide a hand down my face. "Just tell me."

"I don't want to go back to work, and I want to live here with you."

All of the words run together, and it takes my brain a few seconds to process that Nailah is not leaving me.

"I can earn my way. I'm a great cook, and you never have food. I can keep the house clean and manage your schedule. I can do some secretarial work for you and keep all of your flight and client info straight," Nailah rambles her list and lifts a finger for each positive that she names.

I close my hand around her fingers as she finally stops speaking.

"You can stay here, but not for any of those reasons." I peck a kiss across the tip of her hand. "You can stay because I care about you because I'm here for you because you're my family."

A smile cracks through the lines of her worried face.

"I really want to work on me before the baby gets here," she says.

I'm glad that Nailah asked. She was finally feeling more comfortable accepting my help.

"Yoga, counseling, some meditation, a lot of reading about motherhood-"

"Whatever you want to do." I return to my seat, relieved that the hard part is over, and I enjoy Nailah moving about the kitchen.

Mixing a salad, she prattles off more things about the future. Barely able to contain my grin, I listen.

I pull out my phone to look at my calendar app and keep myself from doing the Cha-Cha Slide across the kitchen with joy.

Nailah placed plates on the table before setting down the entrée. I grab the sides from the counter and utensils.

"And once Baby Bug gets here, I want to spend the first few months getting acquainted before I even think about going back. You want tea or water?" Nailah asked, pulling down glasses from the cabinet.

"Tea, and I like your plan." I give a shrug to downplay the top-level thrills of excitement I feel. "When do you want to get married?"

The shattering sound of glass hitting the floor is my first indication that maybe marriage was not a part of her plan.

CHAPTER FIFTY-TWO

Nailah

"This closet is ginormous, Jubilee." I walk through the space that has the same square footage as my entire bedroom and kitchen of my condo.

"Yep. It's big enough to have a wedding in, huh?" Regina spits out.

I took a cleansing breath and then rolled my eyes.

House hunting for Jubilee's new Dallas home has been fun. She plans to keep her home in Austin but wants to be close to me. She is an only child as well, and her mother is in a nursing home.

For some reason, Jubilee had asked Regina to join us in the search. A reason that now annoyed me. I guess she felt the same instant kinship to her that I did.

"Will you drop it?" annoyance dripped through each word. "Tyriq is fine with us not getting married."

"But I'm not," Regina said, tapping the tip of her stiletto against the hardwood floor. "You have the chance for a happily ever after, and you are messing this up for me and my godchild."

I pinch at the bridge of my nose. That night, I was totally surprised when Tyriq didn't yell once I explained to him that I was scared of marriage.

"What if he leaves me again-"

"Did he really ever leave you?" Regina countered before I could complete the question. "The entire time that he was M.I.A, you were still in his home, driving a car that he provided, with access to his family and his Jordan shoe box full of cash stacks."

"How did you- I never told you about that."

Everything that Regina pointed out was true, even the emergency money and credit cards that he left for me.

"Beside the point." She swipes her hand across the air. "I'm sure he'll get tired of trying to convince you to stay before he is actually ready to leave."

Automatically, my hand goes to my chest because that hurts.

"I haven't been around that long, but I did observe something. As a social worker, you walk into family situations and assess the likelihood of danger to a child. You listen and review all of the information and make a judgment call based on that." Jubilee states. "Not considering your life in Brook Bonnet, not considering your fears, but just everything that you know about Tyriq, what judgment call would you make?"

Everything feels like it shifted to the left at that moment. I had been looking at it all wrong. No matter what, in every situation, Tyriq came back for me. I had even stopped talking to Mali once I found out that she was reporting information to him after our split, but he was making sure that I was alright. Even after I rejected his idea of marriage to the tune of breaking glass, he picked up the pieces and made sure that I was unharmed. He had kissed my cheek, mumbled something about oven love, and promised to wait until I was ready.

"Finally," Regina mumbled.

"About time. Now, can we finish finding me a house?"

I have never seen so many mansions in my life. Jubilee took us through about ten city homes with small lots and easy access to the freeway. Then Regina, who was now actually considering the option of her father's arranged marriage idea, made me walk through at least six sprawling country estates spread out over acres of land. She and the mystery groom's wedding gift would be a home of her choosing. We needed a golf buggy to view every last one of the houses that she considered.

Mali's interior design side hustle was taking off. She had partnered with a realtor to stage homes for sale in suburban areas of Dallas. On Saturday, she took me to no less than seven homes that she had been contracted to design. The heavy lifting was already done for each one, and Mali wanted to add accents and take pictures for her website.

"Did you choose yet?" I ask Jubilee.

Mali and I met Regina and Jubilee at the spa after our parade of homes adventure.

"Not yet. They were all so nice. Did you have a favorite?" she asks.

I shrug. "I like city life, but having the freeway as a neighbor is too much for me. I really liked a house that I saw with Mali today."

"Which one?" Her eyes perked open. "I loved the one with the grand staircase and columns."

I shook my head.

"That one reminded me too much of *Gone with the Wind*. I liked that modern brick location with all the windows. I think that it was the fourth house that we visited."

Mali nodded as she picked up her phone.

"That is a nice one," she replied, giving more attention to her phone screen than our actual conversation.

"Who are you texting?"

Mali's fingers freeze in place.

"No one." She tucked her phone away. "You want to ride with me to family game night next week since Tyriq will be out of town?"

"Sure."

"Ooh, they got him!" Regina squealed.

"Who?" I ask.

"I just got a notification that Naeem Matthews was sentenced to a year of jail time and five years of probation. Photographic evidence, medical history, witness accounts, and testimony were turned over to the court, and he made a plea deal."

"The truth always comes to light," Mali adds.

"There is a link to another story about Briana," Regina reads. "A player for the New Mexico Stingers is funding her stay in a therapy camp and supporting her as she recovers from the trauma."

"Damn. She stays having a man." Jubilee throws her hands in the air. "Can I just get one?"

"I thought men would be knocking down doors to get to you?" Mali questions. "You're a supermodel."

"There is never a short supply of men trying to open my legs, but very few of the good kind. The dudes that shoot their shots are often immature and childish. I want a man of substance, not one that just looks good on the outside but is really about something."

"Like Terrence," the dreamy note in Regina's voice catches my attention.

My eyes dart over to my friend as her hand flies to her mouth.

"Did I say that out loud?"

"You like Tyriq's brother Terrence?" I question. "Car fixing, forever in chill mode, Terrence?"

I need to understand.

"He's cute, and so far, these rich assholes haven't worked out." She shrugs. "I was thinking that I should try a regular guy before I walk down the green mile into this marriage that my dad is setting up."

"Terrence isn't just-"

Mali cuts her eyes at me, effectively warning me to close my mouth before I explain to Regina that Terrence is far from poor.

"Can we talk about people that I am not related to?" Mali asks. "This is why I never hang out with girls; they always wanted to talk about my brothers and cousins."

"Don't give up on us, Mali," I chuckle.

"Let me find you the right man, and you won't care who we talk about." As a devious smile spread across Regina's face, I thought about warning Mali to run.

CHAPTER FIFTY-THREE

Nailah

"Did you actually leave your media room today?" Regina's voice blasted through the phone.

"Why are you always so loud? I'm riding around with Mali before we head to game night."

I fidget with the lock control on the door panel of Mali's car before looking out of the window into the dimming sky.

"Good, now smile. I bet that you're over there pouting and looking crazy because you miss Tyriq."

I take a deep breath and slide a hand across my stomach.

"Am not." I am. I lied, but so what? I missed my man.

"You should enjoy your family tonight, Nailah," Regina encouraged.

I did have a family.

"You're right." I give a half grin. I am blessed to have people in my life who care for me.

"I know I'm right, and I'll check on you later."

Regina and I end our call, and I hold the phone near my chest. My friend has her faults, but she is still amazing to me.

When Mali pulled into the circular driveway of the gorgeous two-story home we visited last week, I was surprised.

"I can't believe that this place hasn't been snatched up already. The ground lighting is spectacular."

My eyes roam over the brick structure's manicured lawns, greenery-lined pathway, and large clear windows.

"Yep, it's an excellent home. It should sell pretty quickly, but in the meantime, I need your help to freshen up a few things."

Mali patted a hand against my shoulder.

"Sure."

I admire the curved design of the beautiful entryway. The large front door reminded me of the first door that Tyriq opened for me at the art gallery, but smaller.

My stomach twists a little as we enter, and I scratch at my palm.

The soft jazz playing over the built-in sound system should have been my first indication that something devious was afoot.

When Mali turned to me, and a grin filled her entire face, I still had to question what was happening.

"What is this? Did you bring me to a party?" I glance around the foyer for any other indication of a party. "I hate surprises."

"Because they were never the good kind before." Mali slides an arm through mine before leaning in closer to me. "Just go with it."

I trust my friend and let her guide me through the empty hall and into a large living area. My eyes blink involuntarily and well up with tears before anyone can say a word.

"What are you all doing here?" The words tumble out with more emotion than I want, and my heart constricts.

Each of Tyriq's family members is dressed in white and lined up across the empty room. Art on easels sits next to each group as grins and warm smiles welcome me.

Mama Shirley and Pops stand around a canvas of two hearts.

"Nailah," Mama Shirley spoke. "You will never be on this earth alone again."

Her earnest words nearly caused me to break.

"Everyone has a gift," Mama Shirley continues, her voice strong and commanding. "Your strength is commendable, and your compassion has enriched not only our lives but the lives of children throughout our community. Tonight, we want to give gifts to you."

I cover my mouth with my hand.

"Shirley and I give you our love." Pops linked hands with his wife. "We will also serve as an example of how complicated and wonderful love is."

Joy danced through me as both of his parents took a few steps and wrapped me up in a hug.

The canvas next to Aunt Patricia has multicolored lines painted diagonally across it.

I chuckled because it was straightforward, just like her.

"You are good for my nephew. I didn't always see that, but you look out for him. I'm here to help both of you keep it together and stay on the right track."

Truer words could not be said. Aunt Pat will turn off lights, pull out a Bible verse, perform a background check, and check on anyone who needs it.

Her arms wide, Aunt Pat pulls me against her for a hug. She nuzzles her cheek next to mine and rocks me from side to side.

"I love you, sweetheart. I knew that something was different about you the first day that you walked into my office. You are a part of us now, and we are better for it."

When she released me, I tried not to release any tears.

I looked at Mali, who was bouncing on her toes with giddiness. Her hands were clasped in front of her, and a bright smile cracked her face. She looks like a rainbow could burst out of her at any moment.

The tears win the fight against my eyes.

Terrence, Trystan, and Tyson stepped forward then. Their swagger was turned all the way up. Chad and Cairo group in with the brothers and nod in my direction.

As expected, Chad crossed his eyes and made a goofy face.

My watery chuckle brought smiles to the men.

"We bring you brotherhood and security," Terrence spoke.

Their canvas depicts six men walking off into the sunset. They are in suits standing tall, each with an arm resting on the shoulder of the man standing next to him.

"The brothers got your back no matter what," Trystan states.

I pat my fingers across my lips and blow them a kiss.

Regina stepped forward with Jubilee and Crystal.

"Since day one, you have been my sister. It frustrates me that you can't see how wonderful you are, but the girls and I will be here to remind you of your greatness. We are your sisters, mostly Jubilee, but we give you a bond of honesty and support through whatever happens."

Their picture is a vignette of women in a spa laughing and drinking wine.

Crystal, Jubilee, and Regina each step forward and wrap their arms around me for an embrace.

"Thank you, ladies."

Regina and the ladies moved back near the rest of the family.

The music stopped on a beat.

Mama Shirley held her phone in the air like she was guiding a plane in for a safe landing.

"You even taught me how to use this blue mouth music thing," Shirley added.

Laughter erupted throughout the room, and I fought between choking over cackles or sobs.

"Thank you," I whimper. "I appreciate every one of you."

When the song 'Can't Let Go,' by Anthony Hamilton started, my breath stuttered.

"No," I whisper, my body locking in disbelief. "It can't. He didn't."

I ached for him, but my heart thudded in fear. My first instinct is to run. My feelings are on sensory overload.

Mali clasped my arms to keep me in place.

"You may want to stick around for this," she advised before rubbing circles across my back.

I close my eyes, squeezing out the tears.

I covered my mouth.

I smell him first, and I shake my head.

"Open your eyes, Blade."

I shook my head. "Nope. I can't. You're going to make me cry more. I know it."

He leaned into me, and warmth radiated through me.

"Do you still love me?" his words are short and unsure.

"Yes!" I scream, my eyes popping open. "I never want you to doubt that I love you, Tyriq."

He is a vision when he chuckles. His white suit stood out against the bouquet of multicolored flowers in his hand.

He gave my lips a light brush.

"I know you love me." He swept a gentle finger against the line of my jaw. "I also don't want to overwhelm you. If all of this is making you anxious, we can wait."

The care and concern in his eyes calm me. Nothing bad will happen here, and even if it did, I know that Tyriq would slay dragons for me.

I looked around the room, acknowledging each of the kind, sweet faces, and took a deep breath.

"I'm good," I assured him.

"Now for the real question." Tyriq lowered himself to one knee.

I felt like my heart was going to break through my chest.

"Nailah Le'Mae James, you challenge me, encourage me, support me. You make my days better, and I want that forever. Will you marry me?"

The dysfunctional relationship I developed with my saliva around Tyriq resurfaces as I choke out a tearful "Yes. I'll marry you."

Hollers and hoots filled the room when Tyriq placed a gorgeous ring on my finger. I fell into his arms.

There are three things that our child will know: hugs will happen often, independence is valued, but there is help along the way, and finally, surprises can make sunshine along the way.

About the Author

SUBIRA MILES

Although life can bring hard times that require patience, there are also amazing opportunities that are worth the wait. Subira, which means patience rewarded, has experienced this often in her life. A recurring theme throughout her work, Subira is a living testimony that it gets better.

Subira writes the stories that she wants to read and then shares them with anyone willing to listen or read them. Her stories open the door to her mind for others to experience characters that they will root for and grow to love. Her goal is to share hope through stories that make people feel good.

Subira enjoys simplicity in her spare time: Read. Write. Vibe to music. Eat good food. Repeat.

Join her on this adventure, exploring the worlds she's created and finding a piece of your own story in the characters she developed through patience and love.

Instagram: SubiraMiles

Facebook: Subira Miles Books

TikTok: SiennaOchreBooks

www.ingramcontent.com/pod-product-compliance
Lightning Source LLC
Chambersburg PA
CBHW071118170626
46809CB00002B/408